Bicentennial Summer

A COMING OF AGE JOURNEY ACROSS AMERICA

MARY BERELSON

Published by Blue Pierre Press

Editing, design, and distribution by Bublish

ISBN: 978-1-64704-990-4 (Paperback)
ISBN: 978-1-64704-991-1 (Hardcover)

Dedication

I dedicate this book to my husband, Scott, who has been my unwavering partner for nearly forty years, through thick and thin. He has shared in all the difficulties and rewards that life has offered, with love, patience, and humor. From laughing at all the right places to coming up with the perfect thirty-two-degree reference, he has been my rock and inspiration. Scott is a main character in my real Journal of Life, and his presence has made the scenes richer and more meaningful, certainly more fun. Thanks, honey, for being my greatest supporter.

Devils Tower, Wyoming

Wall, South Dakota

Yellowstone, Wyoming

WALL DRUG

Wells, Nevada

San Francisco, Ca

Auburn, Ca

Mount Rushmore, South Dakota

Salt Lake City, Utah

Truckee, Ca

Grand Canyon, Arizona

Goodnigh Texas

⚠ CAUTION
POISON IVY
POISON OAK

Flagstaff, Arizona

Santa Cruz, Ca

Big Sur, Ca

Bushland, Texas

Los Angeles, Ca

Phoenix, Arizona

Calexico/ Mexicali

BICENTENNIAL SUMMER
ROAD MAP

La Crosse, Wisconsin

Clarendon Hills, Illinois

Sioux Falls, Minnesota

Kirtland, Ohio

Marble Cliff, Ohio

Nashville, Tennessee

Witchita Falls, Texas

Birmingham, Alabama

BLUE PIERRE PRESS

STORIES WITH MILEAGE

PART 1

Home

1

"Reveille" and Ballcock

Dad never quite outgrew his childhood. He still played with model trains, made up goofy nicknames, and treated patriotism like a full-time hobby. He could be spontaneous and silly, and if he had an audience—especially us kids—he'd turn even a chore into a performance. That's probably why I loved him so much. It was also why I was the only one willing to get up at dawn for our flag-raising ceremony.

That spring morning, as usual, it was just the two of us outside. Hopping up and down to stay warm, I marveled at the little clouds puffing from my breath. With each hop, I exhaled dramatically—puff, puff, puff—pretending to smoke an invisible cigarette.

Looking over Dad's shoulder, I noticed that the black paint on the trim around the front door of our little white clapboard house was peeling. That was surprising since we'd just repainted it last summer. Mom said we should've done another coat of paint, but Dad didn't want to spend the extra moola. Apparently, Mom was right.

"You ready, Mary?"

I finished nibbling off a nagging cuticle before saying, "Sure, Dad." He made everything fun, including this early-morning flag ritual of ours, which might have otherwise been miserably cold and tedious.

He smiled at me, pushing his thick glasses up his nose with his middle finger. "Let's go, then."

I stopped hopping up and down, tossing my invisible cigarette butt on the ground and crushing it under my boot, and proceeded to stand at attention. I took our flag ritual seriously. Wetting my lips and lifting the trumpet, I launched into this morning's "Reveille" and "Assembly" while Dad solemnly hoisted Old Glory up the flagpole. He would slowly and methodically use a hand-over-hand motion until the flag reached the round finial at the top and then carefully secure the halyard around the cleat. He liked it to be nice and taut so that the hardware wouldn't clang too much against the pole on windy days.

I blasted out the two military awakening tunes, squinting over the bell of the shiny horn into the sunrise, hoping to spot the pair of horses, Buster and Rascal, in their pasture across the road. Several birds alighted from their overnight perches, squawking their annoyance at the startling disruption of the early-morning silence. You'd think they'd be used to it by now. Undeterred, I played on, loud and clear, maintaining a steady and lively tempo, blasting the crisp staccato passages. I'd been practicing a lot lately, and my band director, Mr. Edwards, suggested that I take a trumpet home to rehearse with, even though I actually played trombone in the eighth-grade jazz band.

Dad stood with his right hand at his temple in a proud salute until I finished. "Wow, Mary, that sounded *ex-tra-or-din-ary* today. You're really improving. You hit those high notes right on!"

I could feel the heat of pride color my cheeks.

It was 1976, the year of the USA's bicentennial anniversary. Americans were extra patriotic. Dad, especially. So that meant I was, too. As a testament to our American spirit, we had erected our flagpole near the top of our steep gravel driveway. It was a real flagpole, like the ones that you'd find at schools or cemeteries or post offices. It was twenty-five feet tall, the mast tapering off up to the ball on top. During the construction of the flagpole, I found out that those balls on top of flagpoles are called finials. A big family secret was that our formal flagpole was topped with a makeshift finial. Instead of having a genuine finial, with a bald eagle clasping a sphere in its sharp talons or

4

simply an inexpensive golden sphere itself, Dad had crowned our flagpole with a toilet float.

Toilet floats, sometimes called ballcocks—a word that made me and my big brother, Skippy, snicker like Buster and Rascal— are those spherical devices that float on the surface of the water in a toilet tank to let the flapper know what to do when you flush. Dad had bought a ballcock for seventy-five cents and let the twins paint it to match the pole. From afar, it looked just right—the straight pole; the red, white, and blue waving in the breeze; and the silvery-white round finial, all with a blue-sky backdrop—but from up close, and if you knew what you were looking for, you could make out the grooves on the painted ball-cock and be reminded that it really belonged in a toilet.

To start our flag ceremony, Dad would whisper in the early mornings, "Mary, wake up," giving me a little shake. Knuckling my bleary eyes and doing a quick arms-over-the-head stretch, I'd hop up, ready to go. I naturally woke up enthusiastically, ready for the day's adventures.

I'd make the bed, smoothing the red bedspread that Grandma Stromp, Dad's mother, had sewn. She had quilted one for all twenty-two of her grandkids, taking into consideration each of our favorite colors. Skippy's was blue, Gerri's green, and Jill's yellow. We three girls could be counted on to have our beds made before we even went to the bathroom in the morning. Skippy somehow got away with never making his bed. Maybe it was because his bedroom was downstairs in the musty basement, or maybe it was because he was too old for my parents to care anymore. Either way, there seemed to be a different set of rules for him—because he was a teenager or because he was a boy; the twins and I couldn't figure out which.

Gerri, Jill, and I handled most of the housework and dishes. That was just how things were. We didn't really mind. To keep things moving and make it more fun, we came up with little games to speed things along, Dad-style. It kind of reminded me of how Mary Poppins got Jane and Michael to clean the nursery by turning it into a game. A little spoonful of sugar really did help the medicine go down. And of course, we always followed our family rule: "Your job's not done till the whole job's done." It felt like a commandment or something. That philosophy, along with "Do not touch what is not yours," pretty much summed up how our house ran.

Skippy seemed to have only one real job: stay out of trouble and not give Mom and Dad, as they liked to say, any more grief. But he wasn't great at that. He stayed out too late gallivanting around and would sneak over to his girlfriend's house at night, smoke grass, and come home thinking incense and minty gum could cover the smell.

A couple of years ago, my parents spent a fortune to fix his crooked teeth, but he hated the braces so much that he didn't even finish the treatment. And no, he didn't go to the orthodontist to get them taken off. Instead, he'd grabbed Dad's pliers from the garage, clamped them onto the brackets, and twisted them off himself.

Dad and Skippy had a tough relationship. For years, getting Skippy up in the mornings had been an ongoing battle between them. Sometimes it was especially tense. There was always the looming threat of missing the school bus if he was late. Because we lived out in the country, the farthest possible distance from our schools, and because Mom started work before we left for school, it was pretty important that none of us ever missed the school bus. If we missed the bus, we missed school.

Dad wasn't often home at suppertime since he had clients to see in the evenings. On Thursdays, he was at choir practice. I'd get my sisters and sometimes Mom to do the flag process in reverse when he wasn't there to do it with me. At night, I'd accompany the flag lowering with "Taps." The twins would help. One of them would pull on the halyard, and the other would wrap it around the cleat after they unfastened the flag. I'd try to play legato, attempting to maintain a warm, stately cadence, allowing the long notes of "Taps" to echo through the valley.

For some reason, even though the twins were allowed to help, Dad picked me over my siblings to be the main assistant in his flag stewardship rituals. He could've chosen his firstborn and his only son, but of course, Skippy wasn't interested. Dad could have shared this special interest with one of the twins, or both, for that matter. But he didn't. He'd selected me.

My lack of a special attribute—being the middle child and one of the girls—made it hard to understand why, out of all his children, he'd come to favor me. But he did. It was obvious. I think it irked my siblings that when he'd tell all of us a story, he'd start off with, "Mary, did I tell you about blah-blah-blah?" or "Blah-blah, Mary, blah-blah-blah." It probably didn't bother Skippy anymore. He was chomping at the bit to move out as soon as he graduated in a few weeks. However, I could see my sisters keeping track of when my name was mentioned and theirs were not. They'd confirm each tally with their identical twin sisters' smirk and almost imperceptible eye rolls and nods. He relied on my responses to and interactions with his stories as if I were the ambassador of his children. I loved that. I thought he was great, and it made me feel special.

We'd cautiously handle the Stars and Stripes, never letting it touch the ground. We were mindful to fold it into a tight triangle, like you're supposed to in the evenings. Even if Gerri or Jill had been the ones doing the special folding, Dad would pass me the flag and direct our gazes westward, toward the setting sun. "Mary, would you have a look at the sunset tonight? God is smiling this evening, isn't he?" I'd agree for all of us, and he'd add, "Would you put this in its special place in the garage until tomorrow morning?"

"Roger that, Dad." I made certain I left it just right. He could be really picky about that.

2

One of These Days

Dad had always dreamed of what he called the Great American Road Trip. He'd talk endlessly about a Boy Scouts expedition he'd gone on at my age, which he felt transformed him. He loved to tell us stories of the train ride from Cleveland, Ohio, all the way to Arizona, where he'd hiked down the Grand Canyon. Throughout all our childhoods, we'd heard about how *ex-tra-or-din-ary* America was. He'd made it sound like magic.

Taking his kids out West became one of his big dreams. We even had a AAA TripTik ready to go. But as the years marched on, the trip never happened. The farthest we ever got was local camping or the occasional visit to Mom's folks in Chicago. Would we ever go? Would he ever stop talking about it and just do it, or would it always be one of those ideas he hinted at, like some far-off fantasy waiting for the perfect moment to come true?

This wasn't the only dream he'd dangled in front of me growing up. He knew I wanted a horse. I wanted a horse so badly, I promised I'd do everything—ride it, brush it, feed it, muck the stalls. I'd even braid its mane and tail into something straight out of a magazine.

"We'll get a horse one of these days," Dad would say. He never said no, just that phrase—*one of these days*. It almost felt like he wanted me to keep asking, like the hope and the anticipation themselves were part of the fun. And hope did persist— right up until the day Mr. Chase, my gorgeous social studies teacher, unknowingly shattered it. In his classroom, he'd hung a poster of a breathtaking snowcapped mountain with a horse, of all things, in the foreground. Underneath, it said: *One of These Days Is None of These Days.*

Wait. What? *One of these days is none of these days?*

My jaw dropped. It hit me like a ton of bricks. There would never be a horse. Why had Dad kept saying otherwise? Why not just tell me no? Was it the money? Was he fooling himself? Did he secretly want a horse, too?

I'd thought and thought, but I couldn't make sense of it. It broke my heart. I kept coming back to his dream of the Great American Road Trip—and finally, I saw it for what it was: a dream teetering on the edge of vanishing, like the horse. I couldn't let that happen. If his dream was going to survive, it had to become mine, too. This summer would be perfect. I'd be starting high school in the fall, and the twins would be heading into middle school. We hadn't picked a summer project, so there was time for it. If we didn't do it now, we probably never would. By the next summer, I'd likely have a job.

So I went all in that spring. I dropped hints, made suggestions, and even helped get that TripTik ready, just in case. With Skippy about to move out, maybe Dad needed this—a way to show us three daughters that he still had it in him to be the real dad he'd always wanted to be. The trip could be his big moment, his proof to himself that he was doing fatherhood right.

Even if I never did get a horse, I wanted this for him. For us.

3

The Checkbooks

Several weeks later, right before school let out for the summer, I woke with a start in the middle of the night, sitting upright in bed as the full moon cast its buttermilk glow through my window, and held still to listen. What was that crashing sound? Was that my dad yelling? I pulled the covers back and tiptoed out of bed, passing the twins' door to better hear what was going on in the living room.

As I started down the hall, I saw my parents' reflections in the mirror hanging near the front door. This mirror allowed you to see all the way to the other side of the living room. Mom had a fistful of little booklets in her hand and was waving them at Dad, her voice tremulous. "Ralph, why do you have all these different families' checkbooks?" She looked at him with eyes so scared and wide open that I could see the whites, even in the semidarkness.

"What the hell are you doing sneaking around in my briefcase?" he slurred, lunging for the booklets and nearly falling over the little coffee table. Why was his voice so strange? I was alarmed to see him going after Mom like that. Crouching down in the hall and keeping quiet, I tried to still my pounding heart. Mom held on to the booklets, turning her back on him so that he couldn't reach them. She flipped through them, looking for something. Their white pages flashed in the moonlight that filtered through the sheer curtains of the living room.

"Johnson? Who are the Johnsons? Why do you have their checkbook?" She opened the next one. "Radners?" She opened another. "Schmidts?" Another. "Powers? Powers! Robert and LeeAnn? LeeAnn is my friend!" She looked up at his defensive face. "Do these people know you have accounts in their names? Ralph, what is this? Why do you have so many different checkbooks?"

Dad shifted from foot to foot, still trying to gain custody of the booklets in Mom's possession, only to be outmaneuvered every time he reached for them. Mom stood on the other side of the coffee table, using it as a shield. "The handwriting in the registries is all the same . . ." She heaved a sigh and smothered a sob with her hand. Her voice was barely above a whisper. "It's all *yours*."

She continued rifling through the booklets, dodging and twisting. Dad kept attempting to snatch them, reaching and grabbing this way and that, but she pivoted out of his grasp, nearly tripping over the table herself. Abruptly, Dad stopped trying to chase her and simply slumped against the wall in an unofficial truce. I stayed quiet.

Mom stared at him for a moment. Then, reassured he was finished chasing her for a time, she sat down heavily on the couch—head drooping and shoulders hunched—and sighed again. Her hands went up to her head, fingers entangling in her curly red hair, as she stared at the many booklets amassed in her lap, trying to make sense of it all. "Have you been rotating money around between the different accounts?"

It soon became clear that while Dad had given up on his pursuit of the booklets, he still wasn't ready to own up to his crimes. "You have no right going through my business papers! How the hell did you find those?" he kept saying, red in the face. "Give them to me!"

His reaction was embarrassing—for him, for Mom. For me.

Was Dad doing something bad? I thought about retreating back to my room, but I was terrified of getting caught—and at this moment, I was afraid any movement at all might give me away.

"That is not the point!" Mom hurled back, returning to life and jumping up. "What have you gotten us into?" On the brink of tears, she slammed the little checkbook registries one by one into his outstretched palms. She punctuated her words with each slap of a booklet. "Why—are—you—hid—ing—this—from—me? I'm your wife! I can *help* you," she supplicated. "You can't charm or sweet-talk your way out of this one!"

He grabbed at the booklets. "Stay out of my business. This is not illegal," he claimed.

Mom scoffed, rolling her eyes. Then, out of nowhere, she surged forward and slapped his hands, causing several of the booklets to go flying. Dad scrambled to gather them up, tripping on the coffee table and crawling on the floor. After returning them to his briefcase, he closed it and dramatically rotated the little dials on the built-in lock with the flourish of a magician.

Mom said, "Are you stealing from Peter to pay Paul?"

Who were Peter and Paul?

My feet were starting to fall asleep from crouching for so long. I wanted my parents to take their fight somewhere else so that I could leave, undetected, but it didn't look like that was going to happen anytime soon.

Dad, suddenly calm, seated with his legs casually crossed at the ankles, explained that it saved everybody time, which freed him up to make additional sales. There was more to it, of course, but it went right over my head, and I couldn't tell if Mom believed him or not. Not knowing how much longer I could remain in that crouched position, I scuttled backward down the hallway, pushing along with my pins-and-needles feet until I was almost out of earshot.

"Ralph, I can't take it anymore," Mom said quietly, sitting back down. That stopped me in my tracks. I strained to catch what came next. I was torn between wanting to hear them and not wanting to hear them. It made me feel grown-up to know what was going on in our family, even the bad stuff.

"What is that supposed to mean?" Dad said, acting surprised. He kicked the briefcase next to the couch, out of sight.

Shaking her head, she said, "I just can't take it."

"Can't take what?" he shot back, even though the fight seemed to have fizzled out of her. "Can't take what? The money I make?"

She considered him for a minute. "Yes. To be frank. The shady way you do your business. The corners you cut. And now this new kiting with the checks." Kiting? Where on earth was I supposed to find out what *kiting* meant? "The late nights away from the family. Do you want me to go on?"

"Sure, bitch. What else?"

I couldn't help but gasp from hearing him call her that. For a few seconds, I wondered if they'd overheard me. They hadn't. I covered my mouth with my hands to prevent a second offense, staying exactly where I was to learn more.

Mom cleared her throat. "Just last week at the twins' school's year-end performance, a woman, the mom of one of the twins' friends, asked Jill if I was a widow. Let that sink in." She paused, eyes locked on him. He started to protest, but she silenced him with a raised index finger. "Somehow you make an appearance every Thursday, without fail, at choir practice, but you don't have the time to be with us at supper." She shook her head. "Or go to the kids' shows. What do you do at night?"

"Oh, not this again. If I've told you once, I've told you a thousand times. Sales!" he shouted. "Sales, sales, and more sales! Do you have any idea—any idea at all—how many times I have to hear *no* for every *yes*? Do you? Do you have any fucking clue?"

Mom whisper-shouted back at him, "We can have this discussion without waking the kids. Be quiet. Please! It's the twins' birthday tomorrow and the first day of their summer break. Let's let them sleep in."

As if he hadn't heard her, he went on loudly, "Of course you don't! You never understand. You've never understood. You have never supported me." He stood up and paced. I was worried he'd spot me, so I backed up again.

"Never? Come on. Ralph, that's not true. I have supported you, and you know it." They both stayed quiet for a moment. That far down the hallway, I couldn't see what they were doing; I could only hear them—or rather, in this moment, hear the deafening silence that followed Mom's words.

Eventually, she took a big breath and said, "We're always in trouble during tax season, and I'm just waiting for the axe to fall.

That's it. I quit." She exhaled. "It's only a matter of time before you're caught. Before we're in serious trouble."

Dad didn't say a word.

I could hear Mom get up off the couch. When she got to her feet, I was able to see her reflection once again in the mirror on the wall and was startled by the severity of her expression.

"I want you out," she said plainly, pointing to the front door, as if he were to leave right then. Afraid that she would meet my gaze in the mirror, I huddled down even farther. "Take your late nights and whatever it is that you do and get out of my house."

"*Your* house?" He stood up and guffawed, mocking her. "You stupid cow."

"Oh, fiddle-faddle." She laughed off his insult like it meant nothing. I couldn't believe he didn't lash out again, though his silence was charged in a way that hinted he was thinking about it. "Now you're just being silly. I may need to get some help from my parents," she confessed, "but it would be doable, and worth it. And it wouldn't be any of your business. I am so unhappy with you and your cheating and infidelities—and now *this*." She gestured to his briefcase. "It's disgusting. You're disgusting. You disgust me," she finished.

"I disgust you? *I* disgust *you*? You disgust me, you frigid bitch!" he spat. "It's no wonder I must find love outside of our marriage. Fine. I'm out of here. You can have this shithole house!" he yelled, officially abandoning any pretense of not waking us kids up. "Maybe I'll take your precious daughters with me and do our Great American Road Trip this summer— without you."

I bet he was surprised when she responded without missing a beat, "Okay. Sounds like a great idea. How about the day after the twins' birthday tomorrow?" I could practically see her practical planning wheels spinning. "I'll help them pack, and you can finally take your dream trip. You and I can use the time as a trial separation to test the waters—"

"Before what?" Dad interrupted. "Test the waters before what?" His voice was softer.

"Before divorce," she replied without hesitation.

14

"Are you serious?" Was that fear or derision I heard in Dad's voice?

Shutting them out, I put my hands over my ears. Divorce! *They can't get divorced!* None of my friends had a broken family. What would they say at church? Having heard enough, I crawled to my room and got back into bed. Laying my head on the pillow and pulling up my quilt, I tried to forget the stuff they said, but my heart was pounding like when we ran the mile during gym class.

They'd argued about money stuff before, but this was different. I'd never heard her ask him to leave, and he'd called her a bitch. Did she really want a divorce? What would happen to me and the twins if Mom and Dad got a divorce?

I took a big soothing breath. I had to put their fight out of my mind.

I started my nighttime trick of calming down. Focusing on my body parts being heavy, I imagined sinking down through the mattress. I imagined my legs melting—toes, feet, ankles, shins, and then my knees. I took long, slow, deep breaths, focusing on nothing else. Ms. Chanel—our super-groovy middle school counselor—had taught us this cool trick last year, and it had served me well ever since. But even so, the thoughts inside my head interrupted the process. What was kiting? What were infidelities? The opposite of fidelity. What was fidelity? I didn't know. Back to my body. Knees, thighs, hips, belly. Breathe in and out. Slowly. The thoughts just kept coming and coming, like waves rolling onto the shore. Actually, more like a swirling tornado getting closer and closer.

"Stop thinking," I silently scolded myself. But *shithole house* and *stupid cow* were repeating in my mind like a skipping record stuck in a groove. I couldn't get my heart rate to slow down. Back to the melting body. Belly, chest, hands, arms, shoulders. Breathe. *Breathe.*

More thoughts, after only about two seconds. Maybe only one. I started thinking about money. We did have enough for the basics but nothing too fancy. We were all really skilled at making do. Making fun out of nothing. Maybe Dad was just doing what he had to do. He did say that what he was doing wasn't illegal, but it sure sounded like it scared Mom to death, which made me afraid, too.

Shoulders, neck, face . . .

Our trip! We'd finally use the TripTik!

At this rate, I was never going to fall asleep.

Usually, I'd fall asleep before I even got up to my head, but those racing, alarming thoughts beat me that night. *Stupid cow. Shithole house.* If they got divorced, it would just be the four of us girls left. I could get the twins to help me raise the flag in the mornings. Even with my eyes closed, I kept seeing the checkbooks, Mom's shaking hands clutching them, the white pages gleaming in the moonlight.

I started all over. Toes, foot, ankle.

PART 2

On The Road

4

The Wave Goodbye

Mom took us shopping at Kmart right after we gobbled up our cereal the next morning. The twins just thought we were enjoying an unprecedented shopping spree in celebration of their birthdays. They had the time of their lives, skipping through the aisles. Gerri even did a cartwheel, but then Mom told her to keep her hands off the filthy floor.

Despite everything, Mom was in an excellent mood. It was as if she was walking on air—as light as a feather after years of carrying a human-size boulder. Was she happy to leave Dad? To break our family apart? Or was it he who broke it? One thing was for sure: she didn't seem sad.

My eyes bugged out when I saw her pull out five twenties at the cash register. I hadn't seen her ever hold that much money before.

As she rifled through her coupon booklet and pulled out several pertinent ones, Jill told the cashier that we were going on the Great American Road Trip the next day. The cashier stared at us with a cockeyed expression, so I explained that my sisters and I were going on a trip with our dad for the whole summer, all the way to the Pacific Ocean in California. She smiled at me but gave Mom a different look.

"You're not going, too, ma'am?" she asked while she rang up our purchases, snapping her gum.

"I am not. I'll be working and holding down the fort. The girls and my husband can finally go do this big dream he's had for years. They won't need me." Only if you really listened for it could you hear any bitterness in her voice, especially on the word *husband*.

We rolled the cart with the bags of goodies to the car. I felt rich.

I wanted to forget about the terrible things Dad had said to Mom. I was happy to just go along as I always had, with him being the fun parent and her being the boring, serious one. Obviously, Mom didn't know I'd overheard their argument, and the twins certainly didn't realize why we were suddenly and out of the blue finally going on our Great American Road Trip, so as the day went on, it became easier for me to pretend things were as they'd been only twenty-four hours ago.

I shook off my clashing feelings as we drove to the army surplus store in Mentor—the bigger town next door—where Mom bought us four mess kits for the trip so that we would each have a tin plate, bowl, cup, and silverware. The silverware set was like a Swiss Army knife, where each of the utensils connected to one base; you could pivot out the fork or spoon or knife depending on the one you wanted to use. So groovy. I loved the silverware and fiddled with mine for the entire drive.

When we got home, Dad was in the garage with his head under the hood of his pride and joy, Blue Pierre, making sure everything was shipshape.

"Hi, troops," he called out brightly. Mom parked her station wagon in the shade of the big poplar tree next to the garage. "Happy birthday, girls!" The twins ran over for a hug from Dad, chitchatting about what they'd gotten and what he'd been doing while we were out. "I had to close up business for the summer, met a couple of clients to settle their accounts and such . . ." I stopped listening as I helped Mom carry the paper bags with our new stuff inside.

When the twins came in, Mom had them climb up to the attic while I held the ladder, and they passed down our rarely used set of pale-yellow Samsonite luggage. She loudly informed us that the luggage had been a gift from TeenTeen and Grandpa Red. "Can you believe these were a wedding gift? That was over seventeen years ago now."

"They look brand new," I remarked.

Mom smiled. "That's how you take care of things."

Placing them on Mom and Dad's bed, Mom orchestrated our packing. We used scissors to cut off the price tags and folded and rolled things neatly to fit. The twins shared the large suitcase, I took the middle-size one, and Dad's stuff went into the small one.

We each laid out our first day's traveling outfit on our bedroom floors. Mom had taught us girls that trick a long time ago. We did it every night before school, setting out the articles of clothing like a flat, two-dimensional person. Even the shoes. That way, you'd remember all the things you needed. It saved us the time of decision-making every morning. Skippy wouldn't do it, though.

Eventually, Dad came bounding in, excited about the preparations. "Blue Pierre is fit as a fiddle and ready to go," he announced, looking at me and anticipating a laugh because "Fit as a Fiddle and Ready to Go" was the name of the piano fingering exercise that I used to practice all the time.

I gave him the response he expected, but I didn't feel it the way I normally did.

*   *   *

After a night of fitful sleep, thoughts racing from excitement and anticipation, the next morning finally arrived. We all bolted out of bed the second the sun rose over Buster and Rascal's corral. Surprisingly, Dad let us hurry up the flag-raising bugle call that morning.

After returning the trumpet to my bedroom, I hollered, "I get the front seat!" I dragged my suitcase behind me and toward the garage. As the older sister, I was generally guaranteed this position. Because the twins were smaller and really did enjoy each other's company best, their relegation to the back seat was obvious, especially for a lengthy trip like this one.

We all piled into Blue Pierre. The squeaky Styrofoam cooler was packed with bologna sandwiches, apples, carrots, chips, cookies, some leftover pink birthday cake from the twins' birth-day, and a big plastic jug of—also pink—Kool-Aid. The luggage was in the trunk. Dad was about to start the engine when sud-denly he paused and instructed us to use the bathroom one last time before departing.

"But I don't have to go," Gerri said, and all of us, groaning at her, replied, "Go anyway!"

"I've just got to check that I've packed something," Dad said before hopping out of the vehicle and cracking open the trunk.

It was hot outside already, so I decided to sit in the shade while I waited. Mom eventually came around the corner, saw that Dad was busy doing something in the trunk of the car, and pulled me aside. We sat on the front porch, the concrete steps refreshingly cold on my bare legs. She took my hand in hers and spoke seriously. "Mary, I want you to keep your eyes open wide on this trip."

"How so?" I asked.

With her other hand, she stroked my cheek, then tucked a loose strand of hair behind my ear, and I could tell she was choos-ing her words carefully. "Well, you know how Dad can be—"

"What do you mean, *how Dad can be?*" I interrupted, trying to hide the scowl that crept across my lips. I suddenly resented her, even though I knew full well what she was hinting at. It was irrational, but part of me wanted to blame her for the fight they'd had, just so I wouldn't have to blame Dad since I'd be together with him so closely for the next several weeks. We'd looked forward to this trip for years, perhaps even over half of my life, and I didn't want their issues poisoning our experi-ence—even though, in many ways, it already had.

She looked at me, brows raised. "Come on."

I stayed silent.

With a sigh of resignation, she said, "Where should I start?" She dropped my hand and began counting off on her fingers. "His overenthusiastic ways, his always being the life of the party, his flamboyant and embarrassing antics, the ooga horn, his loud voice"—she had to continue the counting on her second hand—"his storytelling, the way he flirts with anyone in a skirt. Should I go on?"

"I don't think those are bad things," I reasoned, defending him. "Well . . . maybe the flirting part is kind of icky."

"Oh good, you do see," she said. "He can be self-centered and might not always have your best interests in mind. Just keep yourself and your little sisters safe. I want you to be extra aware of things that are happening." She straightened her oversize, frumpy housedress. "Dad can get out of hand sometimes."

I tried to see things from her point of view. Even though I didn't want to, I knew she wasn't wrong for worrying. Dad was the fun one, so she had no choice but to be the serious one. I supposed somebody had to keep the balance. It made me wonder if, had she married a different kind of husband, she would have been a different kind of mother. Maybe then she could've been the fun one.

"I'm just trying to tell you to keep your eyes open and to trust your instincts if anything doesn't feel right."

"Mo-om." I stretched out the one-syllable word into two. I didn't want to think about all this stuff. I got her point. "Come on, everything's going to be okay. Don't worry. What could go wrong?"

"Now you sound just like him." Even though she laughed, I could tell she was uneasy. "I hope everything will be okay. And it probably will be. But remember, though, that if for any reason—and I do mean *any* reason—you think something is wrong, if you feel uncomfortable or unsafe, please find a pay phone and call me collect. I'll accept the charges." She smiled at me and mussed up my hair. "You are a very, very smart girl, and a long summer stuck in the car with just Dad and the twins might not prove to be a bed of roses, you know."

I thought for a moment and laughed, imagining our body odors amplified in the summer heat and conceding that it indeed might be the opposite of a bed of roses. Even though I thought she was overreacting, I did want to reassure her, so I reached for her hand and squeezed it. "Okay, Mom. I'll be extra aware of things going on and take good care of the girls. I promise to act like their mother."

She squeezed me tightly. Standing up, she smacked me on the derrière, and while brushing away a tear, she said, "I know you'll do your best. You've always been so precocious that I sometimes forget you're still a child yourself."

I felt a strange hybrid of embarrassment and pride. Muttering, I replied, "I'm thirteen, you know."

"I just want you girls to return to me at the end of the summer, safe and sound."

"Don't worry, Mom—"

"I *am* worried," she interrupted. Her shift in energy made it clear that the reality of us girls being under Dad's supervision all summer was officially sinking in. "Worried that he'll make bad decisions and get you all in trouble. Worried that his stupid car will break down, or that he won't feed you all properly, or that you'll run out of money." She reached into the pocket of her dress, pulled out a twenty-dollar bill, and placed it in my palm, spooning her fingers around mine. "Keep this a secret. Tuck it away, just in case you need it." She raked her fingers through her hair, leaving furrows behind. "Oh jeez. You'll probably be fine. But what if . . ." She trailed off when Gerri came back out.

"We'll be okay, Mom." I leaned my head on her shoulder and wrapped my arms around her, accepting the money, but I don't think my reassurances reassured her at all. She shook her head and deliberately lowered her tensed-up shoulders, trying to appear at ease when she wasn't. It seemed just a little too practiced, that movement.

Gerri and Jill skipped over and hugged her and Namo, our dog, goodbye. I don't think Mom had any more worrying words left since she just held on to the little ones for an extra-long amount of time and didn't say much. She and Dad didn't hug and barely said goodbye.

"Okay, kiddos. Here we go. Hop in for the time of your lives!" Dad's voice boomed. He clapped his hands, and I felt a zip of excitement jolt through me. We all piled into the car and did the goodbye wave in our family's traditional manner. The ones who were staying behind would stand in the driveway with upraised arms waving, and the ones departing would wave their hands frantically out the windows and sunroof. Mom dutifully played her part, not even brushing away her tears, waving until we were completely out of sight.

Dad had equipped Blue Pierre—his baby-blue 1967 Peugeot—with an ooga horn, which he blasted continuously as we headed down the driveway. We retracted our arms, and Mom lowered hers. I bet she was shaking her head.

Besides being sad over our departure and the worry and concern she'd just shared with me, I bet another part of her relished the thought of weeks alone without all our explosive and constant energy in the house. We three girls fought about all kinds of things—the single bathroom, especially. I guessed she envisioned the house free of noise and projects and messes and bickering. She was likely imagining weeks of just her and Namo in her nice, clean, quiet house. No jerk of a husband and his unethical ways. Weeks to do whatever she wanted, eat whatever she wanted, whenever she wanted—if she even knew what that was anymore—and not be needed to tend to us. I'm guessing she was looking forward to this summer as much as we were. But on deeper thought, I wondered if there was more to what she might have been thinking.

"Come on, Namo, let's go inside," she'd say, our old Airedale mutt wagging her tail.

* * *

We headed west on Route 6, crossed 306 at the only stoplight in Kirtland, said goodbye to our little town, and got onto Interstate 90. In Cleveland, we could see and smell Lake Erie at Edgewater Park on our right as we rounded Deadman's Curve.

"Pee-*ew!*" said Jill, waving her hand in front of her nose.

"That's dear ol' Cleveland for you," Dad agreed, laughing.

After a few hours, nearing Sandusky, we passed the amusement park we'd been to many times.

"Look! There's Cedar Point! Look!" Gerri hollered as she indicated the spired flags and the skeletons of the roller-coaster rides.

"Can we go to Cedar Point, Dad?" Jill asked.

"Nope."

I saw Jill frown at his curt reply. Dad went on, "We've been to Cedar Point lots of times. This trip is going to be full of new things. Don't you worry, though!" He turned his head toward the back seat. "Girls, this is going to be a trip of a lifetime. We have the TripTik to guide us as far as where we're going in a general sense. Along the way, I'm sure we'll walk into all kinds of adventures. *New* adventures."

"Where are we going first?" Jill asked.

"Grandma and Grandpa's house," Dad said with a weak smile. "They're probably waiting for us. You know how much they love spoiling us—and it's been six months since we visited them in Chicago for Christmas."

He turned around, smiling to himself, his dream coming true even though it took a threat from Mom for him to finally seize it.

5

The Driver's Helper

"Okay, Mare, open the TripTik and orient yourself."

Everybody in our family knew that if you were the front-seat passenger, you were assigned the title of being the Driver's Helper. Dad, of course, was the Driver. He'd always liked to assign job titles to demonstrate the importance of the roles we played and how working together, with no one job being more important than another, was the way to make things go smoothly.

The girls in the back seat were the Food Distributors, which entailed passing out the sandwiches and other snacks and pouring the Kool-Aid. That was a big development for them. I could remember, for what seemed like years, neither of them being able to pour anything without spilling it.

The Driver's Helper's job was key to the smooth operation of the road trip—a big responsibility. There were three main things the Driver's Helper had to do. First, I had to manage the TripTik and maps so that we knew where we were going. And second, there was the business of the CB radio that we used to inform us of local traffic, weather, and the presence of police in the area.

The third job of the Driver's Helper was to oversee the music selections. That might sound like a neat part of the job, being the one who got to choose the music, but I felt weird about being the one to decide what everyone should listen to. I didn't think it was any one person's responsibility to choose for all, so I generally rotated the selection for each of us. Our car had an eight-track tape player, and we had exactly two cassettes with us. I wondered why we hadn't brought a few more. When it was Gerri's turn, she often selected the Statler Brothers' *Holy Bible: Old Testament.* Jill usually chose the other one, the Carpenters' *Now & Then.*

When it was my turn, I would explore stations on the radio. Through these expeditions, I came to learn that the FM stations had better reception when we were near urban areas, and AM stations didn't have good reception for very long, no matter where we were. I tended to stay away from the AM stations and stuck to FM, where there was more unusual music and news channels.

"What does that mean, *paid for by the generous contributions of listeners like you?*" I asked Dad after hearing that phrase for the umpteenth time.

"That means it's a noncommercial station and is different from the normal commercial stations we usually listen to. I think they're doing some fundraising."

Dad loved explaining stuff. If you were ever getting in trouble for something, you could often drop in a well-timed question to veer the conversation away from your misbehavior and onto some other topic he'd love to expound upon.

"The noncommercial stations are the college stations and NPR, the National Public Radio station. They're usually down in the upper eighties and lower nineties on the radio dial. So that makes them kind of easy to find." He glanced my way to see if I was paying attention. "They don't take as many advertisements and are thus free to play what they really want to play, so their programming is more independent but might not be as popular."

"Uh-huh," I added to keep him going. However, my attention started to drift as he droned on.

"Commercial stations get money from advertisers. That's why you hear all those commercials about Dr Pepper and McDonald's and Libby's on the Label along with the songs. You won't hear ads like that on the independent stations."

That reference reminded us of a current television commercial. The three of us interrupted Dad midway through his spiel, in unison, to burst into song. *"When it says Libby's, Libby's, Libby's on the label, label, label, you will like it, like it, like it on the table, table, table."*

"Do you want an answer to your question or not?"

"Okay, sorry." I chuckled, red-faced, and looked back at the girls, who were quietly laughing.

"So radio stations are businesses trying to make a profit . . ." I started to zone out as Dad explained all about the differences between the types of radio stations. I heard my sisters whispering and giggling in the back seat about something or other, and I felt a little jealous that they weren't really expected to listen to Dad as much as I was. So much for being the ambassador of his kids.

Sometimes I wish I wouldn't have asked, but I knew he loved to talk and educate, and what else were we supposed to do in the car for hours on end? It was way better to be in his good graces and try to help maintain a calm environment for all.

Eventually, Dad concluded his monologue, and we all got quiet for a while after that.

Feeling sleepy, I laid my head on the cool window and hummed softly to feel the road vibrations in my throat. Looking up, I noticed we were passing a pair of Harley-Davidsons. Their rumbling noise added to the vibrations I felt. One of the motorcycles had a driver and a passenger—a little kid, I'd guess about eight years old. His helmet must've been too large since I could see it kind of bouncing around.

"Hold on tight," I whispered.

6

The TripTik

In what would come to be a regular daily question, Dad asked, "Hey, Mary, can you find where we are on the map or the TripTik?" Managing the music and entertainment was an important job of the Driver's Helper, but the main responsibility was overseeing the American Automobile Association's custom-built TripTik.

The AAA TripTik was a spiral-bound travel planner, and we used it to navigate our route. We'd visited the AAA travel office several months earlier in optimistic preparation for this trip—which, at the time, we weren't entirely sure would ever happen—and acquired road maps, individual or grouped state guidebooks, and the amazing TripTik.

"Well, hello there, Jenny!" Dad had singsonged by way of a greeting, glancing down at her name tag. I noticed his gaze lingered on the opening of her low-cut blouse. *Ew.* I had blushed with embarrassment. He could be creepy like that. "We're planning a big family trip, and you're just the gal we need to help us."

Dad was practically oozing charisma, still wearing his clip-on sunglasses and with his elbow casually propped on the countertop. Was he trying to look like Warren Beatty in *Bonnie and Clyde*, all cool and stylish? Maybe, but either way, Jenny completely ignored him. In fact, she made a face that looked like she'd just bitten into a lemon, then turned her focus to us, winking at the twins.

"Where are you going?" she'd asked us girls.

Dad had kept on smiling, oblivious.

Jenny's outfit was super groovy. I thought she could've been a dancer on *American Bandstand* with her purple wrap-around maxi skirt and paisley jacket with fringe. Her shoes were wedge high-heeled sandals. A little leather headband around her forehead held her two dark-brown braids in place.

"Well, if we ever go, we'd be leaving Kirtland, heading to my in-laws' in the Chicago area first, then traveling west along the northern part of the country, getting to the Pacific Ocean, and returning along the southern route," Dad informed her.

"Well, that sounds far-out! I'm happy to help. Let's get some details, shall we? You just tell me about the places on your route, and I'll get your TripTik in order for you."

We'd nodded excitedly. It was going to be great to have a personalized map.

"You can come back in a week to pick up the completed TripTik, and I'll use this orange highlighter to mark the route for you, like this one I have ready for another client." She'd showed us a prepared TripTik. It looked so thick and full of adventures. "Ready to start?" I noticed she'd looked exclusively at the three of us kids and not at Dad. "Point A is here in Kirtland, and point B is where?"

"Clarendon Hills, Illinois," Jill said. "That's where Grandma TeenTeen and Grandpa Red live. It's by Chicago."

Jenny settled into the big task as we detailed our trip, telling her about the exotic places we wanted to go to, like Yellowstone and Mount Rushmore and the Great Salt Lake. I especially wanted to see the surfers and swim in the Pacific Ocean. Dad made sure she included Chinatown in San Francisco, too.

"Don't forget the Grand Canyon," he had added.

The following week, as promised, we'd gone back to the travel office to pick up our customized three-volume TripTik.

"This is the biggest TripTik I've ever prepared!" Jenny had boasted, pride evident in her eyes. And true to her word, she'd marked out our route and noted points of interest with her bright-orange highlighter. She'd asked if we would come see her when we got back. At the time, I'd wanted to say it was a trip I doubted would ever actually happen.

When she'd handed me the highlighter, she'd given me a cryptic look. "Be careful out there. Make sure your dad behaves himself." She looked pointedly at Dad, who smiled. Little did I know that the trip would actually take place and that Mom would give me the exact same warning about Dad.

"I will," I'd murmured, and I gave her my word that we'd come back when our trip was over and tell her all about it.

7

My Journal of Life

The first day of driving stretched on endlessly, leaving me wondering how we'd survive weeks of this. But as we cruised westward on I-90, the afternoon sun poured through the sunroof, casting a warm glow over Blue Pierre. Traffic was light, the road smooth, and Dad hummed happily. Gerri and Jill, our expert Food Distributors, passed out snacks without spilling a drop of Kool-Aid, and their duties expanded as we approached Toledo. Armed with a bag of change, they took turns as Toll Payers, perching behind the Driver to toss coins into the baskets with precision.

"Who wants to track the states we pass through?" Dad asked.

As if rehearsed, the back seat erupted with "We do!"

Jill opened her notebook and titled a page *States We've Been In*. She drew columns with the help of her little ruler and labeled them "Date" and "State." Gerri, ever the perfectionist, leaned over her shoulder and said, "Don't you want another column for stuff like what we did there or the weather?"

"Good idea!" Jill added a new column, pausing to think of a title. "Dad, what should I write for this one?"

"How about *miscellaneous*?"

"Holy cow." Jill's eyes widened. "How do you spell that?"

"Try M-I-S-C," Dad said, chuckling.

Gerri wrinkled her nose. "How about calling it Fate? It rhymes with *Date* and *State*."

Dad looked amused by the suggestion. "Sure. Fate is some-thing that happens to people. It's usually out of their control. Perfect for an adventure."

"Excellent idea, Ger-Bear!" I chimed in. "Date, State, Fate—it's great!"

We were all giggles, rhyming nonsense words until Dad's laughter filled the car. Moments like these made me feel like we were the luckiest family alive.

Of course, it hadn't always been sunshine and rhymes. I thought back to the time when Gerri and Jill got stuck in quick-sand down by the creek. Yeah, real quicksand. Skippy and I had saved the day, hauling them out with his cowboy lasso. When we finally made it home, caked in mud from head to toe, Mom was livid. She made us strip down in the yard while trying—and fail-ing—not to laugh as she hosed us off. The patio was so covered in thick mud, it looked like a dozen dirty diapers had sponta-neously detonated.

Oddly, the mud on the patio got me thinking about the chocolate cake incident. I couldn't resist dragging my finger across the frosting before church. When Dad found the gash, he called us into the kitchen, radiating fury as he demanded, "Who ruined Mom's cake?" After a chaotic round of denials, he'd made us write yes-or-no answers on slips of paper. It turned out that Skippy and I had both written *yes*—me confessing to the crime and him just wanting the ordeal to end. We both got punished, but I was the only one stuck writing a report about why honesty matters.

I pulled myself out of my reverie, looking to the left at Dad while he continued driving. He had always wanted to remem-ber everything. Big lessons, little adventures. At some point, that had rubbed off on me, and I'd started to keep track of my own *ex-tra-or-din-ary* experiences, like breaking my arm on a botched rope-swing jump or emceeing the third-grade tal-ent show. But for every real journal entry, there were a dozen half-filled notebooks gathering dust on my "cemetery shelf." I always meant to document my experiences by hand, but I didn't always have the time.

Eventually, I invented My Journal of Life. It wasn't a physical book, just a mental log where I'd store vivid snapshots of my life. In my mind, it was perfect—beautiful entries, intricate illustrations, even flawless penmanship. My Journal of Life let me pause and savor the moment without the pressure of pen and paper. But here's the thing about My Journal of Life: I didn't get to pick what was included. The good, the bad, and the ugly all went in. Like the day Mom folded that twenty-dollar bill into my hand, her voice trembling as she whispered, "Just in case." Or the time I caught Dad ogling Jenny at the TripTik counter, that one crooked tooth denting his bottom lip. My Journal of Life was messy, chaotic, and sometimes painful. But it was mine.

Blue Pierre hit a bump in the road, jolting me back to the present. Dad was humming and smiling, totally in his element. I glanced out the window, the sun painting the horizon gold, and realized I was making a new journal entry right then and there. I wondered what I'd add to My Journal of Life before the trip was over.

8

The Slate

After a few hours, we at last neared the western border of Indiana. At this point, Gerri and Jill had started to doze in the back seat, and I'd slipped into a comfortable silence. I watched acres and acres of green fields roll by.

Eventually, however, Dad broke the silence. "Mary, is there a place coming up soon that's near Michigan where we can cross the border and touch our feet down to add it to our list of states?"

I gave Dad a strange look, which I quickly redirected to the road ahead of us. "We're going to go out of our way just to touch our feet down in more states?"

"Uh-huh." He laughed. "This is supposed to be a fun trip. Plus, we want Jill to have a lot to add to the Slate of Dates, States, and Fates, right?"

"Oh, that's great, Dad," Jill said as she pulled out her notebook and tore out the page. "I'm going to change the title to 'Slate of Dates, States, and Fates.'" She started all over with the correct headings and only had a little to backtrack.

"Groovy, Dad. I love that," I said, warming to the idea. I grabbed the TripTik, flipping through the narrow pages until I found where we were. "Here, let me see. Well, there's a road called Olive Branch Drive that looks close to, um, Galian, Michigan."

"Okay. Make sure to give me about a mile or two notice before we get there. We'll stop for gas and a bathroom break, too," he said.

"It's right by Lake Michigan," I said. "Can we go to the lake?"

"I don't see why not," Dad answered. "Sounds like a hip idea."

We arrived at the enormous lake a half hour later, right before four o'clock, while the sun was still high in the sky and the temperature warm. We changed into our swimsuits and Keds at the lake, holding towels up between the front and back doors of Blue Pierre to make a privacy screen.

When we emerged in our bikinis, Dad whistled and said, "Ooh! Sexy."

We cringed and crossed our arms over our chests, sharing an eye roll and a headshake with one another. We were accustomed to that type of remark from him. I often wondered why we even liked to spend time with him, given that he regularly made such comments. I guess the fun outweighed the icky. It reminded me of my best friend back home, Winnie Gravvers.

She and I were inseparable. We spent a lot of time together riding our bikes to Dairy Queen on hot summer days and swimming in her aboveground pool, acting out *Jaws*. In the winter, you'd find us tobogganing down our neighbor's big hill or playing our favorite board game, Stock Market, on our small dining room table.

By the time Winnie was twelve, Dad had started to refer to her as the sexiest girl on Crary Lane. He didn't even bother calling her Winnie. He'd say, right to her face, "Is the sexiest girl on Crary Lane going to join us this weekend?" Winnie's cheeks would go red, and she'd laugh uneasily. When I heard him speak that way, my skin would feel too tight, and I didn't know where to put my hands or how to make myself smaller. We knew it was wrong for a grown man to call us girls sexy. And I could tell it upset my mom, too. Then he'd be funny or normal again, and I'd forget about the cringeworthy thing he'd said or done.

Our time in Lake Michigan was fun but short-lived. When we were in the water, the waves were like mountains, even though they didn't seem that big at all from the shore. One big frothy wave knocked Gerri over, turning her around like a washing machine tumbling dirty socks. After sputtering to the surface, she was ready to get going.

"Come on, girls! Let's get back on the road," said Dad. "We still have a ways to go before we get to Teen's."

We quickly got back into our dry clothes, shivering despite the heat. The twins arranged our wet swimsuits and one small towel on the ledge behind the back seat to dry out. Knowing that we wouldn't be doing much laundry on the road, we didn't want mildewy suits and towels.

Jill pulled out her book and grabbed her pencil. Even though Blue Pierre was bounding along, she did a great job, neatly detailing our stop: *6/21/76 | Michigan | Swam in Lake Michigan.* I decided to make a new entry to My Journal of Life, adding the mental image of the lake's massive body reflecting the hard gold of the sun. It was so big; it felt like how I suspected the ocean to be. Then I tried in vain to forget Dad's remarks about us girls being sexy, using a mental eraser to scrub away his words, replacing them with dialogue that felt more acceptable. More paternal. I decided on "You girls look great!"

But it didn't work.

I knew, in my heart, that I'd remember he'd said that. What was worse was that I knew I'd also remember the way it had made me feel—that somehow I'd felt complimented by the remark, even if everything about it seemed so wrong that it'd made my skin crawl.

The entry documenting this trip in My Journal of Life wasn't off to a great start.

9

Banana Splits and Sundaes

When we arrived at TeenTeen and Grandpa Red's house on Mohawk Drive in the late afternoon, they came out and greeted us with outstretched arms. They were careful not to drop the ashes from their cigarettes on us as we hugged. Grandpa Red somehow had a knack for not letting his ashes fall, even though they got up to about an inch in length. It didn't seem possible that gravity wouldn't pull down the ash when it got that long. He would always flick it in the nick of time.

Within fifteen minutes of being inside, my eyes were already watering and stinging from the lingering haze of smoke woven into every surface—the floral wallpaper, the polished floorboards, the popcorn ceiling, and the emerald-green velvet upholstery that still held a faint trace of past holiday gatherings. Curiosity compelled me to scratch a fingernail over the textured wallpaper, and it came away with a gummy, dark residue, a silent testament to years of unhurried conversations over coffee and cigarettes. Even so, I didn't mind. My love for my grandparents eclipsed it all.

After the hugs and kisses and several rounds of *How are you?* and *Look how much you've grown!*, Grandpa Red said with a boom, "Must've been a long time in the car! Anyone want an ice-cream sundae or a banana split before supper?" We stared back at him in open shock. Noticing as much, he gave us all a sly wink and added in a whisper, "Don't worry. We won't let your mom know."

I knew it—I just *knew* it. I knew they'd have some awesome treat for us. It didn't matter if we were visiting them for a week at Christmas or at any other time of the year—it was always the same: they always had a surprise in store for us.

We followed him inside the house and skipped to the basement. I held his hand down the stairs—his arthritic, nicotine-stained fingers enveloping my red, nail-bitten ones. By the time I helped Grandpa Red carry a gallon of Neapolitan ice cream from the freezer upstairs to the kitchen, Gerri and Jill had already helped TeenTeen gather everything for banana splits. The yellow countertops—either faded from age or stained by cigarette smoke, who knew?—were covered with colorful toppings. A glass of bright-red maraschino cherries stood next to a lineup of squeeze bottles filled with chocolate, caramel, and strawberry sauces. There was a bunch of perfectly ripe bananas and a can of salted peanuts, too.

Grandpa Red plunked the ice cream down on the countertop's remaining space and used a knife to slice into the cardboard box, opening it. The twins and I stood there, mouths watering.

Grandpa turned to Dad and casually asked, "How's my daughter?"

Dad didn't miss a beat. "She's great. Probably enjoying this alone time."

"I'm sure she is," TeenTeen added with raised brows, and this generated a laugh among the adults for a moment. I didn't laugh at all. I looked at them curiously, wondering if Mom had told them about her and Dad taking a break from each other for the summer or if they just thought we were finally taking this trip that he'd dreamed about for ages.

They didn't reveal their hand either way, and neither did Dad, who acted as though nothing at all was out of the norm. If I were Grandpa Red or TeenTeen, though, I'd be a little more suspicious about Mom's absence.

10

Big Red, the Tricycle

After devouring our banana splits and sundaes, it was still light out, and TeenTeen asked if we wanted to take her grown-up tricycle, Big Red, out for a spin while she finished making supper.

"That would be great, TeenTeen!" I said. She led us into the garage and told us that Grandpa Red had pumped up the three tires and made sure everything was well oiled, greased up, tightened, and safe. Usually, we brought our own bikes with us, strapping them to the top of the station wagon, but for this Great American Road Trip with Blue Pierre, we'd decided to leave them behind.

The existence of Big Red, the Tricycle, never struck me as unusual, but the more I observed that no other grown-ups had tricycles, the more I realized what a rarity it was. TeenTeen's explanation was that after a certain age, she just couldn't ride a regular bike anymore. "I'm too old to keep trying to balance, but I do enjoy a good pedal!" she'd declared, and that was that. So, for her birthday a few years back, Grandpa Red bought her a grown-up-size bright-red tricycle.

She called it Big Red, which was a funny name for the tricycle because it was also Grandpa Red's nickname at work before he retired. Grandpa Red was a large Irish man, and like his many brothers and sisters, he used to have bright-red hair. It wasn't a suitable nickname anymore, though. Big White would be more fitting.

Big Red, the Tricycle, had blue streamers extending from the ends of the handlebars; a bell you could ding to warn others that you were coming; and a white wicker basket hanging off the front, where you could carry library books and other little stuff. In the back were collapsible wire baskets that were meant to hold paper grocery sacks.

"Let's lower the baskets in the back so that I can ride Gerri and Jill around. TeenTeen, do you have a towel we could use to keep the twins' legs away from the pokey edges of the baskets?" I asked, and after a brief nod, she went back into the house and returned with a small folded blanket.

As we started to pedal away, she called after us, "You make sure to be back in less than an hour and to stay in our Blackhawk Heights! Do not go out onto East Chicago Avenue. You hear? It's much too busy for you three to be out there. Mary, you remember what happened last time."

"Yes, TeenTeen," I murmured.

"Stick to our roads and sidewalks in Blackhawk Heights. Hear?" she repeated.

"Yes, TeenTeen, we promise," I said, thinking back to the time, on one of my first solo Big Red Trike rides, when I got lost and the police brought me back to their place. They had loaded Big Red into the trunk of their cruiser with the wheels and handlebars sticking out and the trunk lid bouncing around, even though they had tied it down with some twine. The cops let me sit in the front seat and showed me what the different dials and fancy radios up there were for.

Even though where TeenTeen and Grandpa Red lived wasn't a big city, it was way bigger than our little town in Ohio. It even had sidewalks! Where we were from, the country roads were wide and gravelly, and they got oiled once a summer to keep the dust down.

Sidewalks were a novelty. I loved zigzagging between the sidewalk and the road, weaving in and out at the driveways. Sometimes there were tree roots pushing up the concrete, creating little ramps you could launch from.

"Mary! Be careful on those tree roots! It's bumpy back here!" Jill hollered when we bounced over one on a small descent. "Ow!" she screamed. I tried to turn around to see if she was serious, but the sudden movement made me jerk the handlebars, and we careened off the sidewalk and then back on, hitting another root, sending them bouncing even higher before landing on the sharp edges in back. I guess the protective blanket idea didn't really pan out.

"Sorry, Jill!" I yelled, turning my head so that she could hear me—a lock of hair whipped its way into my open mouth, stifling my words. I spat it out. "*Sorry,* I said."

The brake pads squealed when I squeezed the stiff brake lever and pedaled backward as quickly as possible. Gerri reached her arm around Jill in comfort while Jill scowled at me as we finally came to a stop.

"What?" I said. "How many times do I have to say it? I. Am. Sorry."

"You did it on purpose!" Jill accused me.

"I did not. It was an accident. We were going too fast." Seeing that she was close to tears and was rubbing her derrière, I repeated, "Sorry, Jill."

We rearranged the blanket, and I watched where I was going more carefully for the remainder of the ride back to TeenTeen's. When we approached her house on the last fun downhill section, I noticed TeenTeen's halo of cigarette smoke before I saw her step out into the driveway, checking her tiny gold watch. "I see you've made it just in time. It's pert near an hour now," she said, giving the twins a pat on their heads as they dismounted. Jill rubbed her sore derrière. Gerri hopped off and opened their garage door, and I rolled Big Red into its parking spot.

11

Have a Good Night, Mare

After supper and a card game of euchre, Grandpa Red asked Jillerri to give him a hand. He called either or both of them Jillerri, a combination of Jill and Gerri, because he still couldn't tell them apart, even though he'd known them for ten years. Come on, Grandpa Red! Identical twins don't look *exactly* alike. Besides, it wasn't like they dressed identically, too.

I thought it was cool that Mom always enforced a sense of individuality between them, which was, of course, appropriate because they were quite different in personality, despite being twins. They didn't act alike at all. Jill was more like me—kind of bossy and direct. That's probably why she and I fought more than Gerri and I did. Gerri was kinder and liked it when everyone got along. Jill was a little bigger and had a rounder face, and her glasses were the hexagon ones. Her nickname was Bread Buns because she was softer. Gerri, in contrast, was slighter and shorter, and she sported the squarer frames. She was Biscuit Buns because she was kind of bony. Most people couldn't tell them apart, but Grandpa Red was family. He should have been able to.

"Mary and Jillerri," he said, nodding across the room, "would you girls care to arrange the cigarettes and books of matches in the smoker?"

They had a special piece of furniture dedicated entirely to the storage of their smoking materials, which they kept near the base of the stairs. While the twins reorganized the books of matches, I stocked the lower drawers with the red-and-white packages of Viceroy cigarettes, arranging them in an alternating pattern: red, white, red, white. They looked like checkerboard American flag stripes.

After organizing the smoker, we went upstairs to bed. Gerri and Jill used Aunt Viv's old bedroom, which had two twin beds—twins for the twins, we called it. The room had a slanted ceiling, and you had to be careful not to bonk your head. Dad slept downstairs on the couch. Grandpa Red and TeenTeen had separate rooms, and I got to sleep with TeenTeen.

After brushing my teeth, I joined her in her room. While I got into my nightgown, she took off her wig and placed it carefully on the white Styrofoam head on her dresser. She took off the little pantyhose cap and placed it next to the head. Her glasses were resting lens-side up on the nightstand. Then she removed her dentures and put them in a little plastic container with water. I opened the package of Efferdent and dropped the two tablets into the container to bubble and fizz overnight. Next, she removed her bra with the prosthetic breast and put on her little nightgown.

Grandma TeenTeen looked much smaller and frailer when she removed all those parts. Giving me a kiss on the cheek and then pulling the cord on the bedside lamp, she said, "You have a good night, Mare." But without her teeth, it sounded like "Ooh 'ave a goo' nigh', Mare."

"You have sweet dreams, TeenTeen." I giggled.

"Twi nah ooh ick me ooh muh is ime," she gummed. We had done this verbal routine so many times before, I knew she meant, "Try not to kick me too much this time."

"Try not to snore too loud," I countered, playing my part in our traditional nighttime exchange. "I love you, TeenTeen."

"I uv ooh ooh, 'ary. Now o ooh slee."

I smiled, rolled over, closed my eyes, and did just what she said.

12

Phoebe's Ham Salad

Later the next day, we helped TeenTeen prepare some food for our cooler. She had me fetch the old metal meat grinder in the low cupboard. Stooping down, I lugged out the familiar beast and cringed when I banged the crank on my shin. Every time we used this thing, TeenTeen needed to remind us all that it was the same one her mother, Phoebe, had used.

"All right, girls, go grab those big jars of sweet pickles and Miracle Whip. Mare, the bologna is in the ice chest."

"These two big white paper tubes, TeenTeen?" I asked, bending over and peering into the refrigerator.

"Yep, that's them," she said, swatting my derrière with her cigarette-holding hand. "When I heard you were coming, I had Leroy, my butcher, prepare them special for us." Aha! Mystery solved. Mom *had* called her ahead of time. I sometimes forgot that my mom was also a daughter. She might have called her mom for some advice and sympathy after the big fight I'd overheard. I wondered how much Mom told her. TeenTeen exhaled a plume of smoke while I pulled off the twine and laid the bologna on its opened butcher paper on the counter.

"Warsh your hands, girls, and let's get started," TeenTeen instructed.

Jill grabbed the two big cylinders of bologna. I don't know what came over her, but she raised them over her head like a muscleman lifting dumbbells and sang out, *"My bologna has a first name. It's O-S-C-A-R."*

Not missing a beat, Gerri hopped up from the ladder-back chair and stood next to her twin in the cramped kitchen, chiming in while TeenTeen looked on in surprise. *"My bologna has a second name. It's M-A-Y-E-R."*

I rounded out the trio, positioning myself between the two of them, my arms draped around their narrow shoulders. *"Oh, I love to eat it every day, and if you ask me—why—I'll—say."* We concluded the jingle with a ritardando, then a fermata, and with my nod, we finished off a tempo: *"Cuz Oscar Mayer has a way with B-O-L-O-G-N-A."*

When Jill went to take a bow, those large, slippery tubes of bologna slid right out of her small hands. We all watched them, as though in slow motion, bounce on the table and then onto the floor. One tube of bologna cracked and broke in half. The other whole one slid along the vinyl floor with them, and all three pieces came to a halt near the sink.

Standing with mouths agape, we looked, saucer-eyed, at TeenTeen for her response. Her face was as open as could be, eyebrows shooting up and mouth gaping wide. We held our breath, and then she exploded in what we had come to refer to as the TeenTeen laugh. A raucous guffaw. A loud yet somehow still nearly silent deep-throated cough of a cackle that went on and on. Her dentures made a clicking sound as she bit them back into place. She plopped down in her chair and clutched the hem of her old-fashioned apron, gathering a section and dabbing at the laugh-induced tears in her eyes.

"Well, I'll be damned! Two and two are four and shit is eight!" She gasped her way through the words, still wheezing with laughter. Wide-eyed and still vaguely afraid we'd get into trouble over this, my sisters and I looked at one another in sheer disbelief. If we'd pulled this at home, it wouldn't be good. Dad might've made a show of it being funny, but Mom certainly wouldn't have tolerated the tomfoolery we'd so openly displayed.

"I was just fixin' to tell Jill to put that bologna down in case she got butterfingers before y'all started your little song. And lo and behold . . ." TeenTeen trailed off, dabbing her eyes again, the ash holding on for dear life at the tip of her cigarette. "Did you

47

see them skedaddle across the floor? My Lordy, Lordy, *Lordy*." She wheezed between laughs. "In all my born days!"

Relieved, we exhaled. If she thought it was funny, so did we, and we joined in her hysterics.

After a moment, Jill, with uncharacteristic meekness, collected the pieces of bologna and ran them under water to rinse off the floor germs. TeenTeen got up and helped her dry them off on an embroidered dish towel.

"I'm sorry, TeenTeen," she proffered quietly.

Shaking her head, TeenTeen patted Jill on the shoulder. "Okay. Very nice, girls. Now let's settle down and get cranking here." TeenTeen chuckled, shaking her head again.

"Good one, Teen. I get it. Cranking, right? Cuz we're cranking?" Jill offered.

"Uh-huh." Teen winked at her, then clapped her hands. "Okay! Let's go. Gerri, dump that whole jar of Miracle Whip into the bowl and use a spatula to get every last drop. We'll take turns grinding the bologna since you really need some elbow grease to move that old crank."

Gerri did as she was told, climbing up on the chair to tip the jar of dressing into the big bowl.

"Mary, get your fingers out of your mouth! You just warshed them. Nail-biting is a disgusting habit." She shook her head, and her little brunette wig shifted a bit. "Go warsh them again and then use that sharp knife to cut great big slabs of what's left of the bologna into the proper size to fit into the chute of the grinder while Jill starts the pickles."

TeenTeen sat down to strike a match and puff-puff-puffed a fresh cigarette to life. Once the little red tip was glowing, she pursed her lips, tipped her head back, and exhaled an impressive smoke ring. I thought cigarette smoking was a rather disgusting habit myself, but she adjusted her wig and went on. "I miss your mom. Don't you? Doesn't seem the same without her here."

I walked to the sink to wash my nail-bitten hands, and when I glanced at her, I could see Mom's face behind Teen's glasses and under her wig. There were differences, of course, but their features were remarkably similar. They had the same high cheekbones and straight nose. They even had similar eye colors: a greenish-brown hazel that reminded me of spring.

Seeing Mom in TeenTeen made me miss her even more. How could we have ended up on this trip without her? In fact, I couldn't remember a time when we had ever visited TeenTeen and Grandpa Red without her before. I was so eager to finally go on our trip, after all these years of discussing it, that I hadn't thought about all the ways Mom would have made it better.

"Jill, use that wooden plunger to press the pickles down. When your mom and Vivian were little, we made this ham salad together. Just like my mom and sisters and I used to make when I was knee-high to a grasshopper."

"We miss Mom, too. She does love this stuff." I nodded vaguely at Phoebe's ham salad we were creating and reached over, giving Jill a hand with the plunger. "We hardly ever have it at home. Not ever, really."

TeenTeen nodded, the smoke billowing around her head like a cumulonimbus cloud.

Jill spoke up, adding, "Mom just got a new job, and she said it was hard for her to go on vacation so soon after starting."

"That sounds about right," TeenTeen agreed, a strange look passing over her face. It was dark, sort of like a shadow. "Your mom is the backbone of your family. Always doing the right thing and keeping you guys afloat while your *salesman* father has his ups and downs." She emphasized the word *salesman* with some disdain, like it was a joke, and I couldn't help but be taken aback. Even after the fight I'd seen between Mom and Dad, it somehow still felt wrong to criticize his job. I'd never heard TeenTeen talk about Dad this way. TeenTeen was Mom's mom, and I bet she'd be mighty angry if she knew Dad had called her daughter a stupid cow and a frigid bitch.

"That's true," I acknowledged in a whisper, cranking the handle while Jill pushed the bologna down the chute.

"Don't get me wrong," TeenTeen backpedaled, "I know your dad is full of life, and you have a lot of fun with him."

"Yeah, and she said she wanted the peace and quiet of a summer alone, with just her and Namo," Gerri added, putting the spatula into the sink and screwing the lid back on the empty jar. The twins sounded so dispassionate as they made Mom's excuses. I didn't think they had a clue about what was really going on. After a pause, Gerri added, "Skippy just moved out. You heard about that, right?"

"Yes, I heard about that," TeenTeen answered, tapping her cigarette into the ashtray on the counter.

"I wonder what Mom's doing right now," I said, trying to shift my thoughts toward something ordinary and normal, away from the very real and frightening possibility of Mom and Dad getting a divorce. I had to keep that scary secret away from the girls. Gerri and Jill seemed to think for a moment before we all three talked over one another.

"Probably missing us like crazy," Jill said, right as Gerri blurted, "Probably watching *Jeopardy!*"

"Probably eating bread and butter," I guessed, and we all laughed.

"No, popcorn," Jill amended.

"With butter!" Gerri added. We were all quiet for a moment. Then Gerri added, "I like Mom's popcorn."

The twins held hands for a second, and even though they tried to act like it was no big deal, I could tell they both felt it. Gerri's eyes looked a little shiny, like she might cry, and Jill gave her fingers a quick squeeze. It must be amazing to have a twin who just gets you like that—who can make you feel better without even saying a word.

"Let's stop boo-hooing about your mom not being here and get back to work," TeenTeen instructed with a cheerful clap. As we cranked, the large yellow ceramic bowl filled up with the extruded bologna, spilling over the creamy dressing and pickle bits in a way that made it look like a miniature Mount Everest.

"Just about done," TeenTeen said. "Give it the last ingredient."

We all glanced happily at one another and blew a kiss into the bowl like we'd done many times before. I stood at the sink, washing the dishes, and saw Dad and Grandpa Red in the backyard trimming the hedges. Unfortunately, I was too far away to catch their expressions. Were they talking about Mom right now, too? Did Grandpa Red also know? Not unless TeenTeen told him. Why would Dad tattle on himself to Grandpa Red?

Gerri and Jill opened the screen door and called out, "Grandpa Red! Dad! Come and get it! Lunch will be ready in about five minutes."

They let the flimsy screen door bang shut. TeenTeen frowned.

The twins came back to the kitchen and gathered six mismatched plates while I extracted several slices of Wonder Bread from its bag with the distinctive yellow, blue, and red balloons. I think TeenTeen went out and bought Wonder Bread special for us. I didn't like it much. I thought it was too doughy, preferring the old-fashioned, tougher kind that TeenTeen made from scratch with her stinky sourdough starter.

Using a butter knife, TeenTeen slathered the *deyishous* concoction we'd created onto the slices of Wonder Bread, making the sandwiches. In our family, food was either *deyishous* or *deyacky*, descriptors born during Skippy's toddlerhood. The sweet, crunchy, tangy bite of the pickles was a startling contrast to the smooth, salty bologna and the rich, sweet creaminess of the Miracle Whip. That, along with some Dan Dee potato chips and apple slices, made for a great lunch. Everyone had seconds. Even though this didn't seem that special, I closed my eyes and concentrated, adding this experience to My Journal of Life because sometimes the mundane stuff needs to be remembered, too.

Like I told TeenTeen, we didn't really have Phoebe's ham salad at our house with Mom. To make it, you needed that big industrial-strength hand-cranking meat grinder. As I ate my sandwich, I wondered when it was time for a mother to hand down kitchen heirlooms to a daughter.

"TeenTeen?" I inquired between bites. "When did Great-Grandma Phoebe pass down that huge meat grinder to you?"

"Huh," she said, brows furrowed, thinking.

Grandpa Red mirrored her facial expression and said, "When was that, Vernatine?" I saw him considering the question, what with his eyes looking up into his head and all. "I recall Ma Phoebe making a big thing out of it. Remember?

There was some scuttlebutt about whether you or your sister Clara would get it."

"You're right, Red. I believe it was just after we got married . . . ," she said, trailing off. Before I could ask when it'd be Mom or Vivian's turn, the adults started talking about hedge trimming and other landscaping stuff that had nothing to do with the meat grinder.

I chewed my lip, lost in thought. Mom and Dad had gotten married ages ago—years and years had passed since then. The chance to give her the meat grinder had long since slipped by. I wondered if TeenTeen had a specific reason for keeping it from Mom.

My imagination ran wild, and I pictured her feelings being hurt because her oldest daughter had moved hundreds of miles away to be near her husband's family instead of staying close. Maybe holding on to the grinder was her way of getting back at her.

While I watched the rest of them munching away on Phoebe's ham salad, I somehow found myself referencing My Journal of Life entry where Mom and I were driving home in her Thunderbird after she'd picked me up from volleyball practice sometime last fall. For some reason, the twins were not with us—we were alone. As we drove down Sperry Road, she told me, out of the blue, that she was a virgin when she got married. I remember this conversation like it happened yesterday, the shock of the comment cementing it into my memory. She calmly told me that because she left her family so quickly, having only known Dad for a short time, her aunts thought she must've been in the family way and suspected that she was fleeing to avoid the humiliation. She'd looked over at me, coughed out an embarrassed laugh, and gave a shrug. I was taken aback and didn't know what to say. What a strange thing to tell me.

"That wasn't the truth at all," she'd added quietly. "It was actually the opposite. We got married quickly because we couldn't wait to have sexual intercourse." I'd felt my face go completely red at this, and I couldn't believe Mom thought it necessary to give me so much detail. "We both wanted—your father, too—to be virgins when we got married."

She'd exhaled hard, like a weight had been lifted.

Why did she tell me that?

We endured a rather awkward silence before she made a left onto Dewey Road and pulled into our driveway. After shifting the car into park, she reached over and grabbed my hand, her manicured nails in sharp contrast to my red and raw fingertips. "I just wanted you to know, Mary, that your father and I wanted to save ourselves for marriage."

I didn't know what to think. We'd never talked about sex— let alone *their* sex life—before. Sort of like my reaction to Dad calling us girls sexy, I couldn't figure out how I felt. The little girl in me was totally grossed out, but the teenager in me felt proud to be considered old enough for that kind of information.

"Mare?" TeenTeen asked.

"Huh?" I glanced around the table and saw that everyone was looking at me. "What?" They all started laughing. I must have been really absorbed in reviewing My Journal of Life. "What?" I repeated, joining their laughter.

"I asked if you'd like to play bunco with us when we finish up lunch," TeenTeen explained.

"Oh, yeah. Sure. Of course," I answered and collected the twins' and my empty plates. TeenTeen and Dad passed me theirs, too. Grandpa Red was still eating. Both Gerri and Jill got up and started bringing other items to the sink for me and cleared the counters and table. As I washed the dishes and laid them carefully in the little metal drying rack, I found myself thinking about another odd chapter in My Journal of Life.

Mom must have been in some kind of a mood, because only a few weeks after that completely out-of-the-blue conversation about sexual intercourse with Dad, she confided that she thought she'd made a mistake after only a few weeks of being married.

"What do you mean, *a mistake*?" I'd asked. We were sitting on the back porch. It was in the fall of last year, right before it got too chilly, and we watched the lightning bugs blink in the bushes and grass after a heavy rain. Jill and Gerri were playing inside, and Dad was working. God only knew where Skippy was or what he was doing.

She'd shrugged. "Someday you'll understand," she'd said. Then, with a smile, she added, "I was so young. I was only eighteen when I married your dad, you know. He was twenty. But it was all worth it because I had you girls and Skippy."

I tried to think of what I'd be like in five years, at eighteen. I couldn't envision getting married at such a young age. It was weird to think Mom and Dad were willing to do something so official—all because they wanted to perform sexual intercourse.

Did Mom regret getting married to Dad? Was that why she'd brought this up?

I thought about the fight I'd overheard. Dad could be a real schmuck, and it made me feel sorry for Mom. What a mistake she'd made. But she was right: that mistake had created our family, had created me. Growing up and learning your family's ugly truths was hard. Sometimes I just wanted to go back to being a little kid.

After swatting at a fly that was buzzing around my head at the sink, I returned to the present moment in TeenTeen's kitchen. I glanced over and saw that Grandpa Red had taken a huge last bite of his sandwich. I wondered what it must have been like for Mom and Dad to ask him for a loan when they were ready to build their own house out in Kirtland after a couple of years of living with Grandma Stromp. Mom had called Grandma Stromp unwelcoming, which was her nice way of saying that she was probably very hard to live with.

Apparently, Grandpa Red hadn't been too happy about giving them a loan. But he must have done it anyway because otherwise, we'd have grown up crammed into Grandma Stromp's crowded house in downtown Cleveland. *Ew.* I wondered if that was embarrassing for Mom—being married to a husband who couldn't really support a family. But then again, my mom would rather disappear in a puff of smoke than let anyone catch her feeling embarrassed.

She probably thought I didn't notice, but I could see it clear as day: her well-practiced routine of avoidance; over-apologizing;

and light, breezy attempts at acting carefree. I thought again about the moment we'd shared outside while Dad dug around in Blue Pierre's trunk and the twins took one last bathroom trip. The way she'd sighed and readjusted her shoulders. It was less like she was shedding a layer of old skin to become something new and more like she was adding a layer to everything she'd already built up. A new skin, tough as hide.

I looked around the table and wished that we lived closer to TeenTeen and Grandpa Red. Some of my friends' grandparents lived right around the block or in the same town. Those families could share the big events in life like Christmases, weddings, and births. But they also enjoyed the more everyday events, like teeth falling out in first grade, a broken arm from the rope swing, or how many pogo stick hops the grandkids could do. Writing and sending postcards and letters was what we were stuck with. Long-distance telephone calls were too expensive, so people like us had to rely on just the twice- or three-times-a-year visits. Maybe that's what made the trips here so special.

My musings were interrupted when I heard TeenTeen say, "Girls, listen up. Let's take care of business before bunco. Go get your cooler so that we can pack it properly."

Dad and Grandpa Red headed for the garage, and I went out to the covered porch and brought the cooler back to the kitchen sink to pour out the melted water. The twins and TeenTeen packed some small containers of Phoebe's ham salad. TeenTeen told us, "Put ice around each of them. Here's some cheese and salami, too. Also, let's put these corn-bread cupcakes in your picnic basket." She grabbed a dishcloth bundle of the muffins and wrapped a ribbon around the gathered fabric, cinching it tight.

"Corn-bread cupcakes?" My eyes widened. "When did you make those? Did you make them with a can of creamed corn?"

"Never you mind when, and I'm not sharing my secret recipe. Yet." She winked at me. "They're nice and moist and won't crumble too much while you eat them in the car. But better be careful with them, all the same." She puffed out a big cloud of

55

smoke from her Viceroy. "Use these napkins, and do not wipe your hands on your pants or on your dad's nice car seats!"

She also stocked the small basket with items that wouldn't spoil, like Saltines and chips and raisins and hard little apples and pears. She placed four large, perfectly ripe peaches on top of everything. We filled our jug with bright-orange Kool-Aid, adding cracked ice cubes from the tray in her freezer. After we put the basket near the door and moved the cooler and jug into their garage freezer, we sat down at the table, and she pulled out the dice and scorepad we needed for bunco.

"Can we please have some Dentyne, TeenTeen?" I asked a little cautiously after my sixteen-point roll. Gerri and Jill tittered at the rhyme.

"Can we please have some Dentyne, TeenTeen?" they parroted in unison.

Chuckling, TeenTeen hoisted herself out of her chair, reached into her big stash hidden in the tea canister, and presented each of us with two packs of the spicy cinnamon chewing gum. The twins' eyes were as wide as silver dollars. TeenTeen usually didn't like sharing her gum, saying that it was for grownups only, the bright cinnamon too strong for our children's mouths. I liked the cinnamon. I had stolen sticks of gum many times over the years but never a whole pack—and certainly not two. I'd always gotten away with it.

"Make it last, hear?" she instructed. We each pocketed our two packs of gum, grinning like thieves at one another.

13

Chocolate Chips

Teen Teen's gum wasn't the only thing I used to steal. For some reason, I got a thrill out of taking things and not getting caught. I'm not proud of it or anything, but the rush always seemed to outweigh the guilt. Stealing became something I did all the time. It was freeing to simply take something that I wanted without consequence, something I'd otherwise never get. I wondered if I'd ever grow out of it. Once, a few years back, my stealing even managed to ruin an entire weekend.

Aunt Vivian had come home from college specifically to visit us, and she'd promised that we'd bake chocolate chip cookies. The thing was, she hadn't specified when, exactly, we were going to do this. After she arrived, she was taking her sweet time getting settled in, and I couldn't wait any longer. I was drawn to chocolate like a magnet to metal and had guessed that the chocolate chips were stored up high in the baking cupboard. When the grown-ups were in the dining room playing euchre, I set up my little sisters with some coloring books. Skippy was out playing with one of the neighborhood kids. The coast was clear. I snuck into the kitchen, found the chocolate chips right where I'd expected them to be, and took a handful. I figured I was taking just enough to satisfy my craving and also go unnoticed. But of course, the chocolate was too *deyishous* to only take a few, so I ended up eating a bunch.

"When are you all going to make those cookies?" Dad asked maybe an hour or so later, giving the deck a dramatic shuffle.

"Pretty soon," answered Aunt Viv. "Come on, Mare. Want to give me a hand?"

I went into the kitchen with her. She reached up into the cupboard, grabbed the half-filled bag, and frowned at it for a few seconds, openly puzzled. "Hey, where did all the chocolate chips go?"

Rats! Even from the other room, Dad had heard her. "What? What do you mean?"

Aunt Viv shook the bag again, as though somehow the missing chocolate chips would emerge out of thin air. I kept my eyes averted to the floor. Now that I'm older, I realize that made me look as guilty as I was, and perhaps that's why Aunt Viv targeted me right away.

Or maybe it was the fact that I had chocolate on my chin.

Either way, she started to say, "I think we've got a thief—"

I don't know what came over me, but I grabbed ahold of Aunt Viv's wrist and squeezed, eyes so wide, they were probably bulging out of my head. If Dad learned I'd eaten half a bag of chocolate chips that weren't even mine, he'd hit the roof.

Recognizing the please-don't-tell-on-me look on my face, she said, "Oh, never mind." But Dad could tell something was up. He came charging into the kitchen like an angry bull, upsetting the card table on his way out of the dining room.

Unlike Aunt Viv, Dad was familiar with my stealing habit. "Mary, do you know what happened to the chocolate chips?" he shouted, his eyes bulging now.

"No." I looked down, not meeting his angry gaze.

"Are you sure about that?" he pressed.

"Yes," I muttered.

"Then where are they?" he demanded while Vivian stepped forward and put her arm around my shoulder. Gerri and Jill came to the kitchen door when they heard the commotion. So did Mom and TeenTeen and Grandpa Red.

Feeling backed into a corner, I spat back, "How should I know?" His eyes flashed. *Uh-oh.* That was not going to fly. Stealing was one thing, but lying was another. I could already hear the lecture I was about to get—and in front of everyone in the house, no less. How mortifying. Getting caught, especially by Dad, was the worst. He meted out a severe punishment. Not only did I have to write a sincere two-paragraph letter of apology to TeenTeen and Aunt Viv, but my jail time was served in the chilly basement—two hours of solitary confinement to think about my misbehavior. He made me take off my shoes and socks so that I would be cold. Everyone had to forfeit going to the bowling alley that afternoon due to my naughtiness. The cookies were never baked.

I distinctly recall the whole family being embarrassed by his extremism.

Aunt Viv was especially upset. From downstairs, I'd heard her yelling, "Ralph, come on! Give it a break. It was only a little chocolate, for pity's sake! We want to go bowling! I gave up my weekend at Northwestern for this."

When I emerged two hours later from the dark, cold basement, my sentence served, I expected everybody to be angry with me. Instead, they were obviously on edge and skittish around Dad—the twins, in particular. Jill sucked her thumb even though she'd stopped doing that years earlier, and Gerri chewed on the ends of her hair. Skippy, who had since returned home, made an excuse to leave and stayed out all evening. Mom did what Mom always does: she put on her pretend happy face, and I wondered if she thought she was fooling anyone.

I shook off that old embarrassing entry in My Journal of Life and pulled out a stick from the pack of gum TeenTeen had given us. It was time to prepare to leave. Everyone was already collecting the bags and food and packing Blue Pierre.

I walked out to the driveway, stuffing the stick of gum into my mouth. Dad and Grandpa Red didn't hear me approach. Even though they were talking quietly, I could sense the tension between them—there was something about Dad's shoulders looking slumped and Grandpa Red looking taller. Now was my chance to figure out if Grandpa Red knew anything about Mom and Dad's separation.

Thinking fast, I ducked behind Grandpa's car and stopped chewing my gum, determined to stay quiet. This wouldn't end well at all if I was caught eavesdropping.

"Ralph, that's a big request," I heard Grandpa Red say. "And why are you asking so late in the game? Have sales been down recently?"

Dad looked ashamed and quietly murmured, "Well, Jim. Yes. Actually, sales *have* been down."

"And this trip? You weren't planning on really going this summer until Ginny kicked you out?"

Dang! Did Grandpa Red just say that?

Even from my hiding place, I could see the blush creeping up Dad's cheeks, making him as red as Grandpa's nickname.

Grandpa Red looked irritated. His cigarette trembled in his hand, the ash clinging on in a way that seemed to defy physics. He shook his head and added, "I wish you would have just stayed at the *Plain Dealer*, working your way up in the printing department. You would have been a journeyman by now, making a decent salary."

"I sometimes think that, too," Dad conceded. "But that's not what's happening, is it?"

"How much do you think you'll need?"

"A-an even grand would make the whole trip nicer," Dad stuttered.

"One thousand dollars?" Grandpa Red admonished, eyes wide. I noticed the ash of his cigarette slump off, as though on cue. "Ralph, are you kidding? How did you plan this trip and not have the financials in order?"

"I'm sorry, Jim," Dad whined. "This trip kind of snuck up on me." Grandpa grunted like he was about to reply, but before he could, Dad said, "I know you never thought I was good enough for your precious daughter, and here is just another example, right?"

I clapped a hand over my mouth, stunned. I barely let myself breathe.

"Well, those are your words, Ralph," Grandpa Red quietly replied. The breeze blew the pollen in their front flower patch, and I felt a sneeze coming. Oh no! I didn't want to be discovered. I pinched my nose tight and swallowed back the sneeze, pushing the chewing gum into my cheek.

Grandpa Red cleared his throat. "Ralph, I thought you might ask for some money, so I withdrew five hundred dollars yesterday from my savings in case of this eventuality." I peeked around the car again in time to catch Grandpa Red's expression. It was hard to read. It sort of looked like he was eating something spoiled without complaining about it.

"You thought I'd be asking for money?" Dad echoed.

"Come on, Ralph. It's not like this isn't uncommon," Grandpa Red remarked, and I understood then what the look on his face was: he was trying to hide the disgust he felt at bailing out his daughter's husband once again. This had happened before.

"You took out five hundred?" Dad went on hopefully.

Grandpa Red reached into his back pocket, pulled out his wallet, and extracted two crisp one-hundred-dollar bills. My eyes widened as he handed over another several twenties and extended them to Dad, who accepted the bills. Even though his head was bowed, I saw a shameless smile spread across his face, and even I felt a wave of revulsion for my father.

"Thanks so much, Jim," he whispered. Grandpa Red nodded and lit a new cigarette with the dying one. Dad quickly pocketed the money. As if on cue, TeenTeen and the twins came bounding out of the front door.

"Now you take good care of my granddaughters, Ralph," TeenTeen ordered. "And, girls, you look out for your father. Be careful." Wagging her head, she whispered, thinking only the three of us could hear, "If you ask me, I still think this trip is a harebrained, cockamamie idea." Her volume increased. "Traipsing across the country like gypsies for weeks on end, and God knows what—"

My eyes shot up when I heard Dad mutter under his breath, "No one asked you." He caught my eye, winked, and smiled back at me—his favorite, the daughter he could rely on. I didn't return the smile, not after what I'd just seen him do with Grandpa Red.

"Come now, Verna," Grandpa Red interrupted, wrapping his arm around her shoulders and pulling her toward him. She leaned in, the cigarette smoke rushing from their nostrils, making them look like human dragons. I wondered if she knew about the five hundred dollars. "Drive safe, Ralph," he said to Dad, patting him on the shoulder.

I responded for us all. "We'll take care of one another and be careful, Grandpa Red. Don't worry." Everyone hugged and kissed goodbye. Dad and Grandpa Red only shook hands. We did the wave goodbye through the car windows and open sunroof as we drove off, the cigarette smoke curlicuing from their hands as they waved in return. When we were out of sight, Dad finally stopped ooga-ing.

Once we got on the road, Jill pulled out her notebook. I asked what she wrote. "*6/22/76–6/25/76 | Illinois | TT & GPR— Banana splits, Big Red bike ride, Phoebe's ham salad. I dropped the bologna on the floor. Two packs of Dentyne!*"

"Good details," I complimented, then laughed.

14

Breaker, Breaker, One Nine

We weaved our way out of sidewalks and suburbia and merged onto I-90, heading toward Wisconsin. I stared blankly out at the fields of perfectly organized rows of corn, trying to put the episode of Dad and Grandpa Red out of my mind, but somehow, I just couldn't.

That memory got stored in My Journal of Life; I'll never forget it now.

"Can you get on the horn and find out what the police presence is in this area?" Dad asked me. "I want to put the pedal to the metal and hammer down this morning without getting a bear bite," he added, showing off his CB lingo. I looked back and joined the girls in giggling. Jill gave me a wag of her head in a way that said, *Oh, isn't he fancy?*

Working the CB was one of the more important jobs of the Driver's Helper. Our citizens band radio was mounted on Blue Pierre's dashboard near the glove compartment. Because the cord from the handset to the base wasn't very long, it was definitely a front-seat job.

I turned it on and dialed to the public channel. After listening for a bit and trying not to interrupt, I attempted to get some info. Rehearsing in my head, I practiced the words to say before I tried them out on the airwaves, just like I did when I had something important to ask my parents.

"Breaker, breaker, one nine," I said into the mouthpiece. Dad smiled at me while Gerri and Jill snickered. I gave them a look that said, *Don't make me laugh.* "This is Goldilocks, riding shotgun for Blue Pierre. We're heading northwest on I-90, leaving Chi-Town. Any bears in the forest?"

I thought I sounded authentic enough. Asking about bears in the forest was code for whether there were any police nearby. My sisters giggled more. I took my thumb off the mic and joined them.

A man's deep voice replied, "Hey there, Goldilocks, this is Big Tommy. That's a negative copy, Little Muff. Come again." Realizing that I had accidentally let my thumb slip off the mic button on the handset during part of my transmission, I tried again to ask if there were any police around.

"Breaker, breaker, one nine. Hello, Big Tommy. This is Goldilocks checking to hear if there are any Smokey Bears or plain wrappers northwest of the Windy City. We're headed toward Wisconsin on our big road trip around the country."

"Coast is clear on the green-stamp road, little Goldilocks," Big Tommy replied.

"What's the green-stamp road, Dad?" Jill asked.

"I think it's CB talk for a toll road," Dad surmised.

Suddenly, I heard a girl's voice come alive on the channel: "Breaker, one nine. This is Gardener's Flower. Come in, Goldilocks."

My eyes snapped wide. I gripped the mic, looking to Dad for approval. "Dad! Someone is asking me to talk with them. She said my handle!"

"Well, go ahead and answer," he replied, accelerating to pass a ramshackle RV from Kentucky in the slow lane. I would need to remember to highlight Kentucky on the map, but I was too excited by being called out on the radio to do so right then.

"What did she say her name was?" I asked, panicking.

"She said Gardener's Flower, I think," Gerri answered, climbing forward and holding on to the back of the front seat.

"Thanks, Ger," I said. I cleared my throat and pressed down on the mic. "This is Goldilocks to Gardener's Flower. Come in."

"Hi, Goldilocks. Our family is going to Wisconsin, too. We go camping there every summer for a week. There's this groovy

64

campground called Bluebird that we love. What are you doing in Wisconsin?"

I depressed the mic's button and kept it held down this time. "Well, we're on a big road trip, and Wisconsin is on our way west. We're keeping track of how many states we encounter as we travel across the country. We started in Ohio, then Indiana, then Michigan, then Illinois, and here we are now. We're going to Sioux Falls next."

"Oh, that's a nifty idea. Let's do that, too, Maman," we heard Gardener's Flower say.

Then we heard a younger voice say, "Look! Sa-skatch-ee-won! Wow, I never saw a license plate from there before."

That's when we heard the mom say in a fancy, movie star voice, "It's pronounced Saskatchewan. It's a province, which is like a state, in Canada. I don't believe that you have that on your license plate map. Maybe you can write it down below in the margin."

"But it's gone. I can't spell that!"

Their mom said, "S-A-S-K-A-T-C-H-E-W-A-N."

I glanced back at the twins, who were as wide-eyed and thrilled as I was to be talking to another kid on the CB. Gardener's Flower clearly hadn't taken her finger off the mic button.

"She sounds about your age, Mare," Dad said, raising his brows. "I wonder what else you two might have in common."

I thought about it. Gardener's Flower had a sister and a mom. And they were keeping a record of the license plates they spotted, just like we were.

"Goldilocks to Gardener's Flower," I began. "Who are you traveling with? We've got my dad. His handle is Blue Pierre because we're in a blue car made in France. My two little sisters—Tom and Jerry for Gerri, and Jack and Jill for Jill—and then there's me, Goldilocks."

She replied, "Ooh. I like your handles. Those are funny names. In our car, we've got my dad—our last name is Gardener, and we're from New Jersey, which is the Garden State, so he's Gardener. My mom's Weeder, my little sister is Gardener's Bud, and I'm Gardener's Flower."

"Breaker. Breaker." We heard a gruff voice interrupt our conversation. "Hey, Goldilocks and Gardener's Flower. This is Big Tommy. Those are awful cute handles, but here's some friendly trucker's advice. How about you Little Muffs tune in to another channel and have your get-to-know-each-other hag feast in private?" He cackled. "There're too many folks walking the dog here on nineteen. And you might wanna tell Blue Pierre to pull the hammer back cuz there's a crash 'em up ahead, just north of Rockford, and he might wanna roll the double nickels for a bit and brush his teeth and comb his hair. Bring it back?"

Oh no, what did all that mean? I hoped Dad understood the traffic references. I just wanted to get off nineteen and talk to my new friend.

I depressed the mic. "Copy that, Big Tommy. Thanks for the advice. Hey, Gardener's Flower, pick a low number, and let's both dial to that channel, but if we get lost, come back to nineteen. Is that okay, Big Tommy?"

"Roger Wilco, so long as you stay off channel nine. That's strictly for real emergencies," growled Big Tommy.

"How about seven? Meet me on channel seven, Goldilocks," my new friend said.

"Roger that. Over and out," I sent back.

On channel seven, we found each other right away, and there was no other chatter. It was easier to talk without thinking about sounding proper in CB language. I learned that her real name was Meredith and that we both had birthdays in November of '63. Her younger sister, Mallory, was just a little older than my sisters. When the twins heard that, identical radiant smiles spread across their faces. Her dad was a baritone and liked to sing in church just like our dad, a tenor, did. Her mom's name was Adelaide. What a pretty name. And she had an exotic voice.

Talking over the CB was a little odd. The timing was stilted, and sometimes we talked over each other or didn't hold the mic button properly. As we chattered away, we got better at the pacing of our conversation, and Gardener's Flower said, "You should see the cool ponds at Camp Bluebird. That's my favorite part of camping. There are two of them—one for swimming and one for fishing and frog catching. And there are cold-water springs that feed the ponds. That keeps the mosquitos away." Dad had told us that Wisconsin mosquitos were the biggest in the world, so not having them around sounded great.

"Ooh. I love swimming and playing in water. Do they have any trees for climbing?" I asked.

"That's just what I was going to tell you next!" she answered excitedly. "There's a huge maple tree that is perfect for climbing."

"Really?" I looked over, and Gerri and Jill and Dad were all smiling as big as I was.

"Yeah. It has a little tree growing right next to it, and from the big maple's bottom branch, you can reach out to that little tree and slide down like a fireman."

"Wow. That's neato." I paused, not sure of what to say next. We'd talked about our families, what we liked to do, and other get-to-know-you basics.

As we chitchatted on channel seven, I got to daydreaming that it would be cool to go camping with them. They seemed to know more about the area and how to camp than we did. She told us that they had a little pop-up trailer. We had a tent. Not to mention, we all got along really well. The twins took over the CB a couple of times to chat directly with Mallory, and even Dad spoke as Blue Pierre to Gardener about directions and to discuss our locations. To me, camping together felt like a great Fate portion of our Slate of Dates, States, and Fates.

"Hold on a sec, Gardener's Flower," I said, getting off the CB for a moment. I took a deep breath, then looked at Dad. "I know we have plans to spend some time in Sioux Falls before the Mount Rushmore fireworks, but we could do that and still take a few days with the Gardeners to camp at Bluebird with them. Can we ask them?" I saw the girls' faces light up.

Dad looked at me, and being a salesman himself, I could tell he appreciated my attempt.

"Please?" I went on. "Did you hear how fun Camp Bluebird sounds?"

"Yeah, Dad! Did you hear that Mallory said there are arts and crafts for kids?" Gerri chimed in, adding some back-seat support.

Jill joined her. "And there are educational talks about nature and stuff, too! You like that, Dad."

"And there are hiking trails, which is a good thing since we've been sitting for so long in the car," I added. Dad's eyes crinkled as he listened to our pleadings. "You heard about the frogs and the no mosquitos, right?"

"Gosh, girls. You're quite the salesmen. Those are all great points. How do you propose we ask to join them?" he acquiesced.

"Let's just be straightforward," I suggested.

"Yeah, 'member how Mom always says the worst thing they can do is say no. Right?" Jill reminded us.

"And they do seem to like us, and we have so much in common," I said.

"Let's do it, Dad!" Gerri enthused.

"Okay, okay. You've convinced me. Pass me the horn, and I'll broach the subject with their father."

The funny thing was, as soon as Dad spoke to Gardener, it became clear that while we were persuading Dad to let us join them at the campground, they were discussing if they should invite us at the same time. *Perfect!* We'd spend the next few days at a family campground with experienced campers. With no mosquitos! This was turning out to be a good trip so far, and we'd only been on the road for a few days.

15

Camp Bluebird

As soon as we arrived at the campground near La Crosse, Wisconsin, I returned once again to channel seven to say, "This is Goldilocks to Gardener's Flower. We're here! We made it to Camp Bluebird. We're about to sort out our stay with the park host now."

"Roger that, Goldilocks," Gardener's Flower replied. "We got here about ten minutes ago, but I kept the CB on. Maman's already putting out a snack."

"Oh wow. Sounds great," I replied. Then, seeing Dad pull into the park host's drive-through, I said, "Over and out, good buddy. For now." I heard her giggle before the radio silence.

Camp Bluebird sat nestled in the middle of a forest of white fir trees. I bet it looked magical in winter, with snow piling up on the treetops like frosting. But that day, everything was lush and green, with thick vegetation and grasses swaying in the summer breeze.

Dad steered the car up a winding dirt road and pulled up to a small hut that looked like a tiny cabin. As we drove up, a window slid open, and Dad gave the park host a friendly smile. "We're here to camp with a friend for the night," he said.

"Well, in that case, welcome to Bluebird," the park host said. He had a bandana tied around his throat and a tan uniform. "You're in luck, partner, since we're fresh out of sites for the night. Luckily, all of our sites can accommodate two vehicles.

What's the name of your friend? Let's see if I can point you in the right direction."

The four of us answered as one: "The Gardeners." Then we all cracked up, including the park host. He consulted his paperwork and told us that they were in campsite C3. "You're free to get yourselves settled, and if you need anything," he added, handing Dad a pamphlet with various maps and markers on it, "consult this."

Dad took the paper and passed it over to me.

"Free of charge?" Dad clarified, and I thought of the $500—minus the little bit we'd had to spend so far on gas—in his wallet.

The park host winked at the twins in the back seat. "You're not towing a camper," he observed. "If you're just sleeping in a regular tent tonight, I don't see any reason to charge you. How long you staying?"

"Not exactly sure, sir," Dad answered honestly, shrugging and looking over at me. I shrugged back. The twins weren't even listening, being too busy excitedly bouncing up and down on the back seat, making Blue Pierre bob.

"Well, never mind," he said. "Zero cost is zero cost. Enjoy your stay."

"Thank you, sir," Dad said, tipping an invisible hat. We eased away from the park host's hut and started journeying down a dirt road that led deeper into the forest and campground. We quickly found the Gardeners' spot.

Even though we'd never met in person—and only sort of met a couple of hours or so earlier on the CB—it immediately felt like the Gardeners were old friends. We girls were swept up in hellos and hugs. Mrs. Gardener was beautiful; she looked like a model, and her voice kind of sounded European. French, maybe? Their dad was even taller than their mom.

"Ralph," Dad said, extending his hand to Mr. Gardener and looking up—way up. "Pleased to meet you."

"Brian," said Mr. Gardener, reaching down to shake Dad's hand. "It's our pleasure. Thanks for joining us."

"*Je suis enchantée*," said Mrs. Gardener, walking over to say hi to Dad, her hand extended.

I was right—*French.*

Dad didn't hide his thorough once-over of her body, backing up to get a better view. He raised an eyebrow and smirked, like he was saying, *Ooh la la!* He took her outstretched hand in both of his. I thought back to Mom's warning on the front porch and conceded that she was right. He was too flirty. He and Mom might have gotten into a fight, but they weren't divorced yet! What made him think it was okay to flirt with a married woman in front of her husband, when he himself was a married man?

All of it made me cringe.

"I'm the enchanted one," Dad said. I thought that that was a normal thing to say—charming, even—but not with his ogling eyes doing their damage first.

He finally released her hand. She gave him a polite laugh and immediately stepped back as Mr. Gardener stepped forward. Both of their moves were subtle, but I noticed. I prayed that Dad would be on his best behavior for our stay with the Gardeners.

"That's Maman's way of saying pleased to meet you," explained Mallory, reaching out to touch Gerri's braids.

Gerri asked, "Does *maman* mean 'mom'?"

"Of course," Mallory said, giving her a puzzled look, like she should have known that already.

Meredith clarified, "Maman's from Quebec—"

"That's in Canada," interrupted Mallory. "They speak French there."

"Do you speak French?" Jill asked, wiping the hair out of her eyes.

Both sisters responded together: *"Oui. Un peu."*

Mrs. Gardener chuckled and wrapped her long, slender arms around her tall daughters, pulling them close. In her beautiful voice, she said, "That's not true. My daughters speak more than a little French. They're just being modest." She ruffled their heads, and they blushed. We girls made our way to the picnic table while Dad walked over to their camper. Meredith scooted a pad of paper, some Magic Markers, and a cup of water with two paintbrushes in it off to the edge of the picnic table.

"What's that?" I asked. She quickly closed the cover of the sketchbook. Why did some artists hide their work? I wasn't like that. When I played trumpet, I let it ring out loud and clear, blatty mistakes and all.

"Oh, you know. Just a sketch pad. Nothing important," she said, cleaning up the art supplies.

"She's being humble," Mallory said over her shoulder as she grasped the twins' hands and tugged them toward their camper. "She's a pretty good artist."

"Oh, come on. Let me see." I figured that she must really be into her art if she already had it out and they'd only been here for a little while before we arrived. She looked me over and reluctantly opened the sketch pad. "May I?" I asked before turning the pages.

"Okay," she relented.

"Wow," I said, turning the page first to a landscape of a lake beneath a sunset. The technique was impressive but hard to pinpoint. "How do you do this?" I looked up at her face, saw a little grin begin to creep over it, and then brought my gaze back to the beautiful images. "I like the way you seem to use the same technique even though the subjects are so different."

Now the smile had taken over her face. Watching me look at her art, she explained how she would sketch out her idea in pencil and then use the Magic Markers to outline the shapes, criss-crossing the inside of the spaces lightly with the same color. Then she'd take a wet paintbrush—no paint, just water—and blend the colors. The Magic Marker ink would run and spread and basically create a watercolor effect. She had dozens of filled pages.

I realized, in awe, that this was like her visual version of My Journal of Life. There were pictures of her sister sitting at a piano; a honeybee gathering nectar and pollen; and her parents, I guessed, leaning into each other and looking out at a striped sunset. The last entry was at the pencil stage for a new picture—of the campsite, maybe.

"Wow," I repeated. "You're really good."

The compliment made her flush, concealing her freckly cheeks into a solid blush before receding and letting the freckles shine through again.

Our conversation was interrupted when I heard Dad and Mr. Gardener over by their camper.

"That's some setup you have here, Brian," Dad said. That sounded normal, too. Maybe they'd forget Dad's creepy greeting and he wouldn't ruin things between us and our new friends.

It looked like they were just finishing setting up their pop-up camper trailer. I was so envious of how easy and already arranged everything was. The beds just opened and were ready to be snuggled into, with even the pillows in place. There was a kitchen with cute miniature appliances—a sink, a refrigerator, a stove.

"Come on, girls," Dad said, walking toward our car. "Let's set up. Chores before food, right?"

We dragged our bulky canvas tent out of Blue Pierre's trunk, and the four of us wrangled it to standing.

"This thing is a beast," I said, tugging on one of the corners of the heavy fabric.

It took all our might to get the floor of the tent taut. The twins and I took turns hammering the stakes into the soil. After spreading out our sleeping bags and nestling our small bags and suitcases into the corners, we rolled and tied up the window flaps, allowing air to pass through. The fresh Wisconsin breeze was just what it needed, and we got out of there as fast as possible to escape the suffocating and musty smell. We pushed our sweaty hair from our foreheads and squinted into the bright sunlight.

Mrs. Gardener had laid out a red-and-white gingham tablecloth on the picnic table and offered us all some apple slices and cheddar cheese. "Looks like you all could use a snack," she proposed. I loved her accent. I wondered why neither of her daughters really sounded like her. We contributed our crackers and Phoebe's ham salad. Jill walked over to Blue Pierre and returned with the Kool-Aid jug. Mr. Gardener brought out some cold beers, used the bottle opener, and extended an open one toward Dad.

"Gee, thanks, Brian," he said, taking a big swig. "Ooh, that hits the spot!" He wiped his lips and then belched. We girls looked at one another and burst out laughing.

"Da-ad!" I scolded. How would they ever like us if Dad was burping and flirting all over the place? Next thing you knew, he'd be farting loud and clear, competition-style.

"What?" he said sheepishly.

Gerri, Jill, and Mallory sat on one side of the table. Mallory sat between them and looked left and right, comparing them. "You two are identical!" she realized.

"Of course," they replied in unison, in that eerie way twins often do. "We are identical. Identical twins."

Everyone laughed. Meredith and I sat down at the other picnic table, still close enough to hear their conversation.

"What's it like to be a twin?" Mallory asked.

Jill answered with her standard reply. "What's it like to *not* be a twin?"

"Huh. Good point," Mallory said, putting her arms around both of their shoulders and pulling them in close.

Mrs. Gardener surveyed the table and declared, "Lovely! A veritable smorgasbord." She winked at Meredith, but I caught the *Charlotte's Web* reference, too. "What do we have here?" She spread some of the ham salad on a cracker, then took a big bite. "Ooh! This is remarkable. I've never tasted anything like this before. Savory and sweet. What is this?"

This time Gerri replied, the pride evident in her voice: "We made it with our Grandma TeenTeen. It's called Phoebe's ham salad."

Jill chimed in, "It's named after our great-grandma. It's good, huh?"

"Sure is," Mrs. Gardener said, licking her fingers and smacking her lips. "Scrumptious! The pickles add that certain *je ne sais quoi*." She reached for another Saltine.

"What's *je ne sais quoi*?" I inquired, surmising that it meant something like *a little extra something or other*. I twisted the fork out of my Swiss Army silverware set and scooped out some of the ham salad.

74

Mrs. Gardener answered, "It's a French phrase that's used when you can't quite put something into words. The translation of *je ne sais quoi* literally is 'I don't know what,' but it refers to an indefinable, elusive quality, especially a pleasing one. It's like saying, 'The pickles add a certain I-can't-quite-think-of-how-to-describe-it deliciousness.'"

I liked that new phrase. Repeating it in my head, I added it to My Journal of Life for safekeeping and future use. *Je ne sais quoi, je ne sais quoi, je ne sais quoi.*

"Maman, after the snack, can we put on our bathing suits and go to the swimming pond and show Mary and Gerri and Jill around?" Meredith looked at us for confirmation that we'd like to do that. We all nodded like bobbleheads in affirmation. The three of us turned excitedly toward Dad to gauge his response, too. He gave Mrs. Gardener a silent nod of approval.

"Please wear your Keds and take your towels," she answered. They had to wear tennis shoes, too, and I didn't mind the tennis shoe rule since I had suffered so many cut-up toes and soles over the years.

"We're at site C3, so keep that in mind. You'll go past the rec center and bathhouse, and the ponds are on the left," Mr. Gardener said, grabbing several apple slices in his huge hand and pointing in the general direction of the ponds. When he sat on the edge of the picnic table bench, the whole table creaked and shifted.

"Yes, go forward and be your best selves," his wife added, smiling. "We're going to be here for a while, and we want to make friends everywhere we go."

Meredith replied, "Okay, Maman." In my mind, I adopted Mrs. Gardener as my mom, too. My maman. Meredith went on, "We remember where everything is, and we won't go to the frog pond yet. We'll just go to the swimming one today and show these guys the rec center and playground and tether balls and where some of the other stuff is. Okay?" She bounced on her toes and grabbed her towel before asking, "What's for dinner?"

"Maybe on your outing, you girls should round up some roasting sticks. How about we cook some hot dogs over the fire and have corn on the cob and celery tonight? Then we'll have s'mores at the campfire for dessert." We all cheered. This was going to be great. Dad asked if we could donate our remaining corn bread that TeenTeen had packed that morning, and the Gardeners enthusiastically agreed to include it in the night's menu.

"Hot dogs? Hot diggity dog!" Mallory combed her fingers through her messy strawberry-blonde hair and then started singing in her high-pitched voice, "*Oh, I wish I was an Oscar Mayer Weiner. That is what I'd truly love to be.*" The twins, Meredith, and I joined her. "*For if I was an Oscar Mayer Weiner, everyone would be in love with me.*"

We all smiled and laughed. I could tell that our families were going to get along well, assuming that Dad managed to behave. My eyes clicked sideways, finding him. He met my gaze, winking, and I felt sort of bad for being embarrassed by him.

The five of us headed toward the pond, with Meredith and her long strides leading the way. "Come on, girls," she directed as we all marched along in pursuit.

＊ ＊ ＊

After our campfire meal that evening, we encircled the firepit and enjoyed the sticky, messy, *deyishous* s'mores. Only Meredith was adept at not catching her marshmallows on fire. She could transform her treat into golden-brown loveliness, and somehow, she didn't even get sticky. I, on the other hand, liked to peel off the charcoaled husk on the outside, eat it, and then re-roast the gooey center, burn it, and eat that, too. It felt like getting two marshmallows out of one. The rest of us lacked her patience, and we essentially made marshmallow torches and waved them, writing words in cursive and drawing hearts and flowers in the air, before squashing them between Mrs. G's fancy cinnamon-sugar-coated graham crackers, which had been preloaded with Hershey's chocolate.

Now that we all were sitting around the campfire, Dad stood up and asked, "Would you like to hear a story?" This was one of the things I loved about him most. He was excellent at stories—ghost stories, especially. I wondered if he'd tell the scary one about Ichabod Crane and the Headless Horseman or if he'd pick something I'd never heard before.

"Ooh yes, Mr. Stromp," Mallory said. The rest of us kids were still busy stuffing our mouths with s'mores.

"Girls . . ." Dad smiled. "You can call me Ralph. No Mr. Stromp around here." He winked at Mr. and Mrs. Gardener.

"Okay," said Mallory, licking her sticky fingers. "On with the story, then . . . Ralph," she added hesitantly, looking at her parents for consent. Mr. and Mrs. G nodded.

Dad gathered himself; stood up with an exaggerated two-handed push off his knees; and began in a slow, measured, storytelling voice, spreading his arms wide. "Once, long ago, in a distant kingdom, far, far away from here, a king had a beautiful daughter named Penelope."

Nope, this was not the Headless Horseman story—this was a silly one. Meredith and I snuggled against each other on our bench, and the twins and Mallory did the same on their side. Their eyes glinted in the firelight as we all waited quietly for Dad to continue.

"Penelope was the apple of his eye. The king pampered Penelope in every way. She had jewels and riches beyond belief. Crowns and gowns"—he enunciated the words theatrically, emphasizing the rhyme—"encrusted with precious gems. The king intended for her to marry a handsome prince one day. Well, as it turned out, an evil witch, jealous of Penelope's beauty and her father's wealth and power, kidnapped her, spiriting her away in the middle of the night and locking her in her palace's turret. The king offered the witch jewels. He offered her land. He offered her subjects, but no matter what King Henry, for that was his name, offered the evil witch, she would not release his beautiful Penelope."

He took a big breath and paused for a short moment. I looked around to see the girls' and the grown-ups' faces illuminated by the golden glow of the fire. They looked magical. I felt proud of my dad and his storytelling. I glanced at Meredith, and she smiled back at me.

"The witch's palace had a foul moat surrounding its tall stone walls and an imposing drawbridge leading to the mighty doors. Penelope could be seen high up in the turret and was heard calling to her father, 'Come save me, Papa!'"

We were all rapt. I noticed that Meredith's and Mallory's eyes were opened wide and were dilated in the light of the flickering campfire. They were eating up every word he said. This was the first time they had heard my dad tell a story. I guess I took for granted how he could captivate an audience, how people really liked to listen to him.

He continued, dramatizing the princess's high-pitched voice. "'Come save me. Help, help!'"

We were all absolutely silent. Suddenly, the dark outreaches of the campsite around us felt a bit more ominous and chilling. Dad waited for his echoed pleas to fade, looking each of us in the eye for a few seconds before going on. "Not only was the moat filled with frigid, greasy, disgusting, dark water, but also there was a large monster, with enormous gnarled yellow fingers, living in the moat; his only job was to protect the witch and palace at all costs. He would crush anyone trying to cross the drawbridge if they didn't know the magic words."

Mr. and Mrs. G looked at each other curiously when they heard *yellow fingers*. I wondered if they recognized the reference.

"The king made an offering to any man in the kingdom: if he successfully rescued the princess, he would be granted her hand in marriage as well as half the kingdom. As expected, the White Knight volunteered first. He was sure he could save the princess. He was trained and practiced in jousting, and he did not fear the yellow-fingered monster. The White Knight arrived on his beautiful white steed dressed in shimmering armor and galloped with his jousting lance poised toward the witch's castle. As his horse's massive hooves raced onto the heavy wooden drawbridge, the onlookers could hear the witch cackling."

Dad made the story come to life with hand gestures and changing voices. The firelight and the shadows even seemed to bend to his will, cooperating with his tale. As he described the gnarled yellow fingers of the monster, he used his arms to exaggerate their slow-motion ascent.

The twins were sandwiching Mallory on the other side of the firepit, and I saw them reach for each other's hands, preparing for the scary part.

"Suddenly, the large yellow gnarled fingers of the monster reached up and snatched the knight, clasping him and his horse like a floppy rag doll. He twisted and ripped them before pulling them down into the stinky water. The knight's lance snapped like a toothpick. The gathered crowd gasped."

Even though we sisters had heard this story before and were anticipating the silly ending, we gasped, too.

"Next, the Dark Knight gave it his best shot. He wore his heaviest, blackest armor, thinking it would help protect him. Dashing across the drawbridge, he prayed that speed was on his side. He spurred his steed into a fast gallop, its hoofbeats echoing throughout the kingdom. Yet again, however, the gnarled yellow fingers slowly and ominously lifted out of the water, and the Dark Knight was no match for the gruesome monster. He was ripped and pulled to shreds, and his remains were dragged beneath the murky surface of the moat."

He paused to let the tragedy sink in. Clearing his throat, he took a swig of his Old Milwaukee and then slowly resumed the tale.

"Prince after prince and man after man attempted the feat, longing for the princess's hand in marriage and the ensuing wealth and glory. All to no avail. The king was about to give up and lamented to the crowd, 'Is there no one able to rescue my precious Penelope?'"

I was so engrossed in the story that I bit my fingernail in suspense, drawing blood as soon as I tore the cuticle. Meredith saw and gently slapped my hand down. Resting them in my lap and smiling to myself, I was pleased that my new friend was, in a way, taking care of me.

This made me miss Mom. I wondered if she missed me.

When I brought my thoughts back to Penelope's rescue, I peered at the faces of our clustered group of listeners. Every last one of them—and I'm guessing myself included—was glowing. Seriously. Really shining. We sitters were magically alight. Dad was above us all, standing, and the enchantment of the campfire didn't reach to his face. His booming, measured voice sounded like it came from the darkness, encircling us and making the story even scarier.

"Wouldn't you know, a tiny voice was heard, and the crowd opened up, just like the Red Sea allowed Moses and the escaping Hebrew slaves to pass, permitting the court's page to approach the king. 'I'd like to try,' the diminutive page said." Dad had told this story so many times that his performance sounded like he was reading it. He went on, using book words rather than speaking words. "The king guffawed, 'You? Ha! You're puny. You're just a mere page of the court. You have neither the strength nor the size. You don't have the wherewithal to battle the yellow-fingered monster.'

"The small page stood up as tall as he could and countered, 'Begging your pardon, Your Excellency. You have nothing to lose, my lord. I, on the other hand, am risking my life. I need to be assured that if I do indeed save Princess Penelope, you will allow me to marry her and be granted half the kingdom, as promised.'

"The king, knowing how unlikely that would be, vowed that that would be the case. The people murmured and were shocked to watch the small page—a boy, in truth—proceed steadily toward the drawbridge. The crowd roared in protest, 'Noooo!'"

Mallory called out, "No!"

Dad laughed and proceeded with the story. "'Noooo!' roared the crowd. Don't do it. You will meet the same fate as the others.' Disregarding their objections, he slowly stepped toward the castle. The page, adorned in his tricornered hat, moved carefully toward the drawbridge and took brave, confident strides on its wooden surface. The gnarled yellow fingers, in their now-familiar manner, started to lift out of the moat and reach for the page. Those in the crowd cringed and covered their eyes with their hands, many peeking between their fingers to watch the impending gruesome scene. The boy stood his ground and, with his thin arms outstretched in a *V*, shouted in his biggest soprano voice, 'STOP! LET ME PASS!'"

Dad paused dramatically, reading our faces. We waited with bated breath. "Upon hearing these simple magic words," he went on, "the gnarled yellow fingers paused their advance, twisted back on themselves, and receded into the murky water."

We all lowered our shoulders with a relieved sigh as Dad mimed the disappearing hands.

"While those in the crowd stood in shocked silence, their mouths wide open, the page slowly stepped across the drawbridge and entered the massive doorway. The baffled witch moved aside, and within minutes, Penelope and the page emerged to the cheers of the crowd. King Henry was an honest man, and he granted the page Penelope's hand and bequeathed to him half of the kingdom, as promised."

"Thank God," muttered Meredith.

Before he went on to the punch line, Dad paused again. "As the story goes, the princess and the page lived happily ever after, and the witch bothered them no more. The end." He waited a moment, relishing our anticipation.

"That's it?" asked Mallory.

"Well, there is a moral to the story: let your pages do the walking through the yellow fingers."

Mr. and Mrs. Gardener groaned at the corny play on words.

"Get it?" Gerri asked Mallory. "Get it? Do you? It's funny because it's the opposite of *let your fingers do the walking through the Yellow Pages*. You know, from the phone book commercial?"

"Oh wow," said Mallory. "That's a good story. I liked it . . ." She paused before adding Dad's first name. "*Ralph.*"

We tossed our marshmallow roasting sticks into the fire and quietly watched them blaze. Like I said, I had heard that story before, but this night's telling was being added to My Journal of Life. The new listeners' appreciation and the way we all seemed aglow from the campfire were easy to remember. We said good night and headed to the Beast.

16

Lightning Bugs and Frog Races

Camp Bluebird didn't have mosquitos, but it did have lightning bugs. The following night, we girls chased the fireflies around, trying to catch as many as possible. I added a new all-time favorite entry to My Journal of Life about capturing one. I'd kept it cupped in the safe haven of my hands, watching the slow, breath-like blink of it up close. It felt like I was holding a fairy. Then I opened my palms and watched it lift its outer, shell-like protective wings—exposing the delicate wings beneath—before it jumped, herky-jerky, into flight.

After a game of flashlight tag led by Mr. Gardener, we went to bed late. The roots and pebbles that jutted into my back through the sleeping bag and tent floor didn't even bother me, and I barely needed the toes-to-head melting routine before I fell into a deep sleep.

The next morning, after gobbling up some Cheerios with sliced bananas, we five girls took a couple of nets that the Gardeners had brought and went to the fishing pond to hunt frogs while the adults drank their coffees. After the short jaunt on the gravel path that was peppered with puddles and pitted with potholes, we made it to the meadow, where the pond shimmered in the early-morning sunlight. Water lilies, floating in a big armada on the right, were protected by a flank of pussy willows standing at attention on the shore. We kicked off our shoes, dropped the nets at the water's edge, and waded in. The water was cool, and the mud that squished between my toes was even colder.

In less than a minute, Gerri squealed, "Look at this little one!" Mallory and Jill were squatting down next to her near the lily pads. Gerri grabbed the frog and gently held it.

"Ooh, it's red," noted Mallory.

"No, it's green," Jill corrected.

Gerri turned the frog over in her hand. "You're both right. It kind of changes between red and green."

"Yeah," Jill tag-teamed. "Look how it changes when Gerri turns her hand." She reached over to pet the little frog. "Ooh, it's so cold."

"I used to think that frogs were slimy, but they're pretty smooth, aren't they?" Mallory remarked. The twins nodded, their towheads bobbing in unison.

"Ger, are you going to let it go?" I called to her from Meredith's and my spot nearby—only to immediately spy an enormous frog right near Meredith's foot. I lost all interest in Gerri's answer. Nodding at the frog, I whispered, "Meredith, do you see that big frog?"

She looked down to where I was pointing and shrieked. The three little ones rushed over, disturbing the calm water.

"Stay still!" I yelled.

Meredith did not stay still. As she tried to escape the frog, she slipped on the mud and fell, rather ungracefully, into the water. Her long legs made her look like a tipping giraffe. That big ol' bullfrog must have felt the commotion because it jumped right over Meredith, who grabbed at us like a blind person who'd dropped her red-tipped cane. We fell like dominoes into a heap of jumbled arms and legs. That bullfrog was probably gone forever.

Eventually, we untangled ourselves, sitting with our knees sticking out of the shallow water like stepping stones. Jill had a broken pussy willow stalk clinging to her wet hair, and there was a water lily pad perched on Mallory's shoulder. I looked at everyone's faces and turned to a new page in My Journal of Life. I wanted to make sure to capture the detail of how white everyone's smile was, framed by their mud-streaked, laughing-hysterically faces.

Over the course of the next couple of hours, we found dozens of frogs. Toads, too. Mallory got a stick and inscribed a small circle in the mud. She scratched three concentric rings around it. "Let's race," she suggested. "Choose your best frog. First one out of the big circle wins." Scrambling on our hands and knees, we chose our racers. I picked the biggest I could find. Mallory was impatient. "Come on, you guys." She saw that we were ready. "On your mark, get set . . ." We each positioned our frog a few inches above the center circle, and we dropped them on "Go!" All five of us laughed when the racers didn't do a thing.

After a minute of them still not moving, Jill asked, "Can we touch them? You know, to get them to hop?" She looked to Mallory for the rules.

"What do you think, Meredith?" Mallory asked.

"Sure. How about you only get five touches? And you have to keep count of your touches. And no cheating." She looked pointedly at her sister, who raised her eyebrows back at her.

"That's a good idea, Meredith," I said. "You're as smart as you are pretty." That was weird. Why did I say that? An uncomfortable hush fell over us. They all looked at me. I burst into laughter. "I sound like my dad. Gross." They joined in my laughter. Tears were forming in my eyes. Was I crying from embarrassment or just from laughing so hard?

"That's what I was thinking," Meredith agreed. She put a hand on her hip and stared at me.

I tried apologizing, but my words kept tumbling over one another. "Sorry. I just meant I think you're pretty. I love your red hair. My mom has red hair. And such cute freckles." Meredith put her hands over her cheeks, covering her freckles. "And you're smart, too. And you're such a good artist. I love what I've seen in your sketchbook." She smiled. "I bet you're also tough. I'm sorry. I swear I'm not flirting with you." I wiped at my tears and left muddy streaks on my cheeks. "But boy, that is just the kind of creepy remark that my dad would make. Sorry."

"Gosh, Mary," Meredith said. "Don't worry about it. I like that you think I'm pretty."

This whole thing was going from embarrassing to awkward faster than our frogs were jumping.

"Let's race," Gerri said. Somehow, Gerri was the one who could always be counted on to say or do the right thing to get everyone back on track. I gave her a look of gratitude, and she and I shared a nod. We all watched as she reached down to touch her frog's rear end. It hopped twice, then stopped. Everyone touched theirs, resulting in varying levels of hopping success. Feeling relieved that the attention was back on the race, I touched mine, and it didn't even hop. Eventually, Jill's teeny-tiny one crossed the outside ring first.

"I win! I win!" Jill hollered, hopping up and down. "The smallest one won!"

I looked back at the racetrack and saw that my big bullfrog hadn't moved a muscle and was alone in the original circle.

After rinsing all the mud off, we sat on a log to dry before putting our shoes on and making our way back to the campsite for lunch. As we passed the rec center, we stopped to read the agenda of activities for the week.

"Look, there's tie-dyeing tomorrow at one o'clock," I pointed out.

"Yeah, let's make tie-dyed shirts. Mom got us new white T-shirts at Kmart, right?" Gerri asked.

"Yes. There's one for Dad, too," Jill answered.

"We have some, too," Mallory added.

"Oh. Groovy. We can make hippie shirts to fit right in in California," I said.

As we continued our way back to the campsite, our nostrils were assailed by the enticing scent of fried food. My stomach grumbled.

"Where is that smell coming from?" I asked. Meredith told us that we were approaching the snack bar near the end of the recreation center and that her maman only let them go there once every other day while they were camping.

"I'm hungry," Mallory said. "Let's get back soon. I bet Maman has lunch ready."

The three little ones ran ahead of us, holding hands.

"I'm glad I'm wearing these braids today," I said, brushing the flyaway parts that had come loose. The breeze picked up in a gust. "For all three of us, if we don't braid our hair before going swimming and then get into the wind like this, we're sunk."

Meredith laughed. "What do you mean?"

"It just gets so tangled. I once broke a comb in Jill's hair while trying to get the knots out. Sometimes the knots get so bad in the twins' hair that I use scissors to cut them out, which is not a very good idea on stick-straight hair like theirs."

We took turns complaining about ourselves. She hated her hair and did everything she could to get it to lie down, even wearing a stocking cap over her wet hair in the summer to get it under control. She told me it was especially prone to frizziness in the humidity. I, on the other hand, had lank, straight, get-ting-darker-every-year blonde hair like all the kids in my family did. I never liked the phrases *dirty blonde* or *dishwater blonde*, but that was how others described the color of our hair. The more humid it got, the flatter and limper it became.

We laughed that she thought my hair was great and that I envied hers.

"Who cares about your hair?" I said, scoffing. "You have gorgeous long legs like your mom. I'm short and stumpy, which is such a drag because my mom is actually pretty tall. Not tall like your family, but taller than this." I indicated to myself. "I have her big feet and my dad's short height. That's the worst."

It seemed like her complaining about her hair had the effect of making me like mine a little bit more. Maybe my shortness made her tallness feel better. What did Mom say in situations like this? The grass is always greener on the other side.

✳ ✳ ✳

That night, as I wriggled into my sleeping bag, I realized the Beast didn't have that awful musty smell anymore. Being in the fresh Wisconsin air had done wonders for it.

I thought back to what Meredith and I had talked about earlier. Everything I disliked about myself was something she thought was groovy. Weirdly, our self-deprecating comparisons had left us each feeling a little better about ourselves.

I considered Meredith's insecurities. Her frizzy hair, her freckles. Her pale skin. I hadn't thought about any of those things in a negative light. Did she feel the same way about me? My straight hair, my stocky, boyish build? Something told me she hadn't noticed, let alone cared.

Lying there on the hard ground, I made a promise to myself: I was going to stop thinking negative things about myself. Who cared if I was short or had big feet? How you look isn't who you are. Who you are is so much more than the body you live in.

I also decided I wouldn't jump in to cheer other people up whenever they complained about themselves. They needed to figure that out on their own. As I drifted off to sleep, I wondered if I could actually keep these promises—or if I'd be making them over and over for the rest of my life.

17

Blood Sisters

On our last night together, Meredith and I snuck away before supper. We knew we'd only have about thirty minutes before our absence would be noticed—and that our parents wouldn't approve of what we were about to do. They would try to talk us out of it, if not outright forbid it. Once we were out of view of our campsite, I grabbed her hand and said, "Come on! Run! We don't have much time!"

And so we took off, racing like wild animals into the woods, our feet thundering down the packed-dirt pathway that led to the frog pond. Our noses were met with the ripe scents of damp earth and fishy pond water. Panting and trying to catch our breath, we plopped down next to each other on a dry log, gazing at the still water. The spattering of lily pads with their flat white flowers bobbed on the glassy surface. It was the perfect environment for sharing secrets, which was what we were about to do.

We kicked off our Keds and dangled our feet in the cold water. The ripples that circled out from us disturbed the mirrorlike surface of the pond. In the background, crickets chirped, scratching their hypnotic song.

Meredith had swiped her dad's Swiss Army pocketknife and pulled it out of her shorts pocket. She rotated the sharp blade out of the little red base, and it glinted against the twilight sky.

"Here you go," she said, handing it to me.

I regarded the opened knife in my palm, caught off guard by the fact that I would be going first when, for some reason, I'd envisioned Meredith would. With a breath, I nodded, bit my lip, and poked the tip of my left ring finger with the sharp blade. I rotated it a little, like turning a key. A bright-red drop of blood grew in its place, and I felt a wave of relief. That wasn't so bad.

"Your turn," I said, passing the knife.

She put her hand on her lap and held the knife against her finger but hesitated to press down with enough force to draw the required blood. She looked up at me, clearly anguished. "I can't do it," she lamented. "I can't get myself to push hard enough."

"Yes, you can," I countered, trying to keep the blood from dripping off my throbbing finger.

"No!"

"Yes, you can! Come on, do it." She looked at me beseechingly. "We don't have much time. You've got this, Meredith. Just go forward and be your best self," I encouraged, echoing her maman's regular reminder.

We both burst out laughing—a hiatus from the sickening, queasy feeling we had at the notion of cutting ourselves. She placed the edge of the blade on her fingertip and, looking away, pushed down on it hard. I saw her blood bubble up.

"You did it!" I said, and Meredith gave me a sun-bright smile. "Are you ready?"

"Yes," she said, holding up her hand, palm facing me. We pressed the tips of our bloody fingers together and interlaced the rest of our fingers into a two-person single clasp. Our commingled blood rolled in beads down our palms, past our wrists, and dripped onto the postcards we were planning to send to each other.

As we pressed our bloody fingertips together, I said some meaningful words, making them up as I went along. "Blood to blood. Friends forever. We vow our eternal love and devotion to each other and will always remember and cherish our friendship and our blood sisterhood." I paused for effect and to give myself a chance to think of something more to say. "We will never say anything negative about the other or tell each other's secrets. Blood sisters for life and beyond."

We rinsed our bloody hands in the pond, then sucked on our fingertips for a bit.

"Okay," I continued. "For this to be an authentic blood sisterhood, we each have to share the most embarrassing or painful secret about ourselves that no one else knows."

"Really?" Meredith asked, though she looked secretly delighted by the thought.

"Yep." I nodded, grinning. "Do you want to go first, or should I?"

Meredith said, "You go first."

My heart skipped a little faster. This was happening. It wouldn't be easy to voice my secret, but I imagined the relief I'd feel afterward when it was no longer mine, and mine alone, to hold. I'd share the weight of it with a trusted friend—my new blood sister. I'd bottled it up so well for so long. How would I explain this to Meredith?

"Okay. Here goes. You can already tell that my family is weird, right? Well, at least my dad." I expected her to nod in agreement, but she didn't, and part of me was grateful for that. I took a deep, pond-scented breath and spilled the secret into the night. "Right before we left on our trip—actually, the reason we're even on this trip at all—is because my parents got into a huge fight. My mom basically kicked my dad out of the house. She told him that this summer apart was a trial separation to see if they wanted to get divorced when we got back."

Meredith gave me the gasp I was hoping for. "No joke? How have you not told me this already?"

"I know! But it was just too embarrassing to talk about."

"Oh Mare. I wish you would have said something! What happened?" Meredith asked eagerly.

"It started when she found a bunch of checkbooks from other people in his briefcase—"

"Checkbooks?" she interrupted.

"Yeah, checkbooks. My dad must have been doing something bad because he was angry when she confronted him about them. Angry that what he was doing was wrong or angry that he was caught, I couldn't tell which. Maybe both." Meredith nodded. "But it was more than that. I heard them talk about all kinds of stuff that I didn't want to hear."

"Like what? How did you hear them? Did they argue right in front of you? My parents would never do that." An irritating jolt of jealousy zinged through me when I considered how perfect her family was compared to ours.

I recounted the experience of overhearing all the nasty things Dad said to Mom—the fat cow, the frigid bitch, the shithole house—everything. How he mocked her, saying she'd just run to her daddy for help if he left. I whispered the part about him finding love outside their marriage. It all came tumbling out of me, like when you knock the wrong disc from that wobbly plastic Fred Flintstone–looking man we used to play with—the one with the big feet and the stack of red and yellow discs you'd whack with a yellow hammer—and his head wobbles, then crashes down.

"Like he has s-e-x," Meredith spelled the word, eyes wide in the dark, "with other ladies?"

She sounded as shocked as I felt.

"I think that's what that means. So gross." I shook my head. "One of the worst parts about him is he acts so Christian but is the biggest sinner I've ever met!" A little sob startled out of me, like a roosting bird forced into flight. I didn't know it'd been sitting in there all this time. "Sometimes I hate him. Especially lately. Like when I remember this stuff or think about the creepy way he first looked at your mom." I held my head in my hands in shame and sadness.

"It must be so hard to travel with him if you hate him," Meredith said, resting her hand on my rounded shoulders. It was just what I needed to hear. I'd kept this secret to myself, not sharing it with Winnie Gravvers before we left, not with TeenTeen when I had the chance, not with the twins. I hadn't even called Mom collect. I felt alone in my grief. The only thing left to do was bring my biggest fear to life by saying it out loud: "They're going to get a divorce when we get home."

Meredith took her other hand and pulled me into an embrace. The floodgates opened, and I wept with humiliation, the tears and snot streaming from my eyes and nose, wetting Meredith's T-shirt.

I told her I was shocked and how proud I felt of Mom when she called his bluff about taking us three girls with him on his big dream trip. "They had the argument one night; we went shopping and packed the next day; and then the day after that, we were on the road. It all happened so fast, I barely had time to say goodbye to my friends." I got quiet for a moment, trying to think of how to reveal the next part. "Our first stop was in Chicago at my mom's parents' place. We stayed there for a couple of days."

"I remember that ham salad you brought," Meredith said.

"Oh yeah, so that was right before we met. Well, my dad asked Grandpa Red, my mom's dad, to borrow a thousand dollars."

"A thousand dollars? Wow, that's a lot!"

"I know! My grandpa had already withdrawn five hundred dollars for him before we even got there. So that's doubly bad because"—I ticked off the reasons on my fingers—"one, Dad asked for too much, as always, and two, my mom must have told her parents about their fight or at least that she kicked him out or something, because why else would Grandpa Red have withdrawn the money ahead of time, right?"

"Oh Mary." Meredith was quiet for a breath, shaking her head. "I'm so sorry."

"Me too. What a mess."

"Your sisters don't know?"

"Not really. Well, not the details that I just shared with you." We both sat silently for a moment, a pair of lightning bugs blinking near us. "You know what's the worst part?"

"What?" she asked.

"That before I realized what a creepy, s-e-x-addicted, cheating weirdo he was, Dad would have been the one I'd have shared my worries with—but now he's the cause of my worries, and I can't talk to him anymore! And everything he does just bugs the crap out of me. It's like I'm on high alert. He's a hypocrite!"

"Oh, you're right. That really sucks eggs. Especially when you still have such a long trip ahead of you. You're going to

California and then all the way back to Ohio, right?" She thought for a second, then added, "I hope Blue Pierre makes it."

"Oh my God, I know." I felt so emptied out. It felt so good. "Thanks, Meredith."

"For what?"

"Oh, you know, everything. Listening to this god-awful secret, being my blood sister, and just being here when I needed you. What if you never talked back on the CB? I'll miss you like crazy." Another little sob escaped. "Oh God. I'm a wreck."

"No you're not." She sat up straight and clapped her hands. "So is your sorry story over now?" We both laughed, and I appreciated her attempt at lightening the mood. "My turn."

"Oh good. Let's hear it."

"Well, it's not as big as yours or as painful . . ." She gave me a tender look. "Mine is only embarrassing."

"I will never tell," I solemnly agreed and pressed my cut finger to hers, relieved that the attention was on her now.

She lowered her voice, even though the only ones who could hear us were snapping turtles and frogs. Maybe those lightning bugs.

"I practiced kissing with my friend Joanne so we'd be ready for the school dances in seventh grade." She spat out the words like she was afraid she'd lose her nerve if she didn't say them fast enough.

"That makes sense," I said.

"But then we wondered . . . does that make us dykes?"

"What's a dyke?"

She looked at me like I'd just landed from Mars. "You don't know? It's a bad word for a girl who likes other girls."

"Like . . . a homosexual?" I asked, lowering my voice, too.

She nodded. "Yeah. Like a lesbian."

I hesitated. "My dad calls them faggots. But I thought only men could be homosexual."

Her nose scrunched. "That's not a nice word. My parents say people should just mind their own business and let others be how they are. And *faggot*"—she whispered the word—"is mean."

"But you said *dyke* was bad, too. So both are bad words?"

She nodded. "Yeah. You're supposed to say gay or lesbian."

"Hmm. So you kissed a girl? That's a doozy, too. Did you end up kissing any boys in seventh grade, then? You know, after all that practice?"

"Just one. Sebastian Dewey." She giggled. "His lips were dewy."

I joined in her laughter. "Did the practicing help?"

"Honestly?" Meredith laughed. "I don't know."

It dawned on me. "Oh my gosh! I kissed a boy for the first time in seventh grade at a dance, too," I told her. "His name was Vance. Vance at the Dance. It was in the school gym, and it was so dark that kids were making out like crazy. The song was 'Dream Weaver,' and we kissed for the entire song. And he squeezed my derrière, and the kiss was wet. Kind of cool and kind of gross, too."

"Yuck! I love that song, though! It sounds like outer-space music, and it's like thirteen minutes long!" she shrieked, jumping up and grabbing my hands, spinning us around. "That's the song that was playing when I kissed Sebastian Dewey!"

"What? Really? No way. That's outta sight! We both kissed boys for the first time to the same song? That's crazy. I knew we were blood sisters!" I said as we collapsed back down on the log and sat quietly for a moment, letting it all soak in.

"Okay," I said eventually, sighing. "Is that it?"

"I guess so," she said.

"Well, in that case, I think that ends our blood-sister ceremony. We can never tell anyone our secrets," I concluded.

We hugged and laughed a little at the profundity and absurdness of the whole thing. I paused and tried to take in all the sensations of the experience—the twilight, the pond and the lily pads, pretty Meredith. We hurriedly put on our shoes and laced them up.

"We better get a move on," I said.

"Do you think the grown-ups will know what we've been up to?" Meredith wondered.

"Probably not," I answered. "Make sure to put your dad's pocketknife back so that he doesn't find out that it was taken."

"Roger Wilco," Meredith agreed.

We raced back to camp just in time for supper. I hoped no one noticed our cut fingers.

✳ ✳ ✳

Saying goodbye to the Gardeners the next morning brought tears to my eyes and a quiver to my chin. Feeling embarrassed, I brushed them away with the back of my hand, but I was pretty sure that it was obvious I was crying no matter what I did.

Meredith and I held hands, leaning up against the fully packed Blue Pierre. Gerri and Jill looked sad, too, with their thin little faces downcast, their bangs slipping out of their slept-in braids and hiding their eyes. Mallory stood between them with her arms draped across both their shoulders. The novelty of being friends with twins had not worn off in the time we'd spent together.

Even Dad seemed different. He was sluggish, shuffling his feet in the dust, and kept mumbling about last-minute things he had to do before we left, reluctant to say goodbye.

Trying to keep things upbeat, Mrs. G hugged us each tightly. Even Dad. She'd miss us, too.

Mr. G hung back, watching the scene.

It dawned on me that Meredith could've been my best friend if she didn't live so far away. It felt like such a missed opportunity. I reminded myself to cherish all the experiences we'd had, adding them to My Journal of Life.

Dad had let us spend five whole days at Camp Bluebird with the Gardeners.

The previous morning, I'd rolled out of my sleeping bag and started straightening it up. Dad was inside the tent, and I figured I'd thank him for letting us stay here and make new friends. "I know it's been kind of weird starting our trip with such a long stop," I reasoned, "and we're just using the TripTik as a guide, right?"

"It wasn't weird; it was great." Dad smiled. "And we have a long summer ahead of us still."

I loved it when he wasn't being creepy or too disciplinarian. It was nice to just talk and agree about stuff, for once, and I felt an echo of the Dad I thought I knew return. He unbuckled his suitcase and rolled up a previously worn shirt, tucking it inside. I could tell there was more he wanted to say, and since I'd seen a glimpse of the side of him I loved, I was eager to listen. Eventually, locking up his suitcase and turning his eyes to me, he said, "This is only something I'd say to you, Mary, as you're the oldest, but that Mrs. G is one sexy lady, isn't she?"

My heart sank like a stone in a pond.

I couldn't believe he'd just said that—and right after I was giving him the benefit of the doubt.

I remembered what Mom said about Dad chasing anything in a skirt. She was right. I'd thought every guy was a flirt, but Mr. G showed me that wasn't true. Dad's behavior was gross. He talked about women the way Skippy and his friends would, but Dad was way too old to act and talk like a teenage boy. He was a man, for goodness' sake. A married man! A churchgoing, choir-singing, sermon-giving, Christian man. A father.

Being a father should be the straw on the camel's back. The tipping point. The thing that really made a difference. As a father, I'd think he'd want to protect his daughters and, by extension, all girls and, again by extension, all women. But he didn't—and I wasn't sure what to make of that.

Knowing I had to keep everything copacetic for the trip, I exhaled with a sigh and a dismissive shake of the head and went on as though he hadn't made that comment at all. "So, anyway, thank you so much for letting us stay here for so long, Dad."

He sat back on his sleeping bag, nodding. "Well, it has been pretty *ex-tra-ord-in-ary*." Usually, his silly superlative word prompted a smile on my features, but I drew it back and smirked instead. Of course, he didn't notice. He just went on. "We would never have found this place if we hadn't met them. What a swell family. And it's nice having a maman, isn't it?" He air-quoted *maman*, and for a few seconds, we both smiled. "Even if it's not your real mom."

"Yeah," I said softly.

For once, Dad's smile wasn't so sturdy. It seemed to slip. "I do miss your mom."

I was surprised to hear him say that about the fat cow, frigid bitch he'd so callously dismissed just a couple of weeks ago. I thought he didn't like her anymore. I didn't know what to say or how to feel about being his confidante on such adult matters, so I just wiggled my head, not giving a nod or a shake. I glanced at the breathing pile of tangled sleeping bags that was my sisters and said, "I miss Mom, too."

And just like a silver ball in a pinball machine, he'd bounced right off that topic and onto another.

"I think we should be heading out soon. I'd love to get to Sioux Falls well before the Fourth of July to ensure that we'll be at Mount Rushmore on the big day. We have a lot of ground to cover on our trip. Let's look at the TripTik and do some planning this morning after breakfast."

Oh good, back to normal. That sounded like something good dads would say.

Our discussion was interrupted as the distinctive aroma of frying bacon and pancakes wafted toward us, and we knew that Mrs. G was making another *deyishous* breakfast. The Gardeners had brought real maple syrup and real butter with them. At home, we were used to Mrs. Butterworth's syrup and margarine. Mrs. G even had us in the routine of squeezing oranges for fresh orange juice.

I joined Meredith and Mallory at the picnic table. They were taking turns with the oranges. Our quiet good mornings were accompanied by the cheery birdsong of robins and cardinals in the trees, and with the butter-soft sunlight of a new day, it all felt like heaven.

When the twins emerged from our tent, Mallory ran over and swept them up in a big hug. Their sweaty, sleepy hairdos were pale nimbuses encircling their heads. I braided Jill's and then Gerri's hair, and then Mallory wanted hers in braids, too.

When Jill's hair was done, she asked if she could have a turn with the oranges.

Mrs. G invited her over. "Step right up, Jill. Try to get every drop." Then she quoted Anita Bryant: "A day without orange juice is like a day without sunshine." Her beautiful voice made it sound like "uh day weethout or-ahnges eez like uh day weethout sun-sheen." I don't know how to spell English words spoken in a French Canadian accent, but that's more or less the gist of what I was trying to add to My Journal of Life.

That last morning was bittersweet, as we knew we'd be making our goodbyes soon. I took slow bites, trying to prolong our last breakfast together.

"Thank you for taking care of us this week, Mrs. G," I'd said. I had to stifle some tears, and with a lump of pancake in my throat, I told her, "I'll miss you." I gave her a big hug. She hugged me back and then held both of my arms and looked me in the eyes.

"You are so welcome, Miss Mary." When Mrs. G said my name, it sounded like *Marie*. "Does anyone ever call you Marie, Marie, Quite Contrary?" I nodded. "I bet they do," she said in her exotic voice.

"Oh yeah, of course they do. And it's true sometimes, but I'm not always contrary."

"Yes you are," my sisters said, smiling. Gerri licked some syrup off her finger.

"You two, hush up." She winked at the twins before returning her attention to me. "I know you aren't. I think you're smart and a mover and a shaker." She gave me a squeeze before letting go. Wow, that felt good.

18

Crossing the Mississippi

Reluctantly and slowly, we bid farewell to Camp Bluebird and our new friends, the gravel crunching noisily beneath our tires. The Gardener family joined us in our traditional wave good-bye, and even though we were somewhat subdued, Dad didn't refrain from sounding his ooga horn. I know for certain that the neighboring campers, some of them sleeping in, did not appreciate our noisy departure. Breaking the morning silence like that reminded me of blasting out "Reveille" at home.

Our time at Camp Bluebird had made us accustomed to cramming the days with activity from dawn to dark. There, we were either playing hide-and-seek in the woods, or swimming in the pond with the frogs, or climbing trees, or enjoying Mrs. G's cooking and roasting marshmallows over the fire at night with Dad's storytelling. This led to a significant and somewhat dramatic letdown that I had expected but wasn't prepared for.

The silence in the car as we hummed down the interstate felt empty and dull, and the fact that our party had shrunk back down to one of only four just didn't feel right. Nestling back into Blue Pierre felt oddly confining and made us slightly awkward with one another in the tight, enclosed space. Plus, we all felt a little sad. We were almost shy with each other and started the drive quietly.

After a while, we were back to tending to the necessary things, like figuring out where we were on the TripTik and where we were going. I offered Jill a turn on the CB. She climbed over the front seat and, after practicing out loud a few times, inquired, "Breaker, breaker, one nine. This is Jack and Jill. We're leaving La Crosse, Wisconsin, now, heading west on I-90. Any bears in the woods?"

I gave her a big smile. She had said it just right. Uncle Carl from Minnesota told us that the coast was clear, and so we set off toward our next stop feeling footloose and fancy-free.

"It'll be exciting to cross the Mississippi River this morning," Dad said later, breaking the silence we had established. "And then we'll have a long drive across the Great Plains today. This is one of the wider parts of the river."

"I can spell Mississippi with one *i*," Gerri chimed in, covering one of her eyes behind her thick eyeglasses and reciting, "M-I-S-S-I-S-S-I-P-P-I."

"That's a good one, Ger," Jill praised, even though we had heard it a million times before.

Dad seemed to figure it was time for some education. "Did you know that the Mississippi River, along with the Ohio and Missouri Rivers, is the largest river system in North America, traveling over twenty-three hundred miles, all the way to the Gulf of Mexico near New Orleans, Louisiana? It basically cuts the continent in half from north to south." Dad made a slicing motion with his arm, dividing America in two.

"Really?" I murmured. Disregarding my indifference, he went on to explain the importance of waterways for civilization. He pushed his glasses up and continued. I hated to admit it, but when he was like this, I really did like him. It felt like what normal people did. Dads told kids stuff about what they were passing on the road. Regular family talk. No creepy, sexy flirting. I brought my attention back to what he was saying. "Way back before America gained independence from England, there was the Treaty of Paris of 1763—"

"That's exactly two hundred years before my birthday!" I blurted out excitedly. "My birthday is the bicentennial of the Treaty of Paris! Who'd have thunk?"

"May I continue?" Dad huffed.

I shut up. At least his regular fatherly impatience was normal. I was still just grateful enough for that to let this go.

"Well, in Paris, France," Dad went on, eyes on the road, "they signed an agreement—a treaty—and it was all about the Mississippi River. The treaty gave England rights to all the land east of the Mississippi, and the land to the west would go to Spain."

"How do you know all these things, Dad? How can you remember the years of stuff like the Treaty of Paris? Are you making the dates up?" I asked. He grinned. He could change moods quickly like that, and we kids were all experts at shifting gears to keep up with his different temperaments.

"Of course I'm not making up the dates. If I know the date, I include it. I'm in my forties, you know, and I've been around the block a bit," he said with a silly grin. There was something about this that caught my attention. The angle of his face, the cast of the light—it made me see him objectively, as a man in his forties instead of as Dad. I noted the little circular scar on his temple. It was a souvenir of sorts from when a stranger, demanding money, conked him in the head with a wine bottle through the open window of his car back in his early twenties. He'd escaped and, with blood streaming down his face, had driven himself to the Cleveland Clinic. You could touch the scar and feel the perfectly round depression under the skin where the emergency room doctor had literally drilled a hole in his skull to relieve the pressure.

Nodding, I appreciated how true it was that he had indeed been around the block a bit.

19

Oh Ginny, Don't Exaggerate

I stored the TripTik in a cardboard box in the footwell by my feet in Blue Pierre. Today's navigation was going to be easy. It showed that we had about 350 miles to Sioux Falls, and all of it was in a straight line.

There was so much foot space on the passenger side that the box wasn't in my way at all. I treated the box like a librarian would. It contained the TripTik and the guidebooks and maps, organized by the order of our route and lined up with their spines facing up and out. There was a small pencil bag that I had sewn and embroidered with yellow and white daisies on it that even had a zipper, the inclusion of which had pushed my fledgling sewing skills to the limit. I had also packed a spiral-bound notebook and a journal, of course.

For reading, I added two of Laura Ingalls Wilder's books, *Little House on the Prairie* and *Little House in the Big Woods*, which I thought the twins would like. Even though they weren't avid readers like Mom and I were and preferred talking with each other over escaping into stories, I figured that those books might capture their interest eventually. They were about areas we were traveling through and took place from the point of view of a girl their age. And of course, I included my well-worn copies of *Charlotte's Web* by E. B. White and *Pippi Longstocking* by Astrid Lindgren. Maybe between Fern and Pippi, my sisters might actually read something.

Dad had me add John Steinbeck's *Travels with Charley*, which he said had been inspirational to him for this trip, even though we didn't have Namo along with us.

A few weeks before we left, when I was sneaking around in my brother's room, I found an unopened, crisp book. It was called *Zen and the Art of Motorcycle Maintenance*. I didn't think he'd even read it, having been assigned the book in his English class the year before. The Kirtland High School library card—with a due date of last April—was still tucked inside the cover. He must've not turned it in before he graduated. He got away with all kinds of stuff like that.

The title enticed me, so I took the book and hid it in my room. I thought that Zen meant being peaceful and calm. I realized that I was a high-energy, active person, not very Zen, not very peaceful or calm. I knew others thought the same thing about me because people, like my brother, my teachers, and once, even a lady at church, regularly told me to slow down. What was it to them?

We had a motorcycle—a red Honda CB360—and on weekends, Dad and I would often spend time in the garage tinkering with it, fine-tuning the engine or changing the oil. When everything was running smoothly, Dad would take me out on our gravel roads, just for the fun of it.

Once, a couple of years ago, Dad somehow convinced Mom to go on a mini weekend getaway with him all the way to Niagara Falls and back. He'd earned a spot at the Million Dollar Round Table convention, New York Life's big-deal sales-recognition event, and apparently decided the motorcycle was the perfect way to travel. I was stunned when Mom agreed to climb on the back of that little CB360 for such a long journey. Not to mention, Dad wasn't exactly a seasoned rider, and traveling with a passenger would be new territory for him.

Even now, riding in Blue Pierre beside Dad and remembering all this, I couldn't help but laugh at the memory. Neither Mom nor Dad could be described as petite, and that poor little CB360 looked completely overwhelmed carrying the two of them. The shock absorbers were pushed to their absolute limit, groaning under the weight of two full-size adults.

They spent two nights at a fancy hotel while Skippy babysat us at home, and on that Sunday, when they were due to return, we heard repeated honking on the motorcycle's tinny horn. We kids came running, nearly tripping over one another, stamping down the front steps. Before we ran right into her, Mom swung her leg off the bike, removed her helmet with a flourish, and with her hand on her hip, declared, "Well, I hope you enjoyed that, Ralph, because that is the first and last time I am ever doing something like that!" She sighed dramatically. "We nearly died, kids!"

She didn't even give us a chance to ask questions or interrupt. "You know how easily Dad falls asleep?"

We all nodded, recalling how he would drift off during the sermon at church, while watching TV, and even midconversation sometimes. "Well, he nearly killed us earlier today because he fell asleep while driving!" She looked at our startled faces. "Yes, while driving!"

"Oh Ginny, don't exaggerate," Dad said, defending himself.

"Don't you *Oh Ginny* me!" She stop-signed him with her hand. "And I am not exaggerating! You know perfectly well that everything I just said is the god-awful truth!"

She'd tried to keep talking, but Dad reached for her and started hugging and kissing her while she pulled away. He'd told her how much he loved her and that he'd never do anything to hurt her. Mom eventually acquiesced and allowed the hug and kisses to soothe her. I think I heard him whisper that he was sorry for scaring her. Mom giggled a bit. We kids turned away, a little embarrassed by their intimacy. But something was a little strange, a little fake.

Exaggerated, maybe.

It looked like a show to me. Not Mom's part, but Dad's. It was like he was putting on a show for us kids. Like he was acting the role of good husband. His behavior was straight out of a movie or a TV show, and it didn't at all feel authentically him.

But Dad usually overdid things, so maybe it was real.

20

My Turn to Drive

My calculations were a little off, and we needed to drive for nearly seven hours that day on the long, flat stretch of I-90—a wide, smooth four-laner. The landscape through the prairie of Minnesota was flat and never-ending. We passed the time with reading, drawing, singing along with the Carpenters and the Statler Brothers on the stereo, and listening to the CB chatter. At about the fourth or fifth hour, Dad was starting to nod off the way Mom accused him of doing during their motorcycle adventure to Niagara Falls. Not a good thing.

"Hey, Mary. I've been thinking," he said eventually, lifting his glasses to rub his eyes. "You want to drive for a bit?"

We all exclaimed, "What?"

"I'm only thirteen, you know," I reminded him, as though he'd forgotten. After making such a crazy suggestion, perhaps he had.

"Yeah, but you know how to drive. You've practiced at home. I've seen you drive the neighbor's little minibike. You've been listening to the CB and seem to understand what they're talking about. The highway is very straight and very barren and very sparse of traffic." He yawned, and I had no choice but to remember Mom's accusation. What if Dad kept driving and got us all killed?

"Really? *Really?* You want me to drive Blue Pierre?" I asked dubiously, nibbling at the cuticle on my right pinkie finger.

"You can do it," he said. "I can take a little nap, and you'd enjoy it. The twins can help you. Stay just a little over the speed limit. Listen to the CB for important information. You'll be traveling on the southern border of Minnesota basically the whole time. If you see a good place to cross over the border south into Iowa, go for it. And Jill can add it to our Slate of Dates, States, and Fates."

My palms began to sweat. While I was listening to him explain, I glanced back at the twins to see their slack-jawed expressions. I didn't necessarily want to drive, but I felt terrified of what would happen if I didn't. Dad was visibly tired.

He scratched his arm. "If you hear anything alarming or have any big problems, wake me up. Make sure the car doesn't overheat by keeping your eye on this temperature gauge right here, Mary." I leaned over to see where he was pointing to on the dash. "You'll want to make sure to stop before this little hand gets into the red zone."

"Are you serious?" I asked, feeling properly panicked now. What if I drove us straight into a ditch and killed us all? I thought about Mom's warning moments before our departure. Dad's ideas weren't always the best, and I was positive this was an example of just that.

"One hundred percent. I added water to the radiator and checked the water pump earlier, so you should be good to go." He gently patted Blue Pierre's dash. "I'll stay awake for the first part to make sure you've got everything under control before I fall asleep." He also turned to face the back seat and saw Gerri and Jill's shocked expressions. "How about you twins come into the front seat and give Mary some moral support, and I'll stretch out in the back?"

The twins looked at each other with open skepticism on their faces, then tidied up the back seat while Dad pulled off to the side of the highway. We hopped out of the car, each of us running around the vehicle and entering a different door. Gerri and Jill ran around the front of the car and smashed into each other, both dropping to the ground and landing on their derrières like a scene from an old-timey slapstick movie. They burst out laughing.

Meanwhile, I'd found myself in the driver's seat, my knuckles whitening as I readjusted the seat so that I was positioned closer to the steering wheel. Suddenly, I was terrified that a police officer—or a so-called bear in the woods, I supposed—would show up.

"Just continue on I-90 for about another one hundred twenty miles. That's a little over two hours or so. If you find any shade after the hundred miles and I'm still sleeping, why don't you park and explore outside for a bit until I wake up?" he suggested.

Is this for real?

"Sure thing, Dad. I got this. Leave it to me." My words conveyed more confidence than I actually felt—but the fact was, Blue Pierre had an automatic transmission and power brakes and steering. If I was careful, and I would be, then this would be doable. I just needed to *be careful*.

This was definitely going into My Journal of Life.

"Dad, can you spare a pillow from back there? I think I need to be up a little higher," I said while adjusting the side and rearview mirrors. I took stock of the steering wheel and dashboard. We had plenty of gas. The wipers were here, and the blinkers were there. That temperature gauge was right there. The shifter was easy to change from *P* to *D*.

Making sure the coast was clear, I started to slowly ease off the shoulder, spitting up some gravel, and merged smoothly into the slow lane. So far, so good. Accelerating to fifty-five and staying there was all I needed to do. I felt my worry whoosh out the sunroof and open windows. Dad was right. I could do this. This wasn't going to be too hard.

"Good job, Mare. Nice and smooth. Keep it like that. Ger-Bear and Jilly-Bean can take over the TripTik and let you know what's coming up. I don't know why I'm so tired today." Soon, his quiet snoring provided the background to our excited front-seat chatter.

"Oh man! We're doing this!" Jill said. "Mom would *never* let you drive. Never in a million years. I was sad at the beginning when Mom wasn't coming, but I think I like our trip better this way."

Gerri chimed in as if they were one person. "We're doing all kinds of things we wouldn't do if she was here. It wouldn't have been worse," she reasoned, "but this has been so much fun."

Jill took over the TripTik. "Sioux Falls is fifty miles away, Mare," she said, then returned to the discussion about Mom. "Yeah, Ger. Mom's great, but we wouldn't have spent time with Mallory and her family if she was with us. We probably would have done our own family stuff, I think."

"Well, she certainly wouldn't have let me drive, that's for sure!" I added. "This is so far-out. How am I doing?"

"Well, you're staying nice and straight, and I think you're doing a good job of not going slow and fast and slow and fast, which makes me carsick. But too many cars and trucks are passing you." She peered over at the speedometer. "You're only going fifty to fifty-five, and Dad said go a little over the speed limit, so you should try to go a little faster," Gerri suggested.

"Yeah, put the pedal to the metal!" Jill laughed. Her stick-straight blonde hair was the thickest of all of ours, and it looked wild, whipping in the wind. Gerri and I had kept our baseball caps on. Jill's hair would be a big, snarled knot at bedtime, and I knew I'd have to help her untangle it, but the thrill of having the windows and sunroof open was worth it.

As I drove, Jill caught up the Slate of Dates, States, and Fates page.

"What are you writing, Jilly?" Gerri asked.

"So far, *6/25/76 to 6/30/76 | Wisconsin | Bluebird Campground with the Gardeners—Fun camping stuff. 6/30/76 | Minnesota | Drive to Sioux Falls—Mary drove!*" Jill looked over the page and then up at Gerri and me. "Should I write down that you drove, Mare, like Dad said? What if Mom sees this?" She had her pencil eraser poised to rewrite history.

I considered a minute before answering. "Yeah, keep it in," I ultimately decided. "Let's include everything, and we'll just explain ourselves afterward. Plus, it makes a way better story to have the naughty parts in."

The girls nodded, and we fell temporarily into silence. I plugged along at a meager fifty-seven, too afraid to push past sixty—but Gerri was right. I was going too slow. I leaned a little more heavily on the gas pedal, speeding up, and started gaining on a red station wagon.

"Are you going to pass that station wagon?" Jill inquired.

"I'm going to try. Gerri, will you add Pennsylvania to the license plates map?"

I looked over my left shoulder and into the mirrors to prepare to get into the fast lane. No one was coming, so I put on the left blinker, took a deep breath, and went for it. I turned the wheel a little too abruptly, and we zigzagged before I straightened us out.

As we passed the station wagon, we noticed there were kids in the back seat. They pointed at us and started laughing. It made me realize how strange it must be to see three young girls in the front seat, driving a car. Since Dad was lying down, it looked like we'd taken it without permission and were on some sort of a joyride.

As we passed, I put my finger to my lips and shook my head. All three of us glared at those boys in the back seat to keep quiet. For some reason I'll never know, the big brother gave me a huge grin and a thumbs-up and didn't tell his parents. I decided to stay in the slow lane after that, realizing anew that we'd be in big trouble if we were caught.

After a time, Gerri said, "If we want to make a foot-down touch in Iowa, then maybe we should go south on State Route 229, if I'm reading this map right. Wait . . . is Sioux Falls in South Dakota or Iowa? Or both? Jill, help me."

After they conferred and ironed out the difference between Sioux Falls, South Dakota, and Sioux City, Iowa, to the south, they directed me to take the next exit. Even though I thought I had braked hard enough, we took that turn way too fast. The tires squealed, and I was surprised that the force of the turn didn't wake up Dad as he slid across the smooth back seat.

"Mary! Slow down! This isn't a ride at Cedar Point, you know!" Jill yelled. "Or Big Red the Tricycle!"

We drove south across the Minnesota/Iowa border and turned right to exit the interstate and officially ease toward the city. By this point, it was midafternoon. Squinting into the sunlight, I took one hand off the wheel to reach up and adjust the sun visor. At once, I could see again. Much better.

"Should we wake Dad so that he can touch down in Iowa, too?" Gerri wondered, and the three of us glanced at the back seat, where Dad was still snoozing.

"Nah, listen to him snore," I reasoned, enjoying my new role as the Driver. "He's sound asleep. Let's leave him be."

The twins looked at the map and directed me toward Sioux Falls.

I quickly discovered that driving in a town was way more complicated than driving on the open highway. There were so many more variables to contend with, like intersections and stop signs and crosswalks and pedestrians and traffic laws. I hastily found a shady place to park, pulled over, and moved the gear shifter into park. As fun as driving on the interstate was, I felt a wave of relief wash over me at the idea of returning the wheel to Dad now that we were in the city.

As soon as we were fully parked, I wiggled the pillow out from beneath me, rolled my neck, and shook out my clenched hands. I'd been way more tense than I'd realized. One look at the twins, who were quiet but visibly relieved, made me burst out in laughter.

We were apparently *all* more tense than I'd realized.

We laughed and then shushed one another, trying not to wake the sleeping giant in the back seat.

"Wow, that was a trip," I whispered. "Let's get out of here."

21

Discovering David in the Park

We got out, stretched our legs, and walked around a bit, leaving Dad to snooze in the back of Blue Pierre. Gerri, as usual, started doing cartwheels down the path, her limbs a blur of energy, free from a mom's reminders about how dirty everything was.

We wandered along a trail by the Big Sioux River—charmed by its cascading mini waterfalls—until we stumbled upon a sundial in Fawick Park. We read four thirty. We kept walking the trail, loving this feeling of independence, and it wasn't long before we came across a towering statue of a very large, very naked man, and we burst into a fit of giggles.

Gerri read the plaque aloud: "*David* by Michelangelo."

The three of us circled the base of the sculpture, marveling at its strange placement, so close to a highway and almost forgotten in this quiet little park.

"Don't you think it's funny?" I said, squinting up at the massive figure. "Even though it's so famous, it's just kind of . . . here? Like, out in the middle of nowhere?"

Jill grinned. "Yeah, and it's even funnier that David's back is turned on the town. Maybe they didn't want to see his—" She stifled a laugh. "His front thing. So, instead, they get to look at his derrière."

That set us off all over again.

As we wiped tears of laughter from our faces, Gerri tilted her head and asked, "What's that thing he's holding? Is it a slingshot and a stone?" Her eyes widened behind her glasses, piecing it together. "Is this the David from David and Goliath?"

Jill and I shaded our eyes against the sun and craned our necks to follow Gerri's gaze. "Could be," I said. "Let's go get Dad. I bet he knows."

When we returned to Blue Pierre, Dad was awake, hunched under the hood, adding water to the radiator and checking the pump.

"Well, looks like everything's in one piece," he said, straightening up, his hair resembling Alfalfa's from *The Little Rascals*. "How'd she do, girls?"

"Mary's a great driver," Gerri said quickly. "The trip was easy. Nothing went wrong."

I noticed she left out the part about the kids in the station wagon and my slightly too-fast exit.

"You don't say? Good job, honey." Dad threw an arm around my shoulder and gave me a squeeze. "Thanks for taking the wheel. I feel much better now."

"Dad, you've got to see something," Jill said, tugging his hand. "It's down the path—trust me, you'll love it."

We led him to the statue, and he stopped in his tracks, eyebrows raised. "Can you beat that? A sculpture of David out here in the middle of the US of A? *Sin-cére! Sin-cére.* Do you know what that means? 'Without wax.' Let me tell you why that's important."

We sat in the cool grass beneath *David*'s shadow, eager for the story. Dad launched into an art history lesson, explaining how the statue depicted the boy before his battle with Goliath, armed only with a slingshot and a rock. He talked about Michelangelo's obsessive secrecy while carving the statue, how he worked tirelessly for three years under candlelight, away from prying eyes.

"Why all the secrecy?" Jill asked, her curiosity mirroring mine.

Dad shrugged with theatrical flair. "Who knows? Maybe he wanted it to be a surprise, or maybe he was just a peculiar fellow.

What makes this statue so remarkable is how flawless it is—perfectly sculpted, no corrections needed. Back then, lesser sculptors used beeswax mixed with marble dust to patch mistakes. Over time, the wax would melt or crumble, revealing the flaws. But *David*? He didn't need any wax. That's where the word *sincere* comes from—*sin*, meaning 'without,' and *céra*, meaning 'wax.' A *sincere* work of art is one that stands the test of time—no patches, no hidden flaws."

As Dad spoke, I leaned back, letting the sunlight play across my closed eyelids. His words hung in the air, mingling with the sounds of the river and the rustle of leaves. For a moment, everything felt still, timeless.

On the way back to the car, I glanced over my shoulder at *David*, standing tall and proud in the fading afternoon light. It struck me that, like the statue, the best parts of life—the sincere ones—don't need fixing or hiding. They're meant to stand as they are, exposed and real, enduring long after the moments have passed.

22

Rendezvousing at Wall Drug

The next morning, we untangled ourselves from our cramped positions in Blue Pierre; we had parked on a secluded dead-end road and slept for the night. Dad called this car-camping. I struggled out of my sleeping bag and rolled it up. Pressing the button on the trunk to pop it open, I could hear the Big Sioux River nearby, and after cramming the sleeping bag in, I did a big stretch. The rest of the family followed suit, and we were ready to find a bathroom.

Dad offered to take us out to breakfast. That was unusual. He generally didn't like to spend money at restaurants. Well, actually, he generally didn't like to spend money at all. We were accustomed to fashioning meals on the road from the contents of the basket and the cooler, which somehow was never that cool. The ice seemed to melt so quickly, and our cheeses were always sweaty.

"We should call this a luke-warmer, not a cooler," I joked.

"Ha ha, very funny," Dad retorted while the twins twittered their appreciation of my joke. "Let's go out for breakfast, and we'll remember to ask the restaurant for some ice to get our cooler back to being a cooler. Plus, we need some ice for Blue Pierre's water pump."

We decided to leave Blue Pierre in the shade and went for a walk in search of an economical breakfast. It was our lucky day because a new Sambo's restaurant franchise had opened the day before on the corner of Tenth and Thompson. There were banners advertising its grand opening, and it was crowded. We had to wait ten minutes until a table opened up, which was the perfect amount of time for us to go into their bathroom and brush our teeth and hair and wash up. They had a coupon for a free Wham-O Fastback Frisbee with any purchase. We chose a blue one and admired the cartoon tiger licking its chops that was imprinted on the top. Pancakes, sausage, and scrambled eggs made up our meals. Dad even let us order orange juice.

The twins and I didn't waste any time tucking in. The melted butter and hot syrup drizzled over my pancakes felt like an elixir, especially when washed down by a sip of tart orange juice. It wasn't as nice as Mrs. Gardener's breakfast, though. It tasted just as good, sure, but I still ached for Meredith and our new friendship. I soothed myself by thinking about our post-cards and figured maybe we'd at least be pen pals. Either way, I was just glad to have met her, and that wouldn't have been pos-sible if we hadn't embarked on our Great American Road Trip. I opened my mouth to express my gratitude for this trip once again, to reiterate how happy I was that we were finally doing this, but Dad beat me to the punch.

"Can you believe we're doing this, Mare?" He paused and then added, "Twins?" His eyes were wide and his brows raised. "We're actually taking the Great American Road Trip!" He had a piece of sausage speared on his fork. "Consider how many things we've seen already, and it's still only the very beginning."

"I was just about to say that, Dad," I began, but before I could continue, he had waved down our waitress, Laura, to say, "Laura, this has to be the best coffee I've ever tasted." He splayed his hand over his chest to express his conviction, and I scowled, following Laura's line of sight to the mug of drip coffee to which he was referring.

Laura and I seemed to realize the same thing at once: this wasn't about the coffee.

I sat back in the booth, bracing myself. Suddenly, the acidity of the orange juice wasn't agreeing with me anymore. As pre-dicted, Dad gave Laura an open once-over, eyes hovering at her bare legs for a few seconds too long.

"That ruffled apron really does suit you, doesn't it?" he said, flashing an oily smile that was only artificially reciprocated by the waitress. I saw her eyes dart to his wedding band. "It looks very smart over your long legs. You've got *stunning* legs."

I shrunk down lower on the smooth red vinyl booth bench.

"Can I get you anything else?" She ignored his compliment. "Girls? Everything okay with your breakfasts?" We nodded and kind of hung our heads. I took a deep breath, trying to settle my system so that I could enjoy this meal. Dad smiled broadly, clueless.

"Excuse me, Laura?" I said before she walked away.

"Yes?"

"Do you think you could spare some ice?" She looked quizzically at me. "We're on a road trip, and our cooler needs refreshing."

"Let me see what I can arrange," she said.

As she walked away, I noticed that she did have shapely legs, but still. I looked at Dad, who was tipping back the chunky coffee mug, and I couldn't help myself. "Dad! Come on," I chastised, trying to sound playful but sort of failing. "It's only breakfast time—that's way too early to be putting on the creepy charm."

He glanced up from his plate with the most bewildered expression.

I gave him one back. Could he not see it? "Didn't you see how she kind of grimaced when you said her legs were stunning?"

"Huh?" he grunted.

The twins nodded encouragingly, giving me the strength to go on.

"Man! What is wrong with you?" Now that I'd started, I couldn't stop. "Mom told me to keep my eye on you and your flirting, you know." *Uh-oh.*

"She did, did she?" He laughed. Why was everything a joke with him?

"Well," I began, but he shushed me with a lame don't-talk-to-your-father-like-that remark, and I was glad when Laura returned with the check. She had me follow her back to the kitchen and let me scoop out the crushed ice from their enormous ice maker into a box that had previously held cans of peaches.

Walking back to the car, we took turns playing Frisbee and carrying the cumbersome and leaky cardboard box of ice. Whoever wasn't carrying the ice played Frisbee with the others. By the time we got back to Blue Pierre, the front of my tank top and my shorts and socks and shoes were soaking wet, and the twins' Frisbee tosses were greatly improved.

Under Blue Pierre's yawning hood, Dad checked the water pump, put a pack of ice on top of it, and topped off the water in the radiator. He then checked the engine oil and transmission and brake fluids. We were good to go.

✳ ✳ ✳

Heading west across the Badlands on Interstate 90, we sang some songs and played the animal, vegetable, or mineral game some more to pass the long miles.

"Mary, can you turn on the CB? Channel nineteen, okay? Let's listen in," Dad proposed. I reached down and adjusted the little dial on the radio; it crackled to life. We heard the truckers making their usual commentaries and exchanging information. Sometimes it was hard to decipher what they were talking about. It felt kind of awkward listening in on other people's conversations, especially when they got personal.

"This here's Billy the Kid. Come in, Little Lady. Over."

"Copy that, Billy the Kid. Little Lady hears you. It's been a long time, Billy. Over," a woman's voice oozed over the airwaves.

"Well, ain't that a sweet sound? How you been, Little Lady? You know, I've been having me some beaver fever. Over," he drawled.

"Is that so? Maybe I'd be able to help you reduce your temperature. Would you like to rendezvous at the Wall? You still have your big eighteen with that nice cozy cab? Over."

"What's the Wall?" Jill wondered out loud, looking up from the cat's cradle string game she and Gerri were playing. "And what's beaver fever?"

"Is Little Lady a nurse or something?" Gerri inquired.

"I think they must be referring to Wall Drug," Dad deduced. I noticed Dad wasn't looking any of us in the eye. "Haven't you seen the billboards advertising Wall Drug?"

"Pretty hard to miss them," I acknowledged. "I think there's one like every mile or so. They're very colorful. Looks like you can get free cold water and a five-cent coffee there."

"What does rendezvous at the Wall mean?" Gerri persisted.

"I'm guessing that Billy the Kid and Little Lady are friends who are planning to meet at Wall Drug," he surmised.

"But what's beaver fever?" Jill asked again, repeating Gerri's unanswered question.

"I think it's supposed to be a clever CB rhyme for a man being lonely," Dad replied, chuckling. *Ew.*

Gerri shrugged and then suggested that we play the ABC game but only use the Wall Drug billboards for our signs. That was going to be some easy pickings. Right away, Jill shouted out, "*A* is for *and*; *B* is for *boots, buckles,* and *belts*; *C* is for *Cowboy Up*; and *D* is for *Drug*." Four letters from one sign was a good start. We continued our game, arriving at *Z* surprisingly quickly, even finding *Quality* for *Q* and *Xtra Special* for *X*, and we played three more times after that.

Listening to the crackle of the CB was our background noise. We heard about the weather (hot!), the traffic (not much), and the police presence (none around) as we zipped along the highway.

After a while, Dad asked, "Would you girls like to talk to the CBers?"

By way of an answer, I picked up the mic and said, "Breaker, breaker, one nine. This is Goldilocks riding shotgun for Blue Pierre. I have a question for you all. We've just gone past about a hundred Wall Drug billboard signs. We're on a big, long road trip around the country and don't want to miss anything important. How many of you stop at Wall Drug for free cold water or five-cent coffee? Should we stop there?" I'd found that if you asked an open-ended question, you could get a much richer CB response.

"That's an affirmative, Goldilocks, from Mr. Ted. Every time I'm in these parts, I never miss a quick stop at Wall Drug. I recommend checking out the giant jackalope they have in the back." He laughed like it was an inside joke. I wondered what a jackalope was. The twins looked equally puzzled, but I was sure Dad would know.

"I copy you, Goldilocks. This is Tennessee here. I always stop. You might as well give the buffalo burgers a try, and they're famously regarded for their cherry pie and doughnuts."

"Roger that, Goldi. This a here's Rockin' Randy. As Tennessee pointed out, buffalo burgers are tasty, and they have great french fries and milkshakes to go with them. Over."

"Roger Wilco. This is Mr. Ted again. Make sure to take them up on their offer of free cold water. And behind the jacka-lope in the backyard is a dinosaur excavation. I took my kiddos there, and they loved digging in the dirt and finding fossils." The trucker's voice crackled on. "They have a large selection of cowboy boots and Indian trinkets like jewelry and moccasins and blankets. Bought my kiddos some little booties there last summer. Over."

"Let's stop there, girls," Dad suggested. "What do you say?" I hoped Grandpa Red's money was burning a hole in his pocket and he wanted to buy us some souvenirs.

"Yes! Yes! Yes!" we shrieked, bouncing on our seats.

I depressed the mic and thanked the truckers for their rec-ommendations. "Thanks, guys! We'll stop, for sure. Sounds like fun. Over."

We settled down, imagining the adventures we'd have at Wall Drug for only a few breaths before we were interrupted by a familiar voice over the CB radio. "Goldilocks? Goldilocks? Is that you? It's Gardener's Flower!"

What? Could the Gardeners pick up our reception all the way in Wisconsin?

I snatched the mic up so fast that I nearly dropped it. "Gardener's Flower? It's me, Mary! I mean Goldilocks. How can you hear us?" I asked excitedly. "Let's go to our special station."

"Roger Wilco," said Meredith. We tuned to channel seven and continued our conversation. "We're in the car driving west toward Mount Rushmore, too!" Meredith informed us. "Dad let us talk him into following you guys. Can you believe it?" Her voice oozed excitement. I glanced at the twins, and all of us cheered silently. "We had such a good time together—and Camp Bluebird felt empty without you guys around. And Ralph made the fireworks show sound super far-out, so we packed up our camping stuff and left the campground the day after you did. We hoped we'd be able to reach you on the CB, and we did!"

"Oh wowzie wow wow!" I shrieked, bouncing up and down in excitement in the front seat. Gerri and Jill were grinning from ear to ear. The expression on Dad's face, with his eyebrows raised quizzically and his mouth drawn into an impressed smirk, confirmed his appreciation of this news as well. I settled down and pulled myself together, replying on the headset. "Holy Toledo! I can't believe it. We already left Sioux Falls and are now on I-90 again, going toward Mount Rushmore. What's your 10-20? We're almost to Wall Drug. Probably arriving there for free cold water in about a"—I looked over questioningly at Dad—"half hour?" Dad nodded. "Over."

"Roger that," said Meredith. "We're about an hour away, Gardener says. We're in Kadoka, South Dakota. Over."

"This is far-out! See you soon! Over and out!" I squealed.

Gerri remarked, "Looks like we're rendezvousing at Wall Drug, too." I smiled at her, and she reached her hands forward to hold mine. Jill put hers on the pile.

✳ ✳ ✳

Blue Pierre was a vivid blue and, as such, was easy to recognize. We left a spot for Mr. Gardener to park right next to us. Our family had already indulged in Wall Drug's free ice-cold water, and Dad was enjoying the cheap coffee. No wonder Wall Drug was so popular. I hadn't realized how thirsty I was. All four of us went back for seconds.

We walked around to the backyard and started exploring everything there. Just like the truckers said, there was a dinosaur display and an excavation area, along with a large statue of a jackalope to climb and play on. I'd never seen or heard of a jackalope before. Jackalopes have the bodies and heads of large jackrabbits, but they also have horns that look like those of an antelope. The twins and I couldn't quite tell if they were made up or not. There was also an ice-cream kiosk and a shooting range.

"Hey, girls. Walk this way." Dad gestured for us to follow him. "I want to get some action shots of you and the Gardener family. I have a funny idea."

We followed Dad around to Blue Pierre to gather his Super 8 camera. He staged some shots. He was pretty good at making sure that the movie footage he took told a story. We had a little Super 8 splicer and viewing machine at home and had made a few movies during the past year. He was right that it was a lot easier to edit footage if it was already in order and had some signage in it. Planning the sequence ahead of time spared us from having to cut and splice the thin filmstrip.

Our best movie was from last winter, of a snowman. We'd built it, ball by ball, and then added the carrot and coal and hat and scarf. Then we did a kind of time-lapse sequence of the melting. The result was pretty nifty—a jerky, robotic progression. That refreshing ice-cold memory evaporated in the South Dakota heat, and I brought my thoughts back to helping with the movie Dad was making today.

For this story, he started by walking all the way out to the street to get a good wide shot of the whole of Wall Drug, panning slowly from left to right. Then he took a shot of the welcome sign. I knew that he was reading the words twice through in his head—a trick he'd told me about to ensure that the audience had sufficient time to read everything when they watched the final movie. Luckily, he completed that preliminary work before the Gardeners arrived.

When we saw them pull up, we girls ran from the shade of the building toward Meredith and Mallory, who were opening the back-seat doors of their station wagon. They did it at the same time, and it looked like their car was opening its arms for a hug. We embraced and swung one another around. I twirled Meredith. She twirled me. Mallory spun Gerri, then Jill.

"I can't believe we're together!" Meredith and I exclaimed at the same moment. All five of us held hands, jumped up and down giddily, and danced in a circle, smiling our faces off. My cheeks hurt. I discreetly waved my blood-sister finger at Meredith, and she saluted hers back, our secrets safely held between us.

Dad walked toward Mr. and Mrs. Gardener with his hand extended. "Brian! Adelaide, you're looking as lovely as ever today!" They shook hands and hugged their hellos. It looked like we were all family, reuniting. I loved it.

"Dad, can we show them around and take them to the back-yard?" I asked.

"How about letting them get their free ice-cold water first?"

"Okay, okay," I conceded, suppressing my impulse to do a cartwheel.

After their waters and before we five girls explored the backyard and climbed on the jackalope, Dad had us do something funny. He set up so that he had an angle from the left front of their station wagon and had Mr. and Mrs. G and the five of us girls get into their car. We couldn't all fit in the back seat at the same time, of course, but that didn't matter because the idea was that the parents were going to open their doors and get out, and then he'd zoom in toward the back door, and Mallory and Meredith and then the three of us were going to slide out of the left side of the back seat one at a time. After we got out, we'd wave and smile and casually walk past him and then scurry quietly around, out of the camera's sight, and back into the unseen side of the car and then exit on the left again.

Mrs. G positioned herself on the right side of the car, out of the view of the camera's lens, and helped with the quick costume changes. We'd grab a hat or put on a sweater or pull up our hair in a quick ponytail—somehow changing our looks so that it would appear like there were a lot of different people in the car. We each rotated through four times, giving the illusion that there were twenty kids exiting the station wagon. We tried hard not to giggle the whole way through, but that was tough to accomplish.

At the end, the camera would get a close-up shot of Mr. G, who'd look at the now-empty back seat and then to the camera and say, "Is that everyone?" He'd shrug his shoulders, smile into the camera's eye, and declare, "I hope Wall Drug has enough ice-cold water for our big group!" *Scene.*

I knew I always had My Journal of Life, which documented everything perfectly, but it'd be nice to have some more precise footage of this trip, too. This silly movie would be a great memento of the fun we all had together. Times like this made me love and appreciate Dad.

Then, out of left field, a somewhat disturbing thought struck me: *This was short-lived.*

This, of course, wasn't going to last forever. Eventually, I would have to bid Meredith farewell all over again. It was just a cruel repeat of our last day at Camp Bluebird. And then I'd have to return home to . . . To what? Mom and Dad getting divorced?

"What's wrong, Mare?" Meredith asked, noticing the shift in my energy.

"Nothing," I said, shaking my head, determined, for now, to live in the moment. "I'm just happy you're here."

I grabbed her hand and pulled her toward the back of the store, where we admired the turquoise jewelry they had for sale on a rotating display.

23

Buffalo Stare-Down

We planned to convoy through the Badlands of South Dakota, our two vehicles within sight of each other, or at least within CB range, until we got to Mount Rushmore. If we were going to basically be driving side by side, I wondered, *Why not exchange kids for a while?*

"Hey, Dad and Mr. and Mrs. G," I called out, giving them my sweetest smile, "how about we swap Gerri and Jill for Meredith?"

"Two for one, eh?" Mr. G said with a laugh. "Sounds like a bargain." He was such a nice man.

Gerri and Jill excitedly gathered their things and straightened up the back seat of Blue Pierre for us. Meredith collected her bag of stuff and joined me. I decided to sit in the back with her. Dad, now alone in the front seat, pulled out to follow the Gardeners' station wagon and camper trailer. As soon as we were safely on the road, he peered at us through the rearview mirror. "Looks like I'm your chauffeur. Where to, me ladies?"

"Take us to Mount Rushmore, and don't spare the horses, James," I answered in my best British accent. Dad chuckled.

Meredith and I snuggled into the back seat, and she opened her sketchbook, proceeding to show me the picture she'd finished of the two of us, encapsulating the scene of our blood-sister ceremony on the log at the edge of the pond.

"Wow, that's beautiful, Meredith," I complimented.

She smiled at me kind of shyly. She grasped the page by the corner and tore it from the spiral binding.

"Here," she said, extending it to me. "I want you to have it."

"Really? Wow." I accepted the beautiful image. "You're so good! Just look at the way you did the sunset on the horizon." My fingertip trailed over the sunset in question, pointing out the way she'd added watered-down marker sunrays that stretched into the sky. I loved the technique. "I like the way you can't see our faces," I added, pointing at the two figures sitting on the log. "I mean, I like the way you have it looking over us, not at us."

"Yeah, faces are hard," she confessed. "Plus, I was trying to give the feeling that it was a secret."

"That's exactly how it feels," I said, and she smiled. Climbing over the front seat, I slid the paper safely in between the pages of the large atlas to protect it.

As we were driving across the vast volcanic, lunar-esque landscape of the Dakota Badlands, we saw a small herd of about twenty buffalo up ahead, wandering around on the north side of the highway.

"Hey, Mare. Ask the convoy if they want to stop and see the buffalo," Dad suggested.

I leaned over the front seat, my derrière in the air; lifted the CB handset from its cradle; and announced, "Breaker, breaker, oh seven. Let's stop up here and check out the buffalo." We came to a slow halt on the gravel shoulder, kicking up a big dust cloud.

There were bulls with enormous shoulder humps, cows with deep-brown eyes, and calves that either stayed close to their mothers or frolicked together. Gathered at the barbed-wire fence, we watched the beasts graze, their jaws working the stubborn tufts of grass. Meredith brought her sketchbook and pencil with her. She quickly outlined a nearby buffalo, capturing the tilt and size of the head and hump just right.

After a couple of minutes of quietly admiring the herd, Dad slung his camera over his shoulder and strode to the fence, pushing down the barbed wire and stepping over.

"Shh," he whispered, raising his finger to his lips when he caught me looking. "Mary, keep an eye on your sisters."

"Dad, get back here! That bull is huge! He's like a rhinoceros. It's too dangerous to go walking around by them. Come on," I implored.

Ignoring me, he switched on his Super 8, eliciting a quiet humming sound.

"Dad!" I whisper-shouted. He ignored me again.

He panned slowly from left to right, and when he reached us in the camera's viewfinder, he waved to get us to wave back from outside the fence. We all tried to be quiet, so as not to disturb the herd. I'm sure my expression of sheer outrage was not what he was expecting for his movie. Then he boldly walked even closer to the massive creatures, filming the approach. He alternated between looking at the animals in real life and looking at them through the camera's viewfinder, his head bobbing up and down like a chicken pecking for seeds.

He was within about ten feet of a massive bull when the enormous giant gave him a long and meaningful moo—a warning more than a greeting. Dad froze. It was so quiet after the buffalo's bellow that we could hear the whirring hum of the camera and the buzz of the flies. Then the animal raised his front right foot and lowered his head, staring Dad down, like a bull facing a matador. My dad was no matador. The sun glinted off the bull's huge horns. He stomped his hoof twice, kicking up dust. I could feel the ground vibrate. We all gasped.

The buffalo's head swayed back and forth, giving Dad a good look-over. Dad stayed still, his camera whirring away. This time, he didn't break eye contact by glancing down at the camera. He stared straight back, and I wondered if this was threatening to the animal. I thought Dad was about to be killed. My palms broke into a cold sweat—immediately, my brain was flooded with an unwanted montage of Dad being trampled to death and the horror of that happening in front of the Gardeners and the twins. Would I have to use the twenty-dollar bill that Mom had given me to get us all back home safely?

I would never forgive Dad for dying so stupidly!

Fear-induced sweat ran down my underarms and back. Dad remained motionless. *Is he afraid?* I wondered. The bull took another step closer to Dad. Now they were only about five feet apart. The rest of the herd—the smaller bulls, cows, and calves—all turned to observe the interaction, staying just as quiet as the rest of us. Just a random tail switch or ear twitch interrupted the stillness. *Oh my God. Dad is going to get slaughtered,* I thought. That stare-down lasted for what seemed like forever, my heart staccato-ing in my chest as time ticked by. *What would the twins and I do without him?*

Ultimately, that large, shaggy creature gave one more great huff, fluttering his huge nostrils, the expelled blast lifting a flap of Dad's sweaty hair from his forehead. I wondered if the buffalo's breath smelled sweet like the grass. He switched his tail in dismissal and, letting out a huge plop of poop, trudged leisurely away. I looked around and saw that I wasn't the only one who thought that was funny. Mrs. G was covering her mouth, suppressing a laugh.

Served Dad right that the buffalo let out a meadow muffin right in his face. The rest of the herd instinctively trod in their leader's direction. Dad walked backward toward us. He got to the fence, pushed it down again, stepped over it without snagging anything on the barbs, and exclaimed, "Wow! That was incredible! *Ex-tra-ord-in-ary!*"

He beamed, returning the camera to its case, which he kept slung around his neck. He strode with big prideful steps to the cars, with the rest of us in astonished pursuit. I was silently fuming and slammed the door when I got back into Blue Pierre. I felt the angry energy rising in me like a helium balloon. When we got on the road again, I couldn't hold it in anymore and burst out, "Dad, you're kind of crazy. No, you *are* crazy."

"Hey, what are you talking about?"

"You risked your life out there!" I yelled. Meredith stiffened next to me. "That was a real wild animal! It's not like we were at a zoo and they were behind a big moat or something."

"Oh come on. Why are you so upset?"

"You were only about five feet away. Five feet! Or less! I bet you could've touched the one who roared at you. He looked like he was going to trample you to death! He dropped his head a little when he was checking you out! He pounded his hoof."

"Come on, Mare. Settle down."

"Don't come-on-Mare-settle-down me!" I sounded like Mom. "And I bet they're faster than they look. There were eighteen of them! Did you know that? I counted."

"Come on, Mary. Calm down," he said. "Nothing happened."

"You didn't know he wouldn't defend his herd or attack or something. You could have started a stampede! What would the twins and I do if you got gored or trampled to death?" Spittle was flying out of my mouth as I shouted at him, and Meredith had shrunk over to the passenger door. "That was so reckless! You are a fool, you know that? You're like a child. A stupid child." I couldn't believe what I was saying. I had never spoken to him like that; I had never even *thought* those things before.

Meredith looked on with eyebrows raised. We were both surprised by my outburst. Usually, I would just go along with the situation, keeping things copacetic. But something about how careless he had been made me furious. All his silly antics—like the stupid ooga horn, always drawing attention to himself like a rooster crowing at sunrise, loud and impossible to ignore, and the way he made others uncomfortable with his unsolicited attempts at flirting—and just everything about him in general built up inside me like the high-pressure magma splitting the earth's crust before a volcanic eruption.

Once again, I remembered the talk my mom gave me on the porch right before we left. *She was so right. He's ridiculous. When you're a grown-up, things can't always be fun and games! Ugh! I've never felt like this before.* I hated him. He was embarrassing! And I was feeling this in front of my new best friend. The words tumbled out of my mouth in near-perfect order, as though they'd been waiting there for years, and not even my fast-beating heart and tight throat could slow them.

The truth was that I was *mortified* by him. A flash of Mr. and Mrs. Gardener breezed through my mind—Mrs. G's perfect breakfasts and encouraging words, and Mr. G's easygoing nature. They were nothing like my family. My family was so weird. I didn't even care if Mom and Dad got divorced! I wanted to *scream*. Anger washed over me like a tidal wave. I was mad as hell.

Mad was not a feeling that our family was allowed to have. Whenever cause for anger arose, justified or not, we were commanded to go to our rooms and come back out only when we had a happy face on. Our parents insisted that we be a happy family. Or at least *look* like it.

Also, complaining never got us anywhere, so being bored wasn't permitted, either. We'd heard enough times over the years that if you're bored, you're boring. When you're trained like that for years, you get good at squashing anger or other undesirable feelings and donning that approved-of smiling face. As the practice is ingrained, it simply becomes habit, a way of being.

That was why my outburst was so unexpected.

As I fumed, I added this episode to My Journal of Life. Yelling at him made me feel good. Really good. The anger drifted away like a released balloon, leaving me feeling unexpectedly light. Getting the anger out rather than tamping it down was a new experience and much more satisfying than what I'd been used to.

Dad brushed off my concerns with a wave of his hand. Then he turned around, not even looking at the road, and boasted, "Like I said, nothing happened." His grin crinkled his eyes and spread from ear to ear. "They were so calm and mellow, and I got some incredible footage."

Meredith tried to smooth things out. "It's okay, Mary. Everything's okay." She patted my hand and then rested her own on my leg until my shaking subsided. Dad did nothing to reassure me or tell me not to worry or even thank me for my concern. He didn't discipline or punish me for my outburst, either. He remained completely neutral, as though my words meant absolutely nothing to him. Wasn't he supposed to be the one teaching me to be responsible? He didn't do any of the things a good dad should do! He just turned back toward the road and accelerated, with his big happy face on, as though nothing even remotely was the matter. With his arm draped across the top of the front seat, whistling a jaunty tune, he reminded me of Mr. Magoo.

What was wrong with him? How did I not notice this before?

Mr. Magoo, famously oblivious to the chaos behind him, wandered through life, leaving a trail of physical destruction in his wake. My dad was the same—but instead of broken objects, he'd leave behind emotional wreckage. When I got to thinking about it, many examples of how he'd do crazy, dangerous things came to mind. There was the time he'd let us play on the roof of the garage when Gerri and Jill were only four years old. Gerri nearly fell off and would have if Skippy hadn't grabbed her in the nick of time. I thought of the times he'd tie a rope to the back bumper of Mom's station wagon and drag us along in the wooden toboggan, whipping us around on snowy cul-de-sacs, with the sled sometimes tipping over and throwing us out. Once, the toboggan skidded under the car, and I was nearly decapitated. The muffler burned my snowsuit. I wore that same burned-arm snowsuit for the next two years.

When I was younger, I thought of him as adventurous, entertaining, and admirable—not reckless, foolish, or embarrassing. Sure, his immature choices often led to plenty of fun, but this time was different. This time it was too much. I hated him in that moment—hated him so much, I wished Mom *would* divorce him. The thought startled me, but the anger stayed. I glared at his serene face in the rearview mirror, willing him to notice, but he didn't.

Just like Mr. Magoo, he wandered through life, blissfully unaware of the mess he left behind.

24

The Corner of Walk and Don't Walk

I eventually settled down. Even though I was a bit embarrassed to have exploded in such a powerful outburst in front of company, I also felt proud of myself. Meredith knew my qualms with Dad. It was somehow through her mere presence and silent moral support that I didn't stuff everything I'd been feeling back inside and instead let it loose for once. Meredith had reached over and grabbed my hand in hers during my explosion and held on for a long while until our hands were just too sweaty to stay clasped. When we finally let them slip apart, I gave her a big, thankful smile.

We zipped west along Interstate 90. After crossing the brownish-blue Cheyenne River, we were following the Gardeners and could see—even with the bright afternoon sun in our eyes—that their right trailer wheel was starting to wobble.

Mr. G must have felt it at the same time we'd noticed because he started braking hard, but it was too late. The trailer wheel wriggled itself right off. It rolled all on its own off the road and into the gutter, dumping the weight of the trailer hard onto its axle.

"Oh! Son of a gun! Would you look at that?" Dad exclaimed, happy as a clam. He slammed on the brakes and skidded to a stop on the shoulder. He flipped on Blue Pierre's hazard blinkers, then instructed us to get out on the passenger side so that we were away from the highway.

Huh? That was fatherly.

"Mary and Meredith, would you please go fetch the wheel? It looks like it stopped rolling up there and bounced into the ditch past that little shrub." Dad pointed in the general direction of where the wheel might be. I put my new hatred of him aside while Meredith and I ran ahead. It was a long way off, and we returned sweaty and yucky, palms blackened from rolling the wheel. Our bare legs were scratched up from the weeds along the shoulder of the highway. Meredith's mom handed us some paper towels.

"Well, that's something I've never seen before." Dad crouched down to look at the axle. Mr. G peered over his shoulder. Dad nodded at where we'd just come from. "The wheel just went loose and continued rolling."

"Looks pretty bad," Mr. G observed, mouth in a slant. "Now what do we do?"

"Well, we fix it," Dad said simply, craning his neck around to see him and pushing his glasses up his nose. "Obviously. What else would we do?"

"Do you know how to fix that?" Mr. G inquired, skeptical. He folded his extra-tall body down to peer at what Dad was looking at.

"Let's have a look-see and determine what needs repairing," Dad said. He got down on his knees and then rolled over and lay on his back so that he could look up into the wheel well—an action he probably should've taken only after using a jack to hoist the camper up and keep it secure, but I kept that part to myself.

"I think I need some tools," Dad noted.

Eager to get back on the road again, I ran to Blue Pierre and brought out the tool kit we kept in the trunk, pretending everything was okay. I didn't want the rest of the Gardener family—the nice, normal family—to know that I had come unhinged only moments ago in the car. I set the kit down right beside Dad just as Mrs. G offered him a towel.

Dad winked at her and said, "Thanks, sweetie."

I shot Meredith a *See! Look how creepy he is!* sort of look. She returned it with an *I know!* one back.

Dad spread the towel on the dirt, then started to disassemble the axle, placing the ball bearings and broken parts and other greasy bits on it. Mr. G walked to a compartment in the trailer and pulled out a small cardboard box of automotive parts that was stored with the trailer's spare tire.

"Um, look here, Ralph—not sure what all these parts are for, but maybe there's something you need in here," he offered, jiggling the contents of the box and extending it toward Dad, who wiggled out from beneath the axle to take a look. He rummaged around inside the box and seemed surprised and relieved by what he saw in the hodgepodge collection of materials.

"This set of races is exactly what we need," Dad remarked, pulling them out. "How odd you have a spare set."

"Like I said, I'm not sure what they are. Glad you have the parts you need. How do you know so much about mechanics?" Mr. G asked hesitantly.

"Just part of being a man, Brian," Dad said dismissively. Mr. G looked down at his feet while Mrs. G patted his back. I couldn't believe Dad had just said that. He was so rude! The gall was outstanding. Didn't he see that Mr. G was the very definition of a good man? An excellent father and husband? He was tall, had a great job, was good-looking, and was clearly the apple of Mrs. G's eye.

"Check this out, Mare." Dad, oblivious to my disgust over his rudeness, directed my attention to the busted axle. The sweat under my sun hat ran in rivulets down my face, stinging my eyes, and it wasn't until after I'd wiped them away that I realized I'd probably left a tire-black smudge on my face because my hands were filthy. "This kind of axle has the bearing rollers riding directly on the axle shaft itself. You can see how these broken-down bearings wore a groove into the shaft. That's what happened. That's how the wheel wiggled off."

He looked pleased with his diagnosis. As it turned out, the races were the precise thing he needed to complete the rebuilding of the axle. It took him a while of grunting and mumbling and swearing under his breath before he'd managed to reassemble the pieces and add fresh grease—which he had me fetch from Blue Pierre's trunk.

The little girls and Mrs. G set up a snack well away from the road. Jill, the self-proclaimed Kool-Aid Kid, grabbed the jug and our cups while Mrs. G sliced up some apples and salami. The three little girls scratched hopscotch on the ground and played, using stones as markers.

"Okay, just about done here, but I can't get this tight enough without a bigger wrench," Dad announced, wiping his greasy hands on the towel and sliding his glasses up his sweaty face. "We need a trucker's big wrench to tighten this baby up. Mary and Meredith, how'd you like to use this handkerchief, go out to the highway, and flag down a friendly trucker? They usually have good sets of tools." He pulled his hankie out of his pocket and handed it to me. "Your young, sexy bodies might attract someone quicker than an old, ugly coot like me could."

He smirked and winked at us. *Mr. Magoo strikes again.*

I snatched the hankie out of his hand, irritated and mortified all over again, and we ambled over to the edge of the road. The hankie was clean, so I used it to really wipe my face.

Meredith said, "You're right. Your dad is kind of creepy, talking about our sexy bodies like that. And calling my mom sweetie? *Ew.*"

"I know. I'm sorry." My face was so hot, I probably could've fried an egg on it. "He's always like that. I just haven't really noticed how uncomfortable it makes other people before now." I paused, gripping the handkerchief. "What's his problem? He's not normal."

"I wish I could say I disagreed," Meredith replied. It took me a moment to untangle that complicated remark and realize that she *did* agree. That made it even worse. Truer somehow.

"I know! He's horrible. I want to cry," I moaned, covering my face with my sweaty hands.

She went on, "I'm glad my dad didn't hear that about our sexy bodies. He wouldn't like it at all."

I cringed, agreeing with her. But wouldn't you know, Dad was right, I think, because in no time, a trucker did indeed pull over, flinging gravel everywhere as he came to an abrupt stop on the shoulder. And just like Dad said, he had a great big wrench we borrowed to finish the job. When Dad was done tightening the bolts, he passed the giant wrench back to the trucker with a flourish. "Thank you, partner," he said.

The man straightened his cowboy hat and hitched up his sagging pants as he sauntered back to his rig. "Good day to you all," he said in parting.

"Are we good to go, Ralph?" Mrs. G asked.

"Indeed, we are," Dad answered, and I was relieved he didn't call her sweetie again.

"All right, girls. Let's clean up and get a move on," she said.

We packed up and drove west toward Mount Rushmore. It was still a few days until the Fourth of July, so we had time to get there, but we wouldn't make it by the end of the day the way we'd planned. Fixing the trailer took a long time, and we were off schedule.

When we stopped for gas about ten minutes later, Mr. G used the service station's pay phone, untangling the chain to its dangling phone book, and contacted a campground in Rapid City.

"It's on me," he announced when he returned from making the reservation. "As a token of my appreciation for fixing my trailer wheel, Ralph."

"Gee, thanks, Brian. Mighty generous of you," Dad replied, friendly as ever. It was as if he hadn't recently insulted Mr. G to his face about not being manly.

As we approached Rapid City, the heat was really doing a number on poor ol' Blue Pierre. Even with the heater blasting to dissipate the engine's heat and try to prevent it from overheating, it was stop-and-go for a while. We'd drive, and then the water pump would get too hot, so we'd stop and add ice. Wait. Go again.

The water pump that Dad had installed finally quit completely. The adults decided that because it was getting late, we five girls would load up in the Gardeners' station wagon and go with them to the campsite to start setting things up, then Mr. G would drive back and see how Dad was getting along.

Dad was supposed to stay put. But we later found out that after a few minutes, he'd coaxed Blue Pierre into working again. He told us that he'd tried to catch up to us, that he'd called on the CB, but for some reason, we hadn't heard him. Maybe we'd been too loud in the station wagon, or we had accidentally turned it off. We hadn't expected him to ditch the plan.

Well, at that point, Dad had apparently realized that he didn't know where we were, and he'd begun to panic. "Breaker, one nine. Breaker, one nine. This is Blue Pierre. I can't find my three daughters! They're with the Gardener family at a nearby campsite. I can't recall the campsite's name. Please help. Anyone there? Does anyone know what the campgrounds around here are called?"

By that point, he had been driving through town. "I'm literally at the corner of Walk and Don't Walk in Rapid City. The street sign is missing. I'm lost. I can tell that Rapid City is rapidly closing up for the night. Help. Anyone?"

Thankfully, truckers within the twenty-five-mile radius of the CB had assisted by mentioning a few campgrounds. One of the names jogged his memory, and he'd made his way toward us. We hadn't known that he'd left the place where Blue Pierre had broken down, so Mr. G followed the plan and left us at the campsite with Mrs. G. He drove east while Dad was driving west. They saw each other and waved. Mr. G made a U-turn. Dad had ended up following him to reunite with us.

When they got to our campsite, we were already done with supper and were on to the s'mores. Dad plopped down at the picnic table and put his head in his hands, telling us all about the debacle with perfect honesty. I looked on, yet again ashamed, for the first time wishing he'd be more dishonest and keep this mishap to himself. Meanwhile, Jill pulled out the booklet where she kept our Slate of Dates, States, and Fates tally.

"Jilly," Dad said, realizing what she was about to do, "would you mind keeping the fact that I lost you guys out of our summary? I don't want your mom to know about that."

Typical, I thought.

Jill looked at him and said, "How 'bout I put *7/1/76 | South Dakota | Wall Drug with the Gardeners | Buffalo | Car problems: broken trailer axle and overheated Blue Pierre | Campground in Rapid City?*"

"Sounds like a good summary. Thanks, honey," Dad said, the relief evident in his voice.

I was reminded of the guest sermon he'd presented recently at church, which was about this very thing—getting what you deserve. In the sermon, he was comparing the Hindu and Buddhist idea of karma versus the Christian one of facing judgment when you die. He was trying to prove that the Christian way was superior. He'd gone on and on about reaping and sowing. He'd tried to make Christianity and Hinduism and Buddhism sound so different from each other. But I thought that when you came right down to it, they both seemed to say that if you're good, good will come, and if you're bad, bad will come—while you're living this life or the next time around. I'd thought, *Who cares about the details? Just be good to cover all your bases.*

When I tucked into my sleeping bag that night, I chuckled to myself, thinking that what goes around does indeed come around. I fell asleep with a guilty smile on my face, thinking it served Dad right to get scared about losing us after scaring me so badly when he stepped over that barbed-wire fence and stood face-to-face with that massive buffalo.

And maybe whatever happened between him and Mom when we got back to Ohio would be his comeuppance, too.

25

Fireworks

The next morning, I woke up feeling revitalized and was ready to go exploring. I wandered out of our tent to see Dad and the twins sitting at the picnic table. He'd brought out the box we normally kept in the passenger side footwell of our sedan and had opened it to reveal several maps, our TripTik, and a few guidebooks with an array of different-colored paper scraps acting as bookmarks. He spread them across Mrs. Gardener's red-and-white gingham tablecloth just as she exited their camper and offered him a hot mug of coffee.

"Thank you so much, Adelaide." Tendrils of steam curled around his fingers as he grasped the stout mug of coffee she'd just percolated. Dad gave the twins a brief glance, then looked beyond, as if to confirm Mr. G wasn't around—and he wasn't. With the coast clear, Dad did something I couldn't believe: he patted Mrs. G on the derrière.

She swatted his hand away, red-faced and flustered.

"Keep your 'ands to yourzelf, meez-teur!" she snapped and marched off toward her trailer. But she was smiling, too. *People are odd.*

"Good morning, Mary," Dad said, noticing my approach. "Glad we're all up early. I have some ideas I'd like to run by you girls." Pushing his slipping glasses up his nose, he waited until I took a seat at the table with him and the twins.

"Ideas?" Mr. Gardener asked. He and Mrs. Gardener had emerged from their camper without so much as making a sound.

He had one arm around his wife's waist as they stood behind us, the other holding his own mug of coffee. I wondered if he'd seen what Dad had done and was protecting his wife or claiming her as his. *Maybe*, I thought, *she went inside and told him.*

"Why yes," Dad answered, completely unbothered. "I've got a plan for the next few days."

It took every ounce of my control to focus on what Dad was saying—something about caves and Crazy Horse being more impressive than Mount Rushmore—instead of the heat that was radiating from my face, fueled by sheer fury, humiliation, and grief. It was bad enough to openly disrespect Mom—but now he was jeopardizing our budding friendship with the Gardeners.

Mr. Gardener, having retrieved the *Rapid City Journal* from the campground's little store, reported that the weather forecast called for the heat wave to persist, with a bit of a spike tomorrow. Any activity we did outside the next day should keep the heat wave in mind.

"Then can we agree to do the caves tomorrow?" Dad asked. We all nodded, our mouths full of warm raisin-and-brown-sugar-laced oatmeal, and murmured our agreement. "That leaves an extra day for relaxing and staying near camp. What do you say, girls? Gardeners?"

* * *

Over the next couple of days, we explored all the places on Dad's plan.

As usual, he was right. The Crazy Horse memorial—which was a project that planned to sculpt Crazy Horse, Rushmore-style, into granite—was way more impressive than Mount Rushmore itself, but it was only partly done. There was a model available, along with a few signs, that showed the vision for the final project, so you could imagine where the Indian riding the horse was pointing to and what it would look like in the end. I bet they were only 10 percent done. Mr. Gardener said that he thought they'd never finish it.

"The family who is working on the Crazy Horse carving won't accept any money from the US government. All their revenue is from private contributions," Mr. G informed us and added ten dollars to their collection box. "That's why it's taking so long."

Dad's eyes shifted back and forth between Mr. Gardener and Mr. Gardener's ten-dollar donation, visibly put-out. Frowning, he reluctantly—yet at the same time rather flamboyantly—pulled out his wallet and, with a flourish, gave each of us, including Meredith and Mallory, a single to add to the box.

✳ ✳ ✳

Jewel Cave National Monument featured stunning crystal formations. They glittered like diamonds under the glow of the electric lamps. Some of the formations twisted down from the ceiling like frozen waterfalls while others sparkled as if dusted with sugar.

It was slippery in there. Mr. and Mrs. Gardener held hands. So did the twins and Mallory, and even Meredith and I held on to each other. Dad was on his own. Everything felt damp, and now and then, you could hear the distant drips of water falling from the ceiling.

We stepped carefully on the narrow metal walkways, each footstep echoing through the cavern. At some point, when we were separated from the other tourists, I decided to test it out.

"Hello? My name is Mary!"

A half dozen encores of "Hello? My name is Mary!" ricocheted off the walls before fading into nothingness. Likely to the vexation of the adults present, the rest of the kids and Dad joined in the echo-making until an old couple told us to hush.

Hush, hush, hush, hush . . .

We emerged from the caves like blind mole rats seeing light for the first time.

* * *

At last, the Fourth arrived. After a long day at our campsite—with card playing, reading, hopscotching, jumping rope, and games of hide-and-seek and tag—the afternoon was finally here, and we made our way to our previously selected vista point at Mount Rushmore, checking off another item on Dad's list.

"Oh, look at this!" Gerri exclaimed, twirling beneath the entrance to the Avenue of Flags, which led from the Visitors Center to the Mount Rushmore lookout deck. The walkway was lined with fifty-six flags: fifty state flags, one district flag, three territory flags, and two commonwealth flags. Perched above the walkway was Mount Rushmore itself. Everything was arranged to make the sculpture look as incredible as possible, but the presidents' heads were smaller than I expected.

We searched for the Ohio and New Jersey flags. It was easier to find the Ohio flag because of its unique form—it being the only pennant-shaped one.

Jill skipped along next to Gerri, showing off their matching outfits—their blue shirts with white stars finishing off their patriotic getup. I, on the other hand, refused to be pigeonholed into Mom's idea of Kmart originals Stars and Stripes ensembles that she'd bought for the trip. I threw on my blue jean cutoffs, white Keds with blue socks, and a white tank top. My baseball hat was red. Dad, as usual, wore that ridiculous little blue French chapeau that perfectly matched the color of Blue Pierre. He'd also donned his new American flag shirt, which complemented his striped tube socks.

We set up the Gardeners' camp chairs in our special space and spread out a blanket. I could sense the crowd's growing anticipation and excitement for the upcoming spectacle. Dad let us buy ice-cold Cokes from a vendor there. I sipped mine slowly to make it last. I loved the way the slim bottle sweated and kept my hands cool; I rubbed it on my neck every now and again to refresh. We were all relieved when the temperature cooled down as the sun set.

It felt like it took forever before the fireworks finally commenced, but they were sure worth the wait. Holy moly, the show was simply breathtaking. It went on and on—some explosions were right on top of each other, blooming corollas of red, white, and blue. Crash! Bang! Pow! Onomatopoeias everywhere. Throughout the show, I could hear patriotic songs being blasted from the lookout deck's speakers: "You're a Grand Old Flag" and "The Star-Spangled Banner."

My heart swelled, fully gripped by the power of the moment—a big memory I knew I'd log in My Journal of Life and treasure forever. At some point, I gazed up at Dad, who looked as impressed and awestruck as I did. Was that a tear on his cheek? And for the moment, I let go of the fact that he was wearing that stupid blue French chapeau and that he was a cheapskate and that he'd weaseled $500 out of Grandpa Red and that he'd patted Mrs. G's derrière. All I could see was the man he was, a person. My dad, who'd dreamed of this day. We'd *both* dreamed of this day, more than anybody else present, and here it was, happening. As though thinking the same thing, Dad reeled me in and roped his hairy arm over my shoulders, and for the time being, it was just us again—me, as his favorite child, and him, as my favorite parent.

The Gardeners were standing together, holding hands. Gerri and Jill were jumping up and down and laughing their heads off. The crowd was cheering. We had built up this Fourth of July as one of the biggest events of the summer, and it did not disappoint. After the earsplitting grand finale, the clouds of acrid smoke filled the air and whitened the dark sky. Eventually, the oohs and aahs of the spectators died down, and then a hush descended on us all. I think we all felt a little numb afterward, awed by patriotism and extravaganza.

Slowly, we made our way back to our campsite. Crawling into our sleeping bags, we fell asleep quickly, without much talking.

* * *

Sometimes I feel melancholy after a big event comes and goes. The day after the Fourth of July was one of those times. I woke up earlier than everyone else, listening to the gentle snores of the twins and the loud ones blasting out of Dad, and kept my eyes on the ceiling of our tent. The sadness in my body was heavy, like one of those weighted blankets they put on you when you have your teeth x-rayed.

A couple of tears slid down my temples and into my ears. My face was soggy, my armpits smelled stinky, and my hair still carried the scent of sulfur from the fireworks the night before. I felt gross. My legs were hairy, and my belly rolls were hanging out. I bet my breath reeked, too. I was disgusting. But at least I still had Meredith with me for a while longer.

When Dad woke, he roused us with his nontrumpet verbal rendition of "Reveille." "All right, up and at 'em, Adam Ant!" he sang out, clapping his hands, chipper as ever.

Jill groaned, and Gerri rolled over, covering her head with her sleeping bag.

"Come on, up and at 'em. Let's pack up and head out." Dad reached down and gave Gerri a nudge. "Can't wait to see Yellowstone and Old Faithful." More clapping. "Plus, Devils Tower is on our way. We have a lot of driving ahead of us. Come on. Up, up, up."

I sighed, recalling that there were indeed some cool things to look forward to. Dad's constant optimism surprisingly perked up my spirits a bit. My eyes trailed Dad as he excitedly began packing his belongings, and I thought about the fireworks yesterday—the way he'd slung an arm over my shoulder, and it was as if everything had been temporarily brought back to the way things were before I'd overhead his fight with Mom. Maybe that was another reason I was melancholy. Now that the bright lights and music had all faded away, I couldn't forget reality so easily. What was worse was that I couldn't forgive it so easily, either.

The twins finally got up. They knuckled their bleary eyes, and we began the ever-quicker-with-practice process of rolling up the sleeping bags and tent, getting dressed, and loading Blue Pierre. The Gardeners were doing the same with their camper. During the big packing up, Mrs. Gardener whipped together a simple toast and bacon breakfast with fresh coffee for the grown-ups. Boy, would I miss her when we parted ways.

We got back in our cars, switching the kids again. This time Meredith and I climbed into their station wagon, and Gerri, Jill, and Mallory clambered into Blue Pierre with Dad. *Good luck, little ones,* I thought. The Gardeners had laid the back seats down in the station wagon, so Meredith and I had a big bed to sprawl out on. We had pillows and blankets. It was so cozy. Their car had air-conditioning that worked. Such a treat. The Gardeners could store a lot of their stuff in the camper trailer, so it was much roomier in their car than in our cramped Blue Pierre. All our things were jammed into the trunk, and we still had a bunch of other items in the car with us, like the pillows and the cooler and the picnic basket and the cardboard box in the footwell and each of our little activity bags. I tried to appreciate the space and freedom while it lasted.

We followed along behind Blue Pierre, through the twisty roads and craggy walls of Spearfish Canyon, until Devils Tower appeared in the distance.

26

Snowball Fight

We were easily persuaded to check out the Grand Teton National Park en route to Yellowstone, as it was said to be a national treasure not to be missed, according to the young, khaki-clothed park ranger we overheard giving a tour to some folks back at Devils Tower. After soaking in the energy of that giant natural stone skyscraper, straining our necks to see to the top, and marveling at its incredibility, we hiked back to the cars to head west on Teton Park Road.

"Isn't that just crazy?" I heard Gerri comment to Mallory.

"It is! It's just so out of place," Mallory agreed. "Kind of like a giant building."

Jill skipped up to Dad with Mallory and Gerri in tow and pleaded, "Can we switch cars? Please? We want a turn in the cool car." I pressed my lips into a line; I knew she meant the cooler temperature of the Gardeners' station wagon and not cool in a fashionable sense, but it still felt embarrassing to acknowledge Blue Pierre as the inferior choice. Even so, I had to agree with her. I preferred the bed-size back seat with blankets and pillows and the fresh breeze of the air conditioner to top it all off, too.

"Makes no difference to me, sweetie," Dad answered, giving her a sweaty smile and a pat on the back.

Mr. G remarked, "Fine with us." Meredith and I looked at each other, and even though our shirts were stuck to our sweaty torsos, we reluctantly let the little ones have the comfortable ride. They did look wilted.

"*Okay*," I groaned. "At least we'll still be together, Meredith."

She seized my hand as we schlepped over to Blue Pierre, our typical enthusiasm bogged down significantly by something we both realized but couldn't bring ourselves to say out loud: after our trip to Yellowstone, we'd be saying goodbye—possibly forever. They'd be headed back home to New Jersey, and we'd continue toward the Great Salt Lake. Our time together was coming to an end, for real. It would be a redo of Camp Bluebird but without the rare chance of crossing paths once again.

I knew we'd better make the most of it.

"Can we have some Kool-Aid before we change cars?" Mallory asked her mom. Mrs. G nodded. Jill got out the cooler jug and the cups, and we all quenched our thirst.

Mrs. G said, "Here are some ice cubes." She cracked the baby ice tray that she had extracted from their miniature refrigerator that had a little freezer section on top and dropped a couple into our sticky palms. Some we let drip down our necks and backs, and some we added to our drinks. Gerri wet her hair and shook herself like a dog, splashing all of us. Even though we shrieked in surprise, we didn't mind a bit.

When we opened the back door of the car, I could see a cloud of heat escape. It rushed out of the back seat in near-invisible shivers, and I braced myself for the impact. Spreading a blanket across the seat, I said, "Here, Meredith, this will protect our legs from the hot Naugahyde."

"Good idea, Mare," she said. I collected the TripTik and climbed into the back seat with her.

Dad got in and turned the key, and Blue Pierre rumbled to life. This time we were leading our little caravan. The water pump was still not working properly, so Dad turned the heater on, and we opened the roof. This was going to be a long, hot ride.

After a couple of hours with incredible views of the Grand Tetons and their tall, jagged, snow-covered peaks, we passed several old barns linked together in a row, like beads on a necklace. They looked out of place, surrounded by the rolling countryside.

We sat back and admired the barns and farms as we flew by. Our chitchat, plus the open sunroof, seemed to cool down the sweltering afternoon. Meredith and I leaned into each other in the hot back seat and raised our hands over our heads, feeling the wind through the open roof—the current of it as cool and tangible as strumming our fingers through water.

It was a long drive through the Grand Tetons, but we didn't really stop or walk around, except for a short hike near Jenny Lake. The Gardeners pulled in right behind us, and we all took a refreshing dip in the cold water. We didn't even bother to change into our swimsuits—we just waded in and dunked ourselves under with our clothes on. Even so, it was just warm enough outside for us to steam when we got out—the water cold but our bodies still running too hot.

We had a couple of hours of driving to get to Yellowstone. As much as Meredith and I longed for the luxury of air-conditioning, we let the little ones stay with the Gardeners in the cool car. As we drove along, we started going uphill, and I think the higher elevation finally made the temperature lower. It seemed like that had a good effect on Blue Pierre.

"Breaker, oh seven. This is Jack and Jill. Do you copy, Blue Pierre?" we heard over the CB.

Meredith looked at me, and I said, "Go ahead and answer."

"Hi, Jack and Jill. This is Gardener's Flower. What's up?"

"Well, we see some snow on the side of the road—in July! Can you believe it?" Jill revealed, the suggestion made clear by her tone.

"Are you stopping?" Meredith asked. "Let's stop."

Dad told us that he'd be happy to stop and stretch his legs. In a few minutes, we pulled up behind the Gardeners' big station wagon and pop-up trailer. The little girls were already out of the car, raking their hands through the snow and molding it into snowballs. The snow was old, so it was very icy and kind of gray, and it wasn't rolling into big balls very well, but we still had fun.

"Meredith, over here!" I called and grabbed her hand. I pulled her along to one edge of the small open area, our footsteps so deep, they were poking fence-post holes into the snow, the icy crust scratching our ankles. "Let's throw from here. Start making a pile of balls." I turned my attention to the enemy on the other side while I packed several balls to add to our arsenal. "Hey, you guys! Get ready for a snowball fight!"

"No fair!" yelled Mallory. "You two are bigger."

"But there's three of you!" replied Meredith. Everybody, including our parents standing beside the vehicles, nodded at the reasonableness of this fact.

"Mary, what are the rules?" Gerri called.

"Well, how about each side gets five minutes to prepare, and then the war is on? Other than that, no rules!" I shouted.

"No aiming for the head. How about a thirty-second penalty if you hit someone in the head?" Gerri suggested. We negotiated and bargained and used up our five-minute prep time, and then finally, Mr. G stepped in and interjected, "Go!"

There was some coverage on our side provided by a fallen tree. The twins and Mallory had two big boulders. The war was on. Mallory had an excellent arm and hit me and Meredith a couple of times each. Just as I was about to launch a ball at Gerri, I saw a white explosion on Meredith's chest in my periphery. I tried to avenge my hit comrade, but the ball I threw whizzed right past Jill's head—a total miss. I grabbed another ball, and when Jill turned around to take cover behind one of the boulders, I hit her directly in the back of the head with a lucky shot.

Mr. G called over, "Mary, that's a thirty-second penalty!" I sat down behind our log and packed balls until I heard him call, "Time!"

Mrs. G smiled from her position by their station wagon while her husband officiated, and Dad ran around throwing snowballs at each side. He made for a fun zigzagging target, and I think that each of us five girls hit him at least once. Snow in July was crazy and wonderful. I was so glad we stopped.

"Come on, kids, Ralph. Let's get going," suggested Mrs. Gardener. "We've got a bit of a drive to Yellowstone still, and it's getting kind of late." She was right, but we groaned anyway, for the sake of it, and she bowed her head slightly, brows raised. "Come on now. Time to go forward and be our best selves."

We grudgingly threw our last snowballs. I hit Gerri square on the derrière as she walked toward their station wagon.

"Hey!" She glared at me. "War's over, Mary!"

❋ ❋ ❋

We'd made it to Yellowstone. Meredith and I woke up early the next morning. Everybody else was still asleep. The twins had crashed with Mallory in the pop-up trailer with Mr. and Mrs. Gardener. Meredith and I had stayed with Dad under the stars, which wasn't all that bad—a truth made evident by the fact that Dad was still snoring away, despite the sun spilling light over the horizon.

After Meredith and I rolled up our sleeping bags and brushed our teeth, we hung a note like a flag on Blue Pierre's antenna, saying that we were going to explore some of the bright nearby pools.

After tiptoeing our way out of the camp, we traipsed perhaps the length of a football field until reaching the closest aquamarine pool. We'd spotted it yesterday, but it had been too late to visit it, so this one was first on our list.

The smell of sulfur was overpowering, but once you got used to it, it kind of became comforting and familiar, like the stink of a skunk. We stayed on the wooden paths framing the pool, marveling at all the bubbling and steaming.

While we were hiking, Old Faithful, right around the corner, erupted in a violent display of hot water and plumes of steam. The geyser shot up so high in the sky, and with such force, that even water falling back to the earth was pushed up again for a second round.

It was beautiful. Magical, even.

"Wow!" exclaimed Meredith.

Old Faithful was supposedly very regular, but we still weren't expecting it to erupt with us so close by, without warning. We ran toward it. There were very few visitors there at that early hour, and it felt like an exclusive show just for us.

"Oh my God!" I shrieked. It felt special to be one of the few to see its magnificence in the early-morning hours. "Let's go get the others!"

"Yeah, come on!" Meredith grabbed my hand, and we skipped back toward our campsite. If they hurried, they'd be able to see the next eruption: there was one every hour to an hour and a half or so. After a couple of minutes of walking in silence—the early-morning sun still a pale yellow—she looked at me and said, "I don't want to say goodbye to you."

I sighed, the elephant in the room acknowledged. "I know," I agreed miserably. "It's been so nice being together. You've been so helpful as I've been trying to deal with my horrible dad."

"I've been happy to do it," she said. "How are we going to be with just our plain ol' families?"

"I know what you mean, Meredith. It's been so groovy being able to switch cars. I feel like you're my sister now. Like I have a twin, too."

"What are we going to do without each other?" She had tears in her eyes.

"Oh Meredith . . ." I hugged her hard and started to cry, too. We held on to each other like this was a matter of physically letting go. If we just held on tight enough, then we wouldn't be divided.

I knew this entry in My Journal of Life would be one I'd think about a lot in the future, so I made sure to pay extra attention to all the little details—the scent of Meredith's soap-clean hair, the feel of her breathing in my arms, and even the stinky but magical aquamarine pools, with Old Faithful giving us a private show. I didn't want to forget any of it.

"You've become my best friend," she said between sobs. "I won't be able to live without you!"

"Yes you will," I said, comforting her.

But I knew what she meant. We had shared so much over the past couple of weeks with each other, spending 100 percent of our time together. We had really clicked. What would we do without each other? It wouldn't feel the same after we said goodbye. It would just be me and the twins and Dad again. That used to feel like enough, but now that I had Meredith, Dad's weirdness and Gerri and Jill's youngness felt inadequate. I wouldn't have a friend, a real friend, to talk to.

I'd miss her parents, too. They were so normal. Like a family on television. Meanwhile, my family was falling apart. Meredith's company was enough to make me forget that this summer was a trial separation, which might lead to my parents divorcing. That was scary. What would the twins and I do if that happened?

Briefly, I envisioned a future where we'd have to alternate Christmases with Mom and Dad as well as every other holiday. It was a horrid thing to look forward to. It felt like watching a train wreck unfold slowly, and in painstaking detail, and being helpless to stop it.

27

Saying Goodbye

We spent that morning showing the others what we had found at Yellowstone. Old Faithful did its thing another two times. Then we got back to camp and made sure our stuff was in the right cars and packed everything up. Meredith and I deliberately dragged our feet throughout the whole process, as did the twins and Mallory—a fruitless attempt for more time together.

Eventually, though, no matter how long it took me to pack my bags, Mr. Gardener announced that it was time for us to say our goodbyes. "All right, everyone," he said, clapping his hands on his thighs and peering at us all. "The inevitable has arrived. We've had a wonderful time getting to know you all and driving across the country with you."

"Yeah, we sure have," said Mallory sadly, resting her head on Jill's and then on Gerri's head. I noticed the twins start to tear up.

Seeing the same thing, Mrs. G said, "Come on, ladies. Let's promise to write to one another and keep our relationship going via the post. You have each other's addresses, right?" We girls nodded, and I tried to commit Mrs. G's unique accent to memory. "We can remain friends even though we'll be separated by distance."

"It's not the same thing, Mom," Meredith said.

"It's not, Meredith, but it's all we have," I croaked, my voice coming out strangely. I gave her a heartfelt hug and noted an uncomfortable lump in my throat that made it hard to speak. She squeezed me back, and that lump in my throat got bigger.

"Thank you all for driving so far west with us," said Dad. Mr. and Mrs. G nodded. "I'm glad I was there for you when your axle broke and that you were there for us when I lost my girls in Rapid City," he added with a chuckle.

Mr. G stepped forward and shook Dad's hand. "You're a good mechanic, Ralph. I don't know what we'd have done without you."

"I'm sure you'd have figured something out, Brian. It was mighty convenient that you happened to have the exact parts we needed," Dad said, patting Mr. G on the back. We were all quiet for a moment. A raven interrupted the silence with its loud caw.

Then, suddenly, Jill cried, "I don't want to say goodbye!" Gerri gave her a hug and gently pulled her away from Mallory, whose chin was wobbling. They began saying a quiet farewell to each other, and I knew that it was time for my own.

"Camp Bluebird was so wonderful, and I'll always remember our secrets, Mary," said Meredith, choking back a sob. I smiled at her and quietly raised my blood-sister finger at her. She wiggled hers back at me. I hoped nobody could tell what we really meant.

"I liked that story you told us about the yellow fingers, Ralph," said Mallory. "I'll tell that to my friends back home."

"Yeah, that is a funny one." Dad smiled at her. "Make sure to do the voices and hand motions for the best effect."

"I will," she promised, laughing a little at the thought.

Since we were all being sentimental, Gerri turned to Meredith and said, "I've never seen anyone roast such perfect marshmallows as you did, Meredith."

She smiled, and we let go of each other's hands.

"I loved swimming at Camp Bluebird and catching those frogs and lightning bugs," Jill added, reflecting. We all nodded in agreement.

"We have our tie-dyed shirts to remind us of each other," I reminded everyone, and they nodded and murmured their agreement. Then we all got quiet again.

Seeing that we were probably close to being done with our reminiscing, Mrs. G clapped her hands, signaling that it was time to go. "Okay, everyone. Go forward and be your best selves." Even she was kind of choked up, her voice sabotaged by a tight throat. Mr. G put his arm around her. This time Mallory and Meredith didn't groan or grimace at their mom's suggestion. We started to walk away from one another, toward our respective vehicles.

After a few steps, I turned around and said, "Your family has a certain *je ne sais quoi* that I like very much!"

"*Merci beaucoup. Le vôtre aussi.* Yours does, too," Mrs. G said wistfully.

And that was that. As we walked to our cars, we glanced back at the Gardeners one last time. Climbing in, Dad turned the ignition, and Blue Pierre rumbled to life. We made a slow U-turn, parting ways—us heading west, them heading east. Gerri, Jill, and I knelt on the seats, waving out the windows and sunroof while Dad ooga-ed, the Gardener family shrinking with distance—faces fading, arms still fluttering, then nothing but specks, and then not even that.

We settled into silence as we drove. I glanced at Dad, trying to hold on to the flicker of admiration I'd felt during the Fourth of July fireworks. But I couldn't look at him without also seeing the bad things, too. I got flashes of Dad calling Mom a bitch and flirting with Laura at the restaurant, calling my sisters and me sexy, and worst of all, insulting Mr. Gardener about being a man and then fondling Mrs. Gardener when her husband's back was turned.

I will never forget any of those things but especially the last offense. The way Mrs. G flushed, embarrassed, and brushed it off like it didn't matter. Mr. G had come out moments later. There was *no way* she hadn't told him about it. Were they all in their station wagon now, venting about Dad's weird and inappropriate behavior? My chest tightened, anger bubbling beneath the surface. But then, for the first time, the anger gave way to something heavier.

I felt sad.

Sad that Dad wasn't the person I thought he was—and never would be. These weren't things that could be undone with an apology; they were woven into who he was. And yet this was my Great American Road Trip, too. I wasn't going to let him ruin it.

PART 3

On The Road Again

28

Oolitic Sand

"When we get to Idaho Falls, go south on Interstate 15," I told Dad. We'd been driving for around two and half hours from Old Faithful on our way to the Great Salt Lake, winding our way through Wyoming, Montana, Idaho, and finally dipping into Utah.

It was so hot outside; we could see the mirages shimmering just above the asphalt.

"We should hit that intersection in about ten miles," I reported dutifully, "and then we've got about two hundred miles until the Great Salt Lake."

"Can you see an island?" he asked.

"An island? Here?" I asked, looking left and right at the fields on either side of I-15.

"No, silly," he said. "In the Great Salt Lake. On the map."

"Oh." I laughed. "Let me see."

While I looked down at the TripTik, he went on, "My sister Ruth told me that the Great Salt Lake has a lot of annoying biting gnats. They're called no-see-ums. Isn't that funny?"

"Oh great," I said. "No-see-ums sound bad. It'll be horrible for Gerri. You know how her skin can't handle anything— not grass, not scrapes, not bites, not even a sunburn." I thought about our trip so far, and it was remarkable that Gerri hadn't had any flare-ups yet, not even at Camp Bluebird.

"Well, Ruth said there's an island that people go to that has pure white sand and that doesn't have any no-see-ums."

"Really?" I asked. I wondered why Dad didn't talk about Ruth, his oldest sibling, much. I made a note to myself to ask him about that. "Let's find that island." I took a breath and looked down at the TripTik quickly, trying to squelch the nausea and headache that came from too much reading while zipping along as a passenger in a car.

"There's an island called Antelope Island. It says here"—I pressed the spine of the guidebook open—"'Antelope Island is home to free-ranging bison, mule deer, bighorn sheep, pronghorn, and many other desert animals, and millions of birds congregate along the shores surrounding the island, offering unparalleled opportunities for birding.'" I looked up and out at the road for some relief.

"Sounds nice. Is there camping?"

"Hold on." I closed my eyes and rested for a second. "Yes. There are designated campsites, but no dispersed camping."

"Dispersed camping?" he echoed, scoffing. "So that's what the kind of camping we like to do is called, huh? I guess we'll have to book with an official campsite this time, then. Does it mention anything about the white sand?"

"Hold on." I scanned the information in the guidebook about Antelope Island more carefully. "Oh man, it sure does. Listen to this. But I need to read fast and then stop so that I don't get too carsick. So no interrupting, okay?" I looked to the back seat to see if the girls were listening. Surprised to find them sleeping, I wondered why they were so tired.

"Aye, aye, Captain." Dad saluted. In order to settle my system, I took a big breath, but instead of feeling refreshed, I caught a whiff of whatever was going bad in the cooler. Spilled milk? Maybe that cheese we bought way back in Wisconsin? I rested my head on the seat back and closed my eyes for a moment.

"Mare?" Dad looked over.

"Okay, here goes." I started reading rapidly. "'Much of the area on the island anywhere near the beaches is covered with oolitic sand.'" I stumbled on the word *oo-oo-li-tic* and looked back up at the road for a break. I exhaled and went on quickly. "'Oolitic sand is a type of sand found only in a few areas of the world. Most sands are tiny, angular particles of disintegrated rock, but oolitic sand is formed by many concentric layers of calcium carbonate that precipitate around a tiny core of debris, usually brine shrimp fecal pellets.'" I looked away from the words, closed my eyes to ease the headache, and burped. "Excuse me," I said at once. Burping was the best relief for car sickness.

"That's incredible. Tiny shrimp poop sand," Dad summarized, entirely oblivious to how he was torturing me.

"Incredible is one way to describe it, I guess." I laughed and burped again. "Excuse me. I think *disgusting* is a better term."

"Oh come on. What's a little bit of fossilized shrimp poop going to do to you? I bet it's beautiful. Oval white sand. It'll be soft."

"Soft poop sand," I said and put the book back into the box at my feet. We laughed together for a moment. "Maybe let's not tell the twins."

✳ ✳ ✳

Around three hours later, we paid the toll at the Antelope Island Causeway Tollbooth and still had plenty of daylight to spend out on the lake after we set up camp. While we were putting the poles together for the Beast, Gerri remarked, "I wish Mrs. G was setting up some yummy snack—"

"And Mr. G was handing out cold bottles of Old Milwaukee," Dad added wistfully. I laughed.

Jill continued, "Yeah, maybe some peanut butter and jelly sandwiches or—"

"Eggs and bacon," Dad interjected, spreading the bones of the Beast out on a flat spot for us to reassemble it all.

"Maybe some crackers and those little cheese slices she cut," I added, my mouth watering.

"I loved those ants on a log celery sticks she made," Gerri chimed in.

"Don't forget the sliced fruit trays," Jill added.

"Okay, okay. Let's stop this. I feel like a salivating dog," Dad said. "Let's just get the Beast up and then head to the beach. See if there's anything in the basket that could tide you over. We'll pick up some supplies and groceries at the little campground store to make supper."

Jill had brought out the cooler and put it on the picnic table, turning her face away and wrinkling her nose when the lid slipped open. "Ooh, gross!"

Dad went over to the picnic table while she went back to the car and brought out the Kool-Aid jug, then poured us each a tepid glass of sweet green liquid. I hate to admit it, but that warm Kool-Aid hit the spot. Dad examined the contents of the cooler, and even he, lover of blue cheese and bratwurst, agreed that the chunk of offending Colby needed to find a place in a trash can.

After getting our tent arranged and the bedrolls laid out for sleeping that night, we changed into our swimsuits and grabbed our towels. The drive to Bridger Bay Beach on the shores of the Great Salt Lake took only about five minutes, but getting back into the stale and fusty Blue Pierre after all that driving—and the inevitability of occasionally feeling carsick due to all the TripTik reading—wasn't all that appealing. But the reward of swimming in the lake on what was another scorcher of a day was all the motivation we needed.

Upon arrival, we dropped our towels on the white shore. The scent of brine hung in the air. Where the oolitic sand was dry, it felt like walking on bread flour. We didn't waste any time heading out into the Great Salt Lake, which was so shallow, it took a while before we got deep enough to dunk in.

Dad released the Super 8 from its case slung around his neck and shot footage of us bobbing on the surface of the water, as if buoyed by invisible life jackets. We learned that the salt content was so high in the water, it made us more buoyant. Dad passed me the movie camera while he floated on his front and then on his back. "I can float! I've never floated before. I'm a sinker through and through!" He laughed with childlike amusement. "I can float!"

Jill was digging it. "Watch me, guys!" she called. She lay back and bobbed along, her long hair floating around her head like a pale-yellow halo.

Gerri, conversely, was not digging it. "Oooh, it burns. Ow! The cuts on my legs!" She made herself do a quick dunk—just to get it over with, probably—and emerged from the water, sputtering and crying. "It burns my eyes and my mouth and my ears and my front thing and my bottom. I'm getting outta here!"

With that, she slogged out of the water, beelining for the outdoor showers provided for visitors to use as needed. I glanced at Jill, who wasn't affected nearly as badly as Gerri, and wondered how it was possible for two identical twins to respond so differently to the same thing. Wasn't their skin created by the same exact DNA?

Ultimately, I saw Gerri's point. The water was irritating and burning to all the soft and open areas of the body. It stung like crazy. All my mucous membranes felt ablaze, and the mere thought of somebody splashing water into my eyes was frightening. Even so, I floated with Dad and Jill—who didn't seem as perturbed as Gerri and myself—for only a few more minutes before heading to the shore with Gerri.

By the time I'd schlepped out of the lake, I had to run to catch up with her. She'd grabbed her towel and was heading straight for the outdoor shower, which was basically just a hose connected to a suspended barrel of fresh water caged in a lifeguard tower.

"I'm never going in there again!" Gerri screamed, trying frantically to rinse the water from her hair and body. I remembered she was only ten and so far away from home, and Mom, and everything she'd ever known. Mom had told me to take care of the girls. Had I been taking good enough care of them so far? I thought I'd been doing a pretty good job as a big sister but maybe not as a mother. I needed to do better.

"Here, let me give you a hand, okay?" I offered, taking the nozzle from her and rinsing her off. She was tense, but soon her shoulders relaxed, even though she was being sprayed with cold water. "How's that, honey? Better?" I asked. She gave me a side-eye glance. Okay, maybe *honey* was going a bit far.

She collected herself and surprised me with a wet hug. "Thanks, Mare," she said, quietly resting her head on my shoulder. We held each other for a good minute, and then she said, "Here, let me rinse you now."

We found a smooth section of beach, spread our towels, and took a seat. The sand really was soft, as far as sand goes. It didn't have the normal sharp edges or grit of typical sand. I knew it was technically fossilized shrimp poop, but I didn't care, and I didn't tell Gerri. We relaxed on the beach, staying dry and running our fingers and toes through the soft white sand until the diehards in our four-person unit finally came out.

"Wasn't that *ex-tra-or-din-ary*?" Dad exclaimed, shaking his head like a dog does to rid itself of water and splashing us in the process.

"Extraordinarily *horrible*," Gerri said dramatically, wiping her face clean of his salty spray. "Hey! Watch it. I just got clean."

"Don't be such a downer, Gerri," Dad said.

"Dad! Be nice to Gerri. You know how much this water hurts her," I said.

Jill was grinning ear to ear. Her hair was so stiff, it looked like it had been soaked in starch and perched like a big blonde helmet atop her little red face.

"Let's go find the showers, Jilly-Bean," Dad suggested, putting the camera in its case and leaving it with Gerri and me.

"Right-o, Dad," she said as they skipped hand in hand toward the freshwater relief.

✱ ✱ ✱

"Oh, you found it!" Dad exclaimed as I rotated the radio dial and rolled by a clear channel. "Tune that one in, Mare. Let's listen. *Girls*." He shushed the back seat. "Quiet down back there. Let's listen now."

As I fine-tuned the radio dial to lock in the reception, Gerri and Jill gave each other a look that I couldn't quite read. I wondered what private twin communication they shared. Their closeness made me miss Meredith and our secret blood-sister connection. I bet the twins were getting tired of this long road trip, but at least they had each other.

Soon the radio announcer crackled into clarity. "First, the choir sings the deeply reassuring words, 'I believe in Christ . . . to him I'll sing; I'll raise my voice in praise and joy.'"

Dad beamed at us, then returned his gaze to the road. "Good job, Mare. Sounds like they're just starting a concert. After the letdown of not being able to go into the Mormon Temple and Tabernacle, I'm glad to at least hear the choir." He was right; they wouldn't let non-Mormons into their sacred spaces.

"I think it's a church service," Gerri said.

"I think you're right, Ger," said Jill to everyone, only to then whisper, "Boooooring!" to Gerri, elongating the word to emphasize just how tedious she thought it would be. Gerri put her hand up to her mouth to conceal her giggle, but Dad looked back in the rearview mirror with a strict frown on his face, quelling any glee the girls had shared.

With Dad having his way and quiet restored in the car, we all settled down to listen to some church music and the sermon. Dad kept Blue Pierre at a steady sixty miles per hour, trying not to let him overheat as we left Salt Lake City and headed west toward Nevada.

The Mormon Tabernacle Choir really did sound like angels come to Earth—even through the tinny speakers of Blue Pierre. Unlike my little sisters, I didn't find it boring. The harmonies and richness washed over me, and I felt the music penetrate my body and soul. Resting my head on the seat and making my body soft, I enjoyed the soothing words and music and let myself relax.

"Wow, can you hear the amazing acoustics of that place?" Dad remarked. "I've heard that the Tabernacle building has no nails, that all the wood is connected with little wooden dowels. Have you heard the expression it's so quiet you can hear a pin drop?"

"Uh-huh," we three answered together.

"Well, they say that the acoustics are so incredible in there, you *actually* can hear—from the very back of the building—a pin dropped on the altar. That's partly why their choir sounds so beautiful."

We brought our attention back to the broadcast. The preacher continued with a lesson on commitment: "Commitment is the catalyst within us that generates all our talents and emotions in pursuit of a cause. It is the power and force that keeps us going through difficult times, our shield against defeat."

"Are you girls listening?" Dad probed, raising his brows. "This is good stuff."

"Uh-huh," we murmured in unison again. We quietly listened to the rest of the service. The girls had fallen asleep, lulled by the smooth drive and the sweet sounds of the minister and the choir and also likely by their genuine boredom. I stayed awake.

When it was over, Dad turned the radio off, and for a moment, we were both plunged into silence—the only noise being the steady rumble of Blue Pierre's engine as it labored over another scorching-hot road.

"What do you think about what he was saying about commitment?" Dad asked me, keeping his voice down so as not to disturb the twins. I reluctantly roused myself from my almost asleep state, trying to scrounge together a coherent thought.

"Um, well . . ." I stalled. With the twins asleep, it was just Dad and me talking quietly, like a pair of actual adults, and this conversation, I knew, could go anywhere.

A part of me begged to keep everything copacetic. If I returned to the usual impulse to please Dad by regurgitating a response that he was more likely to agree with, then I knew what I'd get out of this exchange: another shallow conversation with Dad that left him feeling validated and me feeling stripped of integrity. A part of me wanted to switch things up, take another path—challenge him, make him see that he wasn't nearly so moral as he thought himself to be.

Ultimately, I decided it didn't matter how I felt. The reality that right now, trapped in this car, was maybe the only time I'd get to have an honest and adult conversation with him was compelling enough—and I couldn't waste this chance.

I cleared my throat. "He said that commitment was a shield against defeat—that all you need is commitment in order to accomplish whatever it is you're committing to, right?"

"That sounds about right." Dad nodded. "I liked what he said about enterprising businessmen and about husbands and parents."

"It made me think about when people get married," I began, clearing my throat and trying my best to stay casual. "They really commit to being married, right? To loving that other person."

"Good point," Dad acknowledged. "Your mother and I have been committed to each other for, let's see . . . it's 1976, and we got married in 1959, so how long is that?"

Of course, a math problem. But I already knew how long they had been married since I had made their anniversary cake this past year and wrote the number in fancy cursive with thinned-out white icing on the chocolate frosting. "Seventeen years. That's a long time."

"Feels like forever." He chuckled. "Commitment in a marriage means being true to your spouse."

"What do you mean, *being true*?" I asked, thinking back to the fight he'd had with Mom right before we'd started this trip and—with a flash of anger—his hand reaching for Mrs. G's derrière.

"You know, the sanctity of marriage . . ." He pursed his lips. "The monogamy . . . that you only have sex with that one person."

I shook my head, trying to rid myself yet again of the image of my parents having sex. It seemed that no matter what I did, Dad was determined to strip my perspective of him as a dad and replace it with him as a full-grown, perverted man.

"But if commitment means that you only love one other person . . ." I paused as I thought about how best to convey what I wanted to say. I knew I'd steered the conversation in this direction deliberately, but the fact that we'd already arrived at this point had taken me off guard. I knew it might be crossing a line, but I went for it anyway because I couldn't find a less abrupt or more creative way to ask, so I kept my eyes straight ahead and said, "Then how do you explain away how you flirt all the time? That can't feel very committed from Mom's point of view."

My heart started to race as soon as the words were off my lips. I didn't regret them, though.

Dad paused for thought. "What do you mean, *flirt*?"

I balked, unable to believe he was acting like he didn't know what I was talking about.

"Oh come on! You flirt with every woman and girl you talk with." I tried to keep things casual, or as casual as a thirteen-year-old girl confronting her father's philandering could be, but already my throat was tight and my palms sweaty. I was getting wound up. "You call Winnie Gravvers the sexiest girl on Crary Lane. You touched Mrs. G's derrière. I saw that, you know." I looked at him to see if my words were having any effect, but it was as if his expression were carved from stone. "You even flirted with that lady, Jenny, at the AAA who made our TripTik. And every waitress we ever see."

Wow, I was being very bold. I'd never ever spoken up about any of these things in such a straightforward way before. Maybe my outburst after the buffalo stare-down had set a precedent, though, because he hadn't shushed me yet. I glanced at him. His silence made me wonder if he was about to blow his top, but he stayed quiet, too.

After a long minute, I said, "Well?"

"I guess you're right," Dad began, pushing his glasses up his sweaty face. Why didn't he tighten those darned glasses so that they wouldn't slide down so much? "Even though what you say is true, and I cannot deny any of it, I am committed to your mother." He swallowed and took a swig out of his plastic Kool-Aid cup. "She's the only one I love, but sometimes men have unmet needs."

Unmet needs? Gross. I closed my eyes and scooted away from him, toward the window. I couldn't be sure if it was his strategy to get me to stop pestering him with questions about this, but it definitely worked. I didn't want to know any more about Dad's unmet needs, and I'd already pushed the limits enough by bringing all that stuff up.

"Commitment is not one of the Ten Commandments, but it is just as important," he went on, and I could feel the change of subject in motion. "You remember them, right?"

"Of course, I remember the Ten Commandments, Dad. I try to follow them. Do you?"

"Yes, I do." Then he went on to list some of them, like I suddenly needed a reminder, even though I'd learned about them millions of times already. "Thou shalt not steal; thou shalt honor thy father and thy mother," he added pointedly. "Thou shalt not take the name of the Lord thy God in vain; thou shalt not bear false witness—that means lying."

I bit back the response I wanted to give him—"Dad, I *know* all this"—only to realize that maybe this reminder wasn't for me. It was for him.

And if it wasn't, then it needed to be, I decided.

"What about thou shalt not covet thy neighbor's wife?" I countered smartly. It was just too easy. *Seems like he set the trap he just walked into.*

"Yep, that's in there, too. The commandments are there as guidelines for our behavior, and fortunately for us sinners, we have the opportunity to ask for forgiveness if we make mistakes and break any of the commandments."

Well, wasn't that convenient?

"Is that how you explain away all your flirting? Cuz flirting the way you do kind of seems to me like coveting thy neighbor's wife."

"Oh come on. Lighten up. I'm just having fun. And the ladies like it." He grinned like a sweaty version of the Cheshire Cat. "It's complimentary."

"Are you sure about that?" I snorted, raising my eyebrows in disbelief. Could he really think that? Didn't he see the way they reacted to his advances? I thought of our TripTik maker, and Laura at the restaurant, and Mrs. G's flustered swatting away of his hand. They didn't seem to think his weird advances were *complimentary.*

"Oh yeah, of course," he said definitively. He shifted in the driver's seat. Seeming satisfied with himself and his little lesson, he stretched his fingers on the steering wheel and rolled his neck in a way that suggested this conversation was over.

I laid my head on the window. I'd said what I'd wanted to, stuff that had been pent up for weeks, only to be left feeling without closure. What was the point of honoring the Ten Commandments if all anybody had to do after violating one was ask for forgiveness?

29

Wendover Will Neon Cowboy

A couple of hours later, the sun had descended past the horizon, casting the world in shades of smoky rust and burnt orange. We'd driven past towering red rock formations that looked like they belonged on another planet. Mars, maybe.

The twins began to rustle, slowly rousing. Jill asked, "Where are we?"

At least she didn't say, with a whine, *Are we there yet?*

"Still in Utah, almost to Nevada," Dad said. "Let's try to make it to Lake Tahoe, or if we don't get that far, we can stop at a motel."

"A motel?" I marveled. "Us? Stay at a motel?"

"Well, maybe we can splurge a little." Dad smiled. "We could take real showers and wash our clothes. Motels usually have a Laundromat. Girls, do we still have change in the toll road bag? We'll need some dimes for the washing machines and dryers."

Jill started to answer that we did when Gerri interrupted, "Oh no. Another lake?"

"Lake Tahoe has fresh water," Dad said, laughing as he tried to convince her that it would be different from the Great Salt Lake we'd visited earlier.

"Oh, that's good," Jill said, looking at her twin and giving her hand a reassuring squeeze. "See? Fresh water, not salt water. It'll be fine, Ger-Bear."

I opened the TripTik, carefully unfolded it to the correct page, and said, "Yeah, we're not going to make it to Lake Tahoe tonight," I said, somewhat to my relief. I was really warming to the idea of staying in a hotel. "It's already seven thirty, and we're just crossing the Utah and Nevada border. Lake Tahoe is way on the other side of Nevada."

I flexed my leg muscles to get comfortable. We'd been sitting a long time. The more I thought about the luxury of an air-conditioned motel with an actual bed to stretch out in, the more I couldn't stomach another night of sweaty car-camping on the side of the road.

"Oh my gosh! Look at that!" Jill pointed to a hard-to-miss, very tall neon cowboy in the distance.

The fluorescent lighting was just starting to become visible in the early evening, outlining the enormous figure. As we got closer, the giant cowboy grew and grew, and so did the words lit up beneath him.

Gerri read, "'Wendover Will Neon Cowboy Welcomes You to West Wendover, Nevada.'"

"Wow, that's quite the welcome," Dad remarked. He pulled Blue Pierre up to the base of the statue, and as we climbed out of the car, we each stretched our bodies to alleviate the stiffness of all that sitting.

Craning our necks to see to the top, Jill said, "Wendover Will is way taller than that *sin-cére David* statue."

"Yeah, and there's no embarrassing private parts right in your face," Gerri said.

I laughed. "He has all the cowboy things. The hat, the gun and belt of bullets, the cowboy shirt and jeans, and the cowboy boots."

"Welcome to Nevada," Dad said. "Let's go a little farther and see if we can find a motel."

✳ ✳ ✳

As we drove into Wells, Nevada, we saw some billboards advertising a local brothel called Madam Donna's.

Jill asked Dad, "What's a brothel?" and he said something about it being a building, like a hotel with a bar and maybe a restaurant and lots of rooms where men could pay women to sleep with them for the night.

"Sleep with them for the night?" Gerri asked, brows raised.

"Yeah, you know, keep them company for the evening." After a pause, he added, "It doesn't even have to be overnight. It could just be for an hour or so."

I stared out the window at the monotonous world flying by. It was too embarrassing to see if he was smiling at me, like I was in on some adult knowledge that he was simplifying for the benefit of my ten-year-old sisters.

"Why would a man want to sleep for just an hour?" Jill asked innocently.

"Maybe he's only a little tired," Gerri offered.

Dad honked out a laugh and then said, "Yeah, maybe he just needs a little rest, a nap."

It was getting harder and harder to stay out of the conversation, but I was determined not to stoke the flames of it any more than we already had.

As if on cue, Jill asked, "Does it cost a lot of money to pay for sleeping with a woman?"

"I think it's reasonably priced," Dad answered, chuckling. *What? Oh my God. Was this happening?*

"Hey," Gerri interjected, "do women ever pay men to sleep with them?" Her question almost seemed scripted, and I hid my grin, happy one of the twins had thought to ask about this. We all took a few breaths, waiting for Dad's response.

"It doesn't seem to work that way, Ger," Dad said. A loud Harley-Davidson came rumbling past us in the fast lane, and I felt relieved when our attention was drawn to that instead of this awkward conversation about paying for s-e-x. But of course, Dad wouldn't let it die. He added, "They call it the oldest profession in the world."

"What is the oldest profession in the world?" The twins' voices were so evenly pitched and in sync that you could barely tell that there were two of them.

"Prostitution," Dad said simply, and I flinched. "That's what the ladies who work in brothels are called—prostitutes."

Was he really giving them a lesson on prostitution? I couldn't believe he was being so candid!

I turned on the radio and started blasting "Tonight's the Night," trying to drown out everything about this conversation. About twenty minutes later, we stumbled upon a Super 8 Motel, and Dad drove Blue Pierre right up to the front door.

"I can't believe that we're going to stay here!" I exclaimed. My mood had shifted for the better. "They'll have hair conditioner. I can't wait to use some! My hair is so flyaway."

Gerri joked, "Hair conditioner and air conditioner!"

"Oh look! They have a swimming pool!" Jill practically screamed. Gerri jumped up and down. Even she, with her sensitive skin, could handle swimming pool water, and the idea of a nice swim to cool off before a proper shower sounded exhilarating to us all.

"Yes! Yes! Yes!" I joined their excitement, clapping.

"Okay. Settle down, girls. Let's go check this out." Dad laughed. We followed him into the reception area, looking around and admiring the rugged Western decor. There was a single wagon wheel perched right beside the front desk, an antelope skull on the wall, and a bearskin rug on the floor. I liked the chandelier made of antlers.

"Hello there, Dolores," Dad singsonged to the receptionist, his eyes lingering on her name tag atop her large bosom. "Aren't you a sight for sore eyes?" She blushed, and I rolled my eyes, thinking about the conversation Dad and I had *just* had about his flirting.

Dad peeled off three ten-dollar bills from his wallet and grandly presented them to Dolores, and as easy as that, we were given two sets of keys for rooms 109 and 111.

Upon seeing the cost, I wondered why we didn't stay at motels more often. Fifteen dollars per room was pretty cheap, even with Grandpa Red's $500 slowly diminishing.

"Okay, girls. I think we all need a good night's rest, but let's pull out some of the stuff from Blue Pierre and start the laundry. Let's also dump out the cooler and food basket and clean them up and rearrange everything a bit. We can go grocery shopping in the morning. They'll have an ice machine to restock the cooler. What do you say?" Dad asked. "And if we put the pedal to the metal, I bet we can get into the pool before it closes at . . . What time does the pool close, Dolores?"

"Ten o'clock," she replied. "You'll have plenty of time. You can use the towels that are at the pool when you're out there, and there are other towels in your rooms. And in the morning, you can come to this room here"—she gestured toward the adjacent area—"and have a little continental breakfast."

"What's a continental breakfast?" Gerri asked.

"Oh, it's just a light breakfast of a couple of baked goods and flirt and jam and coffee." Dolores, visibly shocked at her misspeak, blasted out a loud, nervous chortle and covered her large teeth. "Did I just say 'flirt and jam and coffee'? I meant *fruit* and jam and coffee!" We laughed with her, and I looked pointedly at Dad. *Even she must think he's flirting, making a Freudian slip like that.*

We three girls turned toward the door, and I heard Dad say, "Thanks, darling. Have a good evening." He smiled at Dolores. *Darling? See! Coveting thy neighbor's wife again.*

Dad drove Blue Pierre right up to our adjacent first-floor rooms. I was pleased that we weren't crowding into one room, even though doing so would have been half the price. Not that I was complaining. This was going to be so neat. The twins would share a bed—and I'd get my own! Dad would have his own room. Maybe there'd even be a bathtub, I realized with glee.

Jill grabbed the picnic basket while Dad hefted the sloshing cooler. I helped Gerri sort the contents of the messy back seat into a dirty clothes pile, and we put the errant art and embroidery supplies and papers and other stuff into their proper places. I thought I'd reorganize the cardboard box we kept in the footwell—my unofficial library—so I grabbed that, too. Dad went back outside and pulled the sleeping bags from the trunk, and we helped shake them out and then draped them over the metal railing to air out. We each grabbed our suitcases and bags and brought them into our motel rooms.

"Can we start the laundry and go to the pool while the clothes wash and then come out and put them in the dryer after we swim?" I suggested.

"Sounds like a perfect plan, Mare," Dad said. "Doesn't seem like anyone else is using the washing machines right now anyway."

"What about supper?" Gerri said.

"Yeah. Our tummies are grumbling," Jill agreed.

"Well, this place doesn't have a real restaurant, and it is getting kind of late. Could we make do with whatever is left in the cooler and basket?" he asked.

I rummaged around in our food stores, and we were able to scrabble together a meal of sorts from Kool-Aid, chips, the last of the sweaty cheese, shriveling-up apples, a little salami, some crackers, and peanuts. After this, there was no food left. We'd eaten everything.

The pool made for the perfect ending to our long day. The water felt silky and warm, especially compared to the nasty, painful water of the Great Salt Lake we'd suffered through earlier. We splashed one another and competed in handstand contests in the shallow end, seeing who could stay underwater longest. Jill won. I had outgrown the desire to be tossed into the water by Dad, but the twins were still into it. He would make a stirrup out of his hands, and they'd step into it with one foot. He'd heave them up out of the water, catapulting them into the air. They'd crash down with a splash.

At closing time, Dolores came out and told us that it was time to get out of the pool. Wrapping up in the fresh, bleachy motel towels, we exited the pool area, clanging the gate behind us. We made our way to the laundry room, where we put our clean clothes into the dryers, inserted the dimes, and started the machines.

"Do you think our clothes will be okay here until morning?" I asked Dad, a wave of exhaustion coming over me. All I wanted to do now was go to sleep.

Dad seemed to be feeling the same way. "I think so," he said. "Let's go to bed, girls."

He got no arguments from us. He went to his room. After brushing our teeth and rinsing off, we dropped dead into our beds. When Dad finished getting settled, he stopped by our room, knocked on our door, and peeked in. "You gals going to be okay in here all by yourselves?"

"Yeah, we'll be fine," I answered. "We've got each other, and you're just a room away."

"All right, then. Good night," he said, walking over to our beds and giving each of us a kiss on the forehead. As he was leaving, he turned and gestured to a golden chain hanging by the door. "Mary, use this here chain to lock up once I close the door." He paused, then continued, "And I was thinking that if I sleep in and you guys wake up before me and you feel like going grocery shopping, you can take this money." He laid a twenty-dollar bill on the little table along with Blue Pierre's car keys. "And drive down this main road to the grocery store we passed on our way here."

"Really?" The twins and I looked at one another in surprise. Maybe I was too tired to feel anything other than exhausted right then, but I wasn't as panicked by this development as I was the first time I was asked to drive Blue Pierre. Besides, driving a mile down the road would be much easier than driving for a couple of hours on the highway like I'd done before. I could do it.

"Sure. Maybe wear something kind of grown-up and park away from the entrance so that no one sees you coming in. You'll know what to get. We're pretty much out of everything. You can even go swimming if the pool opens before I wake up. Just do all the right things you know how to do."

"Okay, Dad. How about five dollars more?" I said, grinning.

"All right. Here's five more. Actually, here's ten." We wagged his brows. "I'm feeling generous. You guys can really stock up. Good night."

I followed Dad to the door, and as soon as it shut, I inserted the little knob at the end of the chain into the slot and slid it over, as instructed. "Okay, we're locked up, and everything's safe and sound. Are you two okay? Need anything before I come back to bed?"

"I'm good. Good night, Mare," said Gerri.

"Me too. Night, Mare," echoed Jill, giggling.

"You two sound like TeenTeen," I chuckled. "Sweet dreams. Angels on your pillows."

I lay down on my bed. Boy, was it soft compared to the ground in a sleeping bag or sleeping uncomfortably in Blue Pierre.

"Actually, does the window open? It's so stuffy in here even with the air-conditioning," Jill said, waving her hand in front of her nose. Even with the air conditioner on, she was right; it was kind of stale and musty.

"I'll check," I offered, flinging off the satiny comforter. It felt good to mother them. I saw that the window easily slid open, and I cracked it about six inches. The screen would keep out any bugs. "There you go, Jill. That should make it smell nicer in here." The gentle breeze made the flimsy curtain dance. "Isn't this groovy, staying at a motel?"

"Uh-huh," they replied, barely keeping their eyes open.

The little digital alarm clock on the end table radiated 10:20 p.m. with its blocky numbers. I could hear the slight whirring and click as it rotated to 10:21 and then again to 10:22. I didn't even need to do my calming-down body routine. We all fell asleep in minutes.

✳ ✳ ✳

A while later, I rolled and thrashed in bed. The clock showed 12:45 a.m. Jill and Gerri were sleeping, and for a few seconds, I lay there, listening to them breathing. Would it be possible to use the bathroom without waking them up? Maybe I'd also close that window.

After a few more minutes, I decided I had to take my chances and eased out of bed as quietly as possible, tiptoeing over the carpet toward the bathroom. But then I heard sounds coming from the room next to ours—Dad's room. What the heck was he up to at this hour? I paused midstride and looked at the twins to see if the noise had disturbed them, but they were still sound asleep—their arms and legs pretzeled around each other and the sheets all helter-skelter.

I went to the bathroom, where the acoustics of the all-tile walls made Dad's room next door all the easier to overhear. Cocking my head and putting my better ear toward the wall, I listened but couldn't distinguish what I'd heard. Was that a woman's voice? Dad was probably watching TV. Was someone being hurt or crying? It was the middle of the night, for goodness' sake. Wasn't he tired?

Maybe he couldn't sleep without us girls around, especially in a strange place. I wondered if he was regretting his choice to buy two motel rooms instead of one, especially as a man committed to trying to save money—

Committed.

Something about that word made me pull away from the white-tiled wall, get myself together, and storm back to bed. My heart was pounding, though I wasn't fully sure why. My mind spiraled with thoughts of prostitutes and brothels, and I thought, *No, Dad wouldn't dare.* Not after we'd just talked about commitment and the Ten Commandments and not after he'd just told me how much he loves Mom and their marriage, even if it hasn't always been easy.

Television. That was it. He was watching TV.

Probably a drama.

Thinking better of the open window, I got back up, closed and locked it quietly, and then used the thermostat to turn up the air conditioner. The soft whir of its fan was soothing and blocked out all the noise of Dad's TV. Shortly after that, I was asleep again.

30

Charlotte

In the morning, I once again woke before the twins. The alarm clock displayed 6:06 a.m., and there was already a flood of sunlight beating against the blackout curtains, slipping inside in bright, knifelike shafts as the curtains were pushed by the breeze of the air conditioner.

I got out of bed and stretched, quietly making my way to the bathroom. I appreciated the indoor plumbing and warm water from the sink. Peeling the paper off the miniature bar of soap, I washed my hands and face. There was some gardenia-scented body lotion in a little plastic bottle, and I rubbed that on my face and legs. Mmm! It smelled like a flower garden! This whole experience felt like pure luxury compared to our car-camping in Blue Pierre or sleeping like sardines crammed into the Beast.

After a minute, my stomach growled. I was starving, especially after that snack we ate for supper last night. We'd left the clean cooler and basket to dry out overnight. I thought I might take them out to the car to have when we went to the grocery store. I tiptoed to the window, trying not to wake the twins, and pulled the curtain open. Looking out at the parking lot in search of Blue Pierre, I was surprised to see Dad. It was early by anyone's measure. What was he doing with the car? Should I go out and give him a hand?

But just as I was about to abandon the window and exit through the door, I realized that Dad was talking to somebody. He wasn't alone. I waited a moment, and a short, big-haired blonde woman shifted into view. She was standing next to Blue Pierre. What was Dad doing out there? Making certain that the curtain was open only a crack, I spied on them, rubbing my eyes.

The woman looked too fancy for six o'clock in the morning. At once, I got a sinking feeling. This wasn't an ordinary exchange. This wasn't Dad flirting with a random employee of the hotel or something. She wore high-heeled sandals and tight little Levi's cut so short that you could see the bottom of her derrière, and her floral peasant top wasn't buttoned up all the way. She grasped Dad's forearm and giggled like they'd known each other all their lives; he seemed to be shushing her, kind of nudging her away.

I blinked and knuckled my eyes again. With his free hand, I saw Dad wiggle his wallet back into the pocket of his pajama bottoms. Their mouths kept moving, but I couldn't hear a word they were saying.

Suddenly, I was mad at myself for closing this window. Without a second thought, I flipped off the thermostat and slid the window open. Lucky for me, it sailed open as smoothly and silently as a canoe over the flat surface of a pond.

I inched nearer, staying out of sight but remaining close enough to listen in, only for my attention to be drawn back into our hotel room when I saw Jill crawling out of bed. She sleepily stumbled over toward where I was standing.

"What are you doing, Mary?" she asked in a much-too-loud voice. I ducked and wondered if Dad and the woman heard us. Violently shaking my head and putting my index finger to my lips for her to be quiet, I motioned her over with my other hand. "What's going on?" she whispered.

I whispered back, "Dad is out there with a woman!"

"Huh? What woman? Who is it?" She pushed the curtain aside to get a good look.

"Don't let them see us!"

I was sure they had to have heard us already, but so far, it didn't seem like they had—they were still standing together by Blue Pierre, talking as though nothing had happened. Jill crouched down beside me, the two of us peering through a slit in the curtains, ears as close to the open window as possible.

"Thank you for a wonderful time, Ralph," the woman said in a startlingly deep voice as she slid several bills into her bra. I saw a couple of twenties and some more. That was a lot of dough. And that dough, I knew, came from Grandpa Red.

"Shh," Dad whispered back, intimately putting his finger to her lips. They were stained by cherry-red lipstick, which was smeared. "It was very nice making your acquaintance, Charlotte."

Charlotte? Who the hell was Charlotte? His hand reached for her waist, only to sink a little lower, where it lingered. I felt dizzy, sick. Totally confused. Why was he touching her like that? *When* had he made her acquaintance? My mind was racing. I looked at Jill, and she seemed even more confused than I did. Dad gestured toward the road, visibly trying to hurry her along.

"Can't you give me a lift, Ralphie?" Charlotte mewled in that deep voice. *Ralphie?*

"I'd love to, Char, but I'm worried my daughters will wake up." He gestured toward our room. We ducked down again. "I'd hate for them to see the car missing or hear its loud engine starting up. How far do you have to go?"

"Not too far." She pouted. "I'll just use the pay phone there to call Madam Donna. She'll have one of the boys come get me." Charlotte proceeded to strut toward the phone booth at the end of the parking lot, swinging her hips back and forth like a metronome. Dad watched her go as though under hypnosis.

I backed up from the window, completely in shock. Turning my attention to the inside of the room, I nibbled on a nagging cuticle and wrapped a loose strand of hair around my finger. Gerri was still asleep, and even though I was relieved she hadn't witnessed what Jill and I had, I knew it'd be only a matter of time before her twin filled her in on everything.

What a mess.

When I looked back outside, Dad was turning around. Not wanting to disturb the curtain and attract his attention, I quickly dropped down out of sight, pulling Jill with me. We stumbled over the cooler, and I stifled a gasp as I rug-burned my knee on the cheap carpet.

Oh my God, did he see us? Did he hear us?

We stayed crouched there for a moment. I silently rubbed my sore knee but couldn't resist seeing what was going on and slowly raised my head to peek through the window. Jill raised herself with me. Dad didn't notice us there, spying on him. Because his room was closer to the car, he wouldn't have to pass our open window. That was a relief.

As he approached his motel room door, he had a huge smile on his face. My brother would call it a shit-eating grin. He turned and waved to Char, and she gave him a playful toodle-oo, each finger taking its turn in a cascading wave from pinky to thumb.

I looked back at Dad and was repulsed by the sight of him. This wasn't like the disgust I'd felt when I saw him touching Mrs. G's derrière, or flirting with our TripTik maker or restaurant staff, or even Dolores. This was a whole new level of revulsion.

What I'd seen this morning had made an indelible mark on my perspective of my father.

I glared at the sight of him. That cocky expression, the skip in his step, like a burglar who'd just robbed a bank. Thick dark glasses camouflaging his buggy eyes. Receding hairline in front of a shaggy mop of thinning hair. He was shirtless, with gray fuzzy hair on his plump chest and big farmer-tanned arms. Pale, chubby belly hanging over the top of his baggy pinstriped pajama bottoms. Bare feet with his nasty, too-long toenails. Everything about him was gross. How had I ever thought that he was a handsome man?

I stayed frozen at the window until I heard his hotel room door open and close. I let out a held breath and stumbled backward toward my bed until the edge of the mattress buckled my knees. I collapsed, sitting there, unmoving.

Jill sat down quietly with me. She put her head on my shoulder and said, "I'm sleepy."

We heard his toilet flush in the adjacent room and the sink run. Then his bed springs creaked. Wouldn't you know, his loud snores commenced in no time.

What the hell? I think he just had sex with a prostitute.

"Jill." I turned toward her. "It's early. Are you going back to sleep?"

"Well, I was just getting up to go potty before we saw Daddy."

"You want to go back to sleep?"

"Uh-huh," she said, getting up and walking to the bathroom. Afterward, she crawled into bed with Gerri and didn't say another word about what we'd seen. I couldn't help but wonder if she, at her age, was even able to process what had just happened.

I asked, "Are you okay?"

"Uh-huh," she murmured, snuggling into Gerri and falling back to sleep. I hoped she thought the whole thing was just a strange dream and wouldn't ask me any questions about it—and better yet, forget about it altogether and never mention it to Gerri.

I, on the other hand, was wide awake, and it was barely six thirty. The thought of Dad having sex with a prostitute—spending money on something like that when we hardly had enough to buy decent food to feed us on this trip—was infuriating. He'd let us eat all Mrs. G's food without a second thought, refusing to buy us anything decent because it was out of our price range. He was a cheapskate, and yet he could afford *this*!

What was *wrong* with him? My heart was fit to burst thinking about it. Commitment, my fanny! How could he do that? Why did he talk about things one way and then act the opposite? Did he think he'd just get away with it? Ask for forgiveness for his sin? What a cop-out! What a jerk. Oh my God, my dad was a super creep. He had sex with a prostitute in the room right next door to us, his own daughters, on our shared dream of taking the Great American Road Trip! He was ruining everything!

It dawned on me that that was why he'd let us stay in a motel—in separate rooms, even. He'd planned out the whole thing. He probably thought of it when he was explaining what brothels were to the twins. Or maybe he'd had this idea all along. I wanted to scream, but it was too early, and everyone except me was asleep. What was I going to do? I paced the room several times, thinking and thinking, trying to be quiet. Every time I passed the mirror on the wall, I did a double take at my sad face; I was blotchy and red and visibly *not okay*.

I decided to make the bed. After smoothing the silky bedspread over the surface and tightening it over the pillows, I sat down and had the sudden thought that maybe other men had slept with other prostitutes in this very bed. Even though I felt like there was a weight holding me down, the idea of that was enough to get me to jump off. I needed to get out of that room.

Grabbing the key from the end table, I walked to the door and quietly slid the chain lock out of the slot. The door creaked a little, and I heard Gerri and Jill make some waking-up sounds, but they rolled over and stayed asleep. Slipping the key into my pocket, I walked to the laundry room. I hoped that Charlotte wasn't around. I looked toward the phone booth, but she wasn't there. I guessed she had already been picked up. There wasn't a soul out and about except for me. That was good. I didn't think I could face anyone right then, not even a stranger.

I went to the laundry room, opened the dryer's rickety door, and pulled out the dry and wrinkly clothes. We didn't have a basket or anything, so I laid our towels out on the scuffed countertop and overlapped their edges, creating a sling of sorts, then piled the rest of the clothes on top. A pair of Dad's underwear fell on the floor. Considering how gross he was, I wasn't about to touch them. Talk about cooties. I used my toes to grasp the sad gray pair and lifted them up to the pile. Then I wiped my foot off on the mat by the door.

I hefted the bundle into my arms and walked back to our room. The girls were still asleep. That made sense. It was only just after seven.

I began the process of folding and sorting the clothes, but I had a hard time whenever I had to handle one of Dad's pieces. Our family had the rule of "your job's not done until the whole job's done," but I just couldn't make myself touch something that had touched him. He was disgusting—which made *me* feel disgusting. I was mad. Why should his bad behavior rub off on me? He was contagious. I wanted to scream.

When my little sisters saw all our clothes folded except for Dad's, they would wonder what was up with that, so I left some of their clothes unfolded, too. They'd have to help finish the job, and maybe they wouldn't notice that I hadn't done any of his.

Eventually, unbidden tears and sobs emerged as the reality of everything I'd seen this morning tumbled over me like an avalanche. I hadn't overheard Dad watching TV last night—I'd overheard him having s-e-x. This was a ruse, a trick, and he'd played all of us. Lied to all of us.

I had a horrible dad. One with unmet needs.

His needs—his disgusting, revolting, nauseating, repulsive, sickening needs—were met now.

He was a husband! My sisters and I were right next door! *He wasn't even quiet about it, and the walls are thin as paper. He should have gotten a room a few down from us to protect me from the memories that are now seared in* ALL CAPS *and* **Bold!** *in My Journal of Life forever, whether I like it or not.*

Needing to get away and hide my tears, I abandoned the laundry and put on my bathing suit to swim some hard laps and release some of this pain. Before getting to the pool, the idea of running around the perimeter of the motel jumped into my head, and I seized it. My Keds made smacking sounds as I rounded the corner at the back of the motel, expelling some of this pent-up energy with every stride. Thoughts bled through my mind: *He is such a hypocrite. Always spouting off about the right way to be, even giving sermons about that stuff, and then turning around and doing precisely what he says not to do.*

Pound, pound, pound . . .

My steps echoed back from the nearby rolling hills. *And he talks about integrity. Integrity! Integrity, my fanny! Integrity means always taking the high road, being true to your beliefs. He's a wolf in sheep's clothing. He doesn't have a stitch of integrity at all. He's a liar.*

My heart was pounding a mile a minute. What was wrong with him? He was broken. Seriously. He thought he could do whatever he wanted and then just say sorry, like that erases the sin of it? I thought back to our discussion about God. How could God forgive a man who was such a hypocrite and a liar and an adulterer? How could God forgive a man who defiled the Ten Commandments and who would then ask for forgiveness each time, knowing he'd never change and only sin again?

I hoped God *didn't* forgive him.

I came to an abrupt halt at the entrance to the pool area. My heaving lungs felt like they would rip out of my body. I inserted the room key into the lock, and the gate swung open. I was the only one at the pool, which was a relief. I took off my Keds and got ready to jump into the cold water. *He's so juvenile. He's like a six-year-old boy trying to figure out if taking cookies from the cookie jar without permission is right or wrong. No, he's worse! He knows it's wrong, and he's doing it anyway!*

I didn't have a very finessed crawl stroke, but I sure paddled quickly anyway, splashing water everywhere. I reached the other side and gripped the tiled lip of the pool, trying to calm myself with some slow, deep breaths. But I couldn't.

What about Mom?

She was right to kick Dad out. She was right to want a trial separation and a divorce. My crying burbled out of me anew. I tried to stay quiet, but it was hard, so I inhaled a deep breath, submerged my head to drown out my noises, and unleashed an underwater shriek. Any hope they'd had of repairing their marriage and avoiding divorce was officially gone. What a betrayal.

Floating on my back, I began some elementary backstrokes, the easiest and calmest swim stroke out there. With no other swimmers in the pool, it didn't matter if I didn't go in a straight line or knew where I was headed. I floated on the surface of the water like a lily pad, staring up at the bright-blue sky of a new day, and wondered, *What am I going to do? Tell Mom? Keep it a secret?*

How was I going to act when I saw Dad in a couple of hours? I was horrible at keeping secrets. Damn it, this was really bad. I stopped floating and continued with that easy backstroke until I bumped into the side of the pool, the top of my hand scraping against the rough edge, and turned right back around for another lap.

A new and disturbing thought entered my mind: if I told Mom the truth, her marriage to Dad was definitely over. Part of me knew there was no other way, but I also didn't want to feel somehow responsible for their divorce. How could I go on knowing I was the one who told Mom, and that's why she divorced Dad? And if they got divorced, we'd be tossed back and forth like a hot potato between them—meaning I'd have no way of avoiding Dad because he'd share custody of us, and then I'd really be stuck. No matter how I looked at it, there was no good outcome to this—outside of trying my best to dig deep down, bury it, and pretend it didn't happen at all. The whole put-on-a-smiling-face thing.

Mom said she wanted me to call her collect if anything made me uncomfortable or if I needed her or if we were in trouble. This seemed to qualify, but I'd definitely have to tell her the truth then, and that set me back to square one.

As I pulled myself out of the pool, I felt sad to be alone. Meredith wasn't around to talk to. She'd be furious. And Winnie was far away. She'd be mad as hell.

Wrapping the towel around my waist, I made my way back to the motel room. I didn't want this whole thing to go into My Journal of Life, but it was such a huge, unsettling disturbance to my equilibrium that there was no way it wouldn't be an important and unavoidable entry. Already, it felt seared into the pages of My Journal of Life—highlighted in bright yellow and underlined to boot. Dog-eared, even. It would never be forgotten.

We still had regular mundane things to do, like pack Blue Pierre and go grocery shopping and sit in the car with one another for hours on end. I dreaded it with every fiber of my being. I didn't think I could do it. He'd realize I knew about it if I abruptly gave him the cold shoulder. Talk about being stuck between a rock and a hard place. And he'd put me there! What a jerk. A jerk with a happy, shit-eating grin on his self-satisfied face.

31

Squeaky-Clean

I cracked open the door, entering slowly. To my relief, I saw that the girls were still asleep. That gave me a little more time to collect myself. I decided I'd take a bath.

Using the motel's little white-and-blue striped washcloth to scrub vigorously, I made myself squeaky-clean to rid myself of my family's filth. I always suspected that we were pretending to be normal, but now I knew it to be true, without a doubt. What kind of family has a father who hires a prostitute? And furthermore, lets his daughter find out? Aren't prostitutes for bachelors?

Seeing my red and raw skin made me feel better. Maybe not better, but at least it was a different sort of pain—a more physical pain. I drained some of the water and then refilled it with the hottest water I could stand. My poor rug-burned knee throbbed in the heat. With the door closed, and because the bathroom was so small, a cloud of steam descended all the way down to the tub. I sighed, sinking into the folds of it, and told myself I was hidden in a place nobody could find me.

Lying back, I submerged everything except my mouth and nose. The water in my ears muffled everything. My hair floated on the surface. I must have dozed off and then woke with a start, sputtering and coughing and gasping and splashing water everywhere. After nearly drowning, I sat more upright and stewed in that hot water until it got cold. I bet it was over an hour. By the time the girls woke up at almost nine o'clock, I felt slightly better.

Jill walked into the bathroom. "Hey, why is the floor all wet?" she asked as she sat on the pot and peed, knuckling her eyes. I looked at her with a question on my face, but she didn't mention anything about what we'd seen earlier.

"Hurry up, Jilly. I've got to go," Gerri said in her high little voice when she entered the cramped room, also rubbing her eyes. "Hey, why is the floor all wet?" Jill and I both laughed.

"Sorry about that," I said, getting out of the tub and grabbing the towel from the counter. After I dried off, I dropped the towel to the floor to mop up the spill, then hung it back on the rod. "Girls, I started folding the clean clothes. How about you finish it off, and I'll run you two a fresh bath?" I forced myself to act normal, giving them a weak smile. "Do you want to have a bath?"

"Yes!" they cried in unison.

"Bubbles?" I asked. In lieu of real bubble bath, I'd just pour a little of the shampoo under the running water.

"Yes!"

"All right," Gerri said. "I'll start the laundry."

What else could I say that was regular, normal, expected, and big-sisterly?

Clearing my throat, I nodded at Jill and said, "Jill, since Dad's still asleep, and we've probably got some time before the grocery store opens, this might be a good time to catch up on the Slate of Dates, States, and Fates."

"Oh, that's a great idea," she said. "I'll help you in a sec, Ger."

I put my wet bikini back on, along with my pair of freshly laundered cutoffs, and sat at the little desk with Jill. She fetched her notebook, opened it to the correct page, and said, "Uh-oh. I'm way behind. I only got to July first. We're already at . . . what day is it?"

"I think it must be like the, um . . . I don't really know." I chuckled. "Let's figure it out by trying to remember all the last stuff we did."

"Okay. The last entry said Wall Drug and the buffalo thing and the broken trailer and overheated Blue Pierre and sleeping at the campground in Rapid City," Jill reviewed.

"That was the night when Dad lost us," said Gerri as she twisted a pair of Dad's socks into a ball. *Ew. Little did she know . . .*

"Did you include that, Jill?" I asked, even though Dad had asked us to omit it. I pulled on a T-shirt and, with our wide-toothed comb, began to tug on my tangled hair.

"No, I'll add it." I watched her pencil in *Dad lost us. Typical,* I thought. *So irresponsible.*

Looking over her shoulder, I saw that that was on July 1. "All right, then we went to Mount Rushmore and camped there for a few days. Remember the caves and Crazy Horse?"

"Oh yeah," Jill said. "I think I'll add them all together." She wrote: *7/2/76 to 7/4/76 | South Dakota | Camping with the Gardeners—Mount Rushmore area: Crazy Horse, Caves, Fourth of July fireworks.* I wondered why she sometimes used dashes and sometimes colons. But her system made sense. It seemed consistent enough, especially for a ten-year-old. The Slate didn't have too many scribbled-out mistakes.

Gerri asked, "What did we do after the fireworks? And whose shirt is this?" She held up one of the tie-dyes.

"I think that's Dad's," Jill answered. Gerri folded it, then added it to Dad's growing stack. I grabbed a pair of the twins' shorts, folded them, and put them on Gerri's pile.

"Was Devils Tower next?" Jill asked.

"I think so," Gerri added. She grabbed a tank top and held it up to her nose like in a commercial. "Wow, this smells so fresh and clean." Then she answered Jill's question.

I watched Jill document our journey, seemingly unaffected. Had she somehow forgotten about Dad and Charlotte? I couldn't tell. It didn't seem possible. If she could remember everything we'd done over the last few days, surely she had to remember this morning—but she seemed fine. How was everyone else fine but not me?

"Okay. So we left Mount Rushmore on the fifth and then drove there, still with Meredith and her family," I said. "But I think those places are in different states. Deadwood was in South Dakota, but Devils Tower was in Wyoming, I believe."

Jill wrote: *7/5/76 | South Dakota* and *7/6/76 | Wyoming | Devils Tower.*

"Wow. We sure have done a lot of fun things!" she remarked.

Gerri nodded. "Yeah. This is like a trip of a lifetime, isn't it?" *Oh brother.*

It was hard to listen to them sing the praises of this trip, knowing what I now knew. I looked away, not able to hide my true feelings, an upsurge of anger and despair resurfacing again.

"Don't you think, Mare?" Gerri asked.

"Sure," I mumbled. They both stopped what they were doing and stared at me. "What?"

"What's wrong with you?" Gerri asked. "You're never in a bad mood in the morning."

"It's nothing. I'm fine," I said, trying to think of some reason to explain why I was off. I said the first thing I could think of that might make sense to them. "I guess I just miss Mom, and I didn't sleep that well. Let's keep going, Jill," I said, trying to deflect from the real reason for my shift in mood.

"Oh yeah, I miss Mom, too. What do you think she's doing right now?" Gerri asked.

"Working," Jill offered.

"Yeah, she must be at work," I agreed. "I wonder if she misses us."

"I bet she misses us like crazy," Gerri said.

"Maybe not all of us," I replied, my voice clipped, and the twins exchanged a silent glance. I was not doing a very good job of fooling anybody. "All right. Let's get this list done," I added with a clap of my hands. "So we got through July 6. What did we do after Devils Tower?"

Jill looked at me funny. "I think the next thing was Yellowstone and the Old Faithful geyser."

"I think you're right, Jilly-Bean," I said.

"That's when we said goodbye to Mallory. That was sad," Gerri said with an unhappy look on her face.

Jill wrote: *7/7/76 | Wyoming | Yellowstone—Old Faithful Geyser— Said goodbye to Mallory and Meredith and Mr. and Mrs. G.*

"We still have more to go. How did I get so far behind?" she lamented.

"I'll help you stay on track from now on," I offered.

"Me too," Gerri said, smiling at Jill, who gave her a silly smile back. "Laundry's all done." Gerri patted the clean piles, one of which was Dad's. I was briefly seized by the irrational urge to burn each and every article stacked there.

Then, suddenly, it dawned on me that the tap was still on and filling the bathtub.

"Oh dang!" I jumped up. "I hope the bathtub water didn't overflow!"

I ran to the bathroom and found that the water was right at the brim. The shampoo bubbles didn't last, but they did cloud the water.

"Just in time!" I shouted, pulling the plug to drain some of the murky water.

I heard Jill call from the other room, "Let's finish this up! We're almost done."

"Well, it was only yesterday when we went to that horrible lake in Utah," Gerri said, rubbing her arms unconsciously, as though reliving the pain. "The Great Salt Lake."

"Yeah, that's right. It wasn't *that* horrible, though," Jill said, then wrote: *7/8/76 | Utah | The Great Salt Lake—Salty, floaty, white sand | Salt Lake City—Temple and Tabernacle (couldn't go in!)* and then *7/8/76 | Nevada | Wells, Nevada—Stayed at Super 8 Motel— Swimming pool, laundry, took a bath, grocery shopping.* "We're going grocery shopping after our bath, right?" she asked, glancing up at me.

"I think so—and nice job, Jill. You caught us all up." I was impressed that she used her neatest handwriting, despite rushing a bit. "And, Gerri, thanks for finishing the folding."

"Sure thing. But where were your clothes?" she wondered aloud.

"I did them already," I said.

"You only folded your own clothes?" She furrowed her brows and shook her head. "Only yours?" She looked at Jill, who gave her a shrug. "Huh? That's weird."

"I know, sorry about that . . . I guess I just started with mine and didn't have time to finish everything else," I muttered.

"Okay . . . strange." She looked at me again, then seemed to shake it off. "Well, I put Jill's and mine back into our suitcase and bag, and I'll leave Dad's here on the table by the door for him to get. Do you know if he's awake yet?"

"Dad?" I forced myself not to grimace. "I don't think so."

"Jill, I picked out an outfit for you for today," Gerri said with a grin.

"Thanks, Ger-Bear," Jill said.

I was so glad that my little sisters were nice and normal.

"Okay, while you two take a bath—and by the way, do a really good job on unbraiding your hair and shampooing and conditioning it so that it'll be easier to comb—I'll get the sleeping bags from outside and roll them up and get some ice for the cooler. Don't take too long," I instructed. "Here's the detangling comb. Can you guys give each other a hand?"

"Are we really going to go grocery shopping without him? And *drive* there?" Jill asked.

"Yep. I think it'll be fun." Driving without Dad, although scary, seemed way more appealing than driving with him. I still needed more time to compose myself. "We'll buy all the stuff that *we* want. Maybe even get things that he usually doesn't let us have."

"Mary!" the twins said at the same time, shocked.

"What?"

"You're acting so weird this morning!" Gerri remarked. "Are you sure you're okay?"

"I'm fine. I said so already," I barked. Then I changed my voice, making it much more tender. "Go on. Take your bath, and don't dillydally, Silly Sally."

"All right, all right," Jill said, stripping out of her nightgown and walking toward the bathroom. Gerri joined her, and their cute little derrières jiggled as they walked away. *There goes Bread Buns and Biscuit Buns,* I thought. Those nicknames were still suitable after all these years. I heard Gerri say to Jill as they closed the door, "Dad sure is sleeping in."

"Yeah. He was up earlier. But I guess he went back to sleep," Jill said, and I walked over to the bathroom to eavesdrop. If Jill was going to tell her twin anything about Dad and Charlotte, it was going to happen right now.

"What do you mean?" Gerri asked. "He got up already?"

"Me and Mary saw him outside in his pj's by Blue Pierre this morning." She paused, and for a few seconds, all I heard was the residual drip of the bathwater. "I was going to the bathroom and then came back to bed."

"What was he doing outside so early?"

"Heck if I know," Jill answered. I sighed with relief. She wasn't going to tell Gerri. "But there was a pretty lady with makeup on with him. They were saying goodbye."

"Was it Dolores?" Gerri asked.

"The receptionist lady? No, he called her Charlotte," Jill replied.

"Charlotte? What were they doing?" Gerri continued.

My relief nosedived. *Crap.* Now Gerri would know about all this, too. I interrupted. "Hey, girls. Let's get you in the tub before the water gets cold. Come on." I nudged them forward as I tried to think of something else for them to talk about. "How about you guys think about what groceries you'd like. Think big. Let's get lots of yummy, fresh stuff. How exciting. When I get back from doing the sleeping bags, I'd like you to each have ten specific things you want. Okay?" That sounded like something Mom would say.

To my surprise, they took the bait. As I walked away, I heard Jill say, "Strawberries and the graham crackers with cinnamon sugar."

"Yeah," Gerri chimed in. "Let's get Cap'n Crunch."

"Okay, you two. I'll be back soon." I smiled as they reached forward and started to unbraid each other's hair.

Gerri didn't ask any more follow-up questions about Dad. *Phew.* I looked at the notebook and resisted adding something like *Paid for an evening with Charlotte, the prostitute* to Jill's Wells, Nevada, entry. Then I made their bed.

32

Good Morning, Beautiful Daughters

Dad emerged from room 109 almost three hours later. The twins and I were in the parking lot near the car. He had showered, trimmed his beard, and dressed, with his Blue Pierre French chapeau atop his head. I thought his long socks and sandals looked dorky with his Bermuda shorts, but he bounced with a jaunty step anyway, calling out cheerfully, "Good morning, beautiful daughters. How are you on this glorious day? I feel refreshed and rejuvenated. Thank you from the bottom of my heart for permitting me to sleep in today." He bowed and gestured expansively while I blanched and looked away, terrified my anger would show on my face. How could it not?

"No problem, Dad. Our morning has been pretty good," Jill answered for the three of us. "We already went grocery shopping. You'd be proud of Mary's driving."

"Would I?" He smiled at me. I smirked back at him, and he gave me a quizzical look that made me worry he'd already read me like a book. My smirk shuddered. "Is there any change from the thirty dollars?"

Of course he hadn't picked up on my mood. Of course he was more concerned about the money.

Well, Dad, you should've thought about that before buying a prostitute.

"Not a cent," I replied quickly. I shot a discreet look at the twins that told them I wasn't going to return the $6.32 we'd gotten in change. It was tucked away safely in my pocket with Mom's twenty dollars for an emergency. "We spent every last penny." I felt justified in stockpiling some cash just in case he did something else outrageous and we ended up broke!

The twins nodded almost imperceptibly.

"Really?" he asked doubtfully.

"Yes," I blandly stated. "I wouldn't bear false witness, you know." I had my left hand behind my back with my fingers crossed. I wanted to remind him about the Ten Commandments.

"Hmm," he murmured.

Gerri continued with our litany of morning accomplishments. "We restocked the picnic basket and cooler. We got ice from that ice maker you told us about. Grocery shopping was super neat. I don't think anyone knew we drove there by ourselves. We got fruit and vegetables and cheese and some turkey and ham lunch meat—"

"And bread and nuts and raisins," Jill said, finishing Gerri's list, "and Cap'n Crunch and potatoes and the instant coffee you like."

Gerri smiled and went on. "And a can of beans and some milk and some beef jerky and crackers and potato chips—"

This time I interrupted. "And olives. The fancy kind." I let that sink in before adding, "I thought a basket of strawberries would be great, so we got them, too. And we bought two big steaks. I know you only like to get cheap meat, but we thought, *What the heck?* They were on sale and were frozen, so they're kind of keeping the cooler cold until we want to cook them the next time we camp. I thought maybe we'd splurge a little."

"Wow!" He smirked, but I could've sworn he'd broken into a sweat. "Okay."

I couldn't tell if he was irritated or amused that I bought all the things he usually refused us. The olives, the expensive steaks, the strawberries. I didn't care. I truly didn't care anymore and felt liberated to do whatever I liked. It served him right, anyway, letting us kids drive to the market and buy groceries to give him—the adult—time to sleep in after a night spent with a prostitute!

"We used the motel's wet towels to wipe down the inside of Blue Pierre," Jill went on.

"And the windows," Gerri threw in. "And we used that little hand broom to sweep the floorboards."

"Oh yeah, and the books and maps and TripTik in the library box are all reorganized," Jill said. "And we added some more information to our Slate of Dates, States, and Fates."

"That's great news! Maybe I should sleep in more often," Dad said. *Gross,* I thought. "Can I see it?" he asked. Jill got out the notebook and showed him. He laughed at some of the descriptions. "This looks fantastic." He patted her head while she smiled proudly, still eager to get his approval. *Poor girl,* I thought. *If she only knew the truth of what she'd seen earlier.*

"And we folded the laundry and loaded the car. Well, except for your suitcase. Your clean clothes are folded and on the table in our room," Gerri bragged.

"Yeah, we're pretty much ready to go. We even had some of the motel's continental breakfast," Jill reported, slightly stumbling over the pronunciation of *continental*. She gestured to Blue Pierre in the parking lot. "The car is all packed, and we even rolled up the sleeping bags."

"And we went swimming," Gerri told him, then sneezed. "Dad, you missed all the fun."

"Gesundheit. Sure sounds like it," he agreed.

Gerri wiped her nose with the back of her hand. "Can I take the keys back to the motel's office?"

"You betcha. Here's my key—but don't let my door shut. I still need to grab my bag and add those clothes you folded. Besides that, I've already double-checked my room."

My fake smile shivered. He probably had to hide evidence of last night's escapade from us.

"Wow, girls, you are *ex-tra-or-din-ary*," he praised, handing Gerri his key. Then, as she skipped toward the reception area, Dad looked at Jill and me. "I'm proud to be your father."

I bit back my response: *I wish I could say I'm proud to be your daughter, but I'm not.*

Dad smirked. "Someone must have raised you well."

Yes, Mom has done a great job.

It was absolutely typical that he would try to take credit for our achievements and behavior. His thank-you sounded like he was complimenting himself. I had a feeling everything he did or said was going to be cringeworthy or repulsive from now on. I needed to figure out a way to conceal my disdain. We had a long trip to go, and I already felt like my face was as stiff as a mask. It desperately wanted to collapse into a frown or an outright grimace.

Aha, this might work. "Hey, Jill, you want to sit in the front seat for a while? Seems like I've had over my fair share. You can do the CB and radio. After a while, you and Gerri can switch." I looked at her questioning face and added, "I'm really tired. It was kind of *noisy* last night," I said pointedly, avoiding Dad's gaze, "and I didn't sleep that well."

I hoped he felt a little guilty or worried, but he probably didn't.

Dad strolled back to his room, gathering his pile of clothes on the way, and returned with his suitcase. I was already in the back seat. Positioning myself directly behind the driver's seat, I could enjoy being completely out of sight of the rearview mirror for a while. As an added measure, I used a pillow to cover my face, making it clear that I was not to be disturbed. They could figure out how to get to California without me. It was just one straight road, after all. He loaded his suitcase into the trunk and slammed it shut.

When Gerri started to get in the back with me, Dad asked, "Ger, you want to sit up here, too? You two are so little. There's plenty of room."

"Sure!" she exclaimed. Jill scooted over to the center to make room for her.

Nice. Even better for me. I could stretch out all the way now and really get some sleep.

Gerri pulled out the TripTik, which I had already opened to the correct page. "Dad, just go west on I-80 the whole way," she said.

Looking over Gerri's shoulder and dragging her finger along the route, Jill said, "It's about three hundred eighty miles to Lake Tahoe. That's the next place you said, right?"

"Yes, you got it. I think that'll take about five and a half hours of steady driving." He patted Blue Pierre's dash. "Hang in there, old buddy. Fortunately, it does seem a little cooler today."

Dad started Blue Pierre, and the car rumbled to life, its throaty engine vibrating loudly. Gerri asked if she could play the Carpenters' *Now and Then*, and I loved that she turned it up. *Crank it, baby!* Maybe I wouldn't have to listen to Dad talk.

As we left Wells, Nevada, I could see the sign for Donna's Ranch from my prone position. I wondered how Charlotte was doing—if she liked her job. I thought that having sex with abhorrent, disgusting, and loathsome men like my dad could not have been a very good occupation. I found myself thinking about what her answer might have been as a little girl when someone asked her what she dreamed of becoming when she grew up. I bet it wasn't *I'd like to be a prostitute*. I hoped that prostitutes earned really good money to make up for how revolting their job was.

Stretching out, I made myself comfortable. I got lost in the sweet, mellow sound of Karen Carpenter singing "Yesterday Once More." I giggled to myself about the background lyrics that we could never decipher. I'm sure it wasn't *oh-e oo-he's got cooties*, but I thought that sounded just perfect for today.

Before falling fully asleep, I heard Dad quietly ask the girls if something was wrong with me, that I seemed grumpy and grouchy and quiet.

"She's been kind of strange today," Gerri confided softly. "She woke up really early, I think."

I braced myself, a volcano ready to erupt. If Dad said anything like "Maybe she's having her period," I would positively scream.

Jill defended me. "She was kind of quiet, but she's the one who did most of the work today. She got the laundry, and the ice, and organized all these books, and drove us to the grocery store. I think she's just tired."

Thanks, Jilly-Bean, I thought.

"Hmm" was the last thing I heard Dad say.

✱ ✱ ✱

Blue Pierre must have hit a pothole, or Dad must have made an abrupt turn or something, because I woke with a bounce. My sweaty face, stickier than the fingers of a toddler eating cotton candy, made a squelching sound as I peeled my cheek off the back seat. I could sense the long vertical indented stripe on my face, from forehead to mouth, created by the seat's seam. Jill, still in the middle of the front seat between Dad and Gerri, noticed me first.

She turned all the way around, kneeling on the front seat and leaning over its back. "Holy moly, Mary. You slept for four and a half hours!" The sun was shining around her head, the nimbus making her appear angelic. "I missed you. We're almost to Lake . . . Lake what?"

"Tahoe," Dad replied.

"Lake Tahoe," Jill said.

"I missed you, too, Mare," Gerri dittoed, joining her sister in that strange backward-facing position.

"Really?" I said groggily. "I must have been very tired." My sisters' sweetness was going to come in handy in counteracting the torture of being stuck in the same car as Dad.

"I'd say!" Dad remarked. "You stayed asleep even when we stopped to get gas and had a bite to eat in Winnemucca."

"Winnewhata?" I mumbled.

"I know, Mare. Isn't that a funny name?" Gerri said and repeated the exotic word once more. "Winnemucca." She laughed, and Jill joined her.

"Yeah, that's a funny-sounding name in English," said Dad. I sat up, and he looked at me with clueless and innocent eyes

201

through the rearview mirror. I could already tell he was about to dispatch another trivia lesson. "But when we were there picnicking, I asked a local resident what it meant, and she told us that it's a Shoshone and Paiute Indian word and means 'one moccasin.'" He was such a show-off. I bet he didn't even pronounce those tribes' names correctly.

"And you slept through Lovelock," Jill said. She must have been the TripTik master, spouting off the names of the locations en route like that. I didn't know how to reply, so I just stayed quiet.

"Are you hungry? You should grab a bite to eat," Dad said, nodding vaguely at the cooler. "We're just past . . . What was the name of the last town, Jill?"

"Fernley," she piped up.

"Yes, Fernley, and we're almost to Reno. Lake Tahoe is just beyond that. I bet we can do some camping there. Mary, do you remember what that other guidebook called the kind of no-reservation camping we like to do?"

I reached into the cooler that was on the floor and pulled out the grapes, sliding a few into my mouth. Their wet sweetness burst over my tongue. "You mean our car-camping, our cheating camping? Um, I don't remember." I'd have to communicate minimally with him, or my anger would be too obvious. "Did it start with a *D*?" I thought for a moment. "Designated?"

"Oh yes. Good one. *Designated* was for camping at real campsites with reservations and money, but there was another *D* word for just setting up camp and getting out before any rangers see you." Dad chuckled.

"I think it was *dis*-something." I tried to think of words that began with *dis* but could only come up with potential Freudian slips. "Disappointed? Disloyal? Dishonest? Disgraceful? Dispersed? Displaced? Disturbed?"

"Dispersed! Yes, that's it!" He smiled obliviously, Mr. Magoo–style, with no acknowledgment of the other words on my list. Wasn't dispersed camping simply another example of how Dad was violating the commandment "Thou shalt not steal"? I was punished big-time for eating some chocolate chips—forced to spend two hours in solitary confinement in the basement, ruining everyone's holiday—but Dad didn't ever seem to get punished for his multitude of sins, all of which were, without question, much more severe. Plus, I was a kid! He was a grown-up!

I tried to shake it off. The grapes, along with a few crackers and a chunk of cheddar cheese, revived me, and I felt more awake, at least. I washed them down with some lime Kool-Aid and wiped my lips with the back of my hand.

"Mary, you want to sit in front?" Jill asked.

"Nah, I'm fine. I'm liking the breeze back here. Is that okay with you two?"

"Oh yeah!" Gerri answered. "I love it up here. You can see the road much better."

We drove on quietly for a while, and I watched the Sierra Nevada Mountains slowly become ignited by the bright sun as we continued on I-80 past Reno.

"Hey, check that out." Dad pointed to the right, his hand hovering in front of the twins' faces. "That little casino–hotel–gas station joint we're passing right now is called Boomtown. The name comes from the gold-rush days when towns sprang up almost overnight, booming with miners and fortune seekers. Some lasted, but many faded when the gold dried up, and people moved on, hoping for another strike. Pioneers heading west hung signs on their wagons that read CALIFORNIA OR BUST."

We crossed the California state line shortly thereafter, coming upon a sign that read LEAVING NEVADA. WELCOME TO CALIFORNIA, THE GOLDEN STATE. I wanted to know why it was called the Golden State—but not enough to invite Dad to get up on his soapbox again.

I should've known my invitation, or lack thereof, wasn't a concern of his.

"California is called the Golden State in reference to the gold rush of 1849," he began, talking more like a history professor than our dad. "Thousands of fortune seekers flooded this state to strike it rich by finding some gold. They'd shout 'Eureka!' when they discovered some. I think there's a town here in California"—he pronounced it *Cal-i-for-ni-ay*—"that is actually named Eureka."

I let him blabber on to the twins and rested my head on the passenger side of the car's window, noticing steam rising from a natural hot spring on the side of the highway that billowed skyward, creating a white cloud. I wished my upset feeling and Dad's awfulness could float away like that steam.

I heard Dad say, "To get to Lake Tahoe, we have to drive through a little town called Truckee."

After about another fifteen minutes, we exited in central Truckee and pulled up to the Ponderosa grocery store. It was incredible to see how much the geography had changed. No longer were we traversing through miles and miles of the empty sand-colored Nevada wasteland—now we were surrounded by ponderosa pine trees, and it overall felt a bit cooler.

"How about a Coke and we take a stroll down this commercial row?" Dad offered. "It would be nice to stretch our legs and let ol' Blue Pierre take a break, too."

The twins eagerly agreed, and we all ambled along. I let the girls walk close to him, and I either went ahead or lagged behind. "This town is adorable," he said, tipping his head way back and draining the last of his Coke. Of course he let out a loud belch. "Well, excuse me!" The twins giggled, and I ignored him. "Girls, hold on to your empty bottles. We can get our nickel deposits back from that Ponderosa place before we leave."

"Oh look!" Gerri exclaimed. She tugged on Jill's hand, running toward a store called Truckee Five and Dime that looked like a candy store and a toy store combined. When we went inside, we were surprised to see it also had arts and crafts supplies, stationery, wind chimes, Truckee souvenirs, and all sorts of groovy things. "Dad, we haven't bought much on this trip . . . Could we please buy some fun things here? Please?" Gerri asked.

Dad considered her request for a minute, then replied, "How about I give you all ten dollars to last for here and San Francisco?"

"Only ten?" I smirked.

"Maybe fifteen would be better," he agreed, "but you'll need to pace yourselves and not ask for more if you spend it all in one place."

The fifteen would add nicely to that $6.32 change I got from the grocery store back in Wells and Mom's twenty.

Dad dug around in his wallet, as though trying to find a way to renege on his offer, but eventually presented me with three crisp five-dollar bills. "Remember, ration this," he said. He gave me a pointed look and added, "Maybe this will get you out of your funk."

"Maybe it will," I said, extending my hand toward the cash. As soon as he'd put the bills in my open palm, I pulled the money away and added, "Maybe it won't."

I turned my back on him and joined the twins.

We were literally kids in a candy store, marveling at all the options. Jill bought a pack of cigarette gum, a Mad Libs book, and some new colored pencils. Gerri got a jawbreaker, a coloring book and crayons, and some stamps and postcards. Dad bought a little magnetic chess set and a book about the Donner Party. I chose an instruction booklet on crocheting, some yarn, and a hook. I wanted to learn to crochet little animals.

We were finishing up with our purchases when we were interrupted by the piercing whistles of an approaching train. Looong, looong, short, looong, blasted the conductor. Across the road was the cute little train depot, and a moment later, the passenger train chuffed to a halt. We'd never seen a real passenger train up close before, and it took only one look at the twins for us all to wordlessly decide to dash out of the Five and Dime, paper bags clutched in our hands.

Many passengers disembarked as we crossed the narrow road. Some of them were dressed up in fancy clothes and hats, and some looked pretty ragged. There was a big group of hippies, some without shoes and the rest with Jesus sandals. They carried army surplus duffel bags and guitar cases.

"I'm reckoning those hippies are coming from San Francisco. They just can't get over their Summer of Love, even though 1969 was a while ago," Dad said, quick to dismiss them. I sighed, trying to hide the way I bristled over his comment.

As they approached us, one of the young men waved a peace sign at our gawking faces. "Peace, little sisters," he said to me and the twins. *He's quite handsome for a hippie,* I thought—with bright-blue eyes, thick hair, and a sun-kissed complexion. He seemed a lot healthier and happier than I thought a hippie might look. I'd always heard—probably from Dad—that they were rail thin, dirty, and smelled like body odor and patchouli oil.

The handsome hippie smiled at my sisters. Their faces went scarlet.

As the group passed us, I was surprised that Dad, not usually discreet, cupped his hand over his mouth and whispered to us, "Can you smell them? They smell like BO and wacky tobacky." I hated to admit it, but he was right—they did smell pretty bad. A little patchouli oil might've helped.

"Hey, mister," said a girl trailing behind her group. I admired her headband, which matched her long tie-dyed maxi dress. It almost covered her bare feet, and the hem was tattered from being stepped on. "Can you spare some change or a buck?" She smiled her question to Dad specifically.

First, I thought, *Oh brother, you don't know what a cheapskate you're talking to.* Then I wondered if, for once, Dad would show some Christian charity. Or if he'd flirt with her. He was impossible to predict.

"Not for likes of you, miss," he retorted shortly.

What? *What a jerk!* Now he was not only ungenerous and stingy but also prejudiced.

The girl's face fell, and I could tell she was expecting to get a few cents out of him, at least—even if it meant a bit of flirting. I wasn't a fan of her approach, but it didn't matter. For now, Dad was the enemy, and I couldn't stop myself from slighting him.

"Here," I said, stepping between the two of them and glaring at my dad. "Here's a dollar."

Gerri and Jill followed my lead and each took out two quarters and added them to her opened hand while Dad stood back with his hands on his hips, shaking his head. I thought he looked like a dog—especially with his three daughters outdoing him in generosity.

After she pocketed the money, she gave us a little bow with her hands in a prayer position in front of her heart and said, "Namaste." I felt compelled to do something back, so I put my shopping bag between my knees and made my hands touch palm to palm like hers and repeated the pretty word. She looked at me with her glassy, bloodshot eyes, cocked her head, and said, "Groovy."

As we headed back to get our soda pop deposit, Dad scolded us. "What did you do that for, girls? You have just wasted your money! *My* hard-earned money, at that. Those types don't have jobs. They don't make any money, and they just scrounge off decent folk like us."

Decent folks like us? *His* hard-earned money? Who was he kidding? Not me. Grandpa Red had given him a lot of money, and Mom actually made more than he did. Talk about wasting money—didn't he pay for a prostitute just last night? Surely that cost more than the two dollars we'd shared with the namaste girl!

"Do you have something to add, Mary?" Dad asked, using my real name instead of Mare, and ever so fleetingly, I fantasized about saying all that out loud. Letting it spill out of me, puddling all over the floor. It'd feel so good, getting it off my chest, but—

Like any spill, it'd be a mess I'd have to mop up later. And for now, it wasn't worth it.

I bit my tongue and said, "I'm just trying to be a good Christian."

33

Run, Stop, Bury

After leaving the hippies and the toy store and getting my nickel deposit back on Commercial Row in Truckee, I hopped into the back seat of Blue Pierre. The twins gave me identical startled expressions. I smiled back and gave them a little nod. "Go ahead, enjoy the front seat, you two."

They piled into the car, and soon enough, we were flying down the road, the ponderosa pine trees whizzing by like an army of soldiers standing at attention and saluting us as we drove toward Kings Beach. I lifted a hand through the open sunroof, allowing the wind to comb through my fingertips like the cool water of a river, and wondered if it'd be possible to ride in the back seat for the rest of this Great American Road Trip.

The closer we got to the beach, the more I realized the forest swept right to the shoreline. A wall of pine trees framed the lake's perimeter. Nearly there, we approached a little hill on Dolly Varden Avenue in Kings Beach.

"Hold on tight!" Dad said suddenly, grinning. He punched the gas pedal, getting the timing just right to soar over that little hill.

As Jill lifted off the front seat, she yelled, "Ticklebelly!"

Gerri joined in her delight, clapping her hands as she bounced back down next to her after the exhilarating split-second sensation of hovering in the air. The TripTik and other things they had on their laps flew everywhere. That ticklebelly feeling was like when you jump in an elevator while you're coming down, and the floor is farther away from your feet than you expected. Dad would let us do that in his office building back in Cleveland.

I hated to admit it, but that ticklebelly felt amazing. As I bounced into the air, I pretended the jolt shook loose a bit of my anger and disappointment toward Dad. I imagined it fluttering away on the wings of a little black angry angel. When I landed back down, a fraction of my heavy disgust seemed to lift with the impact.

But what was I supposed to do with all these mixed-up feelings? Part of me thought I should tell Mom, confront Dad, and demand we go home. But what good would that do? It would just fast-track their divorce, and I'd be the one to blame—or, at least, feel like I was. Once that ball started rolling, there'd be no stopping it. Then what? I'd be stuck with an angry Dad on the car ride home, and things would get even messier. I'd ruin the trip for everyone—Gerri and Jill included—and I couldn't tell how much Jill understood or if she even understood anything at all. Why drag them into this ugly reality if they didn't have to be?

And as much as I struggled to see this side of him now, Dad was fun. He could be so much fun when he wasn't also being a creep. How could someone be both? The contradiction didn't make sense, and it left me tangled like spaghetti in feelings I didn't know how to handle.

Everything about this felt complicated, like I'd been shoved into a world of grown-up problems I wasn't ready to face. They say ignorance is bliss, and boy did I miss my bliss. I liked being happy. I liked being a kid. This grumpy, bitter version of me—it wasn't who I wanted to be. It felt like such a waste of time and energy. *My* time and energy. Why wasn't our family's trick of putting on a happy face working anymore?

Dad turned to look at me, flashing his lopsided, questioning grin. I'm sure he knew something was bothering me. Maybe he did think I was just on my period or something. That'd be better than the truth. But it still felt unfair—me sitting here, quietly unraveling, while he just Mr. Magoo-ed his way through life, obliviously singing and smiling like nothing was wrong.

This trip was supposed to be a dream come true. *Our* dream come true. It was something we'd looked forward to for years. But instead, here I was, drowning in my own frustration while he was having the time of his life.

While I fumed, we drove along the coastline before making a right turn onto Fox Street, and in four blocks, we were right at the shore of Lake Tahoe. Dad pulled into a shady space in the parking lot of the Kings Beach State Recreation Area below a quivering aspen tree, its oval leaves rustling like green silver dollars in the mild breeze.

When he cut ol' Blue Pierre's engine, the poor heap exhaled a mechanical sigh. I patted its roof in thanks. As we changed into our swimsuits, we could hear it pinging and rattling as it cooled. Dad was busy with something under the hood, and we were spared his usual creepy comments or catcall whistles about our sexy bathing suits.

"Go ahead and bring the twins to the water, Mare," Dad instructed, his head still under the hood. "I'm going to take care of something here." I nodded silently. The twins and I walked barefoot over the decomposed granite sand. It was definitely sharper than that oolitic sand from a few days before. And it was hot in the midday sun.

We did the run-stop-bury technique to prevent our bare feet from being burned. After running for as long as our calloused feet would allow, we'd stop and bury our feet into the cooler, unheated sand below the surface until the burning subsided enough to do it again. Dad brought up the rear in his sandals. As soon as we were within reach of the water, the girls took off their glasses, and we dropped our towels and ran straight into the lake.

What a relief. The water was shockingly cold and refreshing and had little glimmers of gold in it. It was nothing like the murky, tepid water of the Great Salt Lake. The surface of the bright-blue water was as glossy as lacquer. It seemed to sparkle and shimmer in an otherworldly way, and it looked altogether too perfect to exist, like the sort of thing you'd see in a calendar.

Plus, there wasn't an insect in sight.

Lake Tahoe lay cradled in an enormous basin, surrounded by mountain peaks still capped in snow, even in July. The air was so clear, I could see all the way to the other side. It was official: this was the most beautiful lake I had ever seen. It was the opposite of the lukewarm ponds we had back at home, whose thick sludge would get stirred up as soon as you got in, making the water so cloudy, every step felt like risking your foot to some sort of a swamp monster.

We waded in deeper and deeper. You had to walk out really far until it was deep enough to fully submerge. It was like this edge of the lake was a huge shelf. We splashed one another and tried to jump over the little breaking waves or bodysurf them. As we got out to deep water, it looked like the ledge abruptly broke off at the precipice of an underwater cliff. I floated on my belly and looked down, marveling at how deep you could see. I was in heaven. Rolling over and gazing up, I saw two seagulls and wondered how ocean birds had made it all the way to this alpine lake. I floated on my back for a long while and imagined my Dad-hatred washing away with each swell of the waves.

With my ears partly submerged, I could just make out Dad hollering from the shoreline, "Gerri, how are you doing? How does this water feel on your skin?"

She cupped her hands around her mouth, creating a small megaphone. "Way better! This water is perfect!"

We stayed in that cold water for nearly an hour. Eventually, the sky clouded over, reminding us of how much time had passed.

Jill swam over to me and asked, "You getting hungry, Mare?"

"Yeah. How about you?"

"Uh-huh. I'm starving, and I keep getting whiffs of hamburgers and french fries."

"Yeah. Me too," I agreed, turning my nose toward the *deyishous* smells and pushing the wet hair out of my eyes.

Gerri swam over, staying underwater, and tried to scare me by grabbing my ankles. I pretended the ambush worked and screamed, then fell over, splashing the pair of them.

She joined our conversation. "What are you two talking about?"

"Hamburgers and french fries," I said.

"Mmm, that sounds *deyishous* . . . but we just bought all that food. I bet Dad won't let us eat at a restaurant today," Gerri said.

"Yeah, you're probably right. Maybe we can get a milkshake or an ice-cream cone out of him," I said. "Jill, you should ask him when we get out."

"Okay, I will," Jill said, giving a little shiver with her shoulders. It was getting cold standing there waist-deep, rocking with the waves, and it seemed like the wind had picked up. I looked toward the shore and saw Dad lying in the sand. The aspen trees beyond him were swaying even more than before.

Gerri looked at me hesitantly, water dripping from her hair. Jill smiled at her, giving her a nod of encouragement. "Mary, Jill and I were talking . . ."

"Oh yeah? What about?" I tried to sound nonchalant, but I knew what was coming and braced myself for the impact.

"What's wrong? Did something happen?" Gerri went on, eyes immediately dropping down to the water. For a moment, it was quiet. Only the soft rustle of waves and lapping water filled the space between her question and my answer.

"What do you mean?" I asked, trying to buy time.

"You're just not yourself," she said. "You're letting us sit in the front seat, you don't sing along to our favorite songs . . ." Jill stood quietly, not saying a word. Gerri continued, "It started at the motel and then the grocery shopping . . ."

"Yeah," Jill murmured. I attempted to make eye contact with her, but she wouldn't look at me. I guess she was trying to pretend that she didn't know what had upset me, which I thought was a smart move on her part. Or maybe she actually *didn't* know. "Ever since then, you've been so quiet and kind of ignoring Dad."

I tried to keep my face expressionless while I appreciated Jill's acting.

Gerri nodded, encouraged by her twin. "And kind of being a smart aleck, too," she added.

I took a calming breath. I didn't want to burst her bubble. Apparently, I wasn't doing a very good job of hiding it from her.

She still idolized Dad, and I had, too, when I was her age—and she should find out the truth about his lack of integrity on her own, under different circumstances. I didn't have the right to divulge what I knew. If they had both seen him and Charlotte in the parking lot, it would be different. I bet they would have asked him who she was, and certainly, he would have had some creative explaining to do. But that didn't happen, so I was burdened with this all by myself, and I wasn't sure about how Jill was handling what she knew.

Jill looked up. They both were gazing at me with their young, innocent eyes. I needed to make some changes and fast. Racking my brain to figure out what I should say to them, I turned around and examined the distant mountains to stall for some time.

"I'm sorry," I started, figuring out how to lie. I just couldn't tell them the truth. I was getting really good at bearing false witness. "I guess I'm just getting tired of this road trip . . . You know, the long car rides, the sweltering heat, always listening to Dad blab on about everything, him thinking he knows something about every subject. It's just getting irritating, you know?" Maybe I should get them to talk and take the attention off me. "How are you two feeling?"

"Well, I'm still having a good time," Gerri said. "This lake is so nice." She splashed some water at me and Jill. *Brr.*

"Well, I'm still having a good time, too," Jill echoed. "But we do still have a long time to go, don't we?"

"Aren't you two getting cold? Let's get out," I said, tugging on their hands. "You're right, we do have a long way to go. First to San Francisco and the ocean before turning around and heading east."

It dawned on me that if I wasn't going to tell them the truth about why I was upset, then it was time to snap out of it. Just because my trip was ruined didn't mean theirs needed to be ruined, too—and anyway, I was trying to be a better mother to them.

I'd sort out my feelings toward Dad later.

For now, and going forward, I would need to put my theater skills to the test.

I dunked underwater one more time to get my hair out of my face. The twins copied me. We floated face down, using our hands to crawl back, clawing against the rough, sandy bottom of the lake, our legs buoyant behind us. We got all the way to the shore, where Dad was sleeping on his belly in the sun. It looked like he'd gotten a sunburn on his legs and back. I resisted feeling happy about that and told myself that it was just his own karma at work, but a little smirk crossed my face anyway.

Gerri and Jill got close and dripped some water on him. He rolled over and jumped up at the shock, which made me laugh. Laughing felt good. Maybe that's how I could snap out of it. *Laugh more.*

The twins grabbed their towels to dry off, but I didn't want to wipe off the soft and powdery feeling or the little golden specks that were clinging to my skin. I decided to just air-dry.

"Let's get ice cream, girls." Dad smiled, sitting up and brushing the sand off his belly and legs. We three looked at one another and wondered how he could've known we were just about to ask him for that very thing, then followed him to Blue Pierre. I climbed in the back again, as was becoming the new norm, and we headed east on Lakeshore Boulevard.

Right away, we came upon the Char-Pit—which was the source of that *deyishous* hamburger and french fry smell. It sold ice cream, too. We all ordered swirled chocolate and vanilla soft-serve cones and sat under one of their umbrellas at an outside table, trying to lick them up before they melted.

"Let's find a place to do some cheating—I mean dispersed camping—a little farther away from this crowded area," Dad suggested, crunching the bottom of his cake cone. "We still have some charcoal in the trunk that we can use to cook those steaks you bought, Mare. You got potatoes, too, right?"

"Yeah, and we were low on foil, so we got a small roll of that, too," I said, then added, "oh, and some corn on the cob."

Okay. I can do this. I just have to pretend that everything is normal.

214

"That sounds perfect." Jill's mouth was full of ice cream and cone. She wasn't able to eat quickly enough to beat the heat, and her hands were covered in brown-and-white stickiness. I looked at Gerri's hands and saw that they were the same. They both had brown rings around their lips.

"Hey, girls . . ." I laughed. "How about we go use that hose to wash our hands and faces?"

We walked over to the outdoor spigot at the edge of the Char-Pit's parking lot and hosed off before driving down the road. In fifteen minutes, we pulled into the wooded parking lot of Sand Harbor State Park. There were beautiful round granite boulders sitting in the lake, looking like a giant had dropped his marbles into a puddle.

Dad surveyed the scene and pointed to a day-use area on the right. "Yeah, I think we can use one of those grills over there for our supper and then camp out of sight in this little cove here. What do you say?"

"Yeah, let's get on it—I'm starving!" Jill exclaimed. "Can you get the coals started right away? I'll wrap some potatoes and corn in foil."

"I'll help you, Jilly-Bean," her twin offered.

I went to the cooler and got the steaks from the bottom, then peeled off the butcher paper. They were cold but not frozen. Perfect.

When we returned with the food, Dad had the grill ready. "Wow, this is going to be a feast. Let's eat up and hit the hay. I'm beat. You three feel like sleeping under the stars instead of setting up the Beast tonight?" We nodded. "I think it feels warm enough, and if we need to make a quick skedaddle in the morning, it'll be much faster to grab the sleeping bags than the tent."

"Sure, Dad," Jill answered for the three of us.

We enjoyed our feast, and after cleaning up, the coast seemed clear. No one else was around. I snuggled into my sleeping bag. The twins and I looked like caterpillars, squirming and wriggling around to create body-shaped depressions in the sand for our beds. I made a pillow of sand so that my neck was perfectly supported.

Gazing at the upturned bowl of stars overhead, and then at my sisters next to me, and Dad on the other side of this little clearing, I thought that maybe pretending to be normal wasn't going to be too hard after all. Time healed all wounds, Mom would say. I doubted these wounds would heal, but maybe, as time went on, they'd scab over and stop feeling so raw. Plus, at least for now, I could accept that if I wasn't going to call Mom and end this trip early, I had better enjoy what was left of it.

34

Eureka!

Fortunately, we were not discovered illegally camping and made an early getaway the next morning. We shook out our sleeping bags, rolled them up, and quietly put them into the trunk. The girls and I found a place behind one of those giant's marbles on the shore to pee. I'm not sure where Dad went.

Our route took us back through Truckee again, crossing the river and train tracks and passing Commercial Row on our way to the San Francisco Bay Area.

"Look, there's the cool toy store!" Jill pointed.

"And the train station." Gerri gestured out the other window.

In a few minutes, we reached the western edge of Truckee, and from the elevated vantage point of I-80, we could see another beautiful alpine lake down in the valley.

"That's Donner Lake," Dad informed us. "You guys want to have one more swim before we head out of the mountains?"

We all nodded eagerly, loving the idea of another beautiful lake.

"I think after this, we'll be going down through the foothills and then the Sacramento Valley, and then we'll be close to the ocean and San Francisco. So this will be our last opportunity to enjoy these cold and pristine alpine lakes," Dad said. "We're at about seven thousand feet above sea level now, and we'll get down to sea level today."

"Wow! That means we're about halfway through the TripTik," I realized, and Dad smiled.

"Yep, time flies when you're having fun, right?"

"Sure does," Gerri answered.

Dad took the exit, and we descended to Donner Lake. "Okay. Let's make this snappy—not like yesterday at Lake Tahoe, all right? Maybe just like a quick baptism." He chuckled. "I want to get to San Francisco, and it's only about four hours from here if we don't stop too much."

We waded into the equally cold water of Donner Lake. I did a speedy crawl stroke to the swim lines marked by buoys and then returned to shore. This lake also had beautiful gold bits suspended in the water, maybe even more than Lake Tahoe did.

"I love these little gold flecks," I remarked to no one in particular.

"I think they're called fool's gold," Dad said. Then he submerged. The twins were splashing and doing handstands. He sputtered to the surface, grasping the air around his head. "Don't move. Freeze!" he commanded, his tone serious. We froze.

"Why? What happened?" I said, holding still.

"I just dropped my glasses. Son of a gun!" He made a sound that could only be described as something akin to whimpering. "I forgot to take them off. Please don't move. Don't step on them."

He looked naked and vulnerable without them, reminding me of Velma from *Scooby-Doo* with his arms groping around in front of him. For a few breaths, I worried he wouldn't find them and I'd have to drive all the way home because he was as blind as a bat. Lucky for him, the water's clarity was equal to Lake Tahoe's, and his glasses were visible right there on the lake floor, near his feet.

Visible to me, at least. Nothing was visible to him, regardless of the water's clarity.

"Mary," he said somewhat desperately, "can you dive down and get them?"

The twins looked at me expectantly, and I caught Jill's eye for a split second. Eager to adopt the role of fun older sister and doing my best to keep everything copacetic, I said, "Yeah, Dad. I can see them right now. No problem."

Even though I was still mad at him, I took a big breath and decided to do the right thing because it was the right thing. They were only about three feet down, so I easily retrieved them. It did feel good to be helpful rather than mean. Being grumpy just wasn't in my nature—but forgiveness was not going to be as easy as retrieving submerged eyeglasses.

✳ ✳ ✳

When we departed Donner Lake, we headed up Old US Highway 40. Dad, of course, told us all about it as we passed through. "This used to be the main way to get to the Tahoe area way back when, before they constructed the cross-country interstate."

"I-80?" I asked. "Oh, and on the other side of the country, it's also called I-90, right?"

I was in the front seat again, acting almost normal. It was still hard not to look at my dad's rough hands and envision them touching Charlotte the Prostitute, but I was getting better at choking all that back and refocusing on surface-level things.

"That's the one," Dad confirmed. "The cross-country interstate."

We drove up the narrow switchbacks, which were framed by granite cliff faces. There was an arched bridge near the top that we'd stopped at for the spectacular view overlooking Donner Lake from the west side. Wow. Dad nodded generally at the bridge as we drove by. "Donner Lake and Donner Pass—this part of the Sierra Nevada Mountains we're driving through—were named in tribute to the Donner Party's horrendous experience."

I thought back to the store in Truckee, when Dad had bought the book about the Donner Party, and braced myself for another lengthy lecture.

"What kind of *party* has a horrendous experience?" Jill asked, pulling on the back of the front seat to better hear Dad's storytelling.

"It's called the Donner Party. *Party* meaning a group—not *party* meaning a celebration."

"Oh," Jill said. "What happened to them that was horrendous?"

"Well, they were stranded here in the winter, slammed by exceptionally heavy snow, as they were trying to come from the Midwest to Sacramento," Dad started. "It was in the 1840s. One of the groups, the Donner Party, broke away from the rest of the wagon train, trying to take a shortcut. It didn't work out very well for them at all. The other groups made it and didn't get stuck in the snow. I think I read that it was over thirty feet deep. Can you imagine? That's the height of a three-story building! They were starving, and many died." Dad paused, fidgeting with his glasses, eyes locked on the road snaking out before us. "They had to resort to cannibalism."

"Oh no," Gerri said, scooting forward. "That is horrendous." Then she whispered to Jill, "What's cannibalism?"

Her twin shrugged. "I don't know. I'm sure Dad will tell us."

"We can hear you, you know," I said. "Cannibalism is when people eat other people."

Dad laughed at the succinct definition.

"That's disgusting!" Gerri said, visibly disturbed. "They ate each other? People ate people? Gross!"

"Sure is," Dad agreed. "I also read that they ate their leather shoelaces and tried to boil snow for water but had a hard time keeping fires going. There was no dry wood around. So not only were they starving, but they were also freezing."

"That is horrible!" Gerri said, eyeing the cliffs we drove alongside, envisioning that disaster the same way we all were. For a few moments, we sank into the morbid curiosity of it all.

Eventually, Jill asked the question I was thinking: "Did they kill each other and then eat each other or eat people who died already?"

Dad balked, probably shocked to hear his ten-year-old daughter asking for such gory details. "I think the story goes that they—and I don't think it was everyone, but some—ate of the people who had already died from starvation, freezing, or what have you." He paused, and as we continued to drive through the pass, it suddenly felt haunted. "Must've been as horrendous as it sounds."

"Why would they name a place after such a disgusting thing that happened?" I asked, staring out at the cliffs and trying to imagine anything else they could've been named. "Wouldn't Whispering Pines Pass or Blue-Sky Heaven Pass be better names? I would think they'd want to forget about it or sweep it under the rug or something. Know what I mean?"

"I do, and I agree with you to a certain point," said Dad. "But maybe it's to honor the memories of the poor souls who died here. And those who survived did eventually make it through this difficult pass in the mountains, so I suppose the name could be in tribute to them as well." We were all quiet for a bit. Breaking the silence, Dad cleared his throat. "I read that one of the fellows who actually participated in the cannibalism ended up opening a restaurant in Sacramento."

"Oh, that's gross . . . I wonder if his customers knew about his past and questioned what was on the menu." I shivered, trying to shake off the bad story. The twins scooted back into their seat, and we all got quiet again.

After an hour of smooth driving, we came upon a quaint little town called Auburn. Right next to the highway, there was an enormous concrete statue of a kneeling gold miner.

"Would you look at that?" Dad pointed. The gold miner wore a huge concrete hat, and his hands held a large concrete pan to dip into streams, presumably in search of great big concrete gold nuggets.

We were flying down the highway. Blue Pierre must've appreciated the downhill ride. It seemed like the overheating problem was a thing of the past.

Dad missed the exit, took the next one, and whipped around to get us up close and personal with the statue of the gold miner. He retrieved the Super 8 camera and had us climb into the pan. "Get in there, girls. We can pretend that you're gold nuggets!"

The concrete pan was big enough to hold the three of us, and its worn surface suggested we weren't the first tourists with this idea. We girls curled up in ball shapes, as instructed, replicating gold nuggets. Dad started filming.

"Eureka!" we shouted on his cue, holding our arms up in *Y*s.

Yelling that word popped my ears. *Oooh, that feels good.* "My ears just popped," I told them. I didn't even know that they needed to.

"What do you mean, *pop*?" Gerri asked.

"I don't really know; they just feel so much better, and I can hear better."

"It's due to the change in elevation and air pressure," said Dad. "You can encourage your ears to pop by chewing gum or yawning or pinching your nose and closing your mouth and gently blowing, like this." He demonstrated, and the twins followed his lead, their thin cheeks puffing out like Dizzy Gillespie's.

"Oh!" Jill cried. "Mine just popped."

In a couple of seconds, Gerri shouted, "Me too!"

"Son of a pup, mine did, too!" Dad exclaimed.

35

An Upside to Growing Up

The Sacramento Valley was very flat. Acres of farmland stretched seemingly in all directions, for as far as the eye could see. Blocks of fertile green rows and fallow tilled soil spread over the valley like an earth-toned chessboard.

"Mary, this fertile valley is a huge agricultural resource. Guess how much of the entire United States' total produce it produces?" quizzed Dad. "That's funny . . . *produce* it *produces*." He laughed at his own play on words.

"Twenty percent?" I guessed.

"Nope, too low."

"Thirty percent?" Jill said.

"Still too low."

"Forty?" Gerri tried.

"Nope, higher."

"Must be half, then, I think," I offered.

"You got it, Mare. Fifty percent of all of America's produce is grown right here. Isn't that *ex-tra-or-din-ary*? Look over there." He pointed to a great big field occupied by a crop I didn't recognize. The plants were different shades of green, and some were submerged in water while others were dry, appearing like a green-and-gold patchwork quilt.

"What is that?" I asked. "What sort of crop, I mean."

"Rice paddies."

"Wow. Rice paddies? I thought they were only in China or somewhere like that."

"Nope. This area is ideal for growing many different crops." Dad nodded generally at another acre of rice paddies. It looked like a shallow pond, with tufts of bright-green leaves popping right up, sort of like blades of grass. "Rice requires a large, flat, irrigated surface for planting."

"The valley really fits the bill," I said. "Being a flat surface."

"Correct," Dad said. "It's called an alluvial plain."

"Oh, like the Nile River Delta?"

"Yes, just like that." He looked impressed. "Did you notice those orchards back there?" Dad asked, and I nodded, only to look over my shoulder for added measure. Rows of trees had been planted in perfect succession, all of them relatively small. "Those were almonds."

Almond trees! I'd never seen one before.

Pointing to the right side of the highway, Dad said, "And what are those, Gerri and Jill?"

"Oh, I know that one! That's corn," answered Jill.

Gerri chimed in, "Those are sunflowers. They're giant!"

After another hour, the temperature began to cool down even more as we neared the Bay Area. For the first time on this entire trip, except for the few times it'd rained, we rolled up the windows and closed the sunroof.

"Did you ever hear the statement attributed to Mark Twain?" Dad went on. "The one that goes, 'The coldest winter I ever spent was the summer in San Francisco'?"

"What? What does that mean?" Jill asked. "I don't get it."

I bet she thought he was being *atastic*. A couple of years ago, I had said something to Jill, and she asked me if I was being *atastic*. I didn't know what she'd meant. *Fantastic* didn't make sense, and so I was left to assume she'd meant *sarcastic* instead. That silly mispronunciation had stuck with me ever since.

Dad proceeded with his explanation. "Well, evidently, San Francisco has cold summers—which will be a nice change for us."

"I'd say," Gerri agreed. "We've been sweating for weeks. Bring on the cold. I've barely even worn that new sweatshirt Mom got me."

"Me either, Ger-Bear," Jill said.

We entered San Francisco via the Oakland Bay Bridge, which Dad said went from Oakland, then through a tunnel that bored through Yerba Buena Island. Holding our breaths and raising our hands while passing through the tunnel, we emerged a moment later to the cabled part of the silver bridge, where we got a magnificent view of the city.

"Go ahead and hop up on the roof. This is a once-in-a-lifetime experience!" Dad suggested.

We three girls looked at one another, shrugged, and burst out laughing. I scooted up through the sunroof, and the twins joined me on either side. I dug my feet into the back of the front seat for leverage and held on to them as they held on to me, the three of us bristling against the cyclone of fresh wind. Dad stayed in the far-right lane and ooga-ed like a crazy person, and we waved like we were the stars of a parade.

The wind rustled through my hair and clothes, brisk enough to cast chills over my arms, making me feel more awake than I had in days. Everything smelled slightly damp, like wet stone, and my eyes couldn't gobble up the scenery fast enough.

My sisters laughed hysterically beside me, also in awe of the experience, and I glanced down at where my dad was driving and honking. For a heartbeat, time slowed. Mom would never in a million years let us do this. I hoped that no cops would see us, but in a way, I didn't care if they did. I bet Dad would just use his gift of commanding an audience on them, and they'd let us off the hook. Wasn't this what being a kid was supposed to feel like? Trusting your parents blindly and leaning into whatever experience they'd built for you?

I closed my eyes, even though it made me dizzy, and added every single detail of this blissful moment to My Journal of Life.

"Hey, Mare!" Dad hollered.

"What?"

"Slide back down here and take the wheel!"

I dropped down and across the bench seat, nearer to the driver's side, and grasped the steering wheel while Dad shimmied back and stood on the seat. Jill scooted to the center to make room for him. Blue Pierre slowed down a little without anyone pressing the gas pedal.

"Give it the gas!" Dad yelled. "Keep it going. Try to stay at fifty."

It wasn't hard to keep Blue Pierre at that speed, and feeling as liberated as I was—with the burst of adrenaline I had pulsing through my veins—I actually dared to look away from the road and up at where Dad was standing. He'd stretched out his arms, as though beckoning San Francisco to bring it in for a hug. His eyes glistened until they closed, the way mine did, and I wondered if he was adding an entry to his own Journal of Life. What did that journal look like? What was he thinking about?

Before I knew it, we were switching places again, hardly swerving as we did so.

Back on the roof, I yelled and smiled like a fool at my sisters. Looking to the north of the San Francisco Peninsula, we could see the rust-colored red of the Golden Gate Bridge, majestic with its two tall spires. Alcatraz Prison was in the center of the bay. What a view!

"Hey, girls!" Dad yelled and tugged on my leg to get our attention. "Come on in."

We reluctantly slid back into Blue Pierre, our cheeks red from the wind and our hair windblown and wild. I couldn't explain why, but I somehow felt baptized by that experience—as though the wind itself had pulled the heartache out of my chest.

I looked at Dad and hadn't forgotten what he'd done. I hadn't forgiven him, either, and I didn't think that I ever would. But somehow, for the moment, it felt okay to see him for exactly what he was and for exactly what he wasn't.

Dad wasn't the hero I'd thought he was. He was just a person.

✳ ✳ ✳

Dad took an early exit at Fremont Street and then turned right until we got to the water's edge, almost underneath the bridge we were just on. The water stretched outward, reflecting the golden midday sunlight.

"There's the Ferry Building," he said, pointing to the big concrete structure on the water's edge. Its huge clock read 3:10. We drove along the shore on the Embarcadero and passed many piers before stopping at Fisherman's Wharf. Needing to stretch our legs and give Blue Pierre a rest, we strolled along the wide sidewalk. There were all kinds of shops and guys handing out paper flyers advertising shows and stores.

I stopped abruptly, nearly walking into an old couple with matching hats, when I saw a bunch of people gathered around a painted, upright, refrigerator-shaped cardboard box. The hand-painted writing on the front read AUTOMATIC HUMAN JUKEBOX. Peering out the window was a long-haired, rugged, bearded man with a microphone. He could raise and lower the window covering with a little wire that he pulled from the inside.

A kid put a dollar in the bill-changer slot, and the man indicated to the kid that he should select which song he'd like to hear. He then lifted a banged-up trumpet to his lips and blasted out the chorus to the selected song. The kid chose 9D, "When the Saints Go Marching In," and the human jukebox took it away. As a fellow trumpeter, I felt honored to drop a quarter into the coin slot on the other side of the box. Between songs, he heckled the crowd and voiced his negative opinion of Richard Nixon and Spiro Agnew. He ended his rant with "Fucking cheating scumbags!" I laughed, shocked that he'd said that out loud to the crowd. Dad laughed, too, but the twins put their hands over their ears. The human jukebox had a bucket in front labeled PHOTO TAX. Gerri made Dad put in some coins after he'd taken a photo of the three of us standing beside the human jukebox. Before we left, another woman chose a song, 6A, and the man pulled out an alto sax and blasted "There's No Business Like Show Business."

We continued walking down Fisherman's Wharf, overwhelmed by the exotic sights and sounds of the city, the human jukebox's amplified music fading as we got farther away.

At the end of Hyde Street, we saw the cable car turnaround. When the cable cars got to the end of the line, the conductor would get out, and along with the attendant's assistance, they'd release the car from the cable and rotate it 180 degrees, on a huge spinning disc, to turn it around for its return trip.

We bought our tickets, waited in a short line, and got on the next available cable car. My sisters and I settled into our seats and waited for Dad, only to realize he wasn't with us or anywhere in sight.

"Dad?" I said rather loudly, sitting straighter.

"Mary! Look over here!" My eyes darted toward Dad's voice. The twins and I burst into laughter at the same time, realizing that Dad had gotten out the movie camera and was jogging along the side, filming us while the cable car started to move. Strangers began waving, too, amused. I don't think Dad realized how fast the cable car was going to take off, and as soon as we lurched into motion, we were already moving almost too fast for him to keep up with.

"Dad!" I shouted. I was getting flashbacks of him standing face-to-face with that angry buffalo in Yellowstone and worried he'd shrug off my concern now the same way that he did back then. "Throw me the camera and get in!"

To my surprise, he actually tossed me the camera while he sprinted to catch up. I stretched for the hurtling machine, and the twins held on to me to keep me aboard. Grabbing just the strap, I pulled it onto my lap, happy that the camera didn't smack into the polished wooden bench seat.

Dad looked like he was about to have a heart attack the way he was huffing and puffing, and after he grasped the rail and pulled himself on, the conductor said, "Hey, mista! Whatcha name? Where ya from?" I thought he sounded Italian.

Dad panted his way through saying, "I'm Ralph—from Ohio."

"Well, Ralph from Ohio . . ." He paused. "Here in California, we usually get on before the trolley departs. It's an intelligence thing. Have a seat." Ooh! A bunch of people cracked up at that insult, and I felt myself go red in the face. Dad simply smiled his goofy smile and stood up to shake his hand, like the guy wanted to greet him formally or something. "Mista, sit down before ya hurt ya'self."

After several blocks we hopped off the cable car at Lombard Street. The twins and Dad waved to the conductor, but I lowered my head, still far too embarrassed by my idiotic father to join in.

"Hey, girls. Check this out. This is the crookedest street in the world!" Dad happily exclaimed, jumping up and down like a puppy discovering a bone. "Let's walk down the sidewalk and then come back and drive Blue Pierre down it. You can sit on the roof and use the movie camera to take some groovy footage."

We walked down the zigzag sidewalk, turned left, and headed back toward the wharf on Leavenworth.

"Do you know how those cable cars work?" Dad questioned us, using the tone that he always did before diving into a lecture.

I wasn't in the mood for it. "You are so embarrassing!" I scolded, another outburst on the horizon. "Everyone was laughing at you for not getting safely on the cable car like a regular person!"

"Okay," Dad said. He blinked as though he'd already forgotten about the incident and was quick to shrug it off. "But do you know how those cable cars work?"

I sighed. There was no way an old dog like him would ever learn a new trick.

"No, how?" I said, humoring him. I took a breath and then added, "There was no motor or exhaust, I noticed."

The girls were skipping in front of us; they didn't care about how cable cars worked.

"You're right, Mare. The conductor has a handle that he squeezes—when he's not insulting his paying passengers, that is." He laughed. "And then that connects or disconnects to the cables that are always moving beneath the streets. So hooking onto the cable makes it go, and letting go of the cable stops it."

"That's far-out," I said half-heartedly, catching a whiff of some fragrant jasmine. There was a large bush of it growing up a brick fence, and I plucked a sprig of the dainty pink and white flowers. When I inhaled, its little petals fluttered into my nostrils. It was heavenly.

"Oh, now you're a flower child," Dad remarked. He didn't roll his eyes, but I could hear it in the tone of his voice. I didn't care. I liked the flower sprig behind my ear. "When in Rome, I guess. Let's go to the fish market and get shrimp cocktails," he suggested.

When we got to the bottom of the hill, he pointed at a man who was completely covered in silver body paint. Even his hair was silver, and he wore silver clothes and shoes. He stood perfectly still, and had Dad not pointed him out, I might've not noticed him at all.

"Look at that fellow," Dad said.

"He looks like a statue!" Jill said in awe.

"And he doesn't move a muscle," Gerri noted.

"Do people give him money for that?" I asked. I stared at him for a full minute, and he didn't blink, not even once—unless he blinked at exactly the same moment I did and I missed it. I was trying to think whether that was a talent or not. Regardless, I reached for a dime in my pocket and tossed it into the box by his feet.

We crossed the street and entered the wharf area. The overpowering smell of brine and fish and seaweed was strong enough to make my eyes water and was accompanied by a distant chorus of noisy barking seals.

"Can you hear that?" I cocked my head to listen. "Can we get the shrimp cocktails to go and then watch the seals?"

"Sounds like a good idea, but these ones are called sea lions," Dad said with a grin. We ordered four of the spicy shrimp cocktails, each served in a small red-and-white gingham-printed paper boat. The shrimp were arranged neatly, their tails curled slightly. The cocktail sauce, deep red and tangy, was served on the side, along with a lemon wedge and a small plastic bag of oyster crackers. It was a bit of a handful, but the shrimp, with their fresh, briny flavor and the promising kick of the sauce, were worth the effort.

After carefully making our way to the sea lions, we sat on a bench and observed them frolicking and barking in the water and on the barnacle-encrusted crossbeams below the pier. It looked like they were playing king of the pier. They rolled and twisted gracefully in the rising and falling seawater, thoroughly enjoying themselves. Seagulls and pigeons squawked and cooed around us, evidently used to being fed by tourists, but none of us wanted to share.

I squeezed a lemon wedge on top of the small pile of shrimp, then used the plastic fork to spear them and dip them into the cocktail sauce. I ate slowly, trying to make the delicacy last, alternating between shrimp and crackers. The smiles on the twins' faces indicated they were enjoying this unfamiliar treat as much as I was, and Dad's lip smacking revealed the same.

I heard Dad say, "Look at those two homos." He pointed to a couple of men—one tall guy and one short guy—holding hands and walking toward us. "You can see all kinds of queer things here in San Francisco," he said dismissively, as though he'd just borne witness to a carnival freakshow.

"Homos? What's a homo?" the twins asked in mouth-stuffed-with-shrimp unison, as if their voices came from one shared mind.

"Faggot men who love each other." He let that sink in, and at once, I thought of how Meredith said that wasn't a nice word. "Do you get it? Men who 'love' other men," he said, air-quoting *love* and rolling his eyes. "They have relationships with each other—not with women."

Dad paused to gauge our reactions. If he was expecting us to be as disgusted as he was, then he was in for some disappointment. I didn't know about the twins, but I just looked back blankly, thinking again about Meredith's parents and how they didn't believe anything was bad about homosexual men. They suggested it was none of our business, and I agreed. The two homos—as Dad had called them—strolled by, carrying on a conversation until spotting a few baby sea lions and stopping to admire them.

Dad cleared his throat and added loudly, "They're an abomination, in my book, and according to the Bible." He raised his finger, making his point—and I glanced at the two men innocently taking in the sea lions beside us, horrified that they might've overheard. It didn't seem that they had, and I turned my rage on Dad.

"Really?" I said, biting my tongue. *Who are you to condemn someone else's behavior? You're an adulterer!*

Gerri and Jill hid behind me, as if sensing danger. The men began walking toward us again. I was intrigued and stared at them as they approached. They were clean-cut and handsome. Their hairstyles were short, and their blue jeans were tight. The tall one gave me a dazzling smile. I smiled back defiantly—for Dad's benefit. Then he hugged his boyfriend tighter and smiled even broader, almost showing off. The short one said something, and they both laughed. They looked like regular guys to me, even though I had never seen two grown men holding hands romantically like that before.

I swallowed before saying to Dad, "They look pretty harmless to me."

"Well. They're not," he responded quickly, eager to cut them down. "Don't let their good looks deceive you. They're unnatural. Unholy. An abomination. Repugnant. Just think what would happen to humanity if that was the norm," Dad lectured, his face getting as red as Rudolph's nose.

He'd started to raise his voice, and I was terrified he'd say something they would overhear, so I turned to face him, lowering my voice to a respectable level. "Well, it doesn't seem like they're the majority. Far from it. So I guess humanity is safe." I gave him a dull stare, emphasizing *humanity* in a way that made it clear I didn't think it was threatened at all. "It looks like they're minding their own business, but you're the one getting upset. Maybe *you* have the problem, Dad, not them."

I was seeing Dad differently. I had been for a while. When I looked back at him now, I saw a flawed human who was probably the product of his environment—believing the stuff he was told to believe, without question or critical thought.

Of course, I didn't used to think that Dad was perfect, but I had looked up to him, even copying some of his mannerisms and trying to mirror his charisma. I wanted his approval because I'd thought that meant something. I'd thought he had integrity, a good moral standing. Now I wasn't sure of that at all, and it left me with this bottomed-out feeling that wasn't nearly as nice as a ticklebelly.

I knew I'd eventually have to gather the nerve to talk to him about what happened in Wells, Nevada. Just then, I fully realized it was something I had to do. For myself. That would take guts and good timing.

For now, I held Dad's gaze, and I wondered if he was seeing me differently, too. How could he not be? What was he thinking? Probably that I wasn't his favorite daughter anymore or that he wished I'd been left behind with Skippy and removed from the Great American Road Trip.

He didn't say anything like that, though.

Instead, he merely shrugged, looking back at the sea lions as he said, "I'm only aligning with the values of the Bible, Mare. If I'm the one with the problem, then so is God."

✳ ✳ ✳

"Okay! Next stop, the crookedest road in the world—Lombard Street," Dad announced as we shuffled back into Blue Pierre, a grin on his face. "But this time, by car!"

We drove back up to the top of the hill, which took only a few minutes, and then waited in line behind several other motorists. Dad got the camera ready. I climbed out through the sunroof. "Exaggerate the corners," he instructed. "Like, pan back and forth to accentuate the curves. Know what I mean?"

"Okay, Dad. I got it."

He handed me the camera right as the motorists in front of us were driving off. I did my best filming the eight hairpin switchbacks and looked forward to seeing what the camera recorded. I tried to make sure to capture the beautiful flower gardens and picturesque houses.

When we got to the bottom, I slid back down into the car and put the camera back in its case.

"How are you girls doing?" Dad asked. "Tired? Or are you ready to go check out Chinatown?" He didn't wait for our answer. "San Francisco is so incredible. I want to see as much as we can."

"We want to go to Chinatown," Gerri answered for us.

"Can you believe this peninsula is basically a seven-mile by seven-mile square? How many square miles is that, twins?"

"Is that an area problem?" Jill said, asking Gerri more than Dad.

Her twin looked back at her, nodding. "Is it just seven times seven, then?"

"Forty-nine square miles?" Jill guessed, unsure.

"Is that a question or an answer, Jilly-Bean?" Dad inquired, grinning.

"An answer. Forty-nine square miles!" she stated.

"You got it," he confirmed. "You two will be math whizzes, like Mary, in no time." He smiled at me, and I reflexively smiled back. It was hard to hate him—and I was finding that it was even harder to fight with him, seeing as he was so good at shrugging things off.

Dad drove down Columbus through North Beach, which he told us was the Italian part of town. While we waited at a traffic light at Broadway, our gazes were drawn to the larger-than-life neon sign above the Condor Club that was impossible to ignore. The sign featured a big-busted blonde woman with red blinking nipples beneath her black bikini.

"Ooh! Have a look at that," Dad said, as if we had a choice. "That's a striptease bar. See the woman there? That's Carol Doda."

"Hard to miss," I remarked. "She and Wendover Will should meet."

"That's a good one, Mare," Dad said, chuckling. "Carol Doda is very famous."

"What for?" I asked, taking the bait.

"She was the first topless dancer in America. She was a go-go dancer during the sixties," Dad told us. He knew all kinds of disgusting and strange facts. "She was revolutionary."

"Revolutionary? Isn't that word usually reserved for when things get improved? Like, you know, countries gaining independence?" I scoffed. "Doesn't seem like being the first lady to shake her bare boobs for men is an improvement for women."

I heard Gerri and Jill chuckle, and I smirked. Ms. Chanel, my guidance counselor and the sponsor of our middle school's Women's Lib Club, would have been proud of me. I was proud of me. Boy, it felt good to talk back to Dad. He needed to realize he wasn't right all the time. In fact, more often than not, he was wrong.

We drove by the traffic light, leaving Carol Doda's blinking-nipple sign behind, and I wondered if she ever felt ashamed of herself. Maybe she didn't think she was revolutionary, either.

36

Woolly Mammoth

At Portsmouth Square, we grabbed an open parking spot next to the basketball courts, where a heated game was in progress. The area was framed in brick walkways, park benches, and trees. Farther in, I spotted buildings with Chinese-style architecture.

"This place is called the Heart of Chinatown," I announced, reading from the TripTik. "The first American flag raised in San Francisco was here—and Dad, the discovery of gold was announced here in 1848."

"Eureka!" Jill said.

"Eureka!" Gerri repeated.

"That's interesting, Mare," Dad said, parallel parking on the left side of the one-way street before shifting Blue Pierre into park. "You know, after that gold discovery, thousands of Chinese immigrants arrived, many settling right here in Chinatown. They helped build the railroads and shaped the city's culture. It wouldn't be San Francisco without them. Let's go find an authentic Chinese restaurant. Come on, troops."

We locked the car and walked through the park, coming across a statue of a ship rocking on a wild ocean with four golden sails blowing in full wind. I recognized the statue from the TripTik. "That statue is a memorial to Robert Louis Stevenson," I noted.

"Who is that?" Gerri asked.

"He's a very famous Scottish author," Dad interjected. *Should've known he'd take over. He can't resist.* "He wrote *Treasure*

Island and the *Strange Case of Dr. Jekyll and Mr. Hyde*, among other titles. He lived around here for a short time."

"What is *Dr. Jekyll and Mr. Hyde* about?" Jill asked.

"It's about this guy with a split personality," Dad began, his eyes lighting up. "Dr. Jekyll is this calm, respectable doctor, right? So he makes this potion and drinks it to see what happens. And guess what? Boom! Out comes his evil alter ego, Mr. Hyde." Dad shook his hands and made a goofy evil face, which caused us to giggle.

"Wait, what? Like, he turns into a whole different person?" Gerri asked, her eyes wide.

"Exactly! At first, he can control it—switching back and forth between his two personalities of Dr. Jekyll and Mr. Hyde—but," Dad said, leaning in dramatically, "the more he drinks the potion, the harder it gets to control, and Mr. Hyde starts taking over. Things get really bad—like, murder-level bad."

Gerri gasped, her hands flying to her mouth. "Murder? No way!"

"Yep. Eventually, Dr. Jekyll gets so freaked out about what Mr. Hyde might do that he . . ." Dad paused for effect, looking around at us.

"He kills himself?" Jill blurted out, almost whispering.

"That's right," Dad said, nodding. "In the end, they find Mr. Hyde's body, and there's a letter from Dr. Jekyll explaining the whole thing." The twins and I exchanged confused looks, trying to wrap our heads around Dr. Jekyll self-destructing in order to kill Mr. Hyde. "Anyway," Dad continued, "that's the original story. Nowadays, when people say *Jekyll and Hyde*, they mean someone who's like two different people—one nice, one not so nice."

Ha! He just described himself. Dad was just like Dr. Jekyll and Mr. Hyde. He tried to have people think he was like the good doctor, but his prominent streak of Mr. Hyde was always ruining all of Dr. Jekyll's progress. I wondered if he saw that about himself.

"Look at what the inscription says. Gerri," Dad said, turning to her. "Would you read it?"

Poor Ger. Ever since she was in that remedial reading class in third grade, she'd been asked to read stuff aloud by Dad. I guess it was to prove that she got over her reading problems—or to force her to keep practicing. Either way, it was an exercise that was always met with some level of mortification on her end.

"Okay." She took a preparatory breath. "'To be honest, to be kind—to earn a little, to spend a little less, to make upon the whole a family happier for his presence, to renounce when that shall be necessary, and not be '"—she paused to sound out the next word—"'em-bit-tered, to keep a few friends but these without cap-i-tu-la-tion . . .' What's capitulation?"

"It must mean something like keeping your friends, no matter what," I guessed, giving her a nod of encouragement. Jill did the same.

"Oh, okay." She referred back to the plaque. I felt sorry for her, slogging through such old-fashioned verbiage. "'Above all, on the same grim condition, to keep friends with himself—here is a task for all that a man has of for-ti-tude and delicacy.'" She sighed and shook her head. "Too many fancy words for me."

"You did an admirable job reading it, though," said Dad. I understood some of it, and I hoped that Dad would take some of it as advice for how to be a decent man, especially the parts about "to earn a little, to spend a little less" and "to make upon the whole a family happier for his presence."

I really hoped that he did try, but poor him—his Mr. Hyde part was too strong.

"Can we go to the playground before we have supper?" Jill asked.

"Sure thing."

We ran ahead, hopped on the swings, and started pumping. I loved swinging high and leaning way back, my hands grasping the chain all the way down near my legs on the sling seat and looking into the sky, making myself sick with dizziness.

Gerri jumped off her swing, and Jill followed suit. They ran over to the monkey bars and started at opposite sides. When they got to the middle, their customary challenge was to pass each other without dropping off. Laughing, they made it, jumping down when they reached the other side.

We took a sip from the water fountain before crossing over to Clay Street.

The shops and restaurants in Chinatown were filled with exotic objects. There were shop windows displaying rows of baked ducks—golden brown and shiny, featherless, hanging by their necks. I thought it was gross and sort of violent. A short Chinese woman pushed her way past us into the door and, in two minutes, came walking out, grasping a large dead duck by its neck, its feet flopping on one side and its head bobbing on the other. I turned to watch her march up the street with her purposeful little steps, the duck bouncing rhythmically against her leg.

We walked into the next place. It was like that toy store in Truckee, only Chinese-style. There were multicolored silk fabrics, shiny green jade jewelry and carvings, bins of fragrant teas, and unknown baked goods. Plastic toys and fans. Soy sauce, sesame oil, white pepper, cooking wine, ginger root. Chinese zodiac calendars. The twins and I each bought a fan for only fifty cents. Dad got some chow mein noodles. The twins looked wide-eyed at all the eye-catching, colorful vegetables and fruits that were displayed in crates on the sidewalk beneath the dusty awning.

I stopped abruptly at the next shop, fascinated by an enormous carved tusk in the window.

I asked Dad, "Is that an elephant's tusk? It's huge! Do you think an elephant was killed for this artwork? I hope not." I read the price tag and balked. "Holy crap! This is seventy-five thousand dollars! That's so much money for an elephant tusk!"

"Would you believe that it's a mammoth tusk?" Dad said, brows raised.

"Ha! Yeah, right. A mammoth? Like a prehistoric mammoth?" I asked incredulously. "A woolly mammoth?"

"Yes. Crazy, huh? Hard to fathom, I know. But there's a place in Russia where individual mammoths died, and then eventually, the whole species went into extinction about twelve thousand years ago. The people there harvest their remains, since they're long dead, and sell them to the Chinese, who do these incredible carvings."

"I can't believe it. That sounds so far-fetched. The animals died that long ago, and their tusks remained?"

"They were frozen, which preserved more of the animal— not just their tusks but sometimes their whole bodies, along with their skeletons, of course. I read about it in *National Geographic* or saw it on *Mutual of Omaha's Wild Kingdom* years ago. Some of them were so well preserved in the frozen tundra in northern Russia that, if you can believe it, modern Russian hunters could even eat the meat."

"What? Twelve-thousand-year-old meat?" I pondered the unimaginable. "It must be freezing up there."

"I think you were wondering if a live elephant was killed for this art, and the answer is no. Isn't that groovy?" he said while directing my attention toward the tusk. "Look at the carved scene." He squatted down and pointed. "There's an ocean, and boats, and fishermen, and a village, and temples and other pagodas, and people."

"I know. It's super beautiful." I crouched down to get a better look, too. "Can you see that little dog and cat there?" I pointed. "It kind of reminds me of a frozen doll house—a seven-ty-five-thousand-dollar doll house!" Gerri and Jill walked over from the vegetable display. I said, "This tusk is from a woolly mammoth!"

"What? That can't be. They're extinct," Jill said, assuming I was being *atastic*.

Gerri added, "You're tricking us, right?" I explained that we were not as we continued on our way. We perused the Chinatown markets for another half hour, in awe of the foreign trinkets, souvenirs, and architecture. It truly felt as though we'd left the United States of America and were all the way across the globe, in another country.

* * *

Eventually, Dad said, "I'm getting hungry. Let's eat." He gestured toward the Sam Wo Restaurant and said, "What about this place? It looks good."

The twins and I had no reason to object. Despite the Sam Wo looking a bit shabby from the outside—with crooked red lanterns hanging above the door and a torn menu taped to it—the steam-streaked windows revealed the sort of bustling activity within that suggested it wasn't a book to be judged by its cover. But either way, we didn't need convincing. It was the intoxicating smell emanating from the open front door that ultimately lured us in.

A busy woman escorted us past the noisy, steamy, and hectic kitchen on our right to the narrow stairway at the rear of the building, directing us to go upstairs. At the top of the steps, a loud waiter commanded another guest and his party of three to scoot over and make room for us at a long picnic table while he used the cloth he'd tucked into his apron to wipe the surface clean.

He rearranged the condiment jars and plunked down three menus. "You take one, you take one," he said to me and Dad, and then, "and you two copycats share," he said to the twins. "Heavy Duty, you hungry?" he asked me, pinching my cheek. *Heavy Duty?* "We have good food you like."

Dad laughed at the waiter's nickname for me. I didn't think it was funny. "How about you, Four Eye? You hungry like you Heavy Duty Daughter and you Copycat Kids?"

What was up with this guy? He had the whole restaurant laughing at us.

"I Edsel Ford Fong," he said, introducing himself, tapping his chest. "What you like eat? You like try jook? Our specialty."

"What is jook, Edsel?" Dad asked.

"Edsel Ford Fong, Four Eye. Jook is rice porridge. We have fish jook, pork jook, pork and pork organ jook, duck jook, beef jook, liver jook, chicken jook, plain jook." He rattled off the selections as though it were the millionth time he'd done so. It probably was. "You try?"

"What else is there?" I asked, a little afraid of the idea of rice porridge, even if it was their specialty. And the meats sounded kind of gross, especially after seeing the dead ducks hanging in the windows down on the street.

"Heavy Duty no like jook? We have dry mixed noodles, stir-fry noodles, fried rice, soup, curry, chop suey . . ."

"Can I just look at the menu for a minute?" I asked, trying not to be intimidated. "And is there a bathroom?"

"Washroom by stairs. Heavy Duty need minute," he said and turned his attention to another party.

I walked to the bathroom, weaving between the picnic tables and the diners alike, until finding the thin stairwell I'd spotted earlier. The restaurant smelled like rice and butter, which sounded oddly good at the moment, though I wasn't sure I could ask for something as simple as that.

The washroom was a dingy, closet-size room with a flickering light bulb and bright-red wallpaper. I took care of business, still racking my mind for what I'd like to order, and when I emerged a moment later, I practically ran face-first into Edsel Ford Fong, who had finished serving a nearby table.

He raised his brows at me and said loudly, "Heavy Duty no wash hands! Bad girl."

"There's no sink in there. Where can I wash my hands?" I said, my face reddening to match the color of the hot sauce on the table.

"Sink right there." He pointed. I saw the tiny sink there against the wall and went to wash my hands. My sisters started to get up, presumably to use the bathroom, too. "Copycat Kids now copy Heavy Duty."

Dang, what was up with this waiter? Dad thought it was hilarious and didn't mind being called Four Eye and evidently saw no need to defend us. I scooted back to my place at the communal table and whispered to Dad before Edsel Ford Fong returned, "What are you getting?"

"I think I'll try some of the jook. Do you see they also have wonton soup?"

"Oh, they do?" I felt a rush of relief. "I love that. I'll order that."

When the twins came out of the restroom, they went straight to the sink. "Smart Copycats," Edsel Ford Fong sang out. "Now what you like?"

"I'll have the duck jook and some egg rolls to share," Dad answered.

"No, Four Eye. You have fish jook with Chinese doughnut. It better. Heavy Duty?"

I chuckled under my breath. "Can I please have the combination wonton soup?" I said, and I hoped he wouldn't override me the way he did with Dad.

"Heavy Duty want wonton." Thankfully, he wrote that down on his notepad without rebuttal, sharply eyeing the twins next. "How about Copycats? What you like try?"

"Yang chow fried rice, please," said Jill, clearly and confidently. I was impressed.

"And I'll have the chicken chow mein," Gerri ordered.

Somehow he got our orders down to the kitchen, and in practically no time, our food arrived via the dumbwaiter—a little elevator on the other side of the bathroom at the rear of the restaurant. Edsel Ford Fong delivered our meals with a clatter, nearly spilling the wonton soup. The stainless-steel dome-lidded dishes were arranged in the center of the table, and we were given empty plates and bowls so that we could share the entrées.

"You Copycats and Heavy Duty know how use chopsticks? And how about Four Eye Daddy?"

"Oh yes, sir. We sure do," I said, even though we were not that proficient with them.

"Good," he barked. He plonked down four sets of chopsticks and four Chinese spoons for the soup.

"Man, he is one rude waiter," I whispered to my family when he turned his back.

"I think it's part of his schtick. His act. Insulting the customers is a novelty, and I bet it brings them back in droves," Dad guessed, prodding his jook with his chopsticks a few times before scooping some up and plunging it into his mouth.

We all paused, awaiting his assessment.

He nodded and grinned, then took another bite.

I decided to start with a so-called Chinese doughnut. "If you say so," I replied, taking a small bite. I didn't realize how hungry I was, and I'd greatly underestimated how good this food would be. I was quite glad that Edsel Ford Fong bullied Dad into ordering it. Assuming that the doughnut would be sweet, I was surprised by its savory and slightly salty flavor. It had a crispy exterior but was soft and airy on the inside. After submerging a corner of it in the family-size serving bowl of wonton soup, I plopped it in my mouth. I really wanted another, but I was already self-conscious about the nickname Heavy Duty and didn't want to live up to it.

"Ooh, this fried rice is *deyishous*," Jill said, her mouth full. "Here, Mare, try some of this." She spooned some onto my plate.

"Thanks, Jill. Who wants some of the wonton soup?" I asked. They all answered yes, so I ladled out four small bowls and passed them to everyone. We all tried each of the dishes, and there wasn't a single thing that wasn't *deyishous*, even the fish jook. After polishing off all the food, we pushed back from the table.

Edsel Ford Fong cleared our dishes and dropped four fortune cookies onto the table. "You read you fortune fast, Four Eye and Pink Kids. New customer need you seat."

Jill read hers first. "'Be careful who you trust. Salt and sugar look the same.'"

I liked that. Gerri followed. "'Everywhere you choose to go, friendly faces will greet you.'"

"What's yours say, Heavy Duty?" Dad asked jokingly.

"Very funny, Four Eye." I smirked. "Mine is . . ." I started to read it aloud, but my eyes gobbled up the fortune before my mouth could even begin: *It is honorable to stand up for what is right, however unpopular it seems*. I paused, heart beating fast. Was this some sort of sign?

Dad cleared his throat. "Do you need Gerri to read it out loud for you?"

"Ha ha. No," I said quickly, shaking my head. I decided to keep that private, not trusting myself to not just come out and confront Dad about Charlotte. "I'm just sorry it's so plain. It says, 'You will have a long and prosperous life,' and I can't argue with that. What's yours?"

He cracked the last cookie in two and read, "'In this world of contradiction, it's better to be merry than wise.' That suits me."

Oh brother, I thought. *Sure does.*

I folded my real fortune and put it in my pocket. We walked down the stairs, passing the hectic and steamy kitchen, and drifted out the door to the cool outside evening air.

"That was a trip," Dad said, pocketing the change from the fifteen dollars he'd spent on supper.

"That guy was crazy!" Jill tacked on, grinning.

"I've never been to a restaurant like that before," Gerri added.

"I'm so full." I recited TeenTeen's famous poem about over-eating: "I've eaten with the greatest efficiency. I've stuffed myself arousingly. I'm afraid if I eat anymore, I'll burst my trilakentrot." I added, "My *Heavy Duty* trilakentrot." That cracked them all up.

It had gotten dark out, and we made our way back to Blue Pierre under the yellow lights of Portsmouth Square.

"Where are we sleeping tonight, Dad?" Gerri asked.

"You mean, *Where are we sleeping tonight, Four Eye?*" her Copycat said, and we all laughed.

"I think we'll be safe sleeping in Blue Pierre tonight," Dad said. "What do you say?"

We snuggled into our car, Dad using the steering wheel to rest his head, me leaning against the passenger window, and the twins sleeping pushmi-pullyu in the back. We fell asleep in no time, even though the streetlights were bright overhead.

37

Rude Awakening

Tap, tap, tap.

What was that?

I stirred in my sleep, face pressed uncomfortably against the window.

TAP, TAP, TAP. Louder this time. I opened my eyes and saw that a cop was rapping on Dad's window with his billy club. Dang! I sat up in a jiffy, trying to wriggle out of my tangled sleeping bag, and shook Dad's arm. "Dad! Wake up!"

"Huh? What's going on?" He knuckled his eyes, reaching blindly for his glasses and teeth that he had left on the dashboard.

"Look!" I pointed to the sour-faced cop standing outside the window, hunched over, peering inside with a flashlight.

"Son of a pup!" Dad yelped. The twins were also showing signs of life, awakened by the abrupt knocking and my loud shouting. Was sleeping in your car against the law? Based on the way the cop was glaring at us, it had to be.

Dad coughed and tried to straighten up behind the steering wheel. He ran his tongue around his teeth. The cop stood there impatiently, tapping his baton into his hand, his hip cocked. Dad rolled down the driver's window. "Good morning, Officer. Officer O'Neill." He must've read the cop's name on the badge pinned to his chest. "What can I do for you?"

"Good morning, sir," the officer said. "Did you spend the night here in your car with your kids?"

"Is that against the law?" Dad asked.

"Sure is. Did you?"

"What if I said that we didn't spend the night here, that we were . . ." He swallowed, scrambling for an excuse. ". . . just having a rest?" Emboldened by his little story, I guess, he went on. "That we arrived very late and just needed a nap? Is that against the law?"

He is such a liar, I thought. *What if we just faced the consequences of the violation we'd committed? I'd think that a good father would want us to learn that kind of lesson.*

"Sir, that doesn't seem probable. It's five thirty in the morning. Not really napping hours, if you catch my drift." Dad seemed to think for a minute, still scheming. Officer O'Neill squinted into the car, getting a better look at us. "Girls, are you okay? I see from your license plates that you're from Ohio, far from here." He gestured to Dad. "Is this your father?"

I figured I'd answer for the three of us. "Yes, we're from Ohio, and this is our father." He kept examining me, so I continued, running my hands over my unruly, slept-in hair. "We're on a big Great American Road Trip for our summer vacation. We're about halfway done."

"Is that so?" The cop seemed unenthused. "Where's your mom?"

"We left her at home with Namo," Jill chimed in.

"Namo?"

"That's our dog," Gerri explained.

"Sir, can you please step out of the car? Girls, stay put." Dad struggled to untangle himself from his sleeping bag and awkwardly stumbled out of the car, nearly falling into the cop's arms. I cringed at the disaster unfolding before my eyes.

"Jaysus, mister," the cop said, shaking his head. "You're a mess."

"Well, yeah, you could say that."

The cop roughly grasped Dad's arm and began leading him away, near the fence of Portsmouth Square. I guessed he didn't want us to overhear anything. We saw Dad nodding and complying, and it irked me that he could be so respectful when he wanted to be. It proved that he really had more control over his behavior than I'd given him credit for. I couldn't blame Mr. Hyde if Dr. Jekyll was so willing to step aside and let him take over.

I scooted to the center of the front seat, straining to hear what they were saying, and frantically kicked my sleeping bag deep down into the dark footwell.

How bad was this infraction? I thought we'd only get a fine, but the way the officer thought we'd been kidnapped or something had me nervous. That was a lot more serious. I glanced at the rearview mirror and noticed the officer was now shining a bright flashlight in Dad's eyes, going slowly back and forth, and I realized with a jolt that he suspected Dad was drunk.

This wasn't good. Mom was right. This wasn't the first time Dad had put us in an uncomfortable situation on this trip. Jill started to say something, but I shushed her, trying to eavesdrop through the half-open window of the driver's seat. Seemed like Dad was trying to stick to his cockamamie story of not having spent the whole night there. Something about wanting to be here early to join the Chinese people in their tai chi practice. What the heck was he talking about? I bet the cop didn't believe him.

They walked back to Blue Pierre. "Okay, girls. Time to get up from your naps. The tai chi class we've been talking about is ready to start." Huh? The twins' questioning expressions matched mine. "Put on clothes for exercise."

The twins and I glanced at one another, trying not to look as clueless as we felt and go along with Dad's farce. We rolled up the sleeping bags and loaded them into the trunk, rummaging in our suitcases for appropriate clothing. We changed into sweatpants and sweatshirts with our privacy trick between the front and back passenger doors. All the while, the cop stood by, shaking his head in the way Mom would whenever Dad carried on with one of his charades for too long.

He didn't believe Dad's story.

I felt humiliated but terrified. What would happen to us if Dad got arrested?

I had to pee badly and was relieved to see public restrooms in Portsmouth Square on our way to where the people were gathering for their morning practice. We approached the group of about two to three dozen older Chinese people and copied what they were doing while the cop stood off to the side, watching us, arms folded across his chest. I wondered if he didn't have something more important to do. He pulled out his walkie-talkie and said something indecipherable.

We stood on the edge of the congregated group. The tai chi people were executing slow-motion, fluid movements that we tried to copy.

Dad whispered fiercely, "Try to do what they're doing. It might make the difference if we get a ticket or not. Do your best."

I glared at him and sighed.

Yet again, he was putting us in an uncomfortable situation. I wanted to tell him that if we got a ticket for illegally sleeping in our car in the city, *he* was the one to blame, not our tai chi skills—but my relief at hearing *ticket* over *arrest* won me over. I'd play along this time.

This was definitely a My Journal of Life entry. Looking at my little sisters giving it their all made me smile. They weren't half-bad at tai chi. Meanwhile, Dad looked clumsy and uncoordinated, no matter how hard he tried.

I focused on the slow and deliberate movements and really tuned in to my body. After only five minutes, my arms were aching. Tai chi was far-out. I could feel my heart pounding, even though the activity didn't seem that strenuous. I liked it. I *really* liked it.

We stuck with it for the full hour. After about the first fifteen minutes, I saw that our cop was still there watching us. But the next time I looked over, he was gone. Ha! It worked. Dad's lying paid off once again. The cop probably thought the whole thing was absurd. I sure did.

* * *

After we had made our tai chi escape from the cop, we zigzagged through the hilly city to the Mission District, where we ate Mexican breakfast burritos. They were made of chorizo, scrambled eggs, refried beans, avocado, and *pico de gallo*. I'd never had cilantro before. It made the salsa so fresh and light. We didn't have food like that in Ohio.

After saying farewell to beautiful San Francisco, we headed south following the curvy lines of the coast of Highway 1. The fog got so thick that we couldn't see the sun. If I hadn't stayed focused on the road ahead of us, I probably would've been carsick in no time. We parked about ninety minutes later near the Santa Cruz Boardwalk. Even though we'd had breakfast, my stomach growled in response to the smells of fried food and sugary candy floating through the air as we perused the boardwalk on foot.

Before I knew it, Dad was handing out snacks and treats like he'd hit the jackpot.

"I can't believe you bought us cotton candy!" Jill said, licking the stickiness off her fingers one by one. Gerri nodded in silent, mouth-stuffed agreement, shaking her hair behind her shoulders to get it away from the gluey mess.

I tried to channel Meredith's s'mores hygiene by pinching off pieces of the baby-pink and baby-blue candy floss and inserting the sweetness into my mouth without letting my fingers touch my lips. This would keep everything from getting sticky. *So far, so good.*

Dad was gnawing away on a candy apple—its hard red shell breaking into shards when he bit into it. The fallen, cracked pieces shimmered like glass on the asphalt of the amusement park.

"Well, it's not that often you're in sunny California at the famous Santa Cruz Beach Boardwalk, smack-dab on the ocean, is it, girls?" Dad swallowed his bite of apple. "I bought twenty tickets for each of us for rides. Where should we start?"

"Let's start on the Ferris wheel!" Jill pleaded. "That way we can view everything from above and see what else there is to ride."

We couldn't disagree with her logic and began migrating toward it. The boardwalk's Ferris wheel rose high above the ocean, right at the edge of the beach—and I noticed with a jolt that each seat was only suitable for two people.

"I'll ride with you, Jill," I hastily said. Gerri gave me a strange look.

"Okay, Mare," Jill answered.

That left Gerri and Dad as companion passengers. We paid the attendant three tickets each and pocketed the remainder. Jill and I got on first, and while Dad and Gerri were being buckled into their car underneath us, Jill and I swung our legs to get our car to swing.

"Hey, you two, read the signs! No rocking the cars!" the attendant shouted up to us.

Dad laughed. We stopped rocking, the low whine and creak of the car coming to a halt. I tilted my face over the bars holding us in and peered down at Dad and Gerri, who were making conversation as the Ferris wheel bumped them up to seat the next people.

My original goal of pairing up with Jill was to avoid sitting with Dad, but I realized quickly that this unexpectedly led to a rare opportunity for us to speak together alone—with *privacy*—which was almost impossible with twins who stuck to each other like white on rice.

I cleared my throat and thought vaguely of the fortune cookie words I had folded up in my pocket. I hadn't planned for this, but it was now or never.

"Jill, did you tell Gerri about Dad and what you saw at the motel?" I whispered, spitting it all out at once. I don't know what I was anticipating, but I didn't expect her to look away from me so fast, her face all shades of guilty. "I hope not. One of us should stay innocent and unknowing."

"Mary, I'm so sorry." She looked down and wouldn't meet my eyes.

"What? Jill!" I berated. "You promised!"

"I couldn't help it. She knew something was wrong!" Neither of us spoke, and then she added, "Mary, come on. She's my twin, for heaven's sake. Besides, I didn't tell her *everything*."

"You didn't? Well, that's good."

Noticing a little bit of cotton candy stuck to the back of her hand, she licked it off, then looked up at me. "It's partly your fault I told her anything at all, actually."

"How is *your* spilling the beans partly *my* fault?"

"Well, if you weren't acting so weird, she wouldn't have kept asking about it."

Dang. I had to concede that that made sense.

We summited the top of the wheel. All the cars were loaded now, so the attendant was letting it go without stopping for more passengers. We got ticklebellies on the way down. When the timing was just right, we could wave at Dad and Ger. Jill and I halted our conversation as we raised our hands and yelled in delight, taking in the swell of waves, the sunbathers and colorful umbrellas on the shore, the sweet and fried smells, and the bright and gleeful sights of the amusement park. The arcade music was accompanied by bells ringing and callouts for the winners.

After five full revolutions, we dismounted before Gerri and Dad. While we waited, I tried to take advantage of what little time we had left to talk. "So what does Gerri know?"

"Well . . ." Jill hemmed and hawed.

"Come on, the harm's done already. Just tell me."

"Okay," she said. "I told her that we saw a lady with Dad in the morning while she was still asleep and that she was a prostitute and that Dad had paid her."

So Gerri *did* know the full extent of it.

"What? That is everything!" I hissed under my breath. "You said you didn't tell her everything!"

"I didn't! She asked if Dad had paid to sleep with her, why he didn't go to the brothel—cuz, you know, that's what he said brothels were about—and I made up something about it being like a brothel to go and that a prostitute had a sleepover at his hotel room."

A slumber party? Maybe they really didn't have a clue. That would be nice.

"Oh brother. A brothel to go?" I couldn't help suppressing a smirk. That was a good one.

"Yeah. We don't really know what it means, and don't tell me." She put her hand up, reminding me of the stop-sign hand Mom had raised to Dad during their checkbook fight. But I needed to know what she knew, *exactly*, so that I could manage my worry. I'd had enough turmoil going on about the fact that this whole thing even happened, and I didn't want to also be worrying that the twins learned about sex way too young.

"What do you think paying for a prostitute means?" I asked her directly, going for the straightforward approach. I could see Dad and Gerri walking toward us. *Come on,* I thought.

"That a man gives some money to a prostitute"—it sounded like she enjoyed saying this new multisyllabic word—"and she sleeps with him so that he's not lonely. It helps his beaver fever."

Oh my goodness!

That was a wonderfully naive and confused understanding. I wouldn't have to worry about them really comprehending the full meaning of the situation. I thought back to Dad's explanation of beaver fever in Blue Pierre earlier on our trip and realized I'd caught on to the fact that it was a sexual reference, but the twins obviously wouldn't have. This was a welcome relief, but I still had the problem of managing my own true understanding of Dad's depravity—and a selfish part of me was disappointed that, once again, I was alone in this.

"What are we going to do?" I lamented, grasping Jill's shoulders and facing her toward me. We only had a few seconds before Dad and Gerri were upon us. They were holding hands, smiling and laughing and completely oblivious.

"What do you mean, *what are* we *going to do*? You mean, what are *you* going to do. You said that if you end up talking to him about it, you wouldn't let him know that I know. I just want to forget about it. You're more bothered about it than I am."

That's because you don't really understand the full implications, I thought. I envied that innocence, even as her determination to keep it made me feel even more alone. She wasn't secretly worrying about our parents getting divorced, either.

"Okay," I said, resigning myself. "What am *I* going to do?"

I hated all these secrets and keeping track of who knew what, but protecting Gerri was worth all the hassle. I agreed with Jill's suggestion that if I really had to talk to him about it, I should wait for a time when it was just him and me and keep Jill out of it.

The four of us made our way through the throng of people to the Giant Dipper, where we prepared to wait in line for their famous old-fashioned roller coaster. Jill and Gerri were identical in so many ways, but as far as roller coasters were concerned, Gerri was deathly afraid of them while Jill couldn't get enough. Somehow we had convinced Gerri that this roller coaster was super smooth and safe and low-key. We also told her it was called the Big Dipper—her favorite constellation—thinking that her knowing it was actually called the Giant Dipper would make her have qualms about riding it. Go figure, but it worked. She was willing to give it a try.

"I'll ride with Ger," I said, leaving Dad and Jill as a duo. Jill gave me a smirk. The line of people made its way up the ramp toward the loading area. "Since you're being so brave, Ger, want to sit in the front car? You won't have to raise your arms if you don't want to," I assured her, and to all our surprise, she agreed.

Our train approached the loading zone, and I had to get behind her and give her a little push toward the front car. "I can't do it," she groaned, suddenly rooted to the spot. My thoughts rushed to the memory of Meredith trying to slice her fingertip.

"Yes you can. I'll hold your hand if you're scared," I said. She grabbed my hand before we even stepped into the car. "Good job, Ger-Bear."

Dad and Jill loaded up behind us, and Jill reached forward and gave Ger a pat on the shoulder. The attendant came over and made sure that the buzz bars across our laps were secure. Once everyone was fastened in, the roller coaster lurched forward with a big chuff. Gerri shrieked. She was squeezing my hand so tightly that my fingers were losing circulation.

"Ger, take a big breath. You'll be okay. *Really*," I said, trying to dispel her fear. She inhaled and exhaled. "There you go," I said as the train continued its spastic surges forward before smoothing out and ascending the first giant incline. We'd lied. It was not a smooth ride.

Clickety-clackety, clickety-clackety. The lift pulled us upward. I turned my head and saw Dad and Jill, both grinning maniacally from ear to ear.

Dad yelled out just in time, "Girls, take off your glasses!" The three of them grabbed at their eyeglasses and held on to them. Before reaching the summit, I had just a second to remind Gerri that she loved ticklebellies before we hurtled down the first and largest descent.

My stomach fell, and I raised my arms overhead. My hand, clasped to Gerri's, lifted hers up, and to my astonishment, she raised her other one, too, still holding on tight to her glasses. She was going all in. *Way to go, Ger,* I thought. *That's how to really face a fear.* I told myself I would draw from her courage when I finally spoke to Dad.

Zooming along the wooden rails, we banked to the left and then to the right and then through a rapid succession of several smaller hills that gave little ticklebellies at the top of each crest. As we approached the end of the ride, I was laughing my head off and saw that Gerri was, too. The ride had one more hill before it started its jerky brake sequence. It parked itself back at the station a minute later, where we jolted to an abrupt stop.

After lifting off the buzz bar and staggering out of our car, Gerri said, "Let's do that again!"

I laughed and gave her a thumbs-up. We each still had enough tickets, so we walked out and got right back in line.

* * *

For supper we had corn dogs and french fries and took them down to the beach. It was a junk-food junkie kind of day. Dad didn't care about the wait-one-hour-before-swimming rule, so we waded and splashed in the little waves as soon as we finished our corn dogs.

By now, the sun was sinking low, just above the horizon, and the ocean's surface shimmered like a million tiny mirrors reflecting the light. It was so bright I had to turn my back to the waves, squinting and shielding my eyes. It felt a little wrong to look away, though—after all, this was our first time at the ocean.

The beach was incredible, a giant mosaic of colors and life, even smells. Pale sand stretched out beneath a patchwork of human faces, brightly colored towels, umbrellas, and bouncing beach balls. The Santa Cruz Beach Boardwalk loomed in the background, all flashing lights and sounds and the smell of *dey-ishous* carnival foods. Standing there, feeling the water lap at my legs, I realized this was another one of those moments I'd be adding to My Journal of Life.

The ocean wasn't just water; it was alive—vast, endless, and powerful. Its pull tugged at my feet, making me feel small, but in a good way, like being part of something so much bigger than myself. I wrote the words in my head as I stood there: *First time in the ocean—felt like standing at the edge of forever.*

I tried bodysurfing and scraped my thighs and belly on the cold, rough sand. The undertow pulled me right back out, and I was washed off my feet. Sputtering when I came up, I shook my hair and got knocked over again. I learned that it was not a good idea to turn your back on the ocean, even if it meant keeping the sun out of your eyes. The next time I surfaced, I spun around, refusing to be caught off guard again, and it felt like I was an actor on stage, blinded by the spotlight. Farther out, it appeared that the twins and Dad weren't having any more luck holding their ground than I was.

The salty water wasn't as bad as at the Great Salt Lake, thank God, but it sure made our noses run. I kept wiping and blowing my nose. I floated on my back for a while, but the salty water and bright sun were too strong to do that for long. I gave up and paddled to shore, but before I lay down, I saw a full sand dollar just lying right there, begging me to pick it up.

I collected the fragile beach treasure, marveling at its beautiful symmetry before wrapping it in the napkin from my corn dog and hoping I wouldn't break it. Stretching out on the sand and closing my eyes, I added the sand dollar, the beach, and the boardwalk to My Journal of Life before Dad and the twins joined me.

We each had a few tickets left and walked back through the uneven sand to use them up at the carousel nearby. While we waited in line, we noticed that this merry-go-round was quite unique. If you were on one of the hand-carved horses on the outside, you could grab a small metal ring from a dispenser as you passed by on each revolution. Then you were supposed to toss it into a big hole in the wall of the platform, shaped like a clown's mouth. If you made it, the lights and bells would go off. I really wanted to hit the target.

We each selected an outside horse to have a go at collecting and throwing the rings, but in the end, only Gerri succeeded, even though we all had about a dozen chances. There were signs that said not to take the rings, but I snuck one into my pocket—next to the sand dollar and the slip of paper my fortune had been written on—keeping it as a souvenir anyway.

It was starting to get late, and we needed to find someplace to sleep. Before that, though, we drove Blue Pierre to the wharf to get a bird's-eye view of the surfers on Cowell's Beach. The waves would come in sets, and you could see that the surfers must have had rules about who could paddle into the wave to ride it. Only one surfer ended up on any given wave at a time. They would bob along for a long while before the next set came in, and then they seemed to know just where the best place was to catch the wave.

I remember telling Jenny from AAA how I'd wanted to see the surfers—and now I had.

It looked super fun but also very scary, if the tiny bit of unsuccessful bodysurfing I had tried earlier was any indication.

We drove toward Steamer Lane to get a close-up of the surfers getting tubed. I was glad Dad pulled out the Super 8 and took some footage for our ongoing movie.

Dad said it wouldn't be a problem to sleep in or next to Blue Pierre that night since you could see that there were lots of vans and other cars that people seemed to be car-camping in. Santa Cruz was more mellow than San Francisco. "Don't think the likes of Officer O'Neill care about car-campers here," he said, chuckling to himself.

There was a restroom with showers that looked like it was for the surfers and other beachgoers, so the twins and I did a good job washing up that night, shampooing and combing through our hair. We even flossed our teeth.

38

Crumbs of Trust

"*I was talking* to one of the surfers, and he told me that we just *have* to find a private beach in Big Sur." Dad imitated him and gave us the hang-loose hand sign. "That is the best way, dude, to get to know Lady Pacifica," he drawled in surfer-ese. I laughed and rolled my eyes at how weird that sounded coming out of him, the dorkiest dork around.

The ocean's breeze highlighted Dad's need for a haircut. His receding hairline looked even worse with the unruly mop flopping above it. It almost seemed like he had a toupée that was coming unglued or something. To save a buck, I often trimmed his hair for him at home—Mom passing that task along to me when I showed interest a couple of years ago.

I was making a very sincere effort to try to hide my true disgusted feelings toward Dad, but I had a hard time seeing myself combing through his icky hair and cutting it like I used to. I didn't even want to touch him. The very notion gave me shivers I couldn't seem to shake off.

I knew I'd have to confront him soon, but the four of us were always together.

"What's so special about Big Sur?" Jill asked from the back seat, looking up from her notebook.

I turned around in my seat to see what she was doing. "Are you adding to the Slate of Dates, States, and Fates?" I asked her. She started to answer that she was, only for Dad to bore a hole in my periphery with an acid-hot stare.

"Why do you always interrupt, Mary?" he scolded, giving me a frown and a shake of his head, like I should know better. For some reason, this really set me off. *He* should know better! What right did he have to criticize me? I just had a bad interrupting habit—and I was only thirteen. He was much worse than that and a full-grown man!

I sat straight back in my seat and bit my tongue, but I knew I wouldn't be able to hold everything in much longer. I thought maybe I should just blurt it out right now and come what may, as far as Gerri's poor innocence was concerned. Better yet, maybe I'd wait until he started speaking again and then interrupt him with this: YOU HAD SEX WITH A PROSTITUTE! YOU ARE DISGUSTING! YOU LIE AND CHEAT! THE COMMANDMENTS ARE A JOKE TO YOU! YOU ARE A MARRIED MAN WHO LOVES TO GIVE SERMONS ABOUT INTEGRITY AND COMMITMENT, BUT YOU HAVE NO INTEGRITY! YOU ARE HORRIBLE! YOU BETRAYED MY TRUST! YOU BETRAYED MOM! I DON'T HAVE A TRUSTWORTHY FATHER ANYMORE! I MIGHT NOT EVEN HAVE A REAL FAMILY ANYMORE!

"I'll tell you about Big Sur, Jill," he started, clueless of my pounding heart and seething thoughts. "It's a ninety-mile stretch of gorgeous beachfront terrain. Supposedly, it's the most scenic drive in all of California."

I drowned out his lecture about how picturesque Big Sur was as I tried to pull myself together. The best I could do was scoot away from him and lean my head against the window, taking deep breaths and acting as if I were asleep. I wished I could go back to sitting in the back seat, but pretending to be asleep up front wasn't too bad; Dad left me alone, at least.

I must have actually fallen asleep because the next thing I knew, we were pulling off the highway to get a view of the Bixby Creek Bridge. It looked a little like that rainbow bridge we saw back in Truckee, but this one was larger and reached over a harrowing gorge with a big drop to the rugged coastline below. I was glad I woke up in time to see it. And thankfully, the nap had settled me down a little.

"There's a beach here with purple sand," Dad read from the Pacific guidebook he'd rested on Blue Pierre's hood. He looked up at us. "Purple sand, can you believe it?"

"Purple sand?" The twins did their same-speech-at-the-same-time trick. I smiled.

Dad laughed and referred to the guidebook. "Yes. It's from the manganese garnet particles from the water that comes down from the cliff, and there's Keyhole Rock there, too." He squinted at the guidebook's tiny writing while pushing his bifocals up his nose to get a better look.

"What's Keyhole Rock?" Jill asked, shuffling her foot in the gravel shoulder of the road and scaring away a little ground squirrel that was approaching. I crouched down, holding Jill's foot still while offering a cracker crumb I'd found in my sweatshirt pocket for the squirrel. The little creature hesitated, its tiny body tense with uncertainty.

"Shh. Stay still," I whispered.

Dad and the girls fell silent, watching as the squirrel took a few tentative steps toward my outstretched palm. Maybe it was hunger, or maybe it was just curiosity, but after a moment of hesitation, it made its choice—it walked right onto my hand and grabbed the cracker.

I could barely believe it.

Its scratchy little claws startled me, and I almost jerked my hand away on instinct, but I held still. That was the thing about trust—you had to stay steady, even when it felt unnatural. The squirrel sat back on its haunches, grasping the tiny speck of food with its dainty hands, nibbling away like it had always belonged there.

With my free hand, I rummaged in my pocket, searching for more. Another crumb, another offering. That's how it always worked—one step at a time, one small gesture at a time.

I thought about Dad. The way he could flash a grin, say the right thing, and suddenly, I wanted to believe him again. I wondered if I was like this squirrel, too hungry for scraps to see the bigger picture. After it had its fill, the squirrel turned tail and scurried off, vanishing into the trees. It didn't look back.

I exhaled, only just realizing I'd been holding my breath. Wow. Another Journal of Life entry there.

"Holy cow, Mare. That was neat." Dad smiled and winked at me, and I smiled right back as if nothing was amiss. What was wrong with me? I hated that I was so prone to forgiving him so quickly and so obviously in want of his affection. I think a deep, dark part of me still refused to believe that the old Dad I'd always known was dead and replaced by the new Dad I despised.

"So, yeah, this Pfeiffer Beach I was starting to tell you about not only has that purple sand but also a big rock formation in the ocean that has a hole—a keyhole, they call it—that goes right through it. It's supposed to be kind of hard to find, so we'll all want to be on the lookout. And there are some tide pools, it says, too."

Again with their trick, the twins said, "What are tide pools?"

"I've never seen one, but I think they're pockets of stone that have little sea creatures in them. The tide rises and lowers, so sometimes the tide pools are flooded with seawater, and then when the tide goes back out, the water recedes, and a puddle is left."

"That sounds groovy. So if we're there when the tide is low, we can see the animals inside the tide pools, right?" Gerri shifted her weight and reached behind herself to casually pull her bathing suit out of her crack.

"Got a wedgie, Gerri?" I laughed.

"Not anymore!" She glowered at me, irritated.

Dad waited until my teasing was over and said, "Not only can you see them, but you can touch them. There should be starfish and sea anemones—"

Jill interrupted with a snort. "Sea enemies?"

"No, anemones," he corrected, chuckling. "I don't remember the difference between sea urchins and sea anemones, but they're both in tide pools. Their tentacles kind of grab on to you when you touch them." He scratched his temple. "And crabs and mussels and barnacles."

"Come on, Dad. If you've never seen one before, how do you know about them? Is it a been-around-the-block thing?" I challenged.

"Actually, I've just looked at these pictures and read the descriptions from this book." He indicated the guidebook on the hood of the car, whose pages were now fluttering in the wind.

❋ ❋ ❋

We got back on Highway 1 and followed its twisty lines farther south in search of Pfeiffer Beach, but even after forty minutes, we never did come across a sign.

"Let's see if we can find tide pools down there and follow that surfer's advice about locating a private beach," Dad suggested, pulling onto a side street that meandered toward the ocean at a point on the highway that veered away from the shoreline. We coasted along the paved road until its surface changed from asphalt to dirt and gravel. Rumbling along for another quarter mile or so, we were getting closer and closer to the water's edge. The road narrowed, and the car filled with dust through the open windows and roof.

Dad coughed. "Hey, girls—roll up your windows, will you?"

As the road tapered, pricker bushes got close enough to scratch Blue Pierre's sides. They were large, thorny, fruit-bearing bushes, clawing at the car's paint like fingernails raked over a chalkboard. I thought Dad would want to abort this mission for sure, but he kept going.

"Mare," he prompted grumpily. "Your window."

I started cranking it shut, but a branch was too quick. Almost out of nowhere, it snuck inside Blue Pierre, slapping me across the cheek and drawing blood.

"Ouch!" I screeched, touching my face and wincing. "Why are we driving on this road that's not even a road anymore?" I sulked, dabbing a finger over my new cut. I rolled up my window the rest of the way and shut out the shrubs. "Those bushes have to be ruining Blue Pierre's paint job!"

I guess Dad saw my point because he switched the ignition off and rolled to a stop. Dust clouds floated skyward in plumes but eventually settled. Blue Pierre ticked and garbled, as it normally would for a while, but otherwise all I could hear was the moan of the wind.

Or was that the roar of the ocean below?

"Let's walk along the road a bit farther and get to the ocean on foot from here," Dad proposed.

I choose to wear my Dr. Scholl's wooden sandals rather than my Keds. I figured they would be more comfortable to slip on and off once we got to the beach, even though Jill and Gerri argued that our Keds were better walking shoes.

They were right. That was *Mistake Number One*.

The twins put on their jean shorts and T-shirts over their bathing suits and slung their towels across their shoulders. Dad looked kind of the same as they did. I didn't see the logic in wearing extra items of clothing. I'd just get wet in the ocean, and it would be nicer to dry off without additional clothes on, so I took off my outer clothes and wore just my brown bikini.

That was *Mistake Number Two*.

I wrapped my towel around my middle. All four of us put on our baseball hats, and we started down what had devolved from a dirt road into a dirt path. It felt like we were going through a green tunnel, parting the foliage like Moses through the Dead Sea.

"Isn't this an adventure?" Dad said cheerfully. "We should be at the water in no time."

Yeah, sure, I thought *atastically*.

Gerri and Jill didn't even reply—they just stomped along, ducking and trying to avoid the plants swinging back and slapping them like whips. I reached up and felt that the blood on my cheek had dried. My hair was sticking to my sweaty face and neck. I looked back, and everyone was sweating—and I could tell I wasn't the only one who wasn't really enjoying this so-called adventure anymore.

A few minutes later, believe it or not, the path constricted even more—and then it just felt like 100 percent bushwhacking, with no footpath at all.

The shoes I'd chosen were ridiculous, slipping and losing traction. Every once in a while, my foot would slide out and then land on the hard wooden sole crookedly, and I'd cry out in pain and annoyance. I knew I was acting kind of babyish, but there was no guarantee we'd get to the ocean this way, and we practically needed machetes to get through this jungle.

"Dad," I began, voice whiny, "I don't think this is going to get us to the water."

"Nonsense, Mary. We've taken the advice of an experienced local."

"But look at us," I argued, gesturing wildly all around. "We're not even following a trail anymore, and even if we do get to the water, I can't imagine having to hike all the way back to Blue Pierre. What if we get lost without a trail?"

"Trust the process, Mare," Dad said, charging us forward.

At this point, I just wanted to get this over with—whether that meant arriving at the ocean or finally meeting a dead end. Determined, I plunged ahead even faster. I'd led the way for no more than a minute before I needed to come to an immediate and abrupt halt because we were on the precipice of, no joke, about a seventy-foot drop-off to the beautiful and inviting sand and sea below.

"Stop!" I yelled before Jill walked into me and accidentally pushed me over the edge. "We're on a cliff! Stop! Stop!"

I grabbed nearby plants with both hands to hold on. I can't remember feeling that scared about anything ever before. The fear was mixed with gratitude that I had been looking where I was going so that I hadn't just blindly stepped off the ledge. *Holy crap!* As TeenTeen would say, "Two and two are four and shit is eight!"

I staggered backward and fell into the plants, landing on Jill, who dominoed onto Gerri.

Ashes, ashes, we all fall down, I thought as I heard a big galumph out of Dad when he hit the ground, too.

We sat there, astonished, catching our breaths at what could've been a life-ending catastrophe.

I took off my hat, pushed my hair off my face, and wiped the sweat from my brow. When I looked down, I saw that my nearly naked body was lashed with countless scratches that were already beginning to welt and swell. The towel around my middle and the flimsy swimsuit had offered me no protection whatsoever.

I looked back at the twins and was glad to see that their scratches were limited to just their lower legs and forearms. Dad had even worn his tall, nerdy tube socks so that only his knees were a little scraped up. He was the least damaged of us all. I tried not to cry at the disappointment and pain, but I felt a lump form in my throat and my eyes well up. I brushed the tears away gruffly, tried to swallow the lump, and attempted to stand. We were all still tangled, so I plopped back down and waited, catching my breath.

"That was a close one," Dad said, unfazed, even though his daughter—*ME!*—had been two steps away from certain death. "I guess we're not seeing tide pools here."

That's what he was thinking about?

"Why did we do this? This was stupid. Stupid, stupid, stupid!" As I yelled the words, I threw my hands up in the air. I twisted around and looked pointedly at Dad, shaking my head. "So dumb!"

Here was just another example of him not thinking things through, getting us into trouble due to a total lack of forethought. What if I'd tripped at the wrong moment in these stupid shoes and stumbled off this cliff and died on this Great American Road Trip? I'd come so close to that, and yet Dad didn't seem to care at all. This was what Mom was afraid of. This was why she didn't think Dad was competent enough to take us all the way across the country and back in one piece!

What if I'd died? Somehow, I couldn't shake that off. What would Dad have told Mom?

"Get off me, would you, Jill?" I barked. She wriggled away, taken aback at my nastiness. I pushed past them, tripping and falling before stomping toward the car.

Going back was even worse than coming down—as I'd predicted. It was uphill, hotter, the new scratches and abrasions added insult to injury, and there was no hope of an ocean dip at the end. After what seemed like forever, I finally emerged from the thicket and furiously kicked off the stupid Dr. Scholl's sandals and baseball hat I'd donned. I slid straight into my sleeping bag in the back seat, despite the heat. The fabric felt comforting and smooth on my raw and injured skin, and more importantly, I'd once again secured a reprieve from Dad's company.

When Gerri and Jill and Dad finally made it back to the car, I heard them open the trunk. I peeked out to see that they were using our gallon jug of fresh water to rinse off their arms and legs and faces. I answered Dad's question of "Hey, Mare? You want to rinse off your scratched skin?" by burrowing farther into the sleeping bag. Then he said to Gerri, "Go on and ask Miss Grumpy Pants if she wants some water."

I don't know why I told her to buzz off. She hadn't done anything wrong. I refused the water, *Mistake Number Three*, and feigned sleep as the twins climbed into the front and Dad put Blue Pierre in reverse until he could turn around and get us on the road south again.

We drove and drove, sleeping that night—dispersed camping style, of course—in Topanga State Park, just west of Los Angeles. The pounding waves lured us to sleep like a lullaby, but I still lay wide awake for longer than everybody else. My heart was pounding, and my skin was stinging, and all I could do was mentally rehearse how I'd confront Dad. Obviously, I fantasized about making it clear to him that I'd witnessed undeniable evidence of his adultery, but something new had cropped up to the forefront of my mind.

I wanted—no, I *needed*—Dad to show some accountability, for once. I needed him to realize exactly how immature he was as a person. I needed him to know that Mom was right about him and that I was taking her side.

My rehearsal went on for too long, and eventually, I told myself to go to sleep. I rolled over, eyes peering skyward, and wondered why the stars were not visible.

39

Tide Pools

The next morning, Dad woke us up early. There was only a spill of pale yellow bleeding into the sky, along with baby blues, pinks, other pastels, and even a few stubborn stars that peeked out behind the low clouds.

"The tide is low," Dad said. "Let's go check out the pools."

I was amazed that he was going strong. We had arrived at this place after midnight, and now it was just after sunrise. We'd barely slept more than six hours, and I'd gotten even less sleep than that.

Gerri and Jill scrambled out of their bags, gathering their bathing suits. I sighed, thinking over whether or not I wanted to carry yesterday's attitude into today. Like everything else, Dad deserved it, but as he'd proven time and time again on this trip, he was somehow immune to my cold-shouldering—so that meant that the only person I was hurting was myself.

I heaved myself out of the warmth of my sleeping bag, examining my legs. The scratches from yesterday were not as welted and pronounced, but they felt a little itchy. Maybe a dip in the ocean would help.

"Put on your tennis shoes so that you don't cut up your feet on the rough tide pools. I went down there already, and it's pretty rocky." I glanced at Dad. The twins were changing, but I already had my bathing suit on, as I hadn't taken it off yesterday. "I'm sorry we weren't able to get to them in Big Sur, as planned," he said, meeting my eyes. The pure shock of hearing him apologize must've shown on my face, but he didn't seem to react. "I was reading that they were here at Topanga Beach."

I couldn't wait to see the critters in the tide pools. It was going to be like a marine petting zoo. After hurriedly tidying up and getting on our shoes, we ran to the water's edge, which was lined by an extremely rocky perimeter. If it weren't for wearing proper shoes, I was certain these rocks—as razor-sharp as a coral reef—would've sliced up my feet.

Just as Dad said, there were numerous depressions in the rock, currently filled with crystal-clear seawater and marine life.

"Look!" screamed Jill. "There's a starfish in here!"

"Oooh! Yeah, I see it!" Gerri exclaimed. She reached in and touched a yellowish blob that squeezed itself around her finger. "Aah."

"That's an anemone, Gerri," Dad said, laughing.

"That's your *sea enemy*, Ger-Bear!" Her twin giggled. "Look at this one." Jill pointed to a ball that looked like a pincushion; I guessed it was an urchin.

"Don't touch that one, Jill," I said, cautioning her against getting stabbed.

Crouching down, I ran my hand through the seaweed in the pool at my feet, observing a hermit crab scuttling away from my fingers. The pungent smell of the ocean's leftovers was strong in my nostrils.

"Dang! Tide pools are the coolest thing ever!" I looked over at my road-tripping family, and we were all grinning like goons. We spent about an hour exploring the tide pools, each one of us claiming a particular pool as our special one.

"That was the grooviest thing ever, Dad," said Gerri, taking his hand while we walked back to the car. Jill and I followed, also holding hands.

The sun was all the way up now, spreading golden light everywhere, like a fisherman casting out a net. Its rays hit the ocean, breaking into a zillion shiny pieces that somehow fit together into one big glittering mosaic. I looked over at Dad. I couldn't believe he'd gotten up early to scout out the tide pools, trying to ensure that today wasn't another failure.

He was trying to make up for yesterday. And he had. My chest felt tight just looking at him.

Dad was kind of like a mosaic, too—made up of all these different mismatched pieces. Some parts were fun and easygoing, full of jokes and goofy charm. Other parts were sharp and hard, like bits of broken glass—deceitful, petty, hypocritical, and way too sure of himself. But there were softer pieces, too, like kindness and love, and then the cold, jagged parts of his anger. He was a walking contradiction, like water caught between being warm and freezing: thirty-two degrees Celsius, bubbling with energy, and thirty-two degrees Fahrenheit, just about to turn into ice.

It hit me again: people are messy. We're all these weird combinations of good stuff and bad stuff, light and dark, Dr. Jekyll and Mr. Hyde. That didn't make everything Dad did okay—not by a long shot—but somehow it made it easier to see the good parts in him. I started to realize these two extremes could be true at the same time. The good parts didn't have to be eclipsed by the bad. They could coexist. And even if thinking about it hurt, it felt kind of good, too—like figuring out a riddle that'd been driving you crazy for ages.

✳ ✳ ✳

When we returned to Blue Pierre and changed into our car clothes, I climbed into the back seat again, settling in comfortably. Dad glanced at the map. "I was looking this over, and we're very close to Hollywood and Beverly Hills. Want to check out the Hollywood Walk of Fame?"

"What's that?" Gerri asked, snuggling up against him in the front seat.

"The Hollywood Walk of Fame is a historic landmark—but it's not a building," Dad explained, launching into another one of his lectures. "It's a stretch of sidewalk along Hollywood Boulevard, embedded with hundreds of stars. Each star is a tribute to the achievements of actors, directors, producers, musicians—even fictional characters. The stars are made of terrazzo and brass. Terrazzo is crushed marble, pieced together like a mosaic. And I think they're pink!"

"That terrazzo reminds me of how sculptors used to fix their mistakes in carvings," I said, smiling slyly. "You know—the ones that weren't *sin-cére*."

"You remembered!" Dad exclaimed, his face lighting up. I couldn't help but grin back, happy to have pleased him once again.

"I'm excited to see these stars in person," I said, ready to get moving.

We headed north on State Route 27, merged onto the 101 South, exited at Argyle Lane, and parked Blue Pierre in a parallel spot along the street. A few blocks of walking later, we found ourselves on Hollywood Boulevard right in front of Grauman's Chinese Theatre, where the Walk of Fame stars sparkled beneath our feet.

As we strolled along, Dad was eager to show us some of the newest additions from 1976: Captain Kangaroo, Barbra Streisand, and Johnny Cash (his personal favorite). I made a mental note to tell Skippy about Dick Clark. We used to love watching *American Bandstand* on Saturday mornings. TeenTeen would also be thrilled to hear that her beloved Bob Barker, the host of *The Price Is Right*, was honored this year. Personally, I found him creepy. And of course, Mom's favorite, Wayne Newton, had a star, too.

As the twins bounced along Hollywood Boulevard, Gerri suddenly stopped and said, "Isn't it strange that we're skipping across Marilyn Monroe's star, and there's gum stuck right on her little movie camera?" She looked at us, incredulous. "Who would spit gum on Marilyn Monroe?"

Good question.

40

Collect Call and Campho-Phenique

After enjoying lunch at the famous Mel's Diner, where we had grilled cheese sandwiches and chocolate milkshakes, Dad drove us to the nearest gas station to fill up Blue Pierre. My sisters—fired up thanks to all that sugar—spotted an adjacent playground and beelined straight for it.

I'd claimed I was going to use the restroom, but instead I found myself on the opposite side of the dingy building, holding a pay phone receiver in my hand. Before even thinking it through, I'd lifted the handset, untangled the metal cord, listened for the dial tone, and dialed zero for operator assistance. She asked me for the number, and I recited my home phone number.

I bit my thumbnail and looked around to see if Dad or the twins noticed that I wasn't really at the restroom. There was no evidence that they had. Dad was busy getting Blue Pierre filled up and chatting with the attendant, and the twins were amusing themselves on the playground's swing set.

The problem was, I really did have to use the restroom. I should have done so before getting on the phone. I almost hung up, but then I heard the call go through, and I thought to myself, *One ringy-dingy, two ringy-dingy.* The phone was picked up before the third ring. I heaved a sigh of relief.

The operator continued with her slightly robotic *Laugh-In*'s Ernestine the Operator's voice. "I have a collect call from Mary Stromp. Will you accept the charges?"

Even though I was hoping to hear Lily Tomlin's voice finish with "Have I reached the party to whom I am speaking?," I was as happy as a dog with two tails, as Grandpa Red liked to say, when I heard my mom's sweet voice reply, "Yes, of course I will." I could detect the smile in her words and maybe a bit of worry, too.

"Go ahead, young lady," the operator finished, making the connection before she clicked off, leaving Mom and me to ourselves.

"Mom!"

"Mary! Is everything okay? I'm so glad to hear from you! Please tell me you're okay!" She paused, then quickly added, "But if things are not okay, that's okay, too." I giggled at all the *okays*.

"Everything is fine," I said, even though that wasn't true. "I just miss you so much and wanted to hear your voice." That part was true, at least. That lump was growing in my throat again, but I was quick to push it back down.

"Oh goodness gracious, tell me all about what's going on. You guys haven't called me once, and it's been over three weeks! Where are you? It's not like I've been worried sick or anything," she added with a mirthless laugh. "I guess I figured you would have run into some trouble or other and needed my help before now."

"I know! I'm sorry. We're in California, just south of Los Angeles."

"California!" she exclaimed. "South of Los Angeles! Well, I'll be!"

I laughed at her echoing enthusiasm. "We've had some different troubles along the trip, but nothing too bad."

"Tell me, tell me," she said.

"We met a family with two daughters and camped and traveled with them for a while. They were great. They had some car problems. We had some car problems. Everything is fine now, as far as that is concerned, though." I nibbled on my nail while

I thought of what else to tell her and shifted from foot to foot and squeezed my crotch muscles to hold the pee back. "I loved San Francisco, and I hated the Great Salt Lake." Hearing her chuckle, I went on. "I'd like to live in San Francisco when I grow up. Maybe there's a good college out here." No one in our family except Aunt Viv and her husband, Uncle Tom, had been to college, but I somehow knew that I would go.

"We'll see about that," she said. "What else? How was Mount Rushmore?"

"Mount Rushmore? Oh yeah." That seemed like so long ago! "That was on the Fourth of July. The fireworks were great. We were with that other family, so that made it even better." I paused to think for a second, twisting the tangled phone cord around my wrist. "Oh, I wish you would have seen Lake Tahoe or Donner Lake in the Sierra Nevada Mountains. Those were the grooviest!"

"Really? How are the twins?"

"You know . . ." I considered what to say. "They're really being troopers. Keeping smiles on their faces."

"Good. Good."

Looking over the edge of the pay phone attached to the gas station's wall, I saw them doing their customary passing game on the monkey bars. Dad had joined them now and was sitting at the top of the wavy slide, looking like a little boy.

"They really miss you," I said, thinking of their teary eyes back at Grandpa Red and TeenTeen's so early on in our trip. "But they've been really strong and helpful and are trying to be tough about it. Jill has been keeping track of everywhere we've gone, and she hasn't had any problems with her capped tooth. And Gerri, what can I tell you about Gerri?" I thought and thought. "Oh yeah, she hasn't gotten any rashes, but that Great Salt Lake in Utah was pretty hard on her. She and I rinsed off right away."

"Oh golly, my little babies." I heard her sharp intake of breath and wondered if she was crying a bit. Then she said, a little quieter, "Is there a specific reason you're calling now?"

"Actually, yes." I kicked at the gravel on the ground. I could tell her now, I realized. I could let all of it spill out of me—give the weight of it to an actual adult and free myself. But when I spoke, none of those words came out. "Yesterday we tried to get to a private beach here at the Pacific Ocean, but we ended up just pushing through a bunch of bushes and never quite made it to the ocean."

"Yes?"

"Well, to make a long story short, I got all scratched up, and like a dumb-dumb, I didn't rinse off afterward like Dad and the twins did, and now I have a rash everywhere. And it looks like it's getting worse. It's on my arms and the backs of my hands, and my belly and back and neck, but especially on my legs." I heard her gasp. "And it's kind of swollen and hurts where the actual scratches are, but mostly it itches everywhere."

"Oh Mary. That sounds awful. What does the rash look like? Do you think it's poison ivy?"

"I don't know, but the rash is welted where the scratches are and then lots of little red bumps, and when I scratch the itch, a clear liquid oozes out and then makes a yellowy crust, almost like a scab. Mom, it's horrible." This time I kind of choked, and a little sob did burst out, unbidden. I didn't realize this was bothering me so much, but it was. "I look like a leper."

"Oh baby. I wish I could help you and give you a big hug."

So did I.

"I think it does sound like some kind of reaction to whatever plants you touched. Like poison ivy. What does Dad think?"

I laughed, stuffing down my tears. That was a joke. Dad never thought you were sick, even if you were. He believed that kids couldn't have headaches and that stomachaches were for sissies. Back in third grade, when I had made a sling out of a scarf and supported my sore elbow all weekend after I got hurt jumping from the rope swing, he mocked me and said I was faking it. It wasn't until Mom took me to the hospital—two days later!—that the X-ray revealed that I had broken my humerus. I came home with a clumsy and heavy white plaster cast, eager to have the kids at school sign it with Magic Markers. All Dad did was tell me he thought it was funny that I broke my funny bone.

"Dad? You know, he thinks it's not as bad as I'm complaining it is."

"Oh sweet Mary. Your dad is too stoic when it comes to pain, sickness, and injuries. Always has been. Grandma Stromp was like that, and he thinks it's the way to be." She put away her scolding tone and adopted her all-hands-on-deck practical voice. "You listen to me! Tell him that your rash needs immediate attention. If he won't take you to a doctor, then at least he needs to bring you to a pharmacy and get you a big bottle of calamine lotion, some Campho-Phenique, and some baby powder. You should rotate through those remedies to relieve the itch and hopefully heal the rash. Repeat to me the three things to get at the drugstore," she commanded.

"Campho-Phenique, powder, and . . ." I couldn't remember the third.

"Campho-Phenique, powder, and *calamine*."

"Campho-Phenique, powder, and calamine," I recited back. Worried that Dad and the girls would wonder where I had been for so long, I knew I'd have to say goodbye soon—plus, I was about to wet my pants. "Campho-Phenique, powder, and calamine," I said again, counting them off on my fingers. *One, two, three.* I scratched my right shin with my left foot.

"You got it. Campho-Phenique, powder, and calamine. Go tell him right away. Does he know you're calling?"

"No. I don't know why I didn't tell them. I think I wanted you all to myself," I said.

"I understand. If you want to keep it our little secret, that's okay with me, but if you want to let them know you called, that's okay, too."

"Okay, Mom."

"What are the three things you need to get?" she asked, quizzing me one more time.

"Campho-Phenique, powder, and calamine."

"Yes. That's it. You'll remember. And I know it'll be hard, but try to not scratch. It'll just make things worse and maybe spread the rash. Oh yeah, and wash your hands if you do scratch. And don't bite your nails."

I obediently took my index finger out of my mouth.

"It might spread the rash to your face. You don't want that. You're starting high school in a few weeks and will want to be your most beautiful self. You'll feel much better soon." I heard her take a quivering breath. "Can you call me back in a few days and let me know how it's going?"

"Yes." I choked back some tears, and I think she did, too. "I've gotta go, Mom. I love you."

"I love you, too, sweet Mary."

As I hung up, I realized she didn't ask how Dad was. He didn't deserve her at all. How could he betray such a beautiful and caring wife and mother? Repeating in my head *Campho-Phenique, powder, and calamine*, I zoomed to the restroom.

41

Unbearable

As I traipsed across the gas station parking lot to the adjacent playground, I found Dad still playing with the twins. They waved at me, completely oblivious to the fact that I'd been absent for probably fifteen minutes.

"Dad?" I climbed the slide to join him on top.

"Oh, hey, Mary! Want to go down the slide next?" he asked, but I ignored him, launching right into my next statement.

"Mom wants you to take me to a doctor and a drugstore for some remedies for this rash."

"Mom? How does she know about it?" he asked, seeming startled and a little chastened. He went down the slide, and I followed. As we walked toward Blue Pierre, he waved for the girls to come back to the car, and they began barreling toward us.

I hesitated, nibbling my pinkie fingernail—and then, remembering Mom's advice, pulled it out fast and wiped it on my shorts. "Well, I just called her on the pay phone—"

"The pay phone? What pay phone?" He looked around, squinting behind those thick glasses in a scandalized sort of way. "How much did that cost?"

"There's a pay phone right there at the gas station. See?" I pointed. "I called collect."

"Collect? That's expensive!" he scolded with his frown and exasperated eyes. "What did you do that for?"

Was he pouting? Was he worried that I knew about their fight, that she'd told me something? I gritted my teeth. He was upset over a collect call to Mom but completely unbothered by the fact that I almost fell to my death yesterday. Typical.

"Dad, come on. She told me to call collect if I needed her or if we had any problems."

He looked blankly at me, as if I'd just betrayed him. The twins stood next to me, flanking me on each side, intuitively aware of the shift in energy. "Well, we're not having any problems, so why did you call her?" he asked defensively.

"Are you serious? Look at me! I'm hideous! This rash is unbearable!" Saying so made me scratch my right ankle with the top of my left foot.

Dad's eyes narrowed, unconvinced. "It's not that bad. Look at your sisters and me."

He showed me the pale underbellies of his forearms. His scratches were nowhere near as bad as mine, and it was obvious. The girls and I looked at him like he was crazy. My rash was a quantum leap in difference from theirs. The few dots on his arms and legs were minuscule compared with the continents growing and morphing on my entire body. I could even feel them on my scalp.

"Dad, Mary needs to see a doctor," Jill piped up as she reached for my hand. I accepted it, giving hers a squeeze of gratitude.

Gerri replied in solidarity, "I think so, too." She held my other hand.

"Aw, jeez," Dad said dismissively. "You girls are so dramatic."

"Well, if not that, then at least we have to go to a drugstore and get Campho-Phenique, powder, and calamine lotion." I wriggled out of Jill's grasp for a moment and ticked the three items off on my fingers.

"Campho-Phenique, powder, and calamine lotion?" He scoffed. With a shake of his head, he ducked into the car.

"Yep, that's what Mom said. Campho-Phenique, powder, and calamine."

"Well, with the four of you ganging up on me, it seems I have no choice," he muttered as we three scrambled into Blue Pierre. *How was my needing some medical attention us ganging up on him? Maybe Mom divorcing him wouldn't be so bad.*

"Can you pass me the TripTik, Jill?" Dad huffed.

Jill did so, and while he looked something up, she pulled out her notebook and sadly announced, "Looks like we've fallen behind in our Slate again."

"We can catch up, Jilly-Bean," Gerri said, patting her leg. "Let's do it. What was the last place?"

Good ol' Ger. Always trying to keep the peace and keep things light. Even though it had only been two days since San Francisco and the tai chi exercise, we'd done a lot. We helped her remember all the stuff, and she added: *7/13/76 | California/ San Francisco—Officer O'Neill and tai chi/Breakfast burritos | Santa Cruz—beach boardwalk/Ferris wheel/Giant Dipper—tricked Ger-Bear/ Corn dogs and bodysurfing/Surfers/Free camping.*

Dad passed the TripTik back to Jill and asked Gerri to get on the CB.

"What do you want me to find out?" she asked.

"I want you to get some opinions on where to stop in Mexicali for some medical treatment for poison ivy," he answered.

"Mexicali?" she asked, trying out the strange-sounding word.

"Yeah. There are two towns at the border—one called Calexico on the American side and the other, Mexicali, on the Mexican side. I love the way they combine the words *California* and *Mexico*. Aren't those great names?" Dad said. I thought they were, but I let Jill and Gerri do the agreeing and wondered why we'd go to Mexico for a doctor.

Jill must've read my mind. "Why are we going to Mexico for a doctor?"

"Well," Dad explained, "we're very close, and it's got to be cheaper, and I bet the treatment for a *rash* is the same." He said the word *rash* derisively. How could a father mock his child? There was something broken about him. I wondered what had happened to him to make him be like that.

Gerri pulled out the mic, cleared her throat, depressed the button, and said, "Breaker, breaker, one nine. This is Tom and Jerry. Anyone know about a doctor's office in Mexicali? My sister, Goldilocks, is a mess. She has a horrible rash. Actually, we all do, but hers is the worst."

I rolled my eyes and thought that she had overshared that information.

A deep, sonorous voice answered, *"Hola, Tom y Jerry.* Soy Pedro. You go *Dr. Luis y Fernando Carrillo en la Farmacia Paris. El es muy popular, pero podría estar demasiado lleno de estadounidenses que quieren cirugía. Pero podrían indicarle la dirección correcta para encontrar un dermatólogo. ¿Alguien me puede traducir eso?* Over."

Hearing his Spanish answer made me wonder how he could understand what Gerri had asked in English in the first place.

After a short bit, another guy got on and translated. "This here's Arizona. Pedro is telling you to go check out the Farmacia Paris, which is a very popular destination for Americans wanting surgery, and they can tell you where to go to find a dermatologist. And by the way, it's probably poison oak. Over."

Gerri replied, "Thanks, Pedro and Arizona." Then she added, "I mean *gracias.*" After hanging up the mic, she said, "You get all that, Dad?"

"Yep. Paris Pharmacy. Dr. Luis Fernando Carrillo." He rolled his *r*s like they did and smiled to himself, obviously pleased with his plan. "Do you think you can hang in there for another hour or two, Mare? We can kill two birds with one stone there—get you fixed up and check out Mexico." A ridiculous smile took over his face as the idea of going to Mexico was added to his Great American Road Trip.

I wasn't sure if it was worth it to press the matter. Frankly, I was just happy that Dad had agreed to take me somewhere at all, even if it was Mexico. But as we drove an hour south, and as the itching started to drive me crazier than ever, I happened to spot a regular American drugstore en route.

"Dad, please!" I launched forward, pointing at the drugstore before we drove by. "Can we stop there and buy those three things Mom told me to get?" At his hesitation, I added, trying not to whine and not to scratch, "Come on, please? My itching is driving me crazy!"

"Oh all right," he conceded, putting on the blinker and taking the exit. "I'm thirsty anyway."

He drove Blue Pierre into the little parking lot. Poor thing. It kind of choked to a halt. We all walked in, and while the twins each selected a candy bar and a Coke, I gathered the Campho-Phenique, the calamine lotion, and the baby powder. I got the largest sizes of each and was relieved to see that Dad was willing to pay for everything. He added a quart of engine oil to our purchases.

As we approached the counter, Dad started singing "Poison Ivy."

The striking dark-haired girl with bright-blue eyes and a splatter of freckles across her cheeks looked up at our approach to the cash register. Smiling, she sang along to the next part of the song.

What the heck, were we in a musical or something?

Dad laughed and turned on his charm. "You look too young to know a song from the Coasters, miss."

The cashier smiled back, snapped her chewing gum, and said, "Oh, my mom always has the Oldies but Goodies radio station on." I held back a chuckle at her reference to Dad's advanced age. His smile didn't fade at all.

Extracting a hundred-dollar bill from his old, worn-out wallet, he asked her while we dumped our selections on the counter, "Can you break this, honey?"

She looked at the bill, held it up to the light, and scrutinized Dad and the three of us before replying. She looked us up and down and wrinkled her nose when she saw my legs. I cringed, too.

She returned her attention to the bill. "It's not counterfeit, is it?" she asked Dad, as if he would ever answer honestly if it were. She lifted one eyebrow. "You're not trying to pull one over on me, are you?"

Dad smiled wide and shook his head. "Of course not, sweetheart. I'd never." Ha! I knew that must have been one of those bills that Grandpa Red had given Dad way back in Chicago. As if Grandpa Red would have passed a counterfeit bill. That's a laugh.

"Do I look like a guy who'd try to use a counterfeit bill?" Dad opened his eyes wide, trying to appear innocent behind his thick glasses, and I had to conceal a scoff. Now that I knew what he was capable of, I couldn't stop seeing him as *exactly* that sort of a person. "I mean, I've got my daughters here with me and everything."

Like that meant anything! He'd had sex with a prostitute essentially in front of his daughters. His smile looked like it would split his face, his cheeks scrunching his glasses up his nose.

"I guess not, but you never know," she said, caving in, and smiled back, though it did not quite reach her eyes. She added up our purchases, and I secretly thanked Grandpa Red for buying me the medicines and powder.

"Thanks, honey." Dad winked at her as we stepped outside, leaving the cool air-conditioning behind for the sweltering heat. Standing in the shade of the drugstore, we savored our candy and Cokes while Dad checked Blue Pierre's oil and water. He called me over to show me how he checked the oil on the dipstick.

I tipped back the Coke and swallowed the last drops. "Here, Jill." I gave her my empty bottle. "That hit the spot."

Blue Pierre's hood was propped open wide like a crooked yawn. "You see how the black oil is showing that it's on the low side between these two dots on the dipstick?" I bent in and peered under his arm, nodding. "So it needs this quart. You want to pour it in?"

"Okay," I said. The spout for the oil was wrapped in a cloth in the trunk. When I walked to the back of the car, I saw Gerri and Jill return to the store to get our nickel deposits. I located the spout, poked it into one edge of the cylindrical can to make a little hole for the air to go in, and then poked it hard into the other edge to pour the oil out.

As it glugged into the oil reservoir, I imagined that the car was enjoying its drink as much as we'd enjoyed ours. I bet Blue Pierre was thanking Grandpa Red, too.

42

Ungüento

I spread my musty towel on the back seat of Blue Pierre and smoothed the wrinkles out below me. I wasn't sure if I'd like the Campho-Phenique or the calamine lotion better, so I unscrewed the Campho-Phenique bottle's lid first to give it a try.

As soon as I did, an overpowering odor wafted out of the bottle.

Gerri turned around at once, pinching her nostrils shut. "Yuck! What is that smell?"

I sighed, grimacing. "It's the Campho-Phenique," I said. "Sorry."

Jill mimicked her gesture. Even Dad had to turn away. We were attacked mercilessly by the gasoline smell that poured out in a toxic fog. Inside the bottle's lid was a stick that extended into the greasy, pungent liquid. It had a cottony blob on the end of it. I daubed the oily solution all over the left side of my body. It was slippery and smarted my skin at first, but then the cool relief washed over my inflamed skin like dripping ice.

On my right side, I rubbed on the calamine lotion, making sure to really shake the bottle before massaging the Pepto-Bismol-pink liquid all over. It started off cold and then hardened after about two minutes. I rubbed my hands on my shorts, leaving greasy and powdery marks. I was glad that I was sitting on the towel, even though its mildewy smell was making me feel a bit sick, because little chips of the dried lotion were flaking off all over the place. It was strangely satisfying squeezing and flexing my toes, cracking the dried-on liquid.

Looking down at myself, I burst out laughing. One side was glossy and greasy, the other dry and flaky. *Let the experiment begin.* "Hey, you guys. Anyone want to try some of the Campho-Phenique or the calamine lotion?" I asked the front seat, shifting on the towel in back. "They do really help."

"I'll try the calamine lotion," Gerri answered, turning and extending her hand toward me.

"I guess I'll try the stinky stuff," Jill said, reaching back.

I passed the bottles forward, and they applied the medicines on their few dots. Dad said he'd pass on both. Mom was right. He liked being stoic about pain—but to be fair, he really didn't have a lot of it, at least compared to me.

We kept driving east on Interstate 8. I saw tumbleweeds bouncing along the road and thought this was quite a change from the lush forests near Lake Tahoe. We finally reached Calexico, Mexicali's American twin sister. We parked Blue Pierre on the northern side of Calexico's city hall in hopes of giving it a shady resting spot while we walked across the border.

That's right—we were going to *walk* to Mexico.

I hoped no one would notice how disgusting my legs and arms were. I looked leprous. And also a bit obnoxious with my contrasting halves.

Still, we moved excitedly—the twins skipping and me carrying a small tote bag with the new remedies inside it. Dad took confident strides toward the border crossing. We passed through a group of bored-looking army guys, their rifles slung across their backs. Approaching the short, stout guard at the border-crossing booth, I tried to look normal and not draw attention to my skin. I walked behind the twins, using them as shields.

The guard's eyes were shaded by the small brim of his green cap. The name on his chest badge said *Felipe Hernandez.* He asked us—in English, I was relieved to hear—what we were planning on doing in Mexico, where we were going, and if our visit was for business or pleasure.

Dad, smiling wide, said that we were there to see a doctor for our rashes and to have a little lunch. We'd be going back to the States before nighttime.

Felipe Hernandez scrutinized Dad and then asked, "Where's the *mamá*?" Then he gave the three of us kids a once-over.

"Their mother, my *wife*"—Dad emphasized—"is back in the Midwest."

"She no want to come on you vacation?" Felipe Hernandez raised his eyebrows skeptically at this explanation. "*¿Por qúe?*"

"Does that mean *why*?" Dad asked, pasting on his goofy smile.

"*Sí, señor.*" Felipe Hernandez looked amused. Well, his eyes did. You couldn't really see his mouth's expression; it was hidden under the long straight line of the mustache that seemed to cut his young round face in two. "Why your wife no want to go vacation wit you?"

The twins and I looked at one another. *Oh brother.* I wondered if Dad was going to tell this stranger about the awful fight they had before he whisked us away on this dream trip or cultivate yet another lie to get his way.

"Well . . . ," Dad hemmed and hawed. I was surprised he didn't say more.

"Okay. *Chicas.*" He turned and directed the question toward us. "Why your *mamá* no come vacation wit you?"

I looked at Dad and then said, "Well, she stayed home with the dog and couldn't leave work." Felipe Hernandez just looked at me, expecting more. "Dad took us by himself. We've been traveling for weeks. You know, camping and visiting national parks and beaches and stuff like that."

He seemed to consider my reply and took his sweet ol' time before continuing. He played with his long mustache. I realized it probably looked suspicious—some man crossing into another country with three young girls, their mother nowhere to be seen.

"What happen to your skin?" He pointed to my legs.

"I think it's an infection—" I started, shifting uncomfortably on my feet.

Dad interrupted, clearing his throat, "No. No. Not an infection, just a rash from some poisonous plants. Not an infection." He looked at me with stern, reprimanding eyes.

"Poison oak?" the guard asked, twisting the other end of his mustache.

"Yes, *sí*. Poison oak. That's right," Dad agreed. "We want to see a doctor for some medication."

"That is some bad poison oak."

"Can we come on through?" Dad asked hopefully.

Felipe Hernandez finally said, "You come wit me. I find you taxi." We followed his lead as he walked away from the booth. "You go *directamente a la Médica de la Ciudad*." We all needed to take quick steps, even Dad, to keep up as he led us to the main street.

"What about Farmacia Paris?" Gerri asked me and Jill quietly, but Felipe overheard her.

"*¿Farmacia Paris?* You say *Farmacia Paris?*"

Gerri looked back shyly and asked, "*¿Sí?*" Jill nodded in solidarity, taking hold of her hand.

"Farmacia Paris is *para* people who want to change face." When he saw our confused expressions, he added, "Look young. Change face. Bye-bye wrinkles. Make face smooth." He dragged his hands over his round, full-moon face, stretching the surface flat. "No more big ugly nose."

I burst out laughing at his description, and he smiled at me.

I realized he meant that Farmacia Paris was for plastic surgery. *That's where Dad would've taken me if it weren't for the intervention of this border patrol guy!*

A driver hopped out of his green Chevy Nova and opened the back door with a flourish for the three of us. Dad climbed into the passenger seat. Felipe Hernandez told the driver to bring us to the Médica de la Ciudad. Dad asked if the driver would take American money.

"*Sí, señor.* He be happy to take you money." Felipe chuckled along with the driver. As we departed, he patted the taxi like my mom used to pat my head. "*Buena suerte*," he said as we drove off.

The taxi driver played loud mariachi music on the radio. I loved the trumpets harmonizing and the vocalist doing

Mexican-style yodeling. The driver drummed the steering wheel and sang along, winking and smiling at us girls in the universal language of goodwill in the rearview mirror.

We drove down what seemed to be the main thoroughfare. There were colorful shacks, shops, and restaurants lining the south side, but the north side was fronted by large, unadorned, factory-style cinder-block buildings.

In fewer than ten minutes, we arrived at our destination. Dad peeled off two dollars and looked questionably at the driver, gauging if this was an appropriate amount, and the driver gave him an affirmative nod. We climbed out, and the twins and I said our rounds of *gracias* and *adios*. The driver smiled and laughed at what must have been our mispronunciations and effort.

Making our way through the crowded reception area of the Médica de la Ciudad was a testimony to the power of nonverbal gesticulation. With a lot of pointing—and from the apparent trouble I was obviously in—it wasn't difficult for the receptionist to figure out what we were there for.

She took the clipboard back after Dad signed it, and we found a seat in the packed waiting area. Gerri sat on Jill's lap.

In a couple of minutes, a heavyset nurse called us in. "*¿Maria eStromp? ¿Maria eStromp?*" She gave me a reassuring smile as we made our way into the examination room. We followed her down the hall. Dad had on a big grin, watching her wide hips bumping left and right into gurneys, wheelchairs, and other medical equipment lining the sides of the narrow corridor.

When we reached the examination room, she gestured for me to climb onto the table, and then she counted my pulse and took my temperature. When the doctor entered the room, reading from a clipboard, she told him that my *temperatura está un poco elevada.*

He lifted his head, took one look at me, and gasped. Actually *gasped*, then covered his mouth with his hand. *Uh-oh.*

"*Lo siento.* So sorry for my unprofessional reaction. *Lo siento. Buenos días.*" He tried to smile and conceal his apparent shock regarding my predicament. "How are you feeling? Itchy?" Then, as if he just remembered, he added, "My name is Dr. Geraldo Perez."

He approached Dad with an outstretched hand to shake, then gave Gerri and Jill a big smile and pulled out two lollipops from the front pocket of his white lab coat. The twins tore off the wrappers and started sucking.

"What's your name?" he asked me.

"Mary."

"*Ay María, bendita entre las mujeres.* Blessed among women." He did the Catholic thing of crossing himself: spectacles, testicles, wallet, watch. "It's nice to meet you. Your legs and arms look rather uncomfortable." He washed his hands in the little sink in the corner.

"Yes, it's very itchy," I replied, scratching my arm against my side.

"What are you doing to take care of it?"

I thought it must be so groovy to speak two languages. Next year in high school, I would be taking Spanish I. Reaching into the tote bag, I pulled out the Campho-Phenique and calamine lotion bottles. "I also have some baby powder."

He nodded while opening the Campho-Phenique and smelling it, crinkling his nose at the caustic odor. "This work? Make you feel better?" He pulled the stethoscope from his neck and listened to my chest.

I took the instructed big breaths and answered, "I don't really know. I've just started using it. It does feel good when I put it on."

"Mm-hmm," he hummed. "I look?" He gestured toward my body. I nodded assent. While he was examining the rash and noting the patches of crusted blisters, he asked the twins and Dad if they had it, too.

"*Sí, Doctor.*" Dad put the emphasis on the second syllable, trying to sound authentic. *Oh brother.* "But ours is not as bad as Mary's," he added, finally admitting the truth now that a doctor was present.

Gerri jumped in. "After we got scratched up, we all washed off, but Mary just climbed into her sleeping bag."

"Yeah, she didn't rinse it off," Jill agreed.

"Do you still use that *esleeping* bag?" the doctor asked, brows raised. Only then did it dawn on me that I probably shouldn't have, but I was honest and nodded. He looked at Dad and said to me, "Have your *papá* get you a new *esleeping* bag. Throw that one away. It's covered in poison oak oil. You need a new *esleeping* bag."

I asked, "Is it poison oak?"

"Yes. It's poison oak. We call it *hiedra venenosa, literalmente* poisonous ivy. Poisonous ivy, poisonous oak, poisonous sumac—all the same. Just like you call it." The doctor shook his head, then added, "I've never seen anything like this. The severity of this rash is *increíble*. This is the worst case I've ever treated."

"Really?" Dad said, shifting uneasily on his feet. I glared at him, my complaints validated.

"Yes, *de verdad*. Really. She is covered." He gave Dad an accusatory look. "Her legs, her arms. Let me see your *estomago* again." I lifted my shirt, and he shook his head. "This is *horrible*. Where did this happen? For how long you have it?" He parted my hair with his fingers and examined my scalp. "*Dios mio.*"

"A few days ago. Up in California on the coast near Big Sur," I replied.

"I would *generalmente* prescribe *un ungüento*, an ointment, de *corticosteroides anti-inflamatorios*, but I fear you need more than that. You have such a large surface area of contamination, I think you take *un antibiótico oral*, too. Just in case. And I think also something for *el picazón*, the itch—un *anti-histamínico*."

"Does that mean an antihistamine for the itch?" Dad clarified.

"*Sí, señor.*" The doctor mimicked Dad's American accent. "An antihistamine for the itch."

"So a cream and some pills?" Dad said, slapping his hands this way and that, like dusting off the problem. "Sounds good. Where can we get them?"

"The nurse can give them to you on your way out," Dr. Perez answered shortly. I was starting to think he didn't like Dad. "How are the rest of you?" He looked at the twins and Dad, walking over to the little sink to wash his hands again.

Jill answered for them all. "We have a little bit." She rotated her arms out for him to take a look. Gerri and Dad did likewise.

"Ay, I see. Well, I'll send you with more of the *ungüento*." He smiled at the twins.

He called to the nurse and asked her for three tubes of the *ungüento* and a round of the antibiotics and the antihistamine for me. She waddled out and then back into the room, her hands full of what he asked for. I added them to my bag.

Before we were excused, he asked if he could take some photos of my skin. He promised he wouldn't include my face and that it was for medical and educational purposes. I looked at Dad for approval, and when I agreed, the doctor went to the little cupboard above the sink and pulled out his old-fashioned Brownie-style camera and posed me discreetly this way and that, taking some shots.

In only ten minutes, we were exiting the Médica de la Ciudad. I had to say, it was one of the best doctor's visits I'd had. Quick and efficient.

We walked outside, and the smell of grilled meat filled our nostrils. At once, I heard my stomach grumble. We all quickly agreed to try some street tacos. I thought the carne asada tacos were *deyishous*. The twins had *pollo*, chicken. Of course, Dad tried the most disgusting thing they offered, *tacos de lengua*. Tongue tacos.

"You'll never taste something this authentic and Mexican," Dad said, smacking his lips with his mouth full of tongue taco. Regardless of the meat, all the tacos were made with two small soft corn tortillas and were served with a little slice of lime, a tangle of cilantro, and some slices of radish. Gerri couldn't eat her third taco, so I finished it off for her, even though I was still vaguely haunted by the nickname I'd gotten in Chinatown: Heavy Duty. It was worth it, though. Her *pollo* was as salty and as *deyishous* as my carne asada. Man, were they good.

We walked farther down the road, wiping our greasy mouths with the little paper napkins the tacos were served with. Dad pointed to a little shop across the way that had a billboard-size sign with vibrant drawings of enormous popsicles advertising their *paletas, hechas de frutas y nueces. Paletas*, I learned, are real-fruit popsicles.

The temperature was rising. We were all getting thirsty and had a sweet tooth after our savory tacos, and those frozen confections sounded like they would hit the spot. The selection was vast, and I was happy to see that they were labeled in *español* and English. I had *coco*, Gerri tried *piña*, Jill had *fresa*, and Dad ordered *pistacho*. We took turns trying one another's. I liked Jill's strawberry the most, so she traded me for my coconut. I wish we could've had another one. I would've tried the *miél*.

As we started back toward the border crossing, we passed many different sellers of Mexican souvenirs. Even though there were a few in real buildings, some in temporary shacks, and some with carts, they all had pretty much the same wares.

It was at this moment that it fully sunk in that we were in another country, even more exotic than Chinatown had been. This was farther than I'd ever been from Ohio, and Mom felt so far away. For a few seconds, the realization felt almost heart-stopping. What would I do if I actually wanted to go straight home? I'd have so far to travel. What if Dad hadn't taken me to the doctor or had refused to buy me any medication? Would I have been stranded with him, or what? Forced to book a Greyhound bus ride? Thankfully, the bright colors, loud noises, and *dey-ishous*-smelling foods made for great distractions, and I calmed myself by reiterating that I was already on the mend with prescription-level medications. Everything would be all right.

Dad let the twins buy some bobblehead *animalitos* from a young Indian woman who had them, along with some clay jars, umbrellas, and a big pile of rolled-up blankets and hooded jackets displayed on a couple of the beautiful woven blankets in the dust.

The two-inch-tall animals were carved from a seed pit and painted in cheerful colors. They had heads and sometimes tails that wiggled with the slightest vibration and were supposed to predict the coming of an earthquake, since they would flutter from the earth's movement before people could feel it. When you touched the heads, they jiggled like Jell-O. Gerri and Jill were having a blast touching one after the other, getting them all to dance in harmony together.

They chose *un mono*—monkey; *un burro*—donkey; *una tortuga*—turtle; *un elefante*—elephant; *un caballo*—horse; and *un gallo*—rooster. Each one cost only a nickel or a dime. The young woman reached for her baby, who was crawling over her wares. The infant had on a little embroidered dress but nothing on the bottom. Didn't she need a diaper? It made me cringe and wonder whether that baby had peed or pooped on the merchandise before.

Trying to contain the fast-moving little one, the mother brought her up to her chest, lifted her torn T-shirt, and started nursing her. That got the kid to stay still. When her baby had fallen asleep, the mom wrapped a piece of cloth around her as a makeshift diaper, I guessed, and laid her down on the edge of her display. She propped up one of the umbrellas for sale to shade her sleeping child.

Now that I'd enjoyed real-fruit popsicles, fresh tacos, and even bought a souvenir, I figured it was a good time to address a bigger concern: buying a new sleeping bag. I'd been eying the colorful varieties of striped wool Mexican blankets and wanted one of those for myself.

I had learned the phrase *¿Cuánto cuesta?* from the woman selling the *paletas* and asked the nursing mom how much a blanket cost.

She held out two fingers and said, "*Dos dólares.*"

I reached into my pocket and gave her three. She peered at me, and I was startled by her dazzling smile. Her baby stirred, and she reached down and patted her derrière until she settled down again.

"Let's get some of this Mexican candy for the drive," Dad said, reaching down and grabbing several packages of De la Rosa Mazapan and Pulpo de Tamarindo. He paid the young mom, and we started the hot walk back to America—right after I took a quick pause and added a My Journal of Life entry with all the smells, sights, and sounds of Mexicali.

Felipe Hernandez was still at the crossing booth. "*Oye. ¿Cómo va?* What did the doctor say?"

"He gave me some"—what was the word?—"*ungüento?*"

"*Sí, un ungüento, muy bien*. You had *una visita exitosa*? A successful visit?" He seemed to struggle with the word *successful*.

"Yes, I'd say we had an overall successful visit," I answered.

"*Muy bien, muy bien*," he murmured, letting us pass through the border. "*Que les vayan bien*."

"*Gracias*, Felipe Hernandez. Thank you for all your help," I said.

With our bellies filled with tacos and *paletas* and our hands overflowing with little animals, blankets, candies, three tubes of *ungüento*, and boxes of medicines, we bade farewell. I was hoping that the medicines would work.

Nodding to my bag of medication, Dad said, "Would you believe that all this cost less than a doctor's visit would have cost in the US of A?"

"Why is that? Why is it so much cheaper in Mexico?" I asked, hoping he'd give a short reply and not one of his lengthy lecture-style answers. I slung the new Mexican blanket over my shoulders, relishing the scratchy softness of the wool.

"Can I put these candies in that medicine bag of yours? I'll carry it." I happily passed Dad the tote bag, and he rearranged our items before answering. "Well, you see, Mexico is a Latin American country that has a low cost of living."

"Why is the cost of living lower? We're only a mile away from America. How can it be so different?" I asked. "On this side of the border, things seem neater, but over there, it's kind of run-down. And very, like, stark." I searched for the right word. "Sort of industrial. But also kind of colorful and lively. That lady selling the blankets and toys looked so poor."

He shook his head sympathetically. "Yes. Lots of contrasts here, aren't there? The distribution costs and cheap labor contribute to the low prices."

The twins, eager to avoid one of Dad's boring, lengthy replies, galloped off in front of us with their new animal toys. I envied them. I should've known Dad couldn't respond to a question like that with a simple answer.

"Also, the Mexican government has control over the prices of goods that are sold. And they have socialized medicine. In the US, we believe that the individual companies should have control over the costs of what they sell. We Americans love our capitalism." He chuckled, somewhat pompously, and smiled at me. "Rightly so. Did you learn about the differences between capitalism, socialism, and communism in your social studies class last year?"

"Not really," I replied. The truth was, we might have studied the differences, but I certainly hadn't managed to log any of that away. I realized, suddenly, that we were just reverting to our old habit of him explaining things with me blindly listening. I'd have to research capitalism, socialism, and communism and the differences among them once I'd gotten home to establish my own opinion.

"Karl Marx, the founder of socialism, said, 'From each according to his ability, to each according to his need,'" Dad announced, like he was quoting a bumper sticker. "Nice idea, right? Everyone chips in what they can, and the needy folks— the crippled, the retarded, and whoever else—get more because, well, they need more."

I frowned. The way he lumped people together like that made me uncomfortable, though I couldn't exactly explain why. I'd heard those words before, but they sounded... off. Crude, maybe. Or just careless. Like he wasn't really thinking about real people.

"I mean... it kind of makes sense," I said slowly, "but doesn't it seem unfair to the people who do work hard? Like, why would someone bother trying if they just got the same as someone who didn't?"

Dad raised an eyebrow, amused. I could tell he liked where this was going.

"Would their money just go to the people who couldn't work?" I added, thinking of the woman in Mexicali with the diaper-less baby crawling across her blanket display. She'd looked exhausted, selling her things in the dust while trying to keep the baby from chewing on a corner of fabric. She was working. Really working. If I made more money someday, would helping her out be unfair?

"Exactly. And that's why I say you've got a capitalist brain," he said, grinning. "You believe in rewards for effort. For brains. For ability."

That sounded too tidy. Too black-and-white. "I guess so," I muttered.

I used to love these conversations with Dad. I used to think we were two of a kind. But now, during this trip, every talk peeled something back, showed me we weren't quite the same. Not really. Not anymore. Maybe we never had been.

Well, it made it even harder to respect his opinions.

43

Confrontation

Dad and I walked silently behind the twins—who continued to skip and play ahead of us—for a few minutes before I spotted a shop I recognized and realized, with a jolt, that we had about a half dozen blocks to go until we'd make it back to where we'd parked Blue Pierre.

My heart beat a little faster. *Maybe this is the time. Maybe it's the only time I'll get.*

I wanted it over and out. I took a big breath and considered how I would start. Despite all the mental rehearsing I'd done, I couldn't recall a single line of the script I'd settled on—but every passing second was precious. I didn't have time to hesitate.

I shifted the heavy blanket from one shoulder to the other, letting it scratch my itchy arms, and eventually settled it over my left—where Dad was standing. It served as a makeshift shield as I took a deep breath, cleared my throat, and whispered, "Dad?"

"Yeah, sweetie? What is it?" Typical. There he was, being sweet and fatherly, right when that was the last thing I needed from him.

Suddenly, it was as though the whole confession was stuck in my chest. Once I told him what I knew, our relationship would never be the same.

"What's on your mind, Mare?" he asked. *Okay, you can do this,* I told myself. We stopped when we got to the next intersection, looking both ways. A convertible drove by, kicking up dust in its wake. The passenger turned and smiled at me, gave me a little wave, her red scarf flapping around her head. Somehow, that gave me courage.

We crossed the street, and I whispered, *"Jill-and-I-saw-you-with-Charlotte-in-the-morning-at-the-motel-in-Wells."* The words rushed out of my body like the water from a broken dam. Oh my God, it felt great to finally get it out there. I could feel the weight lifting off my shoulders. For a breath, it was almost as though I was being tugged up in the air by a bundle of helium balloons— floating above every step, walking on the moon.

Now all I had to do was sit back and receive Dad's apology. The worst was over.

We walked a few steps, and I gave him time. He was probably carefully selecting his next words, trying to find the right thing to say. It wasn't until I looked up at him and saw that his brows were furrowed behind his glasses in a completely bamboozled sort of way that I felt my stomach drop.

"Charlotte? Who's Charlotte?" he had the audacity to say.

Was he stalling or denying, or was it that he didn't remember her name?

"Come on," I said. "Charlotte." He still didn't seem to remember. "The pros-ti-tute?" I reminded him bluntly, stretching out the uncomfortable word. This time, I saw a shift in his eyes. He deflated, gaze dropping to the sidewalk.

"You did, huh?" he replied so quietly I barely heard him.

"Yep. Jill didn't know what was happening, and I sent her back to bed cuz it was only six o'clock in the morning and she was practically sleepwalking." I let that settle before adding, "But I know what I saw, and I know what it meant."

He pressed his lips together sheepishly.

"Dad, how could you?" Hot tears started rolling out of my eyes, and at first I was disappointed in myself for crying. But this was cathartic, too. It had been building up for a long time, and it felt good to rid myself of it. It's not like he hadn't seen me cry before.

Dad tried to put his arm around me, but I shrugged him off—violently.

When he still didn't respond, I said, "Well?"

He gathered himself and started to speak. "I don't owe you an explanation—"

"What? Yes you do!" I yelled, startling the twins, who turned around to see what was going on. I waved them off, putting on a pretend smile. Jill's eyes widened a bit. She grabbed Gerri's hand and tugged her along—and I suspected she knew what was going down. I realized I'd betrayed her request to stay out of this; I wasn't supposed to tell Dad she'd seen anything, but somehow, it felt like honesty was the only way to go. Full honesty.

"Actually, I don't," he replied neutrally, "but I'll try to anyway." He cleared his throat. "Mary, you must know that a man has needs." He paused. "Sexual needs."

"Dad, that's disgusting. You're married," I insisted.

"But I had been without your mother for many weeks by the time we were in Wells."

"What about the Ten Commandments and being a Christian and being faithful to your wife?" My voice rose and cracked with my demanding questions. "You committed adultery!"

Dad slowed our pace, letting the distance between us and the twins grow a little. "Let's keep it down and not upset your sisters, okay?"

For once, we agreed on something. I nodded, slowing my pace, but I noticed Jill look over her shoulder again and give me a microscopic nod before roping an arm around Gerri and frolicking off, footloose and fancy-free.

"But, Dad, it's just that . . ." I shook my head at the memory and disgust I felt. I couldn't finish the thought. I didn't need to.

Dad sighed. "I can try to explain," he offered again.

I didn't want an explanation, and I did want one at the same time.

"Go for it," I suggested, roughly wiping my eyes with the back of my hand and shifting the heavy blanket back to the first shoulder.

"Let me carry the blanket," he volunteered.

"No, I don't need your help. Just tell me what you want to tell me," I huffed. My legs and arms, for the first time in days, weren't itching like crazy. It was like my whole body was numb.

"Well, it reminds me of how you can't keep away from sweets." What? Was he comparing *adultery* to *overeating*? "Even though you know you shouldn't, that you should resist, that eating too much makes you Heavy Duty, as Edsel Ford Fong said . . ." He snickered.

How could he think this was funny? Was he kidding me? *And* calling me fat? He must've seen the way my lip curled up in horror and my eyes shone with tears and blatant incredulity because he immediately changed tactics—which was surprising for Mr. Magoo himself.

"You know I love your mom, but she and I have an understanding." He paused, searching for how to word his response. "Your mom doesn't have the . . . How should I phrase this? She doesn't have the same intensity of need as I do. So we have an understanding . . ."

"An understanding?" I scoffed. I remembered Mom calling this cheating and infidelity in their fight before this trip. That didn't sound like an understanding.

"Yes. An understanding—an agreement. I can pursue other women as long as I don't flaunt it in front of her and am discreet about it."

"Seriously? Mom knew? Mom *knows*? She's okay with this?" I knew she knew, but I wanted him to admit it. I looked down and noticed a dandelion growing out of the asphalt. Somehow, just like how the lady with the red scarf had given me courage, the tenacity of that little weed, its life force striving against all odds, also gave me some hope. "I find that hard to believe, Dad. Besides, you weren't very discreet in Wells with Charlotte. You were just there right outside our window in the motel's parking lot, paying her in your pajamas, hurrying her away."

He let that sink in for a bit as we both walked along in silence for another twenty paces, my feet dragging on the hot, sandy asphalt of Heber Avenue. The blanket was making me sweat. I pushed my stringy hair off my sticky face. "Oh Dad. I think it's disgusting and bad and hypocritical of you."

"What do you mean, *hypocritical*?"

I couldn't help but scoff. Was he seeing this conversation as just another one of our meaning-of-life discussions, encouraging me to expound my position? Was he approaching this like a debate, trying to find flaws in my hypothetical argument?

I pinned him in place with a hard stare. "You preach at church about being honest and faithful, for Pete's sake! And you talk about integrity and stuff like that. How am I supposed to believe anything you say when you're such a liar?" The word seemed to ring in the air. *Liar.*

"Well," he considered. "I mean those things I preach about."

"Then why don't you follow your own rules?" I shot back.

"Maybe I'm preaching to myself, too."

"That's bullshit." I was shocked he didn't rebuke my cussing—and grateful. It made this feel like a real adult conversation, at least a little bit.

"I can see your point. I do try to be discreet about my extra-marital affairs."

"Affairs, like . . . plural? Dad, how many have there been?"

He didn't answer right away. "Well, if we're going for full honesty here, I'd say dozens."

I moaned and stopped, dropped the blanket, crouched down to my rash-scabby knees, and knelt there for a moment, rocking back and forth, hands covering my head. Dad put his hand on my back, and I scooted away. I buried my face into the colorful stripes and quietly screamed, "Don't touch me!"

I crouched there for a while, unraveling.

Eventually, I collected myself and got back up. I wiped my face again, shook out the blanket, then said, "Dozens? Who? Do I know these women? Mrs. Glauber—my piano teacher? Mrs. Frato – from Sunday School? Your clients? *Dozens?*" I moaned.

"Well, yes, dozens," he conceded, as though we were discussing unfortunate facts that were fully and completely outside of our control—not things he'd done deliberately. That he'd even talked about with Mom! *Supposedly.* I knew that even if they'd come to an *understanding*, she couldn't have been happy about all this. *No way.* "Maybe it's better that you don't know exactly who,"

301

he said in a rare display of maturity and wisdom. "Mom knows about them and forgives me; I ask God for forgiveness, too."

I considered what he said before replying. We pressed on in our slow walk, meandering back to the car now at a snail's pace. "That is such a cop-out. It just makes sinning okay. Why even have the Ten Commandments if all you have to do is say sorry after messing up and breaking them?"

"I guess they're just guides."

We continued in silence. There were only a few more blocks until we got to the car.

The twins looked back when we reached the next intersection. Dad called out and pointed, "I think one more block straight and then at the next corner—at East Fifth Street—go right."

"All right, Dad!" they called back in harmony, skipping hand in hand. I envied their innocence.

"Are all grown-ups like this?"

"No. I'm special." He laughed. Then, seeing my disappointment in him, added, "Maybe you'll understand when you're older."

"I don't want to grow up, and you ruined my childhood," I pouted. "Do you mean to say that most adults don't follow their marriage vows?"

"No, I'd say they do."

"Why is it okay for you?" I asked, shaking my head over and over, trying to fling this off.

"Like I said, I've always been special." He cleared his throat and adjusted his collar. "Grandma Stromp hated that about me. I was always . . . outside of the rules."

I stared back at him blankly, in shock. Of course he'd hype up his misbehavior and try to make it sound "special." Of course he'd try to twist it into something good, like putting a shiny bow on a steaming-hot pile of dog crap.

He came back from his musing and said, "You're special, too, you know. I can see it in you."

I didn't want to be special. Not like that. Not like him.

Dad inhaled through his nose, then said, "You realize that some of the rules for other people don't apply to you, right? I see how you sometimes lie or cheat, knowing that you can get away with it, or that you consider the bending of a rule to see if it makes sense for you or not."

Oh my God, he had a point, but I wasn't going to admit it now. Besides, this felt a lot like him trying to compare infidelity with me eating sweets again. I might be a lit match capable of burning, but he was a wildfire consuming and wrecking everything in his path without remorse.

I changed the topic. "Does Skippy know?"

"I don't think so," he said. "Just you and me and Mom." Suddenly, he looked panicked. "You didn't tell Mom about this when you called her collect, did you?"

So maybe he *did* feel that it was wrong.

Or maybe he wasn't worried about doing something wrong—just worried he'd get caught.

"I thought you had an understanding?" I parodied his words, brows raised. His expression didn't change, and ultimately, he waited me out. "No. Of course I didn't. I was too embarrassed. I thought I was protecting her by not saying anything, and obviously I didn't think she knew about"—I struggled for a word to encapsulate this whole debacle but failed—"this. But Jill does, sort of. And *dozens* of women," I spat back angrily. I stepped away from him, creating some distance. I could see the Civic Center, where the car was parked. "I can't sit by you in the car for a while. I need to wrap my head around this first."

"Oh, I see." He smacked his forehead dramatically like an I-should've-had-a-V8 gesture. "Now I understand why your behavior since Wells was so different from before. The silences, the rebukes, the sitting in the back seat, the buying whatever you wanted at the grocery store."

"Duh," I said. "Took you a while." He laughed, and reluctantly, I did, too. We were approaching Blue Pierre. Gerri and Jill were already there.

"Dad, give me the keys, please. We're thirsty as heck," Gerri said. "We need water."

Dad reached into his pocket, fumbled his keys out, and tossed them to her. He grasped my shoulder and turned me to face him, quietly adding, "Mare, it's going to be okay. We can talk more about it, if you want, at another time." I looked at his face and regretted the final tear that dripped from my eye. He brushed it off with the tips of his calloused fingers. "You'll forgive me, you'll see. And life will go on as before."

"Don't hold your breath—and I don't think I ever want to talk about this again," I said, shaking my head. I knew life wouldn't go on as before, not for me, at least.

Gerri had unlocked the doors, and she and Jill rolled down the windows to let the heat out. I could tell they knew something was going on, and I was thankful they didn't ask about it. They seemed to also be trying to buy me more time. Thankfully, I didn't need any more.

With a strange sinking feeling, I thought, *It's over. I did it.*

The twins grabbed the jug of water in the trunk, taking long, thirst-quenching gulps. I opened the back door, pulled out the poisonous *esleeping* bag, and tossed it on the ground, sliding in with my new Mexican blanket. I felt exhausted, emotionally and physically.

Gerri and Jill climbed into the front. They were giggling, oblivious to the real problems in life. They arranged their six little *animalitos* on the dash above the CB radio. Dad picked up the discarded *esleeping* bag and walked across the parking lot to a garbage can near the door of the city hall. He looked around and then shoved it into the little opening. I wished I didn't think that I wanted some of that poison oak oil to rub off on him, but I did.

Dad returned with a—could it be embarrassed?—grin. I doubted it. Before getting into the car, he also took a huge swig of the water. After filling up Blue Pierre's radiator with the same water, he found a washcloth in the back, wet it, and passed it along with the tote of the medicines and bottles to me. "Here, Mare. Take care of yourself. Wipe your face and body down. Take your medicine and dose up."

It was funny, my reaction. Dad's empathy was so hard to come by that when I finally got ahold of a taste of it, I felt like I could cry all over again. Why couldn't he just be good? Was it really so hard for him to just be good?

I was glad to take some orders and wash my tear-streaked face and the dust from the patches of rashes. I tried not to scratch the itch with the cloth, but boy, was it tempting. I popped out two pills, one antibiotic and one antihistamine, and downed them with a cup of hot grape Kool-Aid.

As I started applying some of the greasy *ungüento*, Dad asked Jill to pass him the map. "Looks like we're not on our TripTik course anymore. Let's see which route is the best way out of here." He rubbed his hands, spread out the map, then folded it neatly into the square we needed.

PART 4

New Adventures

44

Pomegranates and Avocados

I didn't want to be the Driver's Helper anymore. I just wanted to go to sleep. To disappear. To be an irresponsible, naive child—not a teenager who understood grown-up bullshit. This whole thing made me fearful of adulthood.

"Let's go to my older sister's—your aunt Ruth's—near Phoenix," Dad said, maybe even a little quietly. Was he subdued, too? Maybe this trip was wearing on him as well. Passing the map to Jill, he said, "We'll just travel east on I-8 and then go north on State Route 85 after Gila Bend." He pointed at the route. "Twins, keep your eyes out for that turn. It'll be in about three hours. Then east on I-10. Let's do it."

"Roger that, Dad. We start with 8, then 85, Gila Bend, then 10," Jill recited. It was a relief to see she was taking over the Driver's Helper's duties, even if a part of me felt aggravated by that. She'd seen what I'd seen. How could she not hate Dad for it? Even if she didn't know the full extent, she had to realize that what he'd done was some kind of betrayal of Mom.

I sighed, shrugging it off. She was a kid. I'd let this go.

We hadn't ever met our aunt Ruth and uncle Hartery or our three cousins, Ronnie, Rosalind, and Randy, before. We'd sent them school photos and Christmas cards, and they'd sent us ones, too, but that was the extent of our relationship. I wondered if Aunt Ruth was special like Dad. I hoped not. I'd like to be with a nice family.

Putting Blue Pierre into drive, he said, "We've been on the road, nonstop, go, go, go, for weeks on end. Let's go to my sister's place and have a rest. Maybe we'll stay there for a week or so." He looked at the twins, who smiled back. "I can work on the car, get Blue Pierre cleaned up and ready for the rest of the trip. I think Ruth has a swimming pool, and she can nurse you back to health, Mare. I think she is a nurse, actually. Looks like you need some taking care of."

The twins hopped up and down. Jill said, "A pool? Far-out!" Dad laughed.

Gerri agreed. "Dy-no-mite!" She clapped in time to the three syllables. "Maybe we can sleep in a real bed!"

I knew just how they felt. This rest was much needed for many reasons, and it would get us out of the car and give us a break before we tackled the rest of the trip home.

Lying in the back seat, I felt the weight of everything I'd faced over the past few weeks crash down on me—like a cartoon anvil falling from the sky, straight out of a Wile E. Coyote scene. And now I had told Dad how I felt and what I'd seen, adding even more emotional weight to the fact that I was physically sick—with a fever, no less. Spending a week in a house, with a bed and a pool, with someone taking care of me, sounded divine. I was ready for a break from acting grown-up and needed some babying.

I opened the bottle, took a big whiff, and applied some more Campho-Phenique, whose smell was growing on me. I didn't want any to get on my new blanket, so I used the dirty towel again. It dawned on me that we'd be able to do our laundry at Aunt Ruth's house. I dozed off to that comforting thought, thinking of how many times we'd hand-washed our underwear and socks and other clothes, resulting in subpar freshness levels.

The twins must have helped Dad with the navigation because the next thing I knew, it was starting to get dark, and we were pulling up to their house in Scottsdale, Arizona. They had a cute one-story ranch with a low roof and a red door smack-dab in the middle of two symmetrical halves.

We gathered some of our things, crunched up their pebbled pathway, and approached their fancy red door.

Gerri asked, "When's the last time you saw Aunt Ruth, Dad?"

Dad hung his head a little. "I think she was pregnant with her third kid, Randy. There was a reunion in Cleveland, if I'm remembering correctly, and she and Hartery brought their little ones. Randy was just a babe in arms then. We only had Skippy back then."

"How old is Randy now?" Jill asked, shifting the load in her arms.

Dad thought for a second. "Fifteen. Sixteen. Maybe."

"How much older is Ruth than you, Dad?" Jill asked.

"She's the oldest sister, and I'm the baby of my brothers and sisters. She's ten years older than me."

"Wow, she's a lot older! And you haven't seen her in over sixteen or seventeen years? Holy cow," I remarked. I looked at my sisters, illuminated by the front porch's yellowish light, and wondered if we'd hardly ever see each other when we grew up. I couldn't imagine.

"Well, yeah, that's how it goes sometimes," Dad replied with a dismissive shrug. He took a big breath and exhaled a bigger sigh, then knocked on the door. We heard some moving around inside and saw a small, compact woman—Aunt Ruth, I assumed—peer out the long frosted window on the side of the red door. She slowly raised both hands to her mouth and shook her head in shock.

She flung the door open. She was dressed in a housecoat—a kind of floral robe—with little pink scuffs on her feet. Her rosy apple cheeks reminded me of a younger Grandma Stromp.

Aunt Ruth exclaimed, "Ralph? *Ralphie?*" The twins and I laughed, hearing him referred to as Ralphie. He grinned back at us with an exaggerated wink. "Is that you? What in the Sam Hill are you doing here? My goodness. Where's Ginny?" She looked over his shoulder toward the car and ran her hand over her hair, smoothing down the flyaways. "Heavens to Betsy!"

"It's good to see you, Ruthie-Roo." Dad smiled wider.

"Ruthie-Roo!" She chortled. "I can't remember the last time I heard that. My, my."

Wringing her hands, she looked at us. "This must be Mary and the twins, Jill and Gerri. My goodness gracious. No Ralph Jr.?" We stood outside, shifting self-consciously from foot to foot. The only sound we heard was the buzzing wings of the moths encircling the light overhead. "Come in, come in. Where are my manners? Is your mother in the car?"

She reached for Dad and squeezed him hard. He told her that Mom was back in Ohio. She gave him a curious look as we shuffled in past her. She called out, "Hartery, Hartery. Come see what the cat dragged in." I looked at us closely and had to agree with her that we looked incredibly grubby and worse for wear—like something a cat would drag in.

Uncle Hartery must have thought she'd really meant that their cat had dragged in something. His voice was so deep, it nearly reverberated through the walls. "What is it? A mouse? A rabbit? What did Ricochet catch this time?" We heard footsteps, and then he entered the front area of their home, looking up from a worn copy of *Sleeping Murder* by Agatha Christie, its cover folded under. His hair was disheveled and sticking straight up like he had been running his hands through it, and his lanky body seemed too tall for his pajamas. His eyes widened in disbelief, as though he were face-to-face with Santa Claus. "Ralph? Is that you? By gum!" He looked over Dad's shoulder. "Where's Ginny?"

He and Dad shook hands and did an awkward kind of clapping-on-the-back hug. Dad told him, too, that Mom stayed home. Scratching his cheek, Uncle Hartery folded himself down to the twins' height. "And who do we have here?"

"I'm Jill," she said, "and this is Gerri, and this is Mary."

"Pleased to meet you." My hand felt swallowed whole when he clasped it in greeting. "You can call us Uncle Hartery and Aunt Ruth."

"Hi, Uncle Hartery and Aunt Ruth," we three said in unison.

"Girls, are you hungry?" Our new aunt motioned for us to follow her into the kitchen. We all trailed after her, abandoning the cozy living room. I liked the plump floral sofa, the contrasting throw pillows, and the brass lamps that cast off a steeped yellow light.

Everything seemed so comfortable. There was a television set, but it wasn't on. The remote was on what appeared to be an antique coffee table, stationed beside a few other trinkets. It was organized, calm, and inviting—and I knew I was really going to love staying here for a while. I *hoped* they'd let us stay. It dawned on me that we'd shown up on their doorstep without warning, and that wasn't the politest thing to do.

In the kitchen was a colorful Mexican-looking ceramic fruit bowl on the center of the counter, under a set of windows with green plaid curtains, that instantly caught my eye. It was filled with oranges, lemons, and several similarly sized red and green fruits.

"What are those?" I asked, pointing to the fruit.

"Those? The oranges, lemons, pomegranates, and avocados?"

"Are the pomegranates the red ones?" Jill asked for all of us. Dad stood in the doorway, leaning on the frame.

"Yes, ma'am. We have an orange tree, a lemon tree, an avocado tree, and a pomegranate tree in the backyard," she boasted.

"That's right, girls," echoed Uncle Hartery. "The fruits and leaves fall into the pool all the time. Maybe tomorrow you could help me strain them off the surface."

"Can we swim?" I asked hopefully.

"Of course."

While we were talking, Aunt Ruth had peeled and sectioned some oranges, arranged them on a plate, and pushed them toward us. Then she sliced one of the green fruits in half, took a knife and whacked it into the center pit, popped it out, and scraped the soft flesh into a bowl.

"What are those?" Dad asked.

"You've never had an avocado before?" She chuckled. "Well, you're in for a treat. I'll fix us up some guacamole."

"We had guacamole with a Mexican breakfast burrito in San Francisco, but I didn't think it came from a fruit," I said, shocked. The avocado certainly didn't look like any fruit I'd

313

come upon before—it was covered in a thin, leathery skin, and there wasn't any juice. It'd seemed savory, not sweet.

While she mashed up the green avocado with a fork and added a bit of diced onions and tomatoes, she explained that in Spanish, an avocado is called an *aguacate*, and *mole* meant "mixed up." So *guacamole* meant a mashed-up avocado.

Uncle Hartery went to the cupboard and pulled out a bag of corn chips, and we used them to scoop up the guacamole. *Wow*. I must've looked starved since I kept dipping chip after chip into the *deyishous* mush.

She then showed us how to peel a pomegranate. "Look here. You slice the top off like this and then drag the knife down the ridges where each section divides. See?" She turned the red fruit inside out over a bowl, and the pink seeds dropped out in droves. We looked at the bowl and then up at her. "Try some." She laughed.

We reached in and put several of the seeds into our mouths, surprised by the way they exploded, sort of like a grape, when you bit into them and by their crunchy, wet tanginess.

"Mmm," I said, reaching in and grabbing a bigger handful.

"You should peel off that remaining white membrane," Aunt Ruth said. I did and then popped some more into my mouth. The twins did the same.

Our hands and lips were turning crimson from the juice. While we were enjoying the impromptu fruity feast, Aunt Ruth poured us some milk. As she handed me a glassful, she noticed my legs, and her eyes went wide in surprise. "What happened to your skin?"

I gulped back the milk, and with my mouth full of orange, I said, "The doctor in Mexico says it is the worst case of poison oak he's ever seen."

"I'd say so," she agreed, lips going into a flat line. I saw her gaze hover at my mouth, still full of orange, and realized she probably wanted to remind me not to talk with my mouth full but had restrained herself. "How bad is it?"

Gerri answered for me as I continued eating. "She's covered from head to toe. Both arms and legs, and tummy, and even on her head."

"Oh Mary, what a shame." She reached over and parted my hair. "That looks miserable. Where did you get it? And why are you the only one?"

This time Jill took over. "Well, we have a little bit." She showed our aunt the undersides of her arms and her ankles, where there were a few spots. "We got it in Big Sur when we were trying to get to the Pacific Ocean."

"Yeah. We almost fell off a cliff," Gerri added. "Dad told us to follow a trail that disappeared, but we kept going. Turns out, it led straight to a cliff!"

Uncle Hartery and Aunt Ruth gave him a questioning—dare I say accusatory?—look. Dad had the decency to cringe, appearing somewhat self-conscious. He put his hands in the air in a gesture that said *What?* and shrugged, then reached over and grabbed a couple of orange wedges.

"That sounds," Aunt Ruth said rather dryly, "like quite the adventure."

"We were in search of tide pools," Dad replied casually. "A local had tipped us off. He didn't offer us very good directions, though, did he, girls?"

I bit my tongue. Typical Dad, shifting the blame. "I should take another one of the antibiotics and antihistamines," I said, changing the subject. "Dad, where's the bag?"

"Still in Blue Pierre." He shoveled the rest of his orange into his mouth and also forgot his manners about talking with your mouth full. "Come on. Let's get our stuff unloaded. I'll help."

✳ ✳ ✳

After we bought what we needed from Blue Pierre inside, Aunt Ruth got us settled in their guest bedrooms. I thought it was very generous and Christian of Aunt Ruth and Uncle Hartery to just take us in with open arms. Dad hadn't called them ahead of time, asking if we could stay or anything. They just invited us in, even in our bedraggled state.

Aunt Ruth ushered us into the bathroom to shower. She passed us each a fresh towel and laughed when she saw the three of us burying our noses and inhaling the fresh laundry scent. "You all need some cleaning. You're in kind of a ragamuffin state."

We looked at one another and laughed at the truth in her description.

"Drop your clothes here, and you can wear some old pajamas from Rosalind. I'll do your laundry overnight." Dad was in the doorway, and she gave him another disapproving look. "Ralphie, while they shower, can you get the rest of the dirty clothes? Might as well get it all washed before morning."

Dad turned toward the front door, and before he departed, she asked, "What's your toothbrush situation like?" We showed her our worn-down brushes. "Oh, those will not do, no siree Bob."

She lifted the small bathroom trash can, extending it toward us. We each dropped in our brush. Plink, plink, plink. Reaching into the drawer in the bathroom vanity, she began doling out three new brushes to us—then she looked at Dad, pulled out another, and passed it to him. When she did so, she kind of smacked it into his palm. It reminded me of how Mom had slapped those checkbooks into his hands way back when.

"Thanks, sis."

"Let's get you cleaned up and get some medicine on Mary's rash." She gave Dad a bump with her hip toward the front door. Finally, she had cracked a smile with him. On Dad's way out, Uncle Hartery joined him to help with the dirty laundry.

After our hot showers, Aunt Ruth had me lie down on a queen-size bed and applied the *ungüento* to my legs and arms like a mom tending to a baby's diaper rash. I relaxed into the clean sheets, inhaling a deep breath of their freshly laundered, soapy scent, and relished every second of this. I'd been in need of some coddling, and here it was. I decided I really liked Aunt Ruth.

"Don't worry about getting this on the sheets," she said. "It's all right."

When she'd finished applying the ointment, she flipped me over, pulled the covers up to my neck, and kissed my forehead. The bed was wonderfully comfortable, and the blankets offered the best combination of warmth, coolness, and weight.

Aunt Ruth looked me in the eyes quite seriously. "Can I get you anything else, Mary? Water for the nightstand? Another pillow or blanket?" She fluffed my pillows without even thinking—just pure nurse reflex—as if I'd complain after weeks in Blue Pierre or on the ground

"No, thank you," I said politely. My throat was tight. "I appreciate all this, Aunt Ruth."

"It's no trouble at all, darling. We're thrilled to have you." As soon as Aunt Ruth turned to speak to the twins, I rolled over to lie face down so that she couldn't see my tears; it had been a long time since a real, responsible adult had taken care of me, and it felt like I could finally exhale—like I'd been holding everything together with duct tape and hope.

"Jill and Gerri, do you want to sleep in Rosalind's room down the hall or in here in Randy's room with your big sister? If you sleep in here, you'll have to share the bed."

Without skipping a beat, Jill and Gerri both said in unison, "We'd like to sleep with Mary."

Aunt Ruth's face warmed. "Such good sisters," she commented, then peeled the blankets back once more to tuck them in. She kissed them good night also, and the girls giggled.

"Tomorrow," Aunt Ruth went on, "we'll get to know one another and spend some quality time together. What do you say? Do you play cards?"

"Yes, we do!" Jill chimed in just as Gerri asked, "And can we swim?"

"We can do whatever you like, girls," Aunt Ruth said, grinning. She drifted to the door, flipping off the light switch, and said one more good night.

Again, I felt like crying. This was going to be a nice break. I liked Aunt Ruth already. She seemed like a more solid, caring, female version of Dad—and I loved even more that she didn't shy away from giving him dirty looks when he deserved them.

When Auth Ruth shut the door, it got very quiet. I could hear the adults continue talking in the living room, but it was too jumbled to listen in on. Not a problem for me. Even though I'd napped in the car, I was too exhausted to care. I imagined Aunt Ruth sweeping in like some no-nonsense fairy godmother, wagging her finger at Dad for dragging us across the country like lost kids in a storybook gone wrong.

The cool, smooth sheets caressed my skin, and the fan overhead swirled the air-conditioned air all around. Their cute little tabby cat, Ricochet, tentatively wandered in. He meowed a few times, as though giving us his own personal welcome. The twins and I patted the bed, inviting him up, and Ricochet didn't hesitate to walk on top of me, kneading with his front paws—left, right, left, right—before curling up right under my chin. We were all asleep in no time.

✳ ✳ ✳

The next morning, after using the restroom, the three of us drifted into the kitchen. I could tell that the grown-ups had been up for quite a while by the way the newspapers were strewn here and there. The smells of coffee, some kind of cinnamon-y sweet roll, and bacon flirted with our nostrils and made our tummies grumble.

"Come have a seat," Uncle Hartery said, gesturing to the breakfast nook.

"Hot chocolate, anyone?" Aunt Ruth brought over mugs. "Whipped cream or marshmallows?"

"Marshmallows!" Jill said, beaming. Gerri enthusiastically requested the same thing.

"Whipped cream for me," I said.

"How is your skin feeling this morning, Mary?" Aunt Ruth asked, giving me a smile and Dad a grimace. I loved that Aunt Ruth was advocating so strongly for us. Dad wouldn't listen to anybody, but maybe he'd listen to her. She plopped a generous dollop of homemade whipped cream into my steaming mug of hot chocolate. Had we died and gone to heaven?

"Pretty itchy," I admitted, sipping my drink. "But better. And it felt amazing to sleep in an actual bed with clean sheets! I slept better than I have in weeks."

Aunt Ruth gave Dad another critical look. "I'm not sure I even want to ask about your previous sleeping situations," she said bluntly. "Camping in a tent, I assume?"

"And car-camping!" Gerri said, only for Jill to splice in, "*Dispersed* camping, actually."

"For weeks on end? My, oh my." She sighed, then looked back at me again. "Let me know if there's anything else I can do for your skin, Mary."

"Yes, ma'am," I answered. I'd never said *yes, ma'am* to anyone before, but it just seemed like the proper way to reply to her. "Are you a nurse? Dad said he thought you were."

"Humph! Of course I'm a nurse! How could your father not know about that?" She looked at her husband, who nodded, and then she said to Dad, "Ralph, your self-centeredness makes you oblivious to what's going on in the rest of your family. You've not changed a bit since you were a little boy." *Wow.* Dad looked rebuked but shrugged and didn't say anything. *Typical.* The man was shameless! I gave Dad a similarly severe look, trying to make him take this more seriously, but he'd already returned to casually paging through the newspaper, entirely unbothered. Returning her gaze to me and the twins, she answered, "I've been a nurse for over thirty years. I began in my twenties and am starting to plan for retirement. Just this past year, I've gone down to only three days a week."

Uncle Hartery added, "That doesn't mean anything. Your aunt Ruth is just about the hardest-working woman you'd ever meet. I wish she would relax once in a while." He gave her a tender smile. "She just goes and goes . . . Helping the neighbors, gardening, cleaning, baking, cooking, canning, knitting, crocheting, quilting. I could go on forever. You name it, this woman does it all and keeps as busy as a bee. She's been head nurse over at the medical office, and even though she's gone down to part time, she still does all their administrative work."

I decided then that I wanted to be just like Aunt Ruth.

Aunt Ruth blushed and came over to where her husband was doling out the bacon and gave him a kiss on his stubbly cheek. It almost hurt to see them like that, so loving and respectful of each other. I couldn't recall a single time Dad had complimented Mom in a similar fashion—especially if he wasn't prompted, obligated, or coerced into it. My cousins were lucky. I wondered what it would be like to grow up here, in such a loving family.

Dad said, "And you haven't changed a bit, either, Ruth. Always in charge. I'm guessing you're bossing everyone around still." He laughed, but I could see it struck a nerve with Aunt Ruth based on the way, for a split second, her eyes widened in outrage. "Ruth?" he went on. "Are these Ma's peanut cinnamon buns?" He took a second one from the pan and added it to his plate, dripping some of the glaze onto the countertop. Almost immediately, I saw Aunt Ruth's hand jet forward with a damp towel, wiping away the sticky, sugary mess.

"Yes, indeedy." She watched as he unrolled one of the peanut buns and plopped a bit into his mouth. "That's exactly how you and the other little kids in our family—Buddy, Gretel, and Hank—used to eat them." She wagged her finger at him like I imagined Grandma Stromp would've scolded them decades ago. "Ma did not like that. You little ones would drop peanuts everywhere."

"Wow, a real blast from the past. I remember that. These taste exactly like the ones she used to make on Sunday mornings before church," Dad said.

"Well, that's not surprising. Someone's got to keep the traditions alive. I use the recipe she wrote on this card here and make no changes." She extended the recipe card to her brother for his viewing. "Well, except I use orange juice in the powdered sugar glaze since we have so many oranges here."

"Ma's handwriting," Dad said sentimentally, thumbing the index card.

Even though there was an undercurrent of discontent between them, Ruth put her hand on his shoulder and said, "I miss her, too."

Grandma Stromp, a seventy-six-year-old widow, had passed away alone in her bed in Cleveland two years ago. She'd been the unofficial chauffeur for her group of old lady friends ever since they started losing their eyesight and getting their drivers' licenses taken away. Just the afternoon before she died, she drove one of them to the drugstore and then went to bed as usual. The only reason they found her was because one of her friends was waiting for her at nine o'clock the next morning to drive her to the doctor. When Grandma Stromp didn't show up, the friend called the cops, and they found her in her bed. Cold and stiff. They said it was a stroke or a heart attack, something that hit her suddenly. But how could they know that? When I gazed at her in the casket at the funeral, she didn't look much different from when she'd nap on a Sunday afternoon after church. But then again, I'd never seen a dead person before.

At the time, I'd thought, *Poor Grandma*, but now that I was a little older, I thought the way she'd been strong to the very end was commendable. I wanted to live like that, too. I didn't know Aunt Ruth very well yet, but her energy reminded me of Grandma Stromp's. They were both resilient. They were like wind-up toys that never wound down.

Dad smiled up at Aunt Ruth, and they looked at each other in a way that only siblings do.

After a bit of silence, she asked us girls, "You going to have a Grandma Stromp peanut bun?"

"Yes, ma'am!" we all said in eager harmony, my new way of replying rubbing off on the twins. She laughed at our enthusiasm.

While we were finishing up the bacon and hot chocolate and peanut buns, Uncle Hartery said, "You sleepyheads slept right through Randy coming home last night after working at the pizza parlor and heading out to work at the golf course this morning."

"We did? I didn't hear a thing," Jill said, tipping back her hot chocolate to get every last drop. There was a white streak of marshmallow on her nose, and Gerri reached over and wiped it off, then licked her finger clean.

"Yep, you slept right through his comings and goings. He says he'll be home around three this afternoon and to save some of your energy to swim with him." Uncle Hartery turned to his wife, adding, "He wants to show them how he jumps off the roof into the pool."

"Hartery!" Aunt Ruth scolded. "Don't give them any ideas."

"Okay, girls. No jumping off the roof," he said to us with a wink. "All right, honey?"

Dad laughed as Aunt Ruth gave her husband a perturbed grimace. "Very funny," she said with a smirk.

Uncle Hartery went on, "Randy's working two jobs this summer—dishwasher and golf caddy."

You could hear the pride in his gravelly voice. "He's saving up for a car."

"Good for him," Dad said, lowering the *Arizona Republic* to his lap and folding it neatly in half. "Skippy had two jobs, too, a few summers back—lawn work and busboying at the Bluebird Diner in Mentor. Scraped together just enough for that '59 Austin-Healey Sprite. Bugeye, yeah. Uncle Scrounge let it go for peanuts, but still—kid earned it."

He paused, like maybe he hadn't meant to sound impressed. "Didn't think he had it in him, honestly."

I couldn't tell if that was a compliment or a dig. Probably both.

Aunt Ruth raised an eyebrow. "Richie sold that tiny sports car to Ralph Jr.?"

"For peanuts," Dad said again. Then added, this time with obvious pride, "I've got to hand it to him. He really put time into that car. Eventually got it purring."

"We helped when he painted it that green color," Gerri chimed in, chewing on one of Grandma's peanut buns. Jill nodded, licking crumbs from her lips.

"He took Stacey to the homecoming dance in it," I added. "They decorated the whole thing with streamers. He told me they nearly froze, and Stacey was mad because her fancy hairdo got wrecked by the wind."

"Oh dear," Aunt Ruth said.

Uncle Hartery let out a booming laugh.

"Can I see the funnies?" I asked.

Dad handed over the section. I flipped right to *Archie*, *Peanuts*, and *The Family Circus*. It had been ages since I'd read the comics.

Later that morning, we took a walk around Aunt Ruth's neighborhood while Dad and Uncle Hartery tinkered with Blue Pierre. Aunt Ruth told us Ronnie and Rosalind were grown and out of the house—Ronnie was working at a bank in Las Vegas, and Rosalind was taking a summer college course in nursing. "Just like me," she said proudly. "You'll meet Randy this afternoon."

When we got back to the house, she suggested we go for a swim while she made us some sandwiches. Our bathing suits were on the top of our neatly folded stacks of clean laundry. I wondered when Aunt Ruth could have gotten to that. Uncle Hartery was right—she sure got a lot done, just like her mom, that apple not falling far from the tree. She had made the breakfast and baked the peanut buns and did the laundry all before we had even gotten up for the day. Next, I bet she'd be offering us an opportunity to give Mom a call.

45

Cousin Randy

"I'm home!" we heard our cousin call out, the front door slamming shut behind him.

"How many times have I told you not to slam the front door, son?" Aunt Ruth scolded.

"Sorry, Mom. Where are they?" His eyes darted around the room, his shaggy white-blond hair a blur of motion. He carried with him the scent of fresh air, boyish sweat, and freshly mowed grass. "There they are!"

He spotted us lounging on the love seat and couch, reading and enjoying a moment of luxury. I had just addressed an envelope with a letter to Meredith, telling her all about Aunt Ruth and our trip to Mexico, and had licked the adhesive strip. We straightened up as he came bounding over, pushing his long bangs out of his eyes with his large hands. "Hi, cousins!"

His hands reminded me of massive puppy paws, hinting at how big the dog would be when fully grown. His high-energy enthusiasm seemed at odds with the formal golfing clothes he wore.

I stood, expecting a handshake, but instead, he wrapped me in a bear hug. "You're Mary," he announced, as though I didn't already know. "Hi, Mary! Welcome to Phoenix! And you're the twins!" he added, giving them a tight squeeze, too, lifting them off the ground.

Dad walked in from the kitchen, wiping his hands on his pants.

"Uncle Ralph!" Randy shouted, his face lighting up like he'd spotted a rock star. His voice crackled with excitement as he dashed across the living room.

Dad looked up, startled for a moment, then broke into a grin. "Well, I'll be," he said as Randy reached him. Their handshake turned into a hearty clasp, then melted into a half hug with back slaps that landed like applause.

"Last time I saw you, you were drooling on my shoulder," Dad said, pulling back to get a good look at him. "Now look at you—what are you, six feet tall?"

"Five-ten and still growing," Randy said proudly. "I eat like a horse and work like one, too!"

I watched the two of them chuckling, and for a moment, it felt like one of those heartwarming family scenes. It was kind of nice. And kind of a bummer. I couldn't remember Dad lighting up like that around Skippy.

Dad continued, "Just look at you, dapper in your golfing getup." Golfing getup? What a dork! But Randy didn't seem to think so. His smile stretched as wide as a mile. I bet Dad would've liked to have had a son like Randy. They fit together like jigsaw puzzle pieces within seconds of meeting. Poor Skippy. His and Dad's pieces came from different puzzles, with no way to align. I sent Skippy a telepathic hug and a silent wish for his happiness in his new apartment with Stacey.

"Uncle Ralph, I've always wanted to meet you," I heard Randy say. "My mom has some good stories about you."

"She does?" I asked, looking first at him, then at Aunt Ruth. It dawned on me that she was probably the most valuable person in the world when it came to learning about Dad's childhood. Maybe she could shed some light on why he was the way he was.

"Let's settle down," Aunt Ruth suggested, straightening her apron and calling us into the kitchen. "Who'd like a snack? I have a plate of cheese and crackers." She smacked Randy on the derrière as he bounced past her and hopped onto one of the barstools.

I loved Phoenix. Happy people; normal family; and someone else doing the laundry, preparing meals and snacks, and reliably taking care of the essentials. Furthermore, my rash was feeling better, even if it still looked horrible. The chlorine water from our earlier swim really dried it out and relieved some of the itchiness.

"So, cousins, tell me about yourselves!" Randy commanded, but before we could speak, he went on to ask, "Have you been in the pool yet? I've got to show you how to jump off the roof. You can do a huuuuge cannonball—"

"No, you don't need to show them that," interjected Aunt Ruth. "They're too little, and we don't know their swimming abilities yet."

"Aw, *Mom*," Randy groaned. He gave us a side-eye. "I bet she gives you the swimming test."

Outside of that being relatively self-explanatory, I wasn't sure what it would entail. I did want to tell them all that we'd been swimming in the ocean and had been knocked over several times and that we'd survived. I'd swum hard laps and the backstroke at the motel in Wells. We were pretty good swimmers. But before I could say anything, Randy went on as if suddenly remembering something else.

"Mom! Can I take them to the bounce place after dinner? What's for dinner? Maybe I could take them *out* to dinner? You guys like McDonald's? We could get Big Macs."

"You mean, two all-beef patties," I began, and Gerri and Jill joined me in adding, "special sauce, lettuce, cheese, pickles, onions . . ."

Randy let out a huge laugh before helping us conclude: ". . . on a sesame seed bun!"

"Oh goodness, you kids are as nutty as a fruitcake," Aunt Ruth chided, turning to the sink to rinse off the plate. Even though Randy was what my mom would call a wild child, I could tell Aunt Ruth adored him, even if it was hard to keep up with him. I wondered what kind of student he was and if his teachers liked him or not.

Jill squeezed in the question, "What's the bounce place?"

"Oh man. It's the grooviest place. They have about a dozen, maybe twenty, sunk-in-the-ground trampolines all lined up next to each other. You can bounce from one to the next. You can do front flips and backflips and all kinds of tricks. And it's right by the McDonald's."

"That does sound groovy," I agreed, smiling at him. I looked to Dad. "Can we go?"

"Maybe you should bounce *before* getting hamburgers," said Uncle Hartery, who had walked in the back door, peeling off his well-worn work gloves and laying them on the counter. "Better to have an empty stomach for all that bouncing and then eat afterward."

"Good point, Dad. Last time we went, Thomas Smart and James both puked up their 7-Eleven Slurpees, and—"

"Oh Randy, spare us the details, please!" Aunt Ruth said, pinning him with a critical stare. The twins and I looked at one another and cracked up, then covered our mouths. Even Dad and Uncle Hartery tried to hide their laughter, too.

We ended up being allowed to go with Randy to the bounce place. The folks there knew Randy and let us in at a discounted rate of one dollar for Randy and me and only fifty cents for the twins.

There weren't that many people there that evening, and we kind of had the place to ourselves. The twins and I started out tentatively at first, mastering seat and knee drops before adding back and front drops. Randy showed us how to do tuck jumps and pike jumps, and within a half hour, we were able to do front flips and backflips. We had races, and Gerri was the fastest to cross from one side to the other—even faster than Randy, who liked to jump super high. It was kind of like when Jill's little frog beat the bigger ones back at Camp Bluebird.

"Having fun?" he asked us after a while.

"We sure are! This place is great," I said, falling down inelegantly next to him.

"We love this," Gerri panted. Jill nodded vigorously.

"I'm hungry," I said. "Let's go eat."

"You won't get an argument out of me about that!" said Randy. "I'm always hungry."

Walking on solid ground after we'd finished all that bouncing felt strangely disorienting, like sea legs. My feet stomped as I walked, and the ground felt too hard. That odd sensation gradually wore off as we made our way to the McDonald's next door. The sign read OVER 20 BILLION SERVED.

"I think it's impossible that they've been able to count to over twenty billion," Randy remarked. I couldn't fault him on that. Seemed impossible.

We ordered Big Macs, french fries, and vanilla shakes for $1.35 each. Dad had given Randy a five-dollar bill before we left. It had just covered our evening's expenses. I was surprised that Dad let us go with just our cousin and that Uncle Hartery had let him borrow the family car. As it turned out, Randy had driven extra cautiously, even making us put on our seat belts. He told us that at the end of the summer, he would have enough money saved to get his very own car and that he would be the grooviest cat in the junior class of Scottsdale High School.

✳ ✳ ✳

The next morning, we congregated in the kitchen, drawn by the *deyishous* smells of breakfast yet again. Dad had arrived first, and when we came through the door, he said, "Good morning, girls. Did you hear the birds this morning?"

I cocked my head to listen, and the birds sang out, on cue.

"Those are our northern mockingbirds. That's ironic, isn't it?" Aunt Ruth chuckled, her cheeks bunching up toward her eyes. "Here we are in the Southwest, and the *northern* mockingbirds are here singing their hearts out every morning."

She poured some orange juice into little jelly jars for us. My mouth watered as the bright aroma drifted toward me.

"I was thinking," she offered, "would you like to call your mom, girls?"

She gave Dad a look I couldn't read. He smiled back. Then, like he couldn't resist, he pulled his eyes off hers and stared directly at me. I wondered if he was worried about how close we'd all become with Aunt Ruth already—and I wondered if he

328

thought I was going to tell her what I knew. A big part of me wished he'd worry that I just might. I would be curious to know about Aunt Ruth's perspective of Dad being "special" and about his "understanding" with Mom. Already, she'd relieved me of all the adult responsibility Dad had dumped on my shoulders, and I knew if I unloaded this on her, she'd do what I wasn't willing to: call Mom, tell her everything, and bring this to an end.

"Is it a workday? I'd love that, but she'll be at work until five o'clock," I said, taking a big bite of one of the egg and cheese English muffin sandwiches she'd made for us.

"Okay. Let's call her at two thirty, which will be five thirty Cleveland time," Aunt Ruth reasoned.

"That sounds great," I said, and I meant it. It'd be good to talk to Mom without being distracted significantly by the need to pee. Or by trying to keep the call secret. And to be in a group. I'd be reluctant to spill the beans in front of an audience.

"We haven't talked to Mom for weeks," Jill chimed in, and once again, Aunt Ruth shot Dad a critical glare. I thought she'd speak up this time, perhaps chastise him in some way, but Gerri interjected. "I miss Mom. I can't wait to talk to her."

"Aunt Ruth, I want to show you something," Jill said.

"What is it, sweetheart?"

Jill dashed from the kitchen and down the hallway, then quickly returned with the Slate of Dates, States, and Fates in hand. "But first I have to do some updating. We've gotta add this resting time in Phoenix with you and Uncle Hartery and Randy." She wrote: *7/16–21/76 | Arizona | Phoenix | Aunt Ruth, Uncle Hartery, and Randy—Swimming pool, trampoline park, McDonald's.*

"Wow, this is one adventure you're having." Aunt Ruth motioned for Uncle Hartery to join her in reviewing the Slate. He put his hand gently on her shoulder, and she covered his hand with hers, patting it lovingly. He peered over her shoulder.

"Nice handwriting," he commented, and Jill beamed. "And funny descriptions: banana splits, bologna, and . . ." His eyes widened. "Mary driving?"

Dad quickly piped in. "Only on a road without traffic." That was a lie, of course, but the moment was too ripe to spoil, so I didn't object. "And only for a short time. She did wonderfully and is a natural. I also taught you how to check the oil levels, didn't I, Mare?" His choppy sentences and defenses made us look more guilty than less.

"Yes, I've learned a lot." I kept his ruse going.

"And look at all these incredible places they've seen," Aunt Ruth added. She finally gave Dad a genuine smile. "You've really given them a wonderful experience, Ralphie—" She caught herself. "Sorry, I mean *Ralph*. Mount Rushmore, Devils Tower, Old Faithful, Lake Tahoe, San Francisco, Santa Cruz, Big Sur . . ." She trailed her finger down Jill's listings, truly awed.

"And the Walk of Fame in LA, tide pools, Mexico," Uncle Hartery went on, shaking his head. "Wow, Ralph. Ruth is right; you've really shown the girls a wide cross section of America."

Dad took his turn grinning like a hero in a tall tale, proud of the adventure he'd given us.

Gerri bragged for him. "Yes, this is the bicentennial year and is a perfect time to take the Great American Road Trip!" She licked her lips, removing some stuck-on egg yolk. "And this is a perfect egg sandwich, Aunt Ruth. Thank you." She popped the last bite into her mouth.

"I agree," her twin said, and, putting on Mrs. G's accent, she added, "It has a certain *je ne sais quoi*." We all laughed. Huh. Even Jill remembered that perfect phrase.

"The Great American Road Trip," Aunt Ruth muttered, as though feeling the words out in her mouth before smiling and nodding silently at Dad. "That sounds exactly like what it's been: the Great American Road Trip."

I felt my heart unexpectedly drop.

Dad and I had been planning this trip for years. And for years, as we mapped out all the places we wanted to go, I told myself it didn't really matter where we ended up. What mattered was spending time with him—the fun parent, my hero, the one I always wanted more of. Looking back, I wonder if I should have been more hesitant. If I should have asked more questions, thought it through. Maybe then I would have realized that some things were better left as dreams. Then again, maybe not.

"Well, I'll be heading to work soon," Uncle Hartery announced, interrupting my thoughts, taking his plate and cup to the sink. "What's on tap for today, folks?"

"I think they should just rest and relax again today," Aunt Ruth answered for us. "Spend some time in the pool. That sort of thing."

We did indeed lounge around the pool, reading books and magazines and drinking fancy ice-cold water that Aunt Ruth flavored with cucumber slices and mint leaves. We swam laps and had handstand and somersault contests. Dad must have appreciated the restful day as well because he ended up taking two naps.

My rash was healing a little bit each day. I was still applying Campho-Phenique, calamine, and the Mexican *ungüento*. The calamine was the most soothing, but I think the sunshine in the day and the medicine at night were what was really doing the trick. Because I didn't like the way the antihistamines made me so sleepy, I'd stopped taking them, but Aunt Ruth told me that even though I was starting to feel better, I had to finish all the antibiotics.

"Hey, girls," Aunt Ruth called to us. "It's just about two thirty. Let's get on the horn and call your mother." We got out of the pool at once, wrapping the clean, plush towels around our waists as we headed inside. I looked around for Dad but couldn't find him anywhere. Perhaps he was taking a conveniently timed third nap.

Aunt Ruth led us to the mustard-colored phone mounted on the kitchen wall. She untangled the long cord and then handed the receiver to Gerri, letting her dial. Gerri messed up the first time and had to do it again. While it was ringing, Jill and I ran to the den, where they had an extension, and picked up the handset. We laid the towels on the chair to keep it dry, then sat down and positioned the phone between our two heads so that we both could hear. After at least four *ring-a-dingies*, we heard Mom pick up.

"Hello?" she questioned, a little out of breath.

"Mom!" Gerri from the kitchen and Jill and I from the den all yelled back at her.

"Well, I'll be," she said, a smile shaping her voice. "Gerri? Jill? Mary? Is that all three of you?"

"And Aunt Ruth," Gerri clarified.

"Aunt Ruth? *Aunt Ruth?* Your father's oldest sister? Are you calling from Phoenix?"

"Yes!" Jill said. "She's great—"

Gerri talked over her twin. "We went to a trampoline bouncing park last night!"

"Trampolines? You don't say," she said. There was an awkward pause where we all tried not to talk over one another. "Mary, did you ever go to a doctor for your rash?"

"Yeah," I said. "We saw a doctor in Mexico."

"Mexico?" She gasped like I'd just said we'd gone to the moon.

"I know, right? Crazy." I shrugged, then added, "The doctor said it was the worst case of poison oak he'd ever seen." Somehow, that seemed impressive to me, but to Mom it might have felt different. Sometimes I had no common sense.

"That's awful! Are you feeling better?" Before I could say more, her tone shifted to something much sharper and more serious. "Wait—why did you go to *Mexico* for a doctor?"

Jill jumped in before I could answer, leaning in close so that I could feel her breath—hot and sweet from the pop she'd been sipping. "Dad thought it'd be a good way to kill two birds with one stone. You know, see Mexico and see a doctor. He said it would be cheaper, too."

Talking to everyone at once, all of us crammed onto two phones and cutting one another off, felt like being on an overloaded CB radio channel.

"Does Namo miss us?" Gerri got in.

I could tell Mom wanted to talk more about Mexico, but she indulged Gerri. "Well, when I asked Namo, she wagged her tail and told me that she could hold out a little longer but wished you'd all come home sooner than later."

I heard Gerri's laughter in our phone's handset and coming through the house, her two voices echoing in stereo.

We caught up on what Skippy was doing and if he ever visited her. Mom said they'd come over for supper twice already. Stacey had brought cupcakes for dessert. Comparing the weather was about the stupidest use of long-distance phone time I could imagine, but we did it anyway. I eventually had a realization, though: I didn't care what we talked about. I just liked hearing Mom's voice, and I think she just liked hearing ours.

After a full ten minutes of reuniting, Mom finally asked, "How is your dad? Is he around?"

"Hi, Ginny," I heard him say. He must've joined Gerri and Aunt Ruth in the kitchen.

"Hello, Ralph." I didn't hear the smile in her voice anymore. "How is your *vacation*?" she asked, adding a strange emphasis to *vacation*.

"So far, so good," he replied rather quickly.

"Mary told me about getting a poison oak rash from trying to get to a beach in California or something?" Mom said, phrasing it as a question.

"Yes, that's true and unfortunate. We didn't realize that we wouldn't be able to access the beach from the path we'd chosen—which a local had directed us to take." Again, I gritted my teeth. Dad's blame-shifting ways were outstanding. "We *all* got scratched up, and Mary stubbornly didn't rinse off like the rest of us, which is why it got so bad. Don't worry—everything is under control."

"I'm not worried," she denied, her words clipped.

Gerri and Aunt Ruth had come into the den, leaving Dad in the kitchen alone.

"Should we hang up?" I asked. "Do you two want to talk privately?"

At the same time, we heard "Yes" from Dad and "No, that's not necessary" from Mom, who went on to say, "I just wanted to know if you three girls were okay."

"They're doing great," Dad said on our behalf. "Aren't you, girls?"

The twins agreed at once, but I stayed silent—caught between the fantasy of telling our mother everything about

333

how Dad had jeopardized our safety repeatedly throughout this trip and how he'd also ruined it with his extramarital affair or agreeing with the twins. I thought back to him telling me that eventually I'd forgive him for what he'd done and that all would go back to normal, and I felt my face radiate heat at the thought. Of course he'd want that. Of course he'd seek out a consequence-free outcome for his reckless, selfish behavior.

"Mary?" Mom said, picking up on the fact that I hadn't answered the question, but Dad quickly took over by saying, "Okay, let me talk to Mom alone for a minute, and then you can get back on and say goodbye."

Reluctantly, we hung up and sat in the den with Aunt Ruth. None of us seemed to know where to look or to put our hands, but it was clear that Aunt Ruth—who sat with her lips pressed in a fine line, eyes locked in Dad's general direction—suspected something wasn't right. I admired her for catching on so quickly. She wasn't easily fooled.

In about three minutes, we heard Dad call out, "Okay, you can pick up the phone now."

We said our goodbyes, and Dad told her that we'd be home in a couple of weeks.

* * *

Randy and Uncle Hartery arrived home at the same time, a little after four thirty. When they came through the front door, Randy was already talking to us. He let the door bang shut again, and Aunt Ruth sighed, shaking her head. I was grateful for the distraction after the phone call. Mom and Dad were no Ruth and Hartery, that's for sure.

"Hey, everyone!" Randy said, a mile a minute like usual. "I have the day off tomorrow, and I was just talking to Dad, who said he could take the day off, too. We were wondering if you'd like to go see the Grand Canyon since you're in Arizona." Our faces must have lit up because he continued enthusiastically without missing a beat, "It's about three and a half hours away. Mom, you work tomorrow, right? Can we take the girls and Uncle Ralph without you?"

"That's fine, son," she answered, straightening the doily beneath a little potted cactus.

"We'll have to leave nice and early. No more sleeping in." He wagged his finger at the three of us, and we grinned. For this, we'd happily get up early. "We'll go to the South Rim on the Kaibab Trail. *Kaibab* is a Paiute word that means 'mountain lying down.' Isn't that far-out? The Grand Canyon is like an invisible upside-down mountain. Kind of. Anyway."

Uncle Hartery tried to get a word in edgewise. "Ralph, I think we'd all fit in our station wagon, and that way your car can keep resting. From what you've told me, it seems like your Peugeot is kind of on its last legs."

Dad seemed a little insulted by this observation but realized Uncle Hartery probably spoke the truth. "Sounds like a great idea. What do you say, girls?"

Gerri answered for all of us. "We'd love to see the Grand Canyon!"

"So," Randy went on, clapping his hands, "do you have good walking shoes?"

Our Keds were getting pretty worn down, but the three of us said yes anyway. What else were we going to do? Buy new ones? Ha! That was a joke. Dad would probably make up an excuse to go against that idea. Either way, we'd make do.

"Good. If we leave early and take water and a picnic, we can arrive there around nine thirty and catch the shuttle from the Visitors Center and then get to the South Kaibab Trailhead. It's less than a mile to Ooh Aah Point. Then we follow a bunch of switchbacks down, down, down—"

I interrupted, "It's actually called Ooh Aah Point?"

"Yeah, cool name," Randy confirmed. "When you get there, you'll look out and be unable to resist saying *ooh, aah*. Groovy, huh?"

"What are switchbacks?" Jill asked.

Dad must've felt left out. He answered, "Switchbacks are a way to manage a steep incline without going straight. Remember

Lombard Street in San Francisco? That little section of road had eight switchbacks. You go one way along the ledge and then switch back in the other direction. Over and over. It makes the distance traveled farther but the slope less severe. You'll really appreciate them on the way back up." He winked at Jill, who got up and fetched her notebook from our bedroom and added: *7/20/76 | Arizona | Grand Canyon/Kaibab Trail, Aah Ooh Point.*

"Good thinking, Jilly-Bean," I said. "Now you're actually ahead on the Slate, but I think it's the *Ooh Aah* Point."

She giggled, then erased and fixed the entry.

The girls and I helped Aunt Ruth prepare a picnic of ham and cheese sandwiches, fruit, carrot and celery sticks, cookies, chips, and drinks. Randy helped Dad and Uncle Hartery get the station wagon ready. I went out to the garage and saw them checking the fluids under the hood and adding jugs of water to the back area. There were backward-facing seats in the rear of the station wagon. The twins would *love* that.

Randy and I came back in, and he went to put on his swim trunks. I was already in my bathing suit, even though it smelled a bit musty, covering the odor and my rash with a long blouse of Aunt Ruth's. With the dads focused on getting the station wagon ready and Aunt Ruth busy in the kitchen, we kids figured that this might be our only chance. Randy and I slipped outside. I went to the pool area while he climbed onto the roof, looking at the back door to make sure Aunt Ruth wouldn't see.

"Call your sisters," he whispered to me. I did as he instructed but didn't really need to. Jill and Gerri emerged from the kitchen just at the perfect time, shading their eyes against the sun. They barreled forward, lining up beside me, and the three of us giggled as Randy got himself ready.

Realizing it was probably inevitable that Aunt Ruth would catch him, Randy shouted, "Cannonball!"

A second later, he launched himself off the roof, gliding forward at least six feet to make it past the pool's edge. He curled up into a ball, plunging into the deep end and splashing the three of us standing there in the sun.

We laughed and applauded enthusiastically. Aunt Ruth, however, wasn't nearly so amused. The door to the kitchen burst open. "Randy! What did I tell you?" she scolded, waving a wooden spoon that she had been stirring the spaghetti sauce with.

"Sorry, Ma," he replied, giving me a wink. She shook her head.

46

A One and a Two and a Three Bee Lee

"Ooh, aah!" We all exaggerated our awestruck appreciation of the Grand Canyon at the lookout. We had been hiking down the Kaibab Trail into the Grand Canyon for about forty minutes. At the Yaki Point, the view of the eastern canyon opened up, and we understood why it was called Ooh Aah Point. That place was *massive*. It really did look like a mountain had been pushed down into the earth, creating an enormous depression.

"This whole thing has been carved by the Colorado River running its course for the past five to six million years. Isn't that *ex-tra-or-din-ary*?" Dad said, putting his hand over his eyes and panning left to right, taking it all in.

The canyon was even more fantastic than Randy had described. You could see inside the earth, and it looked like different layers of browns and reds and oranges and coppers of a multilayered cake. I imagined flavors of cinnamon and clove and nutmeg and pumpkin and brown sugar.

Dad was going crazy with the Super 8, having us pose in various places and arranging our hands in different positions to give the illusion of holding boulders over our heads or supporting the heavy walls of the canyon. In one pose, we pinched our fingers, and it looked like we were holding a miniature tree on the other side of a switchback.

We were still going strong at Cedar Ridge and decided that we could make it to Skeleton Point, where we collapsed on the side of the trail. Uncle Hartery and Dad had divvied up the lunch items from their two knapsacks.

Unzipping them, they passed around the food, and that sandwich was the best I had ever had in my whole life. I'm glad Aunt Ruth had added crispy lettuce. I think when you're physically tired, food tastes better than it normally does. Even the carrots and celery were magnificent. We made a mess of peeling the pomegranates. Aunt Ruth had made it look so easy! We used some of the drinking water to rinse our hands and the sweet fruit juice that had run down our chins. There we were, looking like vampires at Skeleton Point.

Topping off our lunch were the chocolate chip cookies. Feeling blessed, I savored mine, taking tiny nibbles to make it last and picking up the few crumbs that fell on my lap. I couldn't tell what the best part of this entry in My Journal of Life was: the great food, the fun company, or the amazing views.

We lay back and rested for a couple of minutes before Uncle Hartery hopped up, clapped his hands, and exclaimed, "All right, troops, let's do this!"

"Yes, Hartery, I agree," Dad chimed in. "We're fed and rested. Let's march."

I was ready to get climbing, but something held me back. As everybody shouldered their bags and started heading in the other direction—back up out of the canyon—I spied the trail a little farther down, perhaps only ten feet. Something in me wanted to know that I'd ventured the deepest into the canyon, even if only by taking five additional steps. Realizing I probably wouldn't get another chance for the rest of my life to hike the Grand Canyon, I quickly gathered my things and headed the opposite way of everybody else.

One, two, three, four, five . . .

I counted my steps, reaching territory we hadn't yet ventured into, and took one last long look out at the canyon cupped around us.

"What are you doing?" Randy asked. I hadn't realized he was there, and I jumped, startled.

"I just wanted to go down farther into the canyon than my sisters," I whispered, not wanting the twins to hear. But it was too late. Dad, Uncle Hartery, and the twins had walked slower than I had thought and were only perhaps twenty feet away from where I stood.

"What?" Jill asked. I shook my head at Randy.

"She wants to make sure she goes farther down the trail than you," Randy said. *Nice one, Randy,* I thought. *Way to betray me.*

Jill grabbed Gerri's hand, and they ran down two steps past the dusty footprint I'd left.

Oh brother. I ran down two past theirs. We did that over and over.

Dad got out the Super 8, laughing. He had us explain what we were doing.

I wasn't going to lose. Seemed like the twins didn't want to lose, either. We kept at it for about five minutes. Randy and Uncle Hartery helped Dad by assuming perches on different rocks and taking turns with the camera at different angles.

"I went the farthest," I said, tapping my foot in the dust.

"*We* went the farthest," the twins said, hand in hand.

"I went the farthest!" I announced again, smiling up at Randy with the Super 8 in his hand.

"*We* went the farthest!" They giggled, making their footprints and waving at Uncle Hartery, who had his turn.

"Make it a tie," Randy called out.

Gerri said, "Okay. Let's make it a tie. Come on, Mary. We can all line up our steps at the same place." I nodded. "A one and a two and a three bee lee!" On *lee,* we put our footprints down next to one another's. I made sure that my step was on the outside of the curve of the trail so that in actuality, it was farther traveled than theirs, but I didn't tell them that. I'd won.

I was glad we didn't go any farther down and that our bellies were full. What took us an hour and a half to descend took us over three hours to climb back up. When we finally summited, we flopped into the seats of the waiting shuttle bus, dog-tired. Uncle Hartery drove us back to Aunt Ruth's house. I dozed off, resting my head on Randy's shoulder.

✻ ✻ ✻

By the time we'd finally made it back to Scottsdale, I was starving and exhausted. The first thing that met my nose upon arrival was a savory scent that made my mouth water. I realized shortly afterward that it was Aunt Ruth's Crock-Pot recipe from earlier that morning that I was smelling. We washed up quickly and sat down at the table.

"You all look beat," Aunt Ruth remarked. I smiled at her. She was right.

Dad suggested, "How about we rest for another day and then head out the following morning?" He passed me the basket of warm rolls. "We don't want to overstay our welcome."

Aunt Ruth laughed and poured the twins big glasses of milk. "You're still welcome if you'd like to stay longer."

Randy groaned. "Noooo! Don't leave yet! I haven't taken you guys tubing down the Salt River. We have inner tubes and a cooler. I have tomorrow off, too." He took a swig of milk. "You can jump off the cliffs."

"I can't take another day off," said Uncle Hartery. "But you can borrow the station wagon again."

"How about we do that instead of resting tomorrow, and then you can still leave the next day if you really have to?" suggested Randy.

"Yeah, Dad. Let's do it," I said, figuring that we'd rest on the trip home. We had a lot of driving ahead of us to get back to Ohio.

I couldn't believe our time at Aunt Ruth's was coming to an end already. She was so kind, and my rash was getting better by the day. I'd felt more looked after and taken care of than I had not just for this trip, to be honest, but in *years*.

As much as I missed Mom, I wasn't excited about what waited for us at home. Facing the reality of everything Dad had done—not just as far as Charlotte was concerned but about the whole checkbook fight he'd had with Mom and their pending divorce—was overwhelming to think about. Did she feel this trial separation was good for her? I wouldn't blame her if it had been, but I also dreaded the aftermath of such a life-changing decision.

As though on cue, Aunt Ruth stopped in front of me to hand me a plate of *deyishous* food and snapped me back into the present moment. We still had another day of tubing to enjoy tomorrow, and only after that would I let myself refocus on the cold, hard reality of going home.

47

Otters, Waterfalls, and Horses, Oh My!

Just like the day before, we left the house bright and early. Randy had dug out a tie-dyed shirt he'd made back in middle school—amazingly, it still fit. It even sort of matched ours, making us look like a psychedelic team in our swirling bursts of color. *At least we'll have no trouble spotting one another on the river,* I thought.

"We want to get there before everyone else; plus, it gets really hot in the afternoons," Randy said as he drove north on East Indian School Road. "It's a much shorter drive to where we're going today. Only about an hour." He tuned the radio to 104.7 KBUZ, and "Oh, What a Night" by Frankie Valli and the Four Seasons rang out.

I sang along quietly in the back middle seat, the twins bookending me.

Randy and Dad had squeezed two inner tubes into the back of the station wagon and tied four more on top of it last night after supper. I could feel them bouncing around as we drove and hoped they'd done a good job of securing them in place.

"Why do we have six inner tubes for five people?" Gerri asked, leaning to get closer to Randy.

"That's a good question, Ger," he answered, turning the volume down. "I've done this lots of times with my friends. We have the system figured out perfectly. Tying our five tubes around the one center tube that has the cooler in it creates a raft that kind of looks like a daisy. Being combined like that protects us when we go over the waterfalls and basically keeps us together on the lazy sections of the river."

That sounded like a great idea. "Is the water cold?" I asked.

"Of course! Cold and refreshing! And since it's been hotter than a goat's butt in a pepper patch lately, it'll feel great." The twins and I raised our eyes at one another and burst out laughing at that silly phrase. He went on, "Plus, you get to jump off the ledges at Mud Cliffs."

Jill asked, "How high are the cliffs?"

Randy stopped for a second, like he was trying to come up with an answer that'd make sense to a ten-year-old girl. "Not too high," he said, keeping it kind of vague. "You'll all be fine. I'll stay in the water to make sure you're okay."

I'm not certain that was very reassuring to her. I patted her knee. Randy sped up and passed a station wagon that looked just like ours, only theirs had an old white-haired couple in the front seat and two enormous Great Danes bumping into each other in the back.

"Is it salty? It's called the Salt River, right?" Gerri asked nervously, worried that this might be a repeat of the Great Salt Lake experience. Now it was her turn for a reassuring pat on the knee.

"Well, I wouldn't call it salty like the ocean, but it does taste a little salty. It's really soft on your skin, though; that's what I like about it." He scratched his sunburned nose. "It'll probably feel nice on your rash, Mare."

I looked down at my legs and arms; the rash felt so much better. I was still hideous, though. *Yuck.* I looked like a hairless cheetah or leopard, what with the spots still fading. Randy brought me back from my self-loathing. "We brought good drinking water, so you won't have to drink the river water."

"I hate salt water," Gerri said, unconvinced.

"You'll be fine, Ger. It's not like *real* salt water, like I said. You barely notice it," Randy reassured her, then added, "You guys have good sneakers on, right? There are rocks on the bottom, and you don't want to have flimsy sandals. Gotta protect those little piggies." He laughed.

"Yes," Dad replied, "I made sure that we all have on good shoes." He turned around to the back seat and smiled at us. "This will be an adventure, girls. Doesn't the heat here sort of remind you of our time in Mexico? We sure have traveled a long way." Not only the heat but our brightly colored shirts reminded us of the vibrancy of Mexico as well.

It hit me again just how far we'd come—and how much we'd seen. It really had been the trip of a lifetime, even if it didn't look exactly like the one I'd pictured. I thought that our Great American Road Trip would be my chance to bond with Dad—instead, it was my chance to bond with almost everybody but him: the twins, Meredith and the Gardeners, Aunt Ruth and Uncle Hartery, and our cousin Randy.

I was still grateful for this trip, though. Even though I hadn't connected with Dad, and he'd ruined it by paying for a prostitute, I was sure that I'd never forget this summer for as long as I lived. The pages in My Journal of Life were filled to overflowing.

Randy, again, snapped me out of my thoughts.

"And hats, right?" he confirmed, tapping the brim of his Texas Rangers baseball cap.

"Yeah, your mom made sure that we each had a hat with a brim. And we all have on jean shorts over our swimming suits," I added.

"Super-duper," he said. "You're ready as rain."

"Randy, you have as many funny phrases as a cartoon character in a Saturday morning show," I remarked, and this time it was his turn to laugh.

We rode on for a while, the windows down and the radio blasting. Randy was clearly familiar with the area and took all the right turns, and before I knew it, we were pulling into a makeshift parking lot adjacent to the Salt River.

"We're here! Can everyone keep their window rolled down about an inch?" Randy put the station wagon into park, yanked on the emergency break, and jumped out.

Running around the car, he twisted the handle and jerked the back gate open. The wide door swung on its hinge, nearly knocking Jill down. Dad helped, pulling out the inner tubes from the back while Randy unlashed the ones on the roof. They bounced to the ground.

While they were topping off the air in the tubes, I inhaled a deep breath of the cool, dank air wafting off the river. It was a *very* hot day. I didn't think I had ever experienced hotter, drier weather. Earlier, Dad said it was forecasted to be 110 degrees today and that it was perfect for water sports, especially if you did it early, like we were.

"Okay, girls," Randy said. "Each of you carry one of these tubes, and I'll grab the cooler and ice. Uncle Ralph, can you take that bag with the food?" He gestured to the paper sack that the girls and I had helped Aunt Ruth prepare. "We can add it to the cooler when we get down there to the shore."

"Are you going to lock the car?" Dad asked him.

"Oh yeah. Sometimes I'm so forgetful I don't know whether to check my ass or scratch my watch," he said, and we all burst out laughing.

"See? There's another one of your crazy sayings," I pointed out. Randy patted me on the head, then walked around to each door and pushed down the little lock buttons.

I had a moment of sweeping gratitude for what was about to take place today. It was bound to be another great entry in My Journal of Life.

"You each have the small towel my mom gave you, right?" We nodded. "Those come in handy. The tubes get really hot, and you want to protect yourself from the valve stems. Those can poke you if you're not careful while bouncing down the rapids."

I felt my grin falter at this description, and I think the twins reacted similarly. Bouncing down the rapids? That made it sound like they were pretty formidable. There was a lot more to tubing than I'd thought. Randy noticed our concerned faces and said, "It'll be totally groovy. The rapids aren't too scary."

"My girls are brave," Dad bragged. Gerri and Jill smiled at each other nervously.

"No one will get hurt. I really have done it a million times . . ." Randy trailed off as he made his way down to the shore, avoiding the saguaro cacti and their outstretched arms. I had to pause on my way to the shore, taking a closer look at one of them. It was as tall as a tree, and it seemed like it belonged on another planet. I made a quick Journal of Life note.

We traipsed after Randy, the unwieldy tubes banging against our legs. The twins could barely get their skinny little arms around the thick tubes. Jill just let hers go, and it rolled down the hill, somehow missing the cacti. Gerri copied her. And then I did, too. They splashed into the river as we chased after them.

"Here goes nothing," Dad said, bringing up the rear and wrestling with his tube.

Randy wedged the largest inner tube around the cooler, filled it with food, drinks, and ice, and secured the lid with a rope. He lashed five more tubes around it, valve stems down, then looped the excess rope around the handle. Everything was set. Now all that was left was to jump in.

"Ready?" Randy asked, his face lit up with excitement.

"Ready as I'll ever be," I said, stepping into the cold Salt River. The water was immediately knee-deep and ice-cold, but after an initial shriek, I felt my body acclimate to the temperature quickly.

"Did I tell you to be on the lookout for otters and wild horses?" Randy asked us.

"Wild horses? Are you kidding?" I asked, delighted, getting into my tube rather clumsily. It was quite a bit harder to balance my way in than I thought it'd be. The twins and Dad followed suit—Dad helping each twin into their tubes first, then finding the spot Randy assigned him.

There we were, all five of us in a ring around the cooler. I sat in my tube, trying to keep my legs out of the water. I had chills all over. The sun didn't feel so hot anymore; it was more like a friendly warmth, slowly heating me up. I took a deep breath, smelling the fishy water, the sweet honeysuckle, the wet stone, and the unique scent of sunbaked sand.

"Would I kid you?" Randy asked, steering us all into the river's gentle current. "The wild horses are here drinking often, and the otters can be spotted once in a blue moon. Keep an eye out."

By the time we were all loaded up and floating down the river, it dawned on me that except for one group of teenage boys ahead, we were the only ones there. *The early bird does catch the worm.*

We meandered for a short while, drifting around a bend, before the river's surface began to swirl and seethe. Randy recommended that we lift our butts out of the tubes and lie back to avoid bumping our bottoms on the rocks over the rapids.

We got through those first rapids unscathed. They were much calmer than I'd envisioned—certainly nothing we would've bounced over.

The next five minutes were also calm. Jill spotted a sleek little brown creature torpedoing near the bank on the left side of the shore. I spotted another after following her gaze. They looked like a cross between beavers and sea lions.

"Are those otters?" she whispered, pointing.

"I'll be!" Randy sang out. "They sure are! Look how they twist and roll over." He rubbed his eyes as if he couldn't believe he was really seeing them. "That's very rare. You guys are super lucky. Can you see their webbed feet?"

"They look like flippers!" Dad grinned wildly behind his glasses, which were splashed with clear droplets of water. "How *ex-tra-or-din-ary!*"

"I've only ever seen river otters a few times before," Randy revealed. We kicked our legs against the current, trying to slow down so that we could watch the otters a bit longer. Their shiny bodies leaped out of the water, only to arc back in, moving as fast as fish. Then they climbed onto the bank and slithered like snakes through the grass, only to surprise us again by emerging five feet downriver and slicing into the water again.

"Looks like they're playing," Dad observed, and I agreed. That's exactly what they were doing—darting and somersaulting and floating on their backs. I bet they were laughing. They looked like they were having so much fun teasing each other.

As we were carried away down the river, I pretended that they waved goodbye to us. We drifted along in silence for a couple of minutes before Randy said, "The biggest rapids are coming up, but they're not scary or too big—so don't worry."

Was he kidding or just trying to downplay the danger?

The water was already roiling and churning, little whitecaps lapping the surface of the dark river, which narrowed as we got closer to some large boulders. Up ahead, I could see the rapids Randy had forewarned us about. They definitely looked big.

"Hang on tight, everyone! Hold on to your hats and towels! Grab your glasses and the rope on the inner tubes! These are the big ones," Randy commanded, following his own advice step by step, the rest of us doing the same.

Our flowerlike corolla of inner tubes swiveled, and somehow, I was now the one facing the big frothing maw of the rapids. But something in me liked it. I thought back to the Grand Canyon—my urge to hike farther than everybody else. Now I had a chance to be the first to conquer a whitewater rapid head-on. I told myself I'd been through worse.

In the back of my mind, I heard Dad say, *My girls are brave.*

And then, just like that, we were flying—bouncing and jolting in every direction as the inner tubes skipped across the choppy water. My hands clutched the rope too tightly at first, but soon I stopped holding my breath and started laughing.

My grip loosened. This was fun.

I glanced over at the twins. Gerri and Jill looked at me and then at each other, their eyes wide with a mix of shock and thrill as we zipped along, picking up speed.

Up ahead, I saw a three-foot drop over the edge of a mini waterfall.

"Yahoo!" Randy yelped. "Hang on. These are the fun ones. Lift your butts and hold on!"

Right before we dropped over the waterfall, I saw that Dad looked scared. He had removed his glasses and was gripping them in his hand. His Blue Pierre hat was askew, and his receding hairline was prominent in the sunshine. I relished the fact that I looked braver than he did. Perhaps I really was braver, too.

Randy's part of our strapped-together raft went first this time. The twins followed on either side of him. The cooler bobbed along in the center, and as we crested the waterfall, I somehow knew at once that we were in trouble—and so did Dad. The physics of the raft tipping over the waterfall's edge suggested we were about to be slingshot out of our seats—then catapulted into the churning water below.

A quick glance at Dad, who looked panicked, confirmed he could feel it coming, too.

Sure enough, when our rig went over the falls, our side fell hard into the water, dunking us almost all the way under. Then the buoyancy of our inner tubes fought back, shooting both of us into the air. The whole thing was faster and more violent than I'd expected. I flew out of my inner tube, got a parting spank on the derrière—as if the thing were personally offended—and plunged into a fizzy cloud of bubbles

I landed downstream, glad to miss the boulders. I saw a blur of tie-dye as I tumbled over and over. *There goes Dad,* I thought. Randy managed to keep the girls in their tubes and reached for me. The water was loud in my ears, and everything seemed a lot scarier in the water.

I thrust out my hand for Randy's when he passed by, our fingertips nearly grasping each other, but then I felt myself pulled under again. This time I was sucked under by the current, and no matter how hard I kicked my legs, I was completely powerless against it. My knees and thighs got scraped on the riverbed, but all I cared about was not drowning.

Thankfully, the river spat me back up to the surface a moment later. I got turned around under the tubes and bubbled up to the surface again. I imagined myself gracefully surfacing like one of those otters, but in actuality, I was thrashing around like a dying fish, gasping for air. I reached toward our rig, which now was farther downriver, and I barely clamped on to a trailing piece of rope. It must have been that extra length Randy had looped around the cooler handle. It felt as thin as thread, and I thought it would break.

I saw the twins and Randy looking frantically back at me.

Where was Dad? As I inched along that narrow, lifesaving string, my legs continuing in their bashing on the river's bottom, I finally made it back to my inner tube and wrapped my arm around it. I clung on for dear life—the courage I'd had earlier was officially spent. Whipping my head left and right, I searched for Dad, but he was nowhere to be seen.

"Mary! Are you okay?" Gerri yelled. There were tears in her eyes, and I realized that it must have been more dangerous than I'd thought. My hands were shaking.

"Where's Dad?" I screamed back. I caught a glimpse of baby-blue fabric bobbing along near me and grabbed it. It was Dad's hat.

Randy's face looked as white as a sheet.

"I don't see him!" he cried. I couldn't tell if his face was wet from tears or from the water.

"What? You haven't seen him?" I tried to scramble back into my tube, but my arms felt like noodles, and I couldn't pull myself in. Randy reached past Gerri, and with his knee on the cooler, he grabbed the back of my shorts and hoisted me aboard. I seated myself securely back in my inner tube, but even from up there, I couldn't see Dad anywhere.

"Daaad!" the three of us girls called.

"Raaalph!" Randy joined in.

"Daaad!'

"Raaalph!"

This whole catastrophe had lasted only a few minutes, even though it felt like it had happened in slow motion. How could he have just disappeared like that? He had to be somewhere. Was he messing with us? I wouldn't put it past him. Was he going to emerge on the shore and say something stupid like

Where have you been? Had he drowned? Was he going to bob to the surface face down?

"Randy, what do we do?" I asked, still breathless.

"I don't know." That was not reassuring.

"He's a sinker!" I added, suddenly remembering something he'd said at the Great Salt Lake. Fear gripped my chest, and I officially began to panic. "He says he always sinks in the water! What if he got knocked on the head and then sank?"

We floated along in a shocked state while we looked all around. At least the river was calm here. The twins were openly crying now, clutching each other across the cooler.

"What are we going to do without Daddy?" Gerri cried.

"Daaad!" Jill called out again. He was nowhere. How could he just disappear like that?

I looked forward, back, left, right. There was no bright tie-dye to be seen. This couldn't be happening.

"Randy, what do we do?" I asked again. He looked stricken and didn't reply, his eyes transfixed on the passing river in search of Dad.

I began to envision the worst—collecting Dad's waterlogged body in a way that would spare the twins the sight of him, towing him to shore, and then what? Waiting until somebody else tubed down the river and found us? Perhaps Randy would carry on, taking the twins with him and finishing the full circuit in order to get help, but that'd leave me alone with Dad's lifeless body.

Suddenly, I felt myself tearing up, too. This was a *nightmare*. Why hadn't Randy warned us more realistically about the magnitude of the waterfall? He'd told us we'd face rapids, not a three-foot drop off a waterfall—and the physics of that wasn't safe at all!

I started to feel strangely numb, eyes combing the water for any sign of Dad, when, finally, I caught a glimpse of something colorful along the bank—and wouldn't you know, there he was, sitting in the mud, about thirty yards downstream with his knees bent and his head in his hands. His glasses sat askew on his face. Dad's feet were covered in only his socks. He must've lost his shoes. There was blood flowing from his cheek, down his chin and neck. The red of the blood blended into his bright shirt, camouflaged by the tie-dyed swirls.

"Dad!" we screamed in unison. The water was shallow here, and Randy hopped out and pulled our rig over to where he was resting.

"Uncle Ralph, what happened?" he asked for all of us.

"Girls, are you okay?" Dad asked. It was jarring to see him in such a state. "I watched Mary get bounced out when I went flying into the air. Randy, you said these rapids were gentle!"

"I don't think I ever said they were *gentle* . . ."

"It's all right, son," Dad said, clapping him on the back. "Looks like we're all fine, outside of having a bit of a scare. Girls, come here." He wrapped the twins into his open arms, and they continued to sob for a few minutes, still frantic over the whole thing. "Mary?"

I looked up, and he was gesturing for me to bring it in for a hug. I staggered forward onto the soft sand of the bank with him and the twins, joining their embrace, and quickly discovered that my arms and legs were bleeding.

"Those river rocks got you good, too," Dad said, peeling away. "I'm so relieved you're safe."

"Me too, Dad," I said. "We were so scared when we couldn't find you."

"Uncle Ralph," Randy began, tugging our rig onto the shore. It was actually a great spot for a quick breather, with soft sand and shade. "Tell us what happened."

Dad loved being a raconteur. As soon as we were all resting on the bank next to him, he told us how he got ricocheted out, held on tightly to his glasses, ended up underwater and farther downstream than the rest of us, slammed his face into a rock, lost his hat and shoes, and then waited patiently for us to arrive.

I couldn't tell if he was as scared as I was, but if he was, he did a pretty good job of hiding it when he said, "Let's take a break and eat." I passed him his hat, and he used it to wipe the blood from his face and then rinsed it in the river.

Randy apologized over and over, explaining that this late in the season, the rapids were usually not so strong, and the waterfall was normally just a little hill to roll over. It looked like he felt horrible.

"Randy, don't worry about it. We're all fine," I reassured him, even though my legs were going to be bruised, and the cuts were pretty fresh and nasty. With these new injuries, along with the rash still lingering from the poison oak, I definitely looked horrible. But now I didn't care. I was just happy we were all okay. And alive.

"We won't be able to hide this from my eagle-eyed mom," Randy fretted, clearly trying not to cry now. "Look at Ralph's face and Mary's legs. She'll blame me."

Dad's cheek *was* pretty bad.

"Don't worry, son," Dad said again. "We have a long time before we get back home. This cut on my face feels like it's half-hidden by my beard. We'll clean ourselves up, and things won't look so bad when we make it back."

I looked carefully at Dad's face and highly doubted that. His cut was so deep, it might honestly need stitches. There was a flap of cheek hanging open. But I could understand him trying to calm Randy down.

"Let's not add all the details to the Slate, Jill," Gerri offered. She had climbed into Dad's lap, with Jill sitting on the other side. I was so glad that the little ones were unscathed and also calmed now that everybody was safe.

Randy opened the cooler and passed around the canteen. We all had a big swig of fresh water. He distributed the wax-papered sandwiches for lunch, and we ate in silence, the murmuring of the river the only sound for several long minutes.

While we were finishing up our peanut butter and jellies, I looked up and saw a beautiful white horse approach the bank on the other side. It leaned down for a drink, the tips of its silky mane rippling the water's surface. I couldn't believe it. My eyes grew and grew, taking in the unbelievable image. Behind her were another half dozen wild horses coming to their drinking hole.

"Oh my God!" I whispered, clamping a hand over my mouth. My hope of seeing the wild horses had come true! Frantically, I pointed at them, drawing everyone's attention to the amazing sight. We stayed quiet, but our excitement was palpable. "If we hadn't had that little waterfall accident, we probably would have missed the horses!"

That made Randy smile. He took a big bite, finishing off his sandwich.

We watched in amazement as the small herd shook their heads, whipped their manes, snorted, and drank the water. Their long tails swished back and forth. They were all the horse colors—whites and browns and blacks, solids and spotted. Big and small.

"Gorgeous, aren't they, Mare?" Dad observed. I wondered if he was remembering how I'd dreamed of having a horse and thought that this Great American Road Trip was that dream's replacement for me. Probably not. As I stared back at his still-bleeding cheek and dirty T-shirt and dented-up smile, I realized that I didn't get that startling, gut-wrenching stab of betrayal when I looked at him anymore.

All I cared about now was that he was still alive and still my dad.

I smiled, leaned into him, and agreed. "They are."

48

Cliff Jumping

It was weird how easy it was to get back on my inner tube after that super-scary near-death experience. But somehow everything felt . . . brighter. *Better*. I was as happy as a couple of otters playing in the sun and felt as wild and free as a herd of galloping horses.

Who knew almost dying could make you feel so alive?

While I floated down the river, fingers skimming the surface of the cool water, I started thinking about when Dad risked his life during his notorious bison stare-down in Yellowstone. I'd been so mad at him then. The memory made me chuckle now. Grim, but also funny in a way. What if things had turned out differently today? What if we hadn't found him and rescuers had to pull him out of the river? I glanced at Dad. His glasses were still speckled with water, and he was laughing with the twins like nothing had happened.

My anger toward him had vanished—just like that. Washed away in the Salt River along with my fear. He could've died. *We* could've died. But we hadn't. It made me feel small again, but in a good way, like when I'd stood in the ocean for the first time in Santa Cruz. It was the kind of smallness that made you realize you're just a tiny part of something so much bigger. And if I was small, then my anger and hurt were even smaller.

"What's so funny?" Gerri asked, twisting around in her tube to look at me. I hadn't even realized I'd laughed out loud.

"Nothing," I said, smiling. "I was just thinking . . ." I trailed off, but when she kept looking at me, I added, "I'm just glad we're all okay."

Dad smiled at me, his scraped-up face making him look like a pirate. I smiled back for real this time, not just because I had to. Wow, what a relief. I'd been so grumpy and annoyed and angry for so long—and now it was just gone. *Poof.*

"Okay, Randy," I began, "how much farther until we get to the cliffs to dive off?"

He looked tentatively at Dad and then back at me. "You still want to do that? And by the way, it's jumping, not diving. My mom would kill us if she heard that we dove headfirst."

"Yes, I still want to do that!" I called out, shifting my weight in the tube. "Jump, dive, whatever."

"Well, I thought maybe after the little waterfall mishap that nearly *killed you*," he emphasized, shaking his head, "you'd be having second thoughts."

"No way, José! How much longer?"

"It's just around a few more river bends." Randy and Dad exchanged glances, like they were sort of impressed by my attitude. I liked that. "You're full of life, Mare."

"Yes, I am. Thank God," I said, and I meant it. "Any more rapids?"

"Just a couple of little ones." He looked guilty saying that. "*Really*, this time."

"Groovy," I said.

Dad laughed. "You *are* full of life, Mare!"

I tipped my head back into the water. "I guess that's what happens when there are otters and wild horses and when you almost die!"

Our little rig of inner tubes bobbed along for another ten minutes, cruising through slow and quick sections. After an abrupt left turn, we suddenly saw those teenage boys climbing up a gray cliff, little rocks rolling down behind them. There was a hollowed-out section of cliff above them.

"That's where we go to cliff dive. I mean cliff *jump*." Randy pointed. "Mud Cliffs."

The first boy to make it to the jumping spot turned around, faced the water and all those still climbing up for their turn, and screamed, "Geronimo!" He jumped over his pals' heads into the water, knifing into the blue-black deep, feetfirst, his hands held tight against his sides, with hardly a splash. Wow. I'd score him a 9.8.

"Ooh, let's go. Let's do it!" I shouted, smacking my hands together and pulling down Rosalind's old baseball hat. "The water is deep enough that you don't touch the bottom, right?"

"I've jumped hundreds of times and never touched the bottom. Right after you land in the water, you swim off to the side to make room for the next jumpers."

"It sounds too deep for me," said Jill.

"I'll tread water in the landing zone for you twins," Randy reassured them, guiding our strung-together tubes toward the shore. "You little ones have on life vests. You'll be fine. And I'll make sure to help you get to the side if you'd like." Randy's lighthearted enthusiasm brought me away from dwelling on the thought of why Dad, Randy, and I weren't wearing life vests, too—Dad and I could've used their floatiness during our earlier calamity.

We disembarked and stowed our floating contraption on the bank, leaving our hats and their glasses. Stashing everything in the cooler for safekeeping, we scrambled up the cliff wall, avalanching little pebbles and dirt below us. I used my hands to grab on and pulled off more dirt and stones. The twins were behind me, followed by Dad—his feet clad in only socks—and then Randy.

"Hey, careful up there, Mare!" Jill shouted, tucking her head and dodging some little pebbles. I tried to go slower, but I wasn't sure how I could be more careful. Once we all emerged on the jumping-off ledge, we stood there and looked down. It was at least a twenty-foot drop. Maybe thirty. Gazing across the river, the horse herd was barely visible far off in the scrubby desert.

"What's the plan?" Dad asked, looking rather nervous and backing up into the safety of the cliff's interior wall.

"Well, I think that Mary and I should jump first," Randy suggested. "That way, I'm down below waiting for the twins when they jump, and Uncle Ralph, you can stay up here with them in case they change their minds and don't want to jump."

I appreciated his open-ended reasoning. The twins—especially Gerri—were more likely to take a risk if they didn't feel pressured into it.

Randy looked at us, surveying our reactions. My smile was the biggest. I was ready—*more* than ready. I figured I'd be ready even if it were a bigger jump, still high on being alive. The twins, however, didn't look nearly as thrilled, but they also didn't look like they'd change their minds. Maybe Dad's comment on our bravery was buoying their attitudes, too.

Dad's smile, on the other hand, was nonexistent.

Randy tentatively asked, "What do you guys think?" He paused. "You're already up here, and the easiest way down is to jump."

Suddenly, our attention was drawn to the path behind us. The teenagers who'd been climbing and jumping before us had caught up. The one at the lead said, "You guys jumpin' or what?"

"Girls? Uncle Ralph?" Randy prompted.

To my surprise, it was Gerri who said, "Okay, let's do it."

Jill nodded, reaching for Gerri's hand.

This left Dad, who still hadn't answered. He scratched his cut cheek and finally relented with a sigh, shaking out his hands. "Okay," he said, looking at me. "I'm taking a leaf out of Mary's book—she's so full of life, I think she could spare it."

I positively beamed. "You can do it, Dad."

Then, seeing as the line to jump was getting longer behind us, I made my way to the edge of the jumping-off point. The tips of my shoes teetered over the edge, touching nothing but air, and it felt like ticklebellies on a sugar high.

"Want to hold hands?" Randy asked, and I nodded, reaching out to him. He took hold of my hand in his surprisingly warm, dry one. Then, turning to the twins, he said, "Count us down!"

The twins sang out, "A one and a two and a three bee lee!"

Randy and I smiled at each other and jumped on the count. I screamed while my arms flailed, and I tried to keep my legs crossed. We sliced into the water, and he was right—we didn't hit anything on the bottom. As we bobbed back up like corks, he shook his head like a puppy.

"Wow!" I screamed, blinking the water out of my eyes.

"That was dynamite!" he yelled. I knew the twins would have to hurry since the teenagers were already up there, waiting for their next jump. We treaded water and watched them from below as they walked to the edge bravely, holding each other's little hands. Soon we could hear their small voices singing out, "A one and a two and a three bee lee!"

They leaped off the cliff face and splashed into the water near us. Their life vests popped them up even faster than Randy and I had emerged. Gasping and sputtering, they clawed at the surface, reaching toward us.

"You did it! You didn't even hesitate!" Randy shouted, beaming with pride. "I'm so impressed. How old are you girls again?"

"We're ten," they said with their speak-in-unison twin voice, keeping their mouths above the water as they paddled over.

"Ten! That's young to jump off Mud Cliffs!" Randy said, towing them toward the shore. I dog-paddled happily after them. When they were settled, I swam back out to the landing zone, looking up at the jumping-off point for Dad's turn.

But he wasn't there.

"Dad?"

"Uncle Ralph?" Randy called up.

I glanced at the growing line, which was beginning to knot up as more and more teenagers bunched together. Somebody was holding them up, and it must've been Dad, so I shouted again, "Dad, are you there?"

"Yeah!" he said, but not with his confident and boasting voice. He sounded scared.

A few breaths later, I saw Dad emerge at the jumping-off point. He looked down at us, one hand shielding his eyes from the sun's hard glare. I noted the cut on his cheek and how he looked naked without his ever-present glasses. How far could he see? I couldn't decide if his lack of vision was an advantage or a disadvantage. Was it better not to know how far you'd fall?

"What are you doing?" I called up.

"Well . . ." He hesitated. "I'm reconsidering my options!"

One of the adolescent boys near him shouted, "Come on, man. Jump. Have some balls. Your little girls did it." His friends laughed along, which ignited some protective anger in me.

"Shut your trap, young man," Dad said. Then, calling down to us, he said, "I've changed my mind. I'm not jumping."

Randy and I looked at each other, eyebrows raised.

As Dad backed away from the cliff's edge, the group of teenagers groaned. By this time, Gerri and Jill had already climbed back up, scurrying around the line, and reached the jumping-off point all over again. They had snatched Dad's wrists, trying to coerce him into joining them.

"Get out of the way, then, chicken," one of the teenagers said. The rest of the group continued laughing at him. I glared, taken aback. Somebody had just called my dad a chicken. I was sure he wouldn't stand for that.

"Yep, I'm a chicken," he said simply. Of course, he had to add the *bok, bok, bok* sound effect with his hands tucked into his armpits, flapping his arms like wings. That really cracked up the teenagers. He peeled the twins' hands off his wrists and started to descend the trail.

The twins shrugged, unbothered, and got back in line. Soon it was their turn again. With a one and a two and a three bee lee, they leaped, hitting the water at the same time. Just like they did before, they quickly floated to the surface. Randy and I towed them to shore.

We enjoyed a few more jumps. The rush of the free fall was both exhilarating and liberating in a way I hadn't expected. Honestly, I could've stayed there all day. But when Dad eventually made his way down—the way he'd climbed up, which wasn't easy, as Randy had said—we decided to get going. We collected our stored things and drank some water. Randy pushed us off from the shore, and we started drifting downriver again.

After about a half hour, we pulled onto the bank near the road and began disentangling our rig.

"How do we get back?" I asked.

"We hitchhike," Randy said, like it was obvious. At first I thought he was joking, but he looked at me again a second later in a way that suggested he was dead serious.

"Hitchhike?" Gerri said, overtly skeptical. "Isn't that dangerous?"

"How about you three girls go first? I bet there's no one who can take all five of us at once," he said in reply, neglecting to answer Gerri's question.

The twins and I stood on the side of the road, facing oncoming traffic, our thumbs held out in the proper gesture. Only two cars passed us before the third one pulled to a stop.

A gruff, bearded man sporting aviator sunglasses, with a huge Rottweiler in the passenger seat, rolled down his pickup truck's window and said, "I can only take three of you." His voice was about as gravelly as Mud Cliff's ascent.

"Just like I thought," Randy said.

The dog barked, slobber dripping from its jowls. "Down, Ralph," the driver commanded. Ha! We all burst out laughing.

"What's so funny?" the driver asked.

I pointed at Dad. "Our dad's name is Ralph, too."

"I'll be," he said. "I go by Rusty." He held out his hand to Dad for a shake.

Some bolt of rare parental wisdom and caution must've struck Dad because he said, "Okay, the twins and I will go with Rusty and Ralph the Dog." Turning to me, he said, "Mary, you and Randy get the next one."

The three of them climbed into the bed of the truck. Randy hoisted four of our inner tubes into the truck bed with them, along with the cooler, and then slammed the tailgate shut. They took off, and we were left to find our own ride.

He and I waited, our thumbs out, for about another ten minutes before a station wagon with a mom and two kids in the back pulled over. We greeted one another, and she seemed really nice.

"One of you can sit in the front, and the other can sit in the back. We can put the tubes in the way back, too." I was surprised to see that it took about thirty minutes to drive back to the place where we'd parked our car. She dropped us off and wished us well. The kids waved their arms out the windows, saying goodbye.

Dad and the girls were already there, sitting in the shade of Uncle Hartery's station wagon. They were eating the remains of the packed lunch, crunching on apples and carrot sticks. Their three tubes were already tied on the roof.

Dad's cut face was crusting over and looked pretty gruesome. He had taken off his socks and was hobbling around barefoot, wincing when his strikingly white feet were poked by the sharp stones. We headed back to Aunt Ruth's house. I must have dozed off because before I knew it, we were driving south on East Indian School Road and had only another few minutes before we returned for our last night with our aunt, uncle, and cousin.

✳ ✳ ✳

Aunt Ruth took a step back when she saw her baby brother's face. "What in God's name happened to you today, Ralph?" she said, grasping his chin between her index finger and thumb and twisting his head this way and that, examining him at once. "Randy! What happened?"

Randy approached but couldn't get a word in edgewise since Aunt Ruth kept barking at Dad to "Wait a moment!" and "Hold still!" only for Dad to say, "It's fine. I'm all right."

Randy made a hasty retreat down the hallway, escaping while he still could, while his mom pulled out a kitchen chair for Dad. I stepped back to observe the scene unfolding—Ralphie being taken care of by his big sister. I bet this type of interaction had happened many times before between those two.

"You should've gotten out of the water immediately, rinsed and cleaned this, and not exposed the wound to that dirty river water again! This laceration needs stitches." Aunt Ruth looked at Dad in a way that said *This is serious, Ralph.* "You realize you may need a course of antibiotics for this, right? And look at this goose egg growing on the side of your head here." She tapped gently above his ear, finding the place he'd hit his head. Dad winced. "You might have a concussion!"

"Oh come on, sis. I don't have a concussion. And can't you just put a Band-Aid on the cut?" Dad whined. Before my eyes, they had reverted to their childhood selves. Observing them gave me the temporary confusion you feel when watching a movie where actors you know from one film are now cast as completely different characters in a new one.

"Don't you oh-come-on-sis me, young man!" Aunt Ruth had one hand on her hip and the other resting on Dad's shoulder, piloting him toward the table. When he resisted, she fixed him with a truly venomous glare, her eyes blazing. Wow, I hadn't seen that side of Aunt Ruth before! Picking up on the scary energy, the twins made themselves scarce by escaping to the back patio.

Seeing his sister's reaction, Dad complied, sitting in the chair. "You're the nurse," he reasoned.

Aunt Ruth got a stool and climbed up to reach for a dusty bottle that she stored in the cupboard above the refrigerator. She grabbed one of those jelly glasses and poured Dad a big drink of oily pale-amber liquid.

"Drink this," she ordered.

He gave the jar a whiff. "Tequila?"

"Yes, drink up. You need some numbing." Dad drained the glass in one go. She poured another one. He downed that, too. I picked up the discarded jar and inhaled deeply—then coughed.

Ew. It smelled sort of like Campho-Phenique. *Ew.*

Then, just as suddenly as Aunt Ruth's anger had flared up, it was extinguished with a shake of her head. Her capable and compassionate nurse persona took over now that Dad was following orders.

Aunt Ruth hadn't changed out of her white nurse's uniform since she'd gotten home from work. She still had white tennis shoes on over white stockings and that old-fashioned nursing cap perched on her head. She looked like she was from the 1950s.

Digging around in her first-aid kit, she extracted a bottle of something I couldn't identify and daubed its contents in Dad's gash with a cotton ball, which made Dad scrunch up his mouth and eyes. Maybe something to numb it. She went to the bathroom and returned with a razor and shaving cream and proceeded to shave below and around the cut. Dad cringed at every tug.

Lastly, she painted some Neosporin into the wound with a Q-tip, using a tongue depressor to lift the substantial flap of skin away from Dad's cheek to get the medicine in there. That was the first and only time I had to look away. *Gross.*

When Dad winced, she murmured, "There, there. We're almost done."

She used gauze to dry everything. Rummaging around, she located some special Band-Aids that she used almost like stitches. They were super sticky and grabbed onto each side of Dad's cut, holding the cut together. I learned these were called butterfly Band-Aids.

"Are you hurt anywhere else, Ralph?" she asked, looking him over.

"Well, not as bad as that one time when Mama spanked me with the wooden spoon—"

"The one time?" Aunt Ruth covered her laugh with her hand. "Mama sure loved the one with the hole in it that she kept special. The hole made it so that she could swing really fast. Remember?"

"Yes, of course I remember. That's the one that she broke walloping my behind, if I recall correctly." Now it was his turn to laugh, but he stopped quickly since it looked like his closed wound did not appreciate being moved around when he smiled. "I was pretty little for such a big punishment."

"Well, you did deserve it," Aunt Ruth reminded him.

Oh, this was getting juicy.

The twins had wandered back in, and Jill said, "Who deserved what?"

Gerri echoed, "Yeah, who deserved what?"

"Good one, Ruthie-Roo," Dad said. "Now they'll know one of my biggest secrets." He Groucho Marxed his eyebrows, then winced and stopped—still forgetting that moving his face came with painful consequences.

"Tell us why he deserved to be *walloped*, Aunt Ruth," I suggested, using Dad's phrasing.

Jill had opened the refrigerator for some of Aunt Ruth's fancy mint and cucumber water. After Gerri fetched some glasses for everyone, Jill poured, and Aunt Ruth told us about the time that her three youngest brothers had done something that got them in big trouble.

"Hank, Buddy, and Ralphie, aged seven, six, and four, thought it would be a good idea to make some mud pies—it was during the Great Depression, you see."

"What's wrong with making mud pies?" Jill asked.

"What's the Great Depression?" Gerri followed, taking a sip of the cool water.

"Well, during the Great Depression, hardly anyone had any money, and there was a lot of unemployment. So we were lucky, huh, Ralph?"

"Huh? Lucky?" Dad glanced at his big sister with glassy, bloodshot eyes. I'd never seen him look so beat up, ragged, and worn down.

"We were lucky that Papa was a barber and was able to keep his business alive during that time."

"Oh, uh-huh. Everyone still needed their hair cut, beards shaved, and teeth pulled," Dad agreed. His voice sounded slow, the words kind of stringing together. "Too bad he was a nasty drunk who hurt Mom and sometimes Gretel."

Everybody, including the twins, went still. I followed Aunt Ruth's gaze and pieced together what she was also realizing at exactly the same time: Dad's tequila was hitting him hard.

"How many girlfriends did he bring home right in front of Mama?" Dad went on, a dark glint to his glassy eyes. "That cruel son of a—"

"Ralph," Aunt Ruth cut in sharply.

But he wasn't finished. "You know he used to line us up—me, Buddy, Hankie—make us hold out our hands and pick which one got the ruler first?" His voice slurred just slightly, but the bitterness was clear. "Sometimes he made us pull a card from a deck. High card got it first and worse."

Aunt Ruth set her glass down with a soft clink. For a fraction of a second, something flickered across her face—something tight, unreadable. But just as quickly, she smoothed it away and gave a practiced little laugh. She knew how to put on a happy face, too.

"Oh well," she said lightly, as if brushing dust from a windowsill. "We all got through it, didn't we?" She took a sip of her water, her smile as polished as ever.

Dad scoffed, but something in him sputtered, like he wasn't sure whether to keep going or stop. He blinked slowly, then exhaled through his nose. "Yeah. Guess so."

The silence was thick. Even the twins didn't try to break it.

"There's no need to bring that up," Aunt Ruth repeated, snuffing out whatever Dad was going to do with those family secrets. "Well, those three knuckleheads," she went on as if that bomb hadn't just been dropped, "stole some of Mama's raisins and flour and sugar and eggs from the cupboard, and . . ."

I couldn't pay attention to Aunt Ruth's retelling of how they did something with those precious Great Depression ingredients. My mind was reeling with this new information. Grandpa Stromp was a drunk who had girlfriends while he was married?

Dad wasn't an alcoholic, but it did seem like he was cut from the same cloth. Somehow that all felt like a cop-out. We didn't *need* to grow up and be just like our parents, and yet I remembered Dad telling me I was like him, that I was special. And he sure was like Grandma Stromp, too—pretending pain didn't hurt.

Aunt Ruth went on about the boys using those ingredients in a mud pie, but I was writing a new entry in My Journal of Life. I used all caps: I AM MY OWN PERSON. I MAKE UP MY OWN MIND. I DECIDE HOW TO BEHAVE. I CAN BREAK THE CHAIN.

Aunt Ruth finished her story and tidied up the first-aid supplies, sending Dad to bed. I wasn't sure where Randy was or if Uncle Hartery was home from work. I decided against showing Aunt Ruth my legs. The fresh bruises and cuts would just be camouflaged by the scabs and red patches that were already there.

49

Cathedral, Chapel, Crater

The morning we were scheduled to leave ended up being inconveniently timed. It turned out that not only did Randy have an early morning on the golf course to get to, but also Aunt Ruth and Uncle Hartery had early starts, too. Our goodbyes were destined to be made quickly.

Dad had already cleaned out the inside of Blue Pierre and fiddled with the engine and other under-the-hood business, so all we had to do was pack in order to be ready to go. Aunt Ruth had washed the sleeping bags and my Mexican blanket, and we had set up the tent at the beginning of our stay to air out in the hot Arizona sun. Everything felt nice and relatively fresh.

Jill, with Gerri's help, had caught up the Slate: *7/21/76 | Arizona | Phoenix | Salt River tubing and Mud Cliff jumping.* I took a peek and saw that she'd deliberately omitted the injuries and Salt River mishaps, which was probably a good idea.

Aunt Ruth was all business and no emotion when she marched us out to Blue Pierre. She told Dad to drive safely and we girls to be nice to one another. That was it. No tears. No nothing. Which, for some reason, was a little surprising and disappointing, seeing as I was on the verge of tears the whole time and knew I'd miss her a lot. When would we ever see each other again?

Uncle Hartery was much more emotional than his wife, and Randy was his silly self. Instead of doing the wave goodbye while Dad ooga-ed, Randy did backflips in the grass. He must have done a half dozen before we turned the corner. My last view was of him staggering in dizziness on their tidy little front lawn and Uncle Hartery laughing.

"Wasn't that far-out, girls?" Dad remarked. Both the twins and I were crying a little, and all we managed in response were silent nods.

He smiled back at us. "I know how you feel." He brushed away a tear before it ran into the cut on his cheek. "It was a great trip. I haven't seen my sister in ages. Let's agree not to let that much time pass before we see them again, shall we?"

That cushioned the blow a bit.

"Let's head northeast and get home. What do you say, team?" Dad enthused, trying to get us out of our melancholy moods. At this point, the idea of going home felt better and better—even if it did lead us into the unknown territory of possible divorce. I missed Mom and Namo. I missed Winnie. I missed Grandma Stromp's soft quilt. I missed *home*.

I opened the TripTik and turned the road atlas to a page with the whole country on it.

Ohio looked pretty far away still. *Very* far away, actually.

"Let's get to Albuquerque today," Dad suggested. "That's in New Mexico." *Much closer.*

"Albuquerque? That's a funny word." Jill laughed, then repeated it. "*Al-buh-ker-key.*"

Gerri said, "I saw a jerky turkey in Albuquerque."

"A *perky* jerky turkey," Jill amended.

"The perky jerky turkey was on her way to work-y as a clerk-y in murky Albuquerque," I said.

"Quirky," Dad said, chuckling. He smiled in the rearview mirror at the twins; they smiled back. Then he looked at me in the front seat—back in my regular spot. I smiled, too. Our smiles seemed genuine, not put on to hide bad emotions. I realized that this was what *normal* felt like. Then I wondered, *Was he right? Had I forgiven him in time, just like he said I would?*

"This is fun, girls," he said. "Thanks for doing my dream trip with me." Before we could build on his sentimentality, he got straight back to business. "Again, Albuquerque is in New

Mexico. I was studying the map yesterday, and it looks like there are some pretty incredible natural rock formations on our way there."

"What are they called?" I asked, holding up the TripTik. "I'll look for them."

"Cathedral Rock, Chapel of the Holy Cross, and the Meteor Crater Landmark," Dad listed off, using his incredible memory yet again. "The first two are pretty near each other."

I directed him to take Interstate 17 North to Interstate 40 East toward Sedona.

While driving, we listened and sang along to the Carpenters' *Now and Then* 8-track cassette and then the Statler Brothers' *Old Testament*. We belted out the lyrics to "Noah Found Grace in the Eyes of the Lord," with Gerri really getting into it. Blue Pierre was doing great.

The rock formations along our route looked like they had been carved by liquid wind.

In the Red Rock State Park, we observed the Cathedral Rock and the Chapel of the Holy Cross, which was kind of like a church with a cross on top, set into an iron-red cliff face. The church looked far-out, perched so high. It had been built in a way that didn't force the rocks to yield; instead, it seemed like it melted into them or like it'd grown naturally out of the rock on its own.

We drove by Bell Rock shortly after. It wasn't as massive as Devils Tower in Wyoming, but it was still very impressive in its own right and looked sort of like the giant hump of a camel jutting up out of the earth. I got a real kick out of these rock formations. They were so groovy and kind of seemed like they belonged on Jupiter instead of on Earth.

We tried to pass the time with the animal, vegetable, and mineral game and the ABC game, but everyone was a little tired, and we allowed our lack of enthusiasm to be okay. We just let the miles roll past us, soaking in the incredible red rock formations and wide-open highway.

Blue Pierre made some clanging noises from time to time. Dad looked at my questioning expression and said, "Don't worry.

Blue Pierre will be just fine." He patted the dash, giving the car a little caress. "It'll be nice to park tonight and let him rest again."

I hoped so.

We stopped for an ice-cream cone in Flagstaff, Arizona, which didn't have any of the red rocks and instead was occupied by a dense forest and a big purple mountain called Mount Humphreys. It was a cool place, but we were only passing through.

"We'll be going past where a meteor hit the planet fifty thousand years ago," Dad said, finishing his cone. We'd let Blue Pierre sit in the shade for a while after adding more water to the radiator, and that had given us plenty of time to enjoy our ice cream. "Let's get going, and I'll tell you all about it."

"A meteor, Dad?" Gerri asked, licking the last of the ice cream from her lips and getting back into the car. Jill and I did the same. I wiped my sticky hands on my jean shorts and pulled out the *ungüento* to rub on my itchy legs. I already missed Aunt Ruth's pool.

"Well, I remember a bit from when I was a little girl in the Boy Scouts—"

"Da-ad!" the twins called out at once. He had a tradition of telling us stories about his childhood, with the *once upon a time* phrase replaced with *when I was a little girl*.

"How could you be a little *girl* in the *Boy* Scouts?" Gerri laughed.

"Good point." Dad chuckled. "Well, we visited it on the only other trip I've taken out here, plus I read up about it recently in that guide that Mary has there." He pointed to the box of guidebooks that was our makeshift library.

"Let's have it," I said, giving him a genuine smile.

It felt good to have forgiven him. The relief I felt was all for me, not for him. It made me wonder what forgiveness really is. Does the other person even have to be part of it? Does forgiveness demand an apology, or is it just about letting go of the hurt on your own?

"Well, you won't believe how large it is," Dad went on. "The giant bowl-shaped crater—that's the name of an impression left after a meteor hits Earth—is about seven hundred feet deep, over four thousand feet across, and almost two and a half miles in circumference. Can you imagine?"

We shook our heads.

It took a lot longer than you'd expect to reach the crater, but it was worth it. I was glad we'd made the effort to drive out of our way to witness it firsthand. It was as spectacular and as grand as Dad had made it out to be.

Even so, we didn't spend much time there—doing what we coined a "scratch-and-sniff" type of experience. Just a brief surface-level exploration, sort of like the foot-down visits we'd made to certain states earlier in the trip.

We finally made it to Albuquerque, New Mexico, in the early evening. The dry heat—unique to the Southwest, I realized—still beat relentlessly down over us, but we were lucky enough to find a spot in the shade for our night of dispersed camping.

Lying on the ground with my beautifully striped Mexican blanket and using my sweatshirt for a pillow, I tried to do Ms. Chanel's falling-asleep protocol of relaxing my body bit by bit, but all I could think about was how much I missed the comfortable bed and bathroom at Aunt Ruth's house.

50

He's Just a Man

I woke up the following morning to the sound of Dad rustling around outside, splaying a couple of maps over the rocky ground for assessment. Giving up on getting any additional sleep, I sat up, rolling my Mexican blanket off my legs, which I gave a once-over and decided to ignore.

"Hey, Mare," Dad said, chipper as ever, "check this out. The route from here to Amarillo, Texas, is just about straight." He ran a finger along our course, noting the horizontal trajectory. "Should take about six hours. What do you say? Should we follow this route today?"

I rubbed the sleep out of my eyes and peered over his shoulder. "Sounds good to me."

"Great." Dad looked over at the twins. They were still asleep. Their quiet snores were practically inaudible, but it seemed like they were in unison. *Inhale, snorey exhale. Inhale, snorey exhale.* Must have been a twin thing, even in their sleep.

"Mare?"

"Yeah?" I realized Dad had stopped looking at the twins and was staring at me with the sort of expression somebody might have before saying something of importance.

A few breaths of silence funneled into a pause before his response. "I've been thinking about the conversation we had walking back from Mexico—"

I put a hand up. "Dad, do we have to get into it? I told you what I wanted to say."

"Well, I just wanted to tell you how proud I am of you." He spit the words out like he wanted me to hear them. Needed me to, maybe. And as I stared back at him, stunned, he nervously started to fold up the maps he'd spread out before us.

"Proud?" I eventually said. "Are you sure you mean proud? Why? Because I ratted you out for being a disgusting hypocrite?"

"Well, frankly, yes," he said, and we both laughed. "I just think that it was pretty commendable for you to have the guts to get it off your chest and broach the uncomfortable subject with me."

I considered what he said and thought it was out of character for him. "Wow," I said, looking at him suspiciously. "Really?"

"Yep. Even though what I did was wrong in your eyes—"

"In my eyes? I'd say in *anyone's* eyes."

"Okay, what I did was wrong." He paused. "*Period*. You had the courage to deal with it straight on and let me know how you felt about it. I'd say that's honorable. And I wanted to let you know."

"Thanks," I said, and I meant it. But for once, Dad's approval wasn't what I was seeking. I was only happy that somehow, all on my own, I'd found a way to forgive him. To let this go. "I don't agree with what you've done. I still think it's wrong. But I've chosen to let this go—for now, at least. Things may change when we get home."

Dad nodded silently, and we listened to the leaves rustle, the birds sing. I had to confess—this was an aspect that Aunt Ruth's house couldn't beat. It was beautiful out here.

"You said that Jill did see, didn't you?" Dad asked eventually.

"Yes, but I don't think she really understood what was going on. And when I talked to her about it in Santa Cruz, she told me that she'd told Gerri. So they know whatever it is they know. I didn't want to bring it up anymore. I'm glad they're too young to make any real sense out of it."

Dad's brows furrowed. "What do you mean?"

"Well, they think sleeping with someone means *literally* sleeping with someone."

"I kind of wish you were still young enough to think that as well."

"Me too," I said.

Then he went on quietly, "I'm sorry I ruined what you thought of me." To my shock, his eyes dropped to the ground. I was pretty sure I saw real remorse there. "We've always been a team. I've always loved our relationship. I ruined it."

"I appreciate your apology, Dad. I'm coming to learn that people try to do the best they can, and even someone you thought was perfect is just as flawed as everybody else. Sad but true," I said. Then I took a deep breath and said what was eating at me the most. "Dad, I know that you and Mom are on a trial separation this summer and might get divorced when we get back."

He looked at me with a cockeyed expression. "How do you know that? Did your mom tell you when you called her collect before we went to Mexico?"

"No." I looked up at him, now my time to feel guilty. "I heard you guys arguing the night when she found a bunch of checkbooks." Just like my first confession to Dad, this took another incredible weight off my chest. I felt almost like I was walking on the moon again, spared the force of gravity.

But Dad's saddened expression towed me back down again.

"Oh, you heard that? I'll be." He pushed his hands through his hair, took off his glasses, and cleaned the lenses on the bottom of his shirt. "Well, yes. I guess that's what's happening." Replacing them on his face, he said, "Hard to believe."

"We'll be a divorced family," I said, as though that hadn't dawned on him. "None of my friends' parents are divorced. I don't know anybody whose parents are divorced. The only one I know who doesn't have a mom *and* a dad is Winnie, but that's cuz her dad's dead."

"Yes, poor Mrs. Gravers and her kids. That must be tough for them." He cleared his throat. "Well, we're not home yet. And I say we cross that bridge when we get there. For now, we enjoy ourselves."

Gerri and Jill woke up at the same time, and I locked my worries away when I heard them stir. They rolled over and bonked heads with each other and giggled.

"Hello, sleepyheads," Dad said, smiling sweetly at them. They stretched out their arms, then started scrambling out of their sleeping bags.

As we packed our things and got ready to go, I looked at Dad. *Really* looked at him. What I saw surprised me. He was just a man—a regular flawed man like so many other regular flawed men. He just happened to be my father.

51

Poor Ol' Blue Pierre

En route to Amarillo, Blue Pierre began to make a strange clunking noise. We'd all heard Blue Pierre's mechanical rattling before, but this seemed different. We exchanged worried looks with one another. It was coming from under the hood and sounded like a light wheezing.

Dad pulled onto the side of the barren highway. There was no shade in sight, and we were surrounded like a raft at sea, with desert fields edged in barbed wire all around.

When Dad popped the hood, a gust of steam enveloped him. He jumped back.

"Son of a gun! This dratted radiator just keeps leaking the fluid and water." He shook his head and smacked his thigh. "I thought I had fixed it with that additive I poured in back in Phoenix."

Dad glanced at us with an expression I couldn't read.

Worry? Shame? Anger? Helplessness?

He looked terrible with that red gash, crusted over with the start of a dark-brown scab peeking out of the butterfly Band-Aids covering it. A shiner was developing under his eye. And his stubbly, unshaven face added to the overall gruesome effect. He was like a Halloween monster.

While we let the engine cool, we sat in the very, very small sliver of Blue Pierre's shadow and had a snack and some Kool-Aid. The juice from the pomegranates was perfectly sweet, and the oranges were so juicy, it felt like we were drinking them instead of eating them.

Dad paced along the dusty shoulder of the highway, clearly debating what we could possibly do next. I tried to swallow the last of one of Aunt Ruth's oatmeal raisin cookies, but I had a panicky lump in my throat, and I had to choke it down. After twenty minutes in the blazing heat, Dad made us take a good long swig before adding the last of our water jug to the radiator, and we started to once again head east toward Amarillo.

The twins and I looked at one another and shared a shake of the head. This was our signal that now wasn't a time for horsing around or chitchat. We'd let Dad focus and were as quiet as possible while he did so.

I gave them a good once-over. They were so scrawny and disheveled. Their faces were dirty from camping, and I hadn't helped them with their hair since we left Aunt Ruth's.

Jill quietly took out her notebook and started writing. When she was finished, she passed it up to me. I read: *7/22/76 | Arizona and New Mexico | Cathedral Rock, Chapel of the Holy Cross, ice cream in Flagstaff, Painted Desert, meteor crater, camped at Petroglyph National Monument near Amarillo.*

When I passed it back to her, I caught a whiff of my own underarm. I smelled rank. *Ew,* and I bet I had bad breath, too! We hadn't been very diligent about our dental hygiene for the past couple of days. Quickly getting my nose out of my armpit, I tried to act sisterly or motherly and patted her hand. I whispered, "Nice job. Add Bell Rock between Holy Cross and the ice cream."

"Oh yeah, good one. Thanks," she whispered back, flipping her pencil around to fix the entry.

We drove in silence for another ten minutes, listening anxiously to Blue Pierre's complaints—which continued to grow in severity. I looked at Dad from time to time to gauge his reaction, but he didn't reveal anything one way or another.

Eventually, a curtain of steam—or was it smoke this time?—started to gush out from under the hood. As if that weren't enough, Blue Pierre's complaints evolved into a full-blown protest, and everything started to stink with a burned-toast aroma.

"Son of a . . ." Dad pulled Blue Pierre off the road again.

Before rolling to a stop, Blue Pierre made one last screech and then got quiet, the grayish-white cloud still billowing out from under its hood. I glanced back at the twins, and they looked pale and wide-eyed, their grimy, pomegranate-stained fingers intertwined.

"Son of a bitch. Goddamn it!" Dad yelled. "Fuck!"

The girls and I exchanged silent, frightened glances. Dad usually stopped his cussing at *son of a pup* or *son of a gun* or *gosh darn it*. He wasn't big on swearing. This meant that whatever was going on with Blue Pierre was bad. *Really* bad.

Without another word, Dad got out of the car and walked toward Blue Pierre's hood—which was so hot that it cast off shivering heat waves. Dad opened it anyway, swearing some more as he did so. Apparently, he'd burned his fingers.

The three of us got out again but didn't make a sound. Would we be broken down out here in the middle of the desert? We hadn't seen another person for miles, and we'd used the rest of our water for the radiator the last time we'd stopped.

First, Dad moaned, but then he burst out laughing. "Would you look at that? Girls, come over here."

Reluctantly, we walked to the front of the car. Dad appeared maniacal and scary, acting hysterical like that. The three of us stood in a line, with me in the center. We were all holding hands, stickiness be damned.

"Damn it. Damn it. *Damn it*." As the steam tapered off, he peered closer under the hood. "We are up shit creek without a paddle. I've been so focused on keeping the radiator filled with fluid and water that I neglected the engine oil." He burst out laughing again, using that creepy, hysterical cackle that made me worry we weren't just trapped on the side of a highway in the desert but trapped on the side of a highway in the desert with a lunatic. He pointed to the engine block, and even we could see that something was definitely wrong. The engine cover was warped. "I'm so stupid. I just let the engine shoot a rod for lack of oil. What was I thinking?"

"What's that mean?" Gerri asked tentatively. "Shoot a rod?"

Dad took a big breath. "Shooting a rod means that one of the pistons has gotten stuck in its cylinder due to a lack of lubrication."

That didn't sound good. He was right; we were up a creek without a paddle. And out here in the middle of Nowhere, Texas. And in the heat of the day, with the sun directly above us. And with no one around to help. And with hardly anything to drink. And with our fearless leader no longer fearless.

Dad took off his glasses, ran his hands over his face, and entangled them in his wispy hair, then moaned again. We three quietly backed up. He leaned against Blue Pierre and then sank down onto the sandy ground, slumped forward with his hands still cradling his head, and proceeded to have what could only be described as a full-blown meltdown.

Jill dared to ask, "Can't you fix it, Dad?" Gerri looked at her like she was crazy.

"Hell no!" he started to bark back at her. Then he took another big breath, smiled eerily, and said, too slowly and sweetly, "No, I cannot fix it." He put his glasses back on after wiping the sweat from his forehead one more time. "Once a motor is seized, it's pretty much unrepairable. It can't be fixed. The only way Blue Pierre is going to ride again is if the engine is replaced."

He swayed in his seated position, with his arms wrapped around his belly, rocking himself. He wobbled like that for several minutes while I felt like we were melting under the heat of the sun. Then, as if a light switch had been flipped from off to on, he transformed from Mr. Hyde into Dr. Jekyll.

He jumped up, clapped his hands, smacked the sand off his derrière, and shouted, "Let the adventures begin!"

We looked at our crazy father, and I thought he must've been losing his mind.

"Okay. Here we go. I have a plan." He motioned with his beckoning index finger for us to come closer, like revealing the big plan was a secret. "We're going to push Blue Pierre to a service station."

"Push?" I said. "You've got to be kidding." Now it was my turn to moan.

"Yes. Push." I glanced down the long highway. "It's slightly downhill, imperceptibly so, but still," Dad explained. "We'll get Blue Pierre back onto the actual road. I'll put on the hazard blinkers for safety. You three put on your hats and socks and shoes. One of the twins can steer."

They looked up at him incredulously.

He laughed again. "You can do it. The road is practically perfectly straight. Mary and I and whichever one of you is not steering will push. It'll be easier than you think."

I pulled on their hands, and we went back into the car to find our hats and exchange our flimsy flip-flops for the sturdier Keds. We all got ready, and I saw that there was only half a jug of orange Kool-Aid left. I passed it around, and we each took a sizable gulp of the sweet, warm drink.

"Hey, let's leave some of the Kool-Aid, just in case this takes longer than we think," Dad said, an uncomfortable reminder that we had no other water.

We assumed our positions. First, Dad scooted the front seat forward as far as it would go so that Gerri could reach the wheel, offering her a pillow to sit on, too. Then he pointed Jill and me to the back of Blue Pierre, assigning us each a side. The trunk and bumper were too hot to touch, so we used my folded Mexican blanket to protect our hands. He took hold of Blue Pierre at the frame between the front and back seats on the driver's side.

"Okay, Gerri. Shift the car into neutral." She looked at him blankly, nervously. "Move that gear shifter until it says *N*." She did. "The hardest part will be getting poor ol' Blue Pierre up off the shoulder and back onto the pavement. Ger?"

"Yes, Dad?"

"Think of your steering as just going straight. You won't have to turn the wheel much at all. But there is an edge between the shoulder and the road that we have to get over. We're going to start pushing, and I want you to stay on the side, on the shoulder, until we pick up some speed, and then you're going to gently—*gently*—turn the wheel to the left, counterclockwise, to get us back onto the road. I'll be pushing from right here, so I can help you if need be."

"Roger, Dad." She rotated her hands to the left on the still steering wheel, practicing.

Her reply made me think of something.

"Dad," I said, "why don't we use the CB to ask for help?"

"Well, I thought of that, but we're almost out of money, and we've got a long way to get home. If we can push him to a service station, saving the cost and time of waiting for a tow truck, we can find out if the mechanic can locate a replacement engine. That's why we're not using the CB to get help. Are you ready for an adventure?" He looked at us, and I sighed, deep and heavy. It seemed risky. The expensive route was preferable in almost every way, and contacting somebody using the CB meant that we'd probably be out of the heat sooner rather than later, but for some reason, I didn't argue.

"Yes, sir," Jill and I said at the same time, giving him a salute.

"Okay, let's do this." He started us off with "A one and a two and a . . ."

We three joined in with "three bee lee!"

We pushed as hard as we could to get the inertia to break, and I was surprised that it was much easier than I thought it would be. Once Blue Pierre started rolling, Dad said, "Okay, Ger-Bear, start your gradual turning."

She executed the maneuver perfectly, and with a heave, we got Blue Pierre up over the curb and onto the highway again. Once the car was moving along, we hardly had to push. Jill even had to run a bit to keep up. We were speed-walking along. Dad was right: it wasn't that bad.

After a few minutes, Dad started singing "One Fine Day" by the Carpenters. By then, we knew every last lyric of every song on that album, so we all joined in.

Jill and I, at the back, pushed along, marching in step to the rhythm of the song. Singing seemed to make the time go quicker and cool the heat of the sun.

After a while, we decided it was time for the twins to switch spots. The road was as straight as a pin, and there wasn't much real steering to do except just holding the course. Blue Pierre was rolling along slowly enough that Jill was able to run and hop in the passenger side without us stopping, and get herself arranged in the driver's seat, plumping up the pillows, while Gerri scooted out the driver's side door.

Unfortunately for Gerri, her shoelace was undone, and she tripped and landed in a heap on the pavement, giving herself some road rash. *Perfect, another ugly injury.* I could see that she didn't want to cry, but she couldn't hold it back.

"Oh good Lord," Dad said, nearly stepping on her. He scooped her up and pushed her through the back seat's open window. She tumbled into the seat. "Clean up with some of that stuff in Aunt Ruth's medicine bag. Mary, what would you suggest?"

"Gerri, wipe off the sand and grit with a clean T-shirt and daub some of the Campho-Phenique on the scrapes," I instructed, still pushing.

"Okay," Gerri sniffled back, wiping her snotty nose and tear-streaked cheeks with the back of her good hand. She knocked her glasses off in the process. Jill wanted to see what was going on and turned around to see how Gerri was doing. Not being very practiced at the wheel and being distracted by her twin's back-seat activity, she let Blue Pierre drift off to the right.

"Jill, pay attention to the road!" Dad commanded. I could see that there was a slight rise coming and that it wouldn't be a good idea for us to lose momentum.

Gerri let out a yelp when the Campho-Phenique touched her open scrapes. "Mary! You said this stuff didn't sting. It stings like the dickens!"

"Only at the beginning, and then it feels real nice. Isn't it better already?"

She conceded that it was. I wiped the sweat from my brow. Man, was it hot. I could feel the skin on my shoulders and arms burning. I was a little lightheaded as well. There was no shade in sight, however, and my lips felt like they were cracking. Licking them just dried them out more. When I looked over at Dad, I was alarmed to see that he was as red as a pomegranate.

"Dad, how much longer is it until we get to a gas station, do you think?" I asked, panting.

"I'd say it's half again as far, or we're almost halfway there."

Oh brother. He was using that frustrating family expression that basically meant that the end was nowhere in sight. How could he expect us to keep pushing Blue Pierre without a stopping point? Again, I gave his red-as-a-beet face another hard look.

"Maybe we should have another swig of that Kool-Aid," I suggested.

"Okay, but we still need to save some. Everyone, take the smallest amount you can," Dad said.

Jill and Gerri took swigs and then passed it out to us. After Dad had a sip, I couldn't help myself and had what would be considered more than my share. I guiltily passed the container back, which only had about two inches of liquid left.

"Ger, can you hand me that white blouse in my little bag in the front seat?" I asked her.

She crawled over the front seat and dug out my shirt. I hoped it would be just the thing to cool me down. I wished we had some water to soak it in. Dad repositioned his Blue Pierre cap so that the brim was in line with the angle of the sun. I saw that it was drenched with sweat. Two of the three butterfly Band-Aids had slid off his wet face.

Dad let Gerri recover in the car for another minute or so and then asked if she thought she'd be able to get out and help. We were approaching that rise in the road, and we needed all hands on deck.

"Make sure your shoes are tied this time!" I cautioned.

"I know, I know," she said and then climbed out the passenger side. This time, she held on to the door handle and made sure she was steady on her feet before letting go. She had to trot to keep pace with Blue Pierre. I showed her how to bunch her hands into the blanket to protect them from the blistering surface of Blue Pierre. After a few steps, I put my arm around her. She leaned her head on my shoulder while we pushed and stayed there until we were both too sweaty. I gently shoved her off.

The scenery was unchanging to an alarming degree. It felt like being stuck in purgatory, pushing a car at high noon in the desert without any verifiable progress. We were surrounded by barren, sand-colored fields so stereotypical of the Southwest, I was surprised there wasn't a tumbleweed in sight. Everything was yellow, brittle, and presumably dead, despite it being midsummer. I glanced at the road before us. It looked like a dark black rug unfurling into infinity, with heat waves shimmering wildly over it.

I wondered where the crops were. Maybe it was just too dry out here. Maybe I was wrong, and these were more like grazing areas for cows, not fallow fields at all, but I hadn't seen any cattle the whole time we'd been pushing. I was too tired and hot to care enough to ask.

Amazingly, the little bit of help that Gerri provided was enough to get us up to the summit of that small crest. Well, that plus Dad, who had veins popping out in his neck. I could tell that he was really pushing hard. *As he should,* I reminded myself. If it weren't for his cavorting with a prostitute in Wells, then we'd arguably have the money to get on the CB right now, call for help, receive aid, and probably spare ourselves an early heat-induced grave.

"Oh come on! We've got to be almost there already," I whined, reaching a breaking point.

"We're closer than we were," Dad said. His optimism was annoying.

"What if there's not even a gas station around here?"

"There's always a gas station," he concluded. "This is America."

Wouldn't you know, he was right—just over the rise, maybe another mile away, we could see a cluster of massive silo-shaped buildings with a sign that read Welcome to Bushland, Home of the Falcons emblazoned across them. Beneath was a little gas station called the Falcon's Stop, and attached was a business called the Nesting Place. I wasn't sure if there'd be a restaurant, but I was certain they'd have water.

Seeing the end in sight renewed my energy, and in no time, we rolled Blue Pierre into the narrow strip of shade alongside the Falcon's Stop building. Jill couldn't really reach the brake pedal, so at the last minute, Dad hopped into the driver's seat and unceremoniously shoved little Jilly-Bean out of the way, steering the car in and braking to a stop. "Sorry about that, honey. I thought you were going to drive it into the side of the building."

Jill looked relieved. I peered around at the barren service station. There were two fuel pumps under a large flat roof about fifty feet from the small two-bay service garage. Unfortunately, I saw that the Nesting Place wasn't a restaurant but a store of home goods and men's clothes. Its yellow-and-white canvas awning fluttered in the wind and looked dainty and out of place. Home goods and men's clothes in the middle of nowhere? At a service station? Who would the customers be? We hadn't seen a single car or truck in our long pushing trek.

The Falcon's Stop sold a small selection of snacks, like chips and candy bars and gum.

An elderly attendant—Earl, according to the faded tag on his mechanic's shirt—shuffled out when he saw us approach. His knobby hands were huge, his fingernails thick with grime. Everything about him looked like it belonged in an old black-and-white photo: his shirt was gray, his hair was gray, even his fingernails were gray. Wispy strands of long hair failed to hide the pale gray scalp beneath. He might've stepped out of a world where color had given up.

"Well, hello there. What do we have here?" His voice was just as wispy as his hair, which was arranged into a straggly comb-over that flopped to and fro when he spoke.

He took one look at us and shook his head. When I croaked, "Water?," he pointed to a hose on the other side of the building. I ran over to it and pumped the handle. Out came scorching-hot water for about ten seconds before it cooled down. Raising the hose above my head, I let it douse me. The twins were right on my heels. We sprayed one another and took long, long drinks.

I discreetly washed under my arms and my privates, using this opportunity as a shower. I passed the hose to Gerri, who held it for me so that I could rake through my hair with my sore hands, untangling what I could and rinsing off the rest. I wiped my teeth with the hem of my shirt and gargled. She passed the hose to Jill, and they both did the same. I secretly peed, right in my wet clothes, and used the water to rinse everything clean. The water felt so good on my rash-covered legs.

I felt bad that we'd left a large muddy puddle at the edge of the garage, but I figured it would evaporate lickety-split. It took all three of us to depress the pump handle to cut off the flow.

I don't know how Dad resisted coming over to quench his thirst. I know he had worked harder than any of us, doing the majority of the Blue Pierre pushing, but he was busy talking to Earl, and they had their heads together under the hood. They spoke low and seriously, I noticed, but I couldn't hear a word they were saying.

After our impromptu showers, we walked back to see what Dad and Earl were up to.

Earl had a wrench in one hand and four bolts in the other. It looked like he had removed the engine cover. I heard him say, "Well, son. Looky like you done gone and blew a rod clear through the cylinder." He pointed to the bulging side of the engine. "You done gone and seized this puppy up. Ain't no oil left in there. Dry as a bone in this a here desert. Ain't gonna run no more." Earl stepped back to see some kind of car identification, his strange hair bobbing up and down. "I ain't never seen a car like this 'un afore. What it be?"

"It's a Peugeot," Dad replied, with no trace of his usual pride. When he saw that that rang no bell with Earl, he added, "It's from France."

"His name is Blue Pierre," Gerri said a little too brightly.

"Well, Blue Pierre has done seen the last of his days, it looky likes to me. I wouldn't even know where to start huntin' for a motor from France. You do know you're in Texas, right? The US of A?" Earl chuckled and gestured to the wide-open nothingness around us. "An' even if it were a 'Merican vehicle, it'd be a pretty penny up front and a few weeks afore we'd get-cha back on the road."

With a frown, or maybe it was a scowl, Dad walked over to the hose for a drink and a rinse-off, too.

52

Paring Down

The day was so hot that we were almost dry by the time Dad got back, soaking wet from the hose, and told us that we would leave Blue Pierre at Falcon's Stop, along with the better part of our things. This would include the movie camera and film, the majority of our clothes, the food basket and cooler, and most of the books and maps and the TripTik.

When we all looked at him in horror, he said, "We'll be hitchhiking back to Ohio."

No. *Heck no*. There was no way hitchhiking was our only option!

I pulled Dad aside, leaving the twins in the shade while he and I walked over the coarse gravel surrounding the building and ventured back to the muddy reservoir we'd created earlier with our use of the service station's hose.

"Dad," I said earnestly, trying to sound like an adult. "You can't be serious about this."

"I'm the adult here, Mary, and I'm your father, and I'm deadly serious about—"

"Why can't we use the pay phone over there"—I gestured to the battered phone outside the building twenty feet away—"and contact Mom or Grandpa Red or even Aunt Ruth? Why can't we ask somebody for help?"

Dad gave me a razor-sharp critical look. "There are many valid reasons why, Mary, otherwise we would obviously be pursuing—"

"What are your valid reasons?" I pressed. "Humor me."

I guess he'd been thinking about the pros and cons of his decision already because he fired back quickly. "One, we're on the last leg of our trip, and it's not that far." I gave him a *yeah, right* scowl. We were in Texas. That was a long way from Ohio! He ignored me. "Two, we're having an adventure, and hitchhiking fits the bill," he went on, but I could tell that not even he was convinced of the legitimacy of this one. "Just think of all the interesting characters we'll meet along the way."

"Oh brother." I rolled my eyes. "How about this: three, you're embarrassed to ask Mom or Grandpa Red or Aunt Ruth for money or help, and four, you feel like a failure because you're out of money and have a broken-down car out in the middle of nowhere, and five, you're worried about getting home soon because your wife is about to divorce you?"

Ouch. As I gave Dad my very honest rebuttal, I felt sorry for him.

He paused for a second, looked at me, and said, "You're absolutely right. That's why we're hitchhiking. We'll keep this our secret until we get closer to home."

I almost laughed. We were doing this. Was it against our better judgment? Of course. But it was happening.

Dad arranged to leave Blue Pierre with Earl, who charged him ten bucks up front for rental space and another ten dollars a week until we relocated it elsewhere. I glowered at Dad over another example of him justifying the cost of something that was convenient for him—and refusing to justify it for anything or anyone else.

We spent the next half hour going through everything and deciding what we absolutely had to have and what we could leave behind. We'd each have one bag that we could sling over our shoulders, and we'd share my medium-size suitcase for all of our clothes.

Dad tore the road atlas in half so that we were carrying only the eastern part of the country. He said we couldn't take any of the reading books, but I hid *Zen* in my bag because it was the smallest, and I wanted to find out how quality related to living a good life. We pared down Aunt Ruth's medicine kit. I told him that I couldn't live without the Campho-Phenique and *ungüento*.

"What about the sleeping bags and pillows?" Gerri asked while going through the things in the back seat.

"Definitely no for the pillows, and can you twins share one sleeping bag—the smallest one we have? Mary, you bring your blanket. I'll use a towel for my sleeping," Dad said, his head peeking out of the trunk.

Even though we felt like we had pared down a great deal, we still ended up with a large mishmash of luggage: the one suitcase; a pillowcase stuffed with the twins' small sleeping bag, one towel, and the Mexican blanket; four littler bags, one for each of us; and the gallon jug of water that we had refilled with the Falcon's Stop's hose.

Seven pieces in all. Dad carried the maps in his bag. I had the medicines and some other meager toiletries, like toothpaste, a small bottle of shampoo that I'd mixed some detangler into, a sliver of soap, my deodorant, a roll of toilet paper in a sandwich bag along with a few tampons, and a comb to share.

Jill had her notebook with our Slate of Dates, States, and Fates. She added some other paper, colored pencils, and markers. I was glad to see that she'd made a judgment call and tossed in the deck of cards and the dice. I was sure we'd appreciate that at some point.

Gerri toted the dry snack foods like chips and nonchocolate candy bought at the Falcon's Stop, plus the rest of the oranges, the last two pomegranates, and the three avocados we had from Aunt Ruth's fruit trees.

Dad made it clear that each of us needed to be responsible for our own toothbrush and money. He would carry the Swiss Army knife, and we'd each have our little mess kit and utensils. As soon as we'd packed what we could take, Dad was already locking up Blue Pierre and handing Earl the keys.

It hit me again: *This was really happening*.

Donning our jean shorts over our bathing suits and topping off our outfits with clean T-shirts, we were ready. I'd rinsed out that white blouse and tied its sleeves around my waist; the twins did the same with their sweatshirts.

After we'd eaten everything we could from our cooler, Dad's eyes widened, and he turned to us with a maniacal sort of smile as he said, "Are you ladies ready for the adventure of your lives?"

"You're calling hitchhiking from Texas to Ohio the adventure of our lives?" Jill parried.

"Sure. Who do you know who's done something as *ex-tra-or-din-ary* as this? This is a once-in-a-lifetime bicentennial event that you will remember until you the day you die. Just think of the stories you'll be able to tell, even when you're an old great-grandmother." He laughed. "What if you have a first-day-of-school writing assignment about what you did over the summer? Imagine the interesting and mind-blowing things you'll be able to write."

Earl walked out of the shade of the Falcon's Stop wearing a big Stetson cowboy hat. It looked as old as him, the way it was formed perfectly to his head and had a permanent band of darker brown where the years of sweat had pressed a stripe into the leather. He handed each of us girls a small bag of Lay's potato chips, a yellow Laffy Taffy, a package of Bottle Caps, and a Snickers bar. Candy jackpot. We tucked them into our small bags and murmured our gratitude.

"How 'bout I give you a lift into Amarillo and set you on a good path for yer hitchhikin'?" Earl suggested. "I'm about to shut 'er down for the day. There hasn't been a soul in, except y'all, all day."

"Well, only if it isn't any trouble," Dad answered, but he looked thrilled.

"No trouble at all. I'd offer you some supper, but my missus, God rest her soul, passed away from the cancer goin' on two years now, and I ain't got much by way of groceries. I was just gonna fix myself a Hungry-Man TV dinner . . ."

"That's mighty kind of you, Earl," Dad said. "Don't you worry about us. We just had a big meal, and we sure do appreciate the water and you lettin' us park ol' Blue Pierre with you until I come back and figure out what to do with him."

Was Dad copying his accent?

"And thank you," I interjected, "for the chips and candy."

We moved to stand in the snippet of shade provided by the Nesting Place's awning until we heard Earl revving his truck. Its throaty roar startled the ravens that were perched on the roof above the gas pumps.

"This here is my pride and joy," Earl said, backing out. Dad whistled. "She's a 1952 Ford F1 pickup. I call her Betsy."

"She sure is pretty," Jill chimed in. It really was. The curved lines of the truck's oversize fenders stood out like massive smooth muscles, and its candy-apple-red color was so shiny, I could see my reflection staring back at me. Dang, was I a sight. Straggly hair. Ragged expression. The truck's grill looked like a mouth with great big teeth, and the whitewall tires were too clean to exist in this flat, plain desert.

"How 'bout you young 'uns settle on in the bed, and your daddy and me'll ride up here in the cab?"

We loaded the pieces of luggage into the back. The bed had long wooden boards that were laid out like slats between the metal rails. The wood was warm, but the rails were blazing hot. I spread my blanket out for us to sit on, protecting our legs. We scooted into the bed until we were sitting against the cab, facing backward.

"You girls all set?" Earl asked. He saw our simultaneous thumbs-ups through the cab's back window.

Dad stepped onto the metal bar to climb into the passenger side of the cab. Earl was a lot nimbler than his stooped gait suggested, and he hopped right up into the driver's seat. He pulled onto the highway, and our last view of the Falcon's Stop was of Blue Pierre resting forlornly in the shade, shrinking in size as we drove away on the flat, straight road. I pretended to hear the ooga horn saying goodbye.

Being situated in the middle of the three of us made it easy for me to wrap my arms around both of the twins. They felt so small, their bony shoulders poking into my ribs.

"Can you believe this?" I asked.

Gerri leaned into me and said, "Mom would kill him if she knew, I think."

"You got that right," Jill agreed.

"Just think of the stories you can tell," I said, mocking Dad.

"Ha ha. Yeah, great stories," Jill said *atastically*.

We sat in silence for a bit until Blue Pierre was no longer visible.

"He does have a point," Gerri said.

I agreed. "When life gives you lemons, make lemonade, right? Or in our case, when life gives you . . ." I tried to come up with something to lighten the mood. Thinking fast, I dug into Gerri's food bag and extracted an avocado. "When life gives you avocados, make guacamole."

Eventually, we got closer to something like a small town, and the truck pulled over and stopped.

"I think this is where I should drop you off," Earl said. "This way, your next ride can take you in the general direction of your home on either of these major roads." We unloaded our ragtag pieces of luggage and set ourselves up at the junction of 40 East and State Route 287 South.

"Mighty nice of you to get us all the way across Amarillo, Earl. We appreciate it," Dad said, his hand outstretched for a shake, which Earl accepted. "I'll be in touch in a week or so about picking up our car."

"Well, I'll do a little searchin' to see if I can find a Frenchy motor or sumpin' that'll work in there fer you."

"Mighty generous of ya," Dad repeated, grinning. He *was* picking up Texas-speak!

"Thanks, Earl." Gerri approached him tentatively and gave him an awkward hug around his skinny middle. Jill came over and did the same. Not to be left out, I gave him a hug and thanked him, too. He rigidly patted our backs in turn.

"You take care of these here girls, son," he told Dad. "And, girls, eat up those chocolate bars afore they melt."

"We thought of that and already did. Thank you so much. For everything, Earl," I said. With a wobbly about-face, he retreated to his precious Betsy and climbed in. Turning the truck around and heading west, he gave us a wave out the window. We waved back until we couldn't see his shiny old truck anymore. Dad had nothing to ooga with.

PART 5

Have Thumb, Will Travel

53

Have Thumb, Will Travel

"So how do we do this?" I asked, looking around and assessing our situation. Earl had dropped us off somewhere in Amarillo, Texas, in a random parking lot near the highway. A few gas stations and fast-food places dotted the edges of the lot, their neon signs buzzing in the hot air. Trucks rumbled past on I-40, heading east and west, while the wind swept across the flat, open land like it had somewhere to be.

My eyes traveled around our ragtag crew. Our "showers" hadn't really cleaned us up. Our hair was tangled. Our clothes were wrinkly. Our faces were streaked with sweat and grime. I had the leg leprosy thing going on. Dad's face, with the black eye and red gash, was off-putting, to say the least, and better described as terrifying. Gerri's new scrapes added to our overall grotesqueness. Jill was the only one of us who looked normal, but she was getting as skinny as her Biscuit Buns twin—their knobby knees wider than their thighs. It looked like we were starving them.

Mom would be *appalled*.

I shook my head, giving Dad a curt look. "Who in the world would pick us up? We look horrible. *We* wouldn't pick us up."

"Well, let's just do it," Dad proposed. "We'll put out our thumbs and see who comes along. We won't be able to go in a beeline home, of course . . ."

Beelining home was precisely what we all wanted. We couldn't get there soon enough. The idea that we'd now be driving with probably a whole slew of different people—*strang-ers!*—trying to scratch and claw our way back to Ohio was an idea I dreaded. I'm sure our exhausted expressions did not boost Dad's confidence. In fact, after the ease of enjoying Aunt Ruth's house, I was starting to reach my limit—and I think the twins had reached theirs a while ago.

"Don't you remember how quickly we got picked up after jumping the Mud Cliffs with Randy?"

"Wasn't that a little more expected? You know, downriver on a river-rafting river?" I burst out laughing. "River, river, river." Oh my God, I was losing my mind.

He put his hand on my shoulder, grounding my hysteria. "Do you remember the article in the *Plain Dealer* about how I'd hitchhiked to work in Cleveland and left Mom the car for you guys in Kirtland? 'Have Thumb, Will Travel'?" He swept his hand in the air, highlighting the title of the human-interest story. "It was above the fold on the front page of the Daily Life section. Remember? It was a great article about how commonplace and normal hitchhiking has become. This will be a piece of cake."

"Oh my God. A piece of cake? This is more like humble pie! You cannot compare this to that. You were a single man, in a suit, obviously going to work. Not a hobo family of four, without a mom, hundreds and hundreds, maybe over a thousand, miles from home. In Texas. In the heat. We look deranged!" I shot back.

The girls rotated their heads like spectators watching a tennis match.

"Let's just keep our spirits up, and we'll be home in no time," Dad claimed, but I had a very hard time believing we'd be home soon, let alone before the school year started. "Aren't you ready to be home? We just have a few rides between here and there."

"A few rides? Dad!" I shouted, my hands on my hips. Was this the moment I finally decided to contact Mom and get her involved? "We're in Texas. The western part of Texas, I think. Amarillo is on the western side of the state, right? And isn't Texas, like, bigger than the size of most European countries? We have so far to go!"

The twins' heads swiveled again while Dad shot back, "Yes. So let's get started."

Was I ready to go home? Did bears poop in the woods? Did fish swim in the sea? My desperation to return home was reaching an all-time high. It absolutely dwarfed my anxiety about Mom and Dad's possible divorce. I was most *definitely* ready to go home.

Jill said, "I have to go to the bathroom."

"Me too," Gerri added.

Dad looked around. "Aw, jeez. Number one or number two?" he asked.

"One."

"One."

"Okay, let's create a little barrier with our luggage, and you can squat down behind it. If we put the bedding on top of the suitcase and Mary and I stand guard on the outer edges, you should have plenty of privacy."

We had been traveling like this for so long that they didn't even put up resistance, peeing in the parking lot, out in the open, only adding to our look of being a group of disheveled, homeless refugees. We were worse than the hippies! I couldn't believe I'd judged their smell. I was pretty sure I smelled like twenty of them crammed into a small, humid room.

While they were peeing, I added, "And we have hardly any money. I have about twenty dollars plus some change from the groceries—about six bucks more, I think. Gerri? Jill? How much do you have?"

Jill answered while zipping up her jean shorts. "About six."

"Gerri?"

"I think about four dollars."

"That gives us about thirty, plus whatever you have, to get across the whole United States."

"Not the whole United States," Dad mumbled. "Hey. Hold your horses. I thought you said there was no change, Mary. Not a penny."

"I lied. Sorry about that. I'll just ask God for forgiveness for bearing false witness. Don't worry," I retorted.

He looked at me, shook his head, and chuckled. "I have . . ." He counted the money in his wallet. "Ha! Would you believe I have thirty dollars also?"

"You only have thirty dollars? *Whoopie*." Boy, it took everything in my power not to conduct a mini audit on Dad's original $500 to see where it'd all gone. "We have sixty bucks to get from Texas to Ohio." I scoffed, the frenzy inside buoying closer and closer to the surface. This was about as bad as it could get.

"Isn't hitchhiking free?" Gerri asked, presumably trying to be helpful.

Jill jumped in, "And we won't have to buy any gas."

"Good points, Ger-Bear and Jilly Bean." Dad looked at me and took my sad face into his calloused hands. "It's going to be all right. Just put your faith in your dear ol' Dad. We've got this."

I thought back to the hungry ground squirrel on the California coast—the way it took those tiny steps of trust before finally taking the crumb from my hand. I'd written about it in My Journal of Life, noting how trust, like that little creature, moves forward one step at a time. I'd try to do the same.

54

Goodnight, Texas

It was late afternoon, and a gentle breeze had blown away some of the oppressive heat.

We walked out to the side of an on-ramp for State Route 287 South, lined up our luggage, and stood in front of it. Dad told us to scoot together so that we appeared smaller than we were. At first, we were silly and waved our thumbs like royalty in a parade to all passing cars and trucks, trying to have fun with it—but after a while, we ended up just standing there, shoulders slumped, with our thumbs out. Some of the eighteen-wheeler big rigs blasted their air horns but didn't stop to pick us up. I bet over a hundred cars passed us.

"How long do you think until someone stops?" Jill asked Dad after about a half hour.

Before he could answer, a station wagon pulled over onto the shoulder and dusted us from top to toe. Coughing, we picked up our bags and ran up to the open windows on the passenger side.

"Sorry 'bout that, darlins!" sang out the driver. She had a huge blonde hairdo stacked on top of her head, just like Dolly Parton. It nearly grazed the car's ceiling. "Y'all are a sight! Looks like you could use a helpin' hand."

"We sure could!" Dad was as happy as a clam, leaning flirtatiously against her station wagon. How could he not see how ridiculous he looked? "We might be a sight, but you're a sight for sore eyes." I rolled *my* eyes when he winked at her.

"Can you toss your things in the back? Hop on in," she drawled. Dad opened the back of the station wagon and put our stuff around her guitar case back there. He swung the rear door shut. I seized the rare opportunity for us to speak privately and grabbed hold of his arm.

"Dad, can you *please* not flirt with her? Just this once?" I whispered.

I don't know if it was because I missed Mom, or because I was dreading what would happen when we got home, or because I'd finally hit my limit with this entire trip, but I simply couldn't take it anymore. Plus, this lady was helping us, and I didn't want Dad to scare her. Dad looked at me as though he'd never seen me before. Then he gave a curt nod, and that was that.

We three girls slid into the back seat, scooting some empty McDonald's and Burger King bags out of the way and onto the floorboards. Dad opened the front door and sat down. He looked at the country star look-alike. As she got back onto the road, Dad asked, "Has anyone ever told you that you look just like Dolly Parton?"

"Well, of course, sweetie. They call me Jolene. I do an impersonator show in Amarillo to bring in a little extra dough, and I'm on my way home. I just finished a gig." Now it was her turn to wink, but this time, it was directed to us in the back seat. She popped her gum. "Would you girls like a stick of gum?"

Yes, please," I said—TeenTeen's two packs of Dentyne long gone, chewed into oblivion and spit out like exhausted rubber. She reached into her Dolly Parton–size cleavage, pulled out an unopened pack of Juicy Fruit, and passed it back. "Is Jolene your stage name?" I asked.

I extracted a piece, stripped off the wrapper, and popped it into my mouth, then passed the pack to Jill. I put the silver foil wrapper in my pocket for when I'd need to spit it out soon. Juicy Fruit never held its flavor for very long, but it sure worked to get the bad taste out of my mouth.

"It sure is. Clever, huh?"

"Yes, very. I love that song." I smiled and sang out a line.

Jolene finished the lyric. "I always sing that for the encore, and by the way, you have a lovely voice. What's your name, sweetie?"

"I'm Mary. The twins are Gerri and Jill."

"Hi," they said together, giving little waves.

"Pleased to make yer acquaintance," she said in her southern accent.

"I'm Ralph." Dad clearly didn't want to be left out of the beautiful Jolene's attention.

"Where are y'all headed?" she asked.

"We're going back home to Ohio," Jill told her.

"Ohio?" Her eyes bugged out a bit. "Well, I'd say that's a mighty piece down the road. Bless yer hearts. Well, I'm headed home to Goodnight."

"Goodnight? What do you mean? You're headed home to go to sleep?" Gerri asked.

"Well, eventually, darlin'." Jolene giggled. "I mean I'm heading home to Goodnight, Texas. That's the name of where I live."

"Oh, that's funny. I thought you meant you were saying good night." Gerri chuckled, snapping her Juicy Fruit and passing the remaining two pieces in the pack up to Dad. He didn't like to chew gum since it made his dental bridge wiggle around. He laid the Juicy Fruit on the dash.

"Do you have a family?" Jill said.

"Of course I have a family." Jolene laughed. "Everyone has a family. My husband is a long-haul trucker, so he's out of town a lot. He's on a run to Kentucky right now. Too bad you weren't riding along with him. That would've gotten you much closer to home." Like almost everybody on this trip so far, she gave us a pointed look when she asked, "Is your mama in Ohio?"

I answered this time, and the words that came out surprised me. "Yes, she and Dad had a big fight, and we ended up taking an around-the-country road trip with Dad so that they could be apart for a little while."

Dad gave me an incredibly sharp look that clearly said *Don't go airing our dirty laundry!*

But it was too late, and I was too tired to care. I realized that really defined everything about me at the moment: too tired to care. I was too tired to lie, too tired to force a smile, too tired to deal with all of Dad's usual flirtatious antics—

I was just *too tired*.

Anyway, it seemed that Jolene took it in stride.

"I see," she said. "Well, all marriages have issues, don't they?"

Dad nodded and grimaced a bit. Mostly at me. Again: I was too tired to care.

Then she went on to say, "Actually, we have three daughters, just like you, Ralph." She turned to smile at us, her big blonde hair lagging a split second behind, as if moving with a mind of its own. "They're a little bit older than you three. Fortunately, our home's not very far. Just a hop, skip, and a jump down 287 South."

"Well, we appreciate it," Dad said. "It'll be a hop, skip, and a jump closer to home for us, too."

"It'll be almost dark by the time we get there," Jolene said, thinking along the same lines that the four of us probably were. "And as a good Christian woman, I will invite you to spend the night. How does that sound?"

"It sounds very kind," Dad answered. I saw his shoulders relax.

"Ralph, as long as you're not the Ted Bundy type, you can sleep on the couch." She looked at him rather sternly, only half joking. "You're not the Ted Bundy type, are you?"

Dad burst out laughing. "Of course I'm not! I'm traveling around the country with my three little girls, for goodness' sake. And from what I've read, he is much more handsome than I am." He pointed to his face. "Unfortunately, I bashed up my face a couple of days ago in the Salt River, so I look a little worse for wear."

"Just checking." She smiled, but it was a bit stiff. "Girls, you can have a slumber party with my daughters and take a bath or shower. Maybe get a comb through yer hair. Y'all will like my girls. Sheila is sixteen, Shayla is thirteen, and Sheena is twelve."

"Sheila, Shayla, and Sheena?" I asked. "Don't you get their names mixed up?"

"I do admit, in hindsight, that their names might've been a bit of a mistake. Their poor teachers up at the school are always confusin' 'em." She laughed. "Y'all'll think it's funny that their daddy's name is Shane."

I let out a huge laugh and hoped it wasn't rude.

"What's your real name, Jolene?" Dad asked.

"Charlene." We all, including Charlene, burst into laughter.

When we arrived at her house in Goodnight, her daughters were startled to see their mom had a carload of passengers and, as it turned out, overnight guests to boot. The first thing Charlene did was take off her high heels and her Dolly Parton wig. I was surprised to see she had short brown hair underneath that was cut like a man's.

"Sheila," she said, "can you start a big pot of water for some spaghetti while I take this makeup off and get cleaned up?"

Her daughter complied, and Charlene returned sometime later, looking fresh and plain in a white nightgown—nothing like the glamorous Dolly Parton she impersonated. Her chest was even flat. The whole thing, I realized, was a costume. Now she looked like a normal lady, even with that short hairstyle for men.

Charlene tied on an apron. She picked up a wooden spoon, stirred the sauce, then turned around.

"Sheila, how about you lead the lot of them?" she suggested. "Can you show them the shower and help them with their hair? Maybe loan them some nighties to sleep in so that they can keep their clothes for their travels? Better yet, Mary, once you and your sisters get out of your dirty clothes, have Shayla bring them to me so that I can run a load of laundry for y'all."

Charlene smiled at her oldest daughter, who smiled back. As we left the kitchen, I heard her call out to Dad, "Ralph, I pulled out a pair of Shane's pajamas for you to borrow. They're on the couch. Go take a shower in the guest bathroom and leave out your dirty laundry for me to wash with the girls' clothes."

Once we'd all cleaned up, we came back to the kitchen, looking refreshed. Dad, especially. He must have shaved or something. The cut was still visible on his cheek, but it didn't seem as crusty, and his black eye had faded into a sallow kind of yellow. He looked like a little boy swimming in Shane's giant pajamas.

Charlene had baked some garlic bread and tossed a green salad. There was the familiar green cylinder of Kraft Parmesan cheese standing in the center of the large table. We gathered around, each of us pulling up a chair, with Charlene at the head.

"Ralph, would you like to say grace?" she asked, looking to Dad.

Was Charlene an angel? I looked over at her and wondered. Whoever heard of someone just taking in a family of four for the night, making them supper, doing their laundry, and letting them shower and borrow pajamas and sleep over?

"I'd be honored," Dad replied.

* * *

We all slept well that night, exhausted and well fed as we were.

Charlene dropped us off at US 287 and Interstate 20 East the next morning.

"Someone going on either of these routes can get you toward your general direction, I reckon," she told us on the side of the highway. Cars zoomed by. I was dreading another hitchhiking excursion but was so grateful for her hospitality. I stepped forward to shake her hand, but she grabbed me up in a big bear hug. "You mind your dad, now, and take care of your sisters."

Then she did the same to both of the twins and even to Dad.

She hopped back into her station wagon, and with a quick U-turn, a little out-the-window wave, and a toot of her horn, she was gone. Just like that.

I concentrated really hard and tried to create a strong mental image of Jolene/Dolly/Charlene and her little family of girls from Goodnight, Texas, for safekeeping in My Journal of Life.

55

The Sting Operation

"Not sure we'll get picked up by anyone quite as *ex-tra-or-din-ary* as that Charlene," Dad remarked, rebalancing the pillowcase stuffed with our bedding on top of our battered yellow suitcase. I thought of how nice that luggage had been when we'd started off—the barely used wedding gift that it was. Now it looked like something we'd hauled out of a dumpster.

We ended up waiting and waiting by the side of the road. Cars and trucks sped by, and I felt my hope for another Charlene speed by, too.

The days that followed were a blur of short rides and a lot of standing around. They were worse than I could've imagined. Some of the stretches of waiting were painfully long. At one point, after waiting quite literally all afternoon and into dusk, Dad said, in a fit of desperation, "Okay, let's try a different approach and go for sex appeal."

"What?" we all said together, horrified.

"Well, I was just thinking that us looking like a family of four might scare off some prospective rides. So, Mary, I was thinking . . ."

"Yes?" I said, dreading his reply.

"I was thinking that—well, you know—if you've got it, flaunt it, as they say."

I looked at him skeptically. "What are you getting at?"

"Well, how about you stand out here by yourself? We'll scoot back from the road and hide with the luggage, and you stand out here in your bathing suit."

"Dad!" I looked back at him, outraged. "Are you kidding me? Stand out in my bikini?"

"Well, not really." He shrugged. "We've been out here for a long time, and as you said, no one's picking us up. I simply figured we'd try a new approach. You'd just be standing there, Mare. You don't have to do or say anything."

"Then what?" I balked. "Some perv tempted by a thirteen-year-old pulls over to give me a ride, and you guys come jumping out of the bushes and join me?"

Dad laughed nervously, likely caught off guard by the disturbing accuracy of my prediction, and simply shrugged. "Something like that."

"Ew." What was wrong with our world? Then I looked at my sisters and Dad and saw how hot and ragged they were. I felt how hot and ragged I was. Frankly, I was desperate, too. I would do just about anything to get us back home to Mom. Plus, maybe just one of us would attract a ride faster, and one of the twins was out of the question. They were too young. We very well couldn't have them both on the side of the road together, either, though. Dad by himself would be the worst option for a number of reasons—and he was less likely to be picked up altogether, I figured.

Dad had a point. This current approach wasn't working.

We'd have to market ourselves differently.

"Why not?" I said finally, with a small burst of a laugh. "Okay."

Before second-guessing my decision, I took off my shirt, folded it, and passed it along with my blouse to the twins. Straightening my brown crocheted bikini top, I asked, "Should I take off my shorts and stand out here in just my bikini and shoes?"

"If you've got it, flaunt it," Dad said again.

I unzipped my shorts and wriggled out of them, passing them to Jill.

There I was in just my bathing suit with my Keds on. I still looked a mess, though, what with my skin all splotchy and scratched and my hair lank and flat in the humidity. As gross as it was, I all of a sudden worried nobody would want to pick me up. Maybe I wasn't sexy. How embarrassing!

In less time than it would take to brush your teeth, a green Pacer screeched to a halt on the shoulder in front of me. I shot a glance at Dad, and he motioned for me to go check it out. Hiding my nervousness, I approached the car. I'd heard about Ted Bundy, too, so I made sure to stand back far enough that they couldn't grab me if they wanted to.

There were two guys in the car, probably in their twenties, and they smelled like my brother's bedroom. I'd seen Skippy and his friend Dan Dikelis smoke a joint before, so I knew what that purple feather roach clip was for.

"Well, hello," the passenger said. "Need a lift, sugar?" He wore his baseball hat backward and had a five o'clock shadow.

"Where are you two heading?" I asked, trying to inject some confidence into my voice.

"Wichita Falls, Texas," the driver answered. "I'm dropping off my friend Henry here"—he pointed to the passenger with his thumb—"at his old lady's place. I'm Tom."

I didn't know if *old lady* meant his mom, his wife, or his girlfriend. The Pacer was a two-door car with large, rounded wraparound windows in back. Upon first glance, it was hard to say if there was room for four passengers. Henry started to get out of the car, presumably to let me in the back, when Dad and the twins trotted up.

"What the hell?" Henry said, trying to hide the joint, passing it quickly to Tom, who lowered it below the seat. Its fragrant, telltale smoke drifted upward anyway. "Is this some kind of sting operation or something?" He glanced nervously at Tom and then fell back into the car and slammed the door.

"Good morning, fellas," Dad said, placing his hand on the open window ledge, peering inside. He took an exaggerated whiff. "Smells good in here. You guys smokin' the wacky tobacky?"

What? What other secrets did Dad have? What would Mom think?

"Hi, Dad. This is Tom. And this is Henry." I introduced them. "They're going to Wichita Falls, Texas."

"That's well and fine," Dad said at once. Shifting into businessman mode, he gave them a look of contrition and approachability that just didn't jive with his current vagabond-man aesthetic. "I don't want to bust you, and this is not a sting operation or anything like that. We're just a family trying to get closer to home." Dad looked into the Pacer. Now that I had time to actually give it a good once-over, I could tell it was pretty empty in back—tidier than Charlene's station wagon had been, actually. "I betcha we could put two of the girls in the back with me and our luggage, and one could sit in the front with you two. We'd fit, no problem."

"Uh . . ." Tom seemed to be racking his mind for a way to get out of this but was coming up empty. "We were just pulling over for the one girl." He looked at Henry for backup.

"Yeah. Yeah. We thought she might've been a runaway or something," Henry said, trying to round out their explanation. They were convincing nobody.

"Well, that's mighty neighborly of you," Dad said, unfazed. "What do you say? Think we can squeeze in?" They were both shaking their heads. "How far is Wichita Falls?"

"Aw, man. You tricked us." Tom pointed at me.

"Oh come on," I pleaded. "It'll be fun. An adventure."

In the end, he relented, probably thanks to the effects of the Mary Jane. We'd just gotten ourselves a three-hour drive to Wichita.

The back seat was so small that Dad and I could barely fit. Jill sat on Dad's lap, using the towel between them to absorb the sweat. I yanked on the towel, trying to position it between myself and Dad so that I could keep my legs off his. The front had two bucket seats, so Gerri, the smallest, our little Biscuit Buns, couldn't sit between them but rather sat on Henry's lap.

The luggage obscured the back window. We each held on to our individual bags, which had our lunch sacks from Charlene.

Pacers do not have windows that open in back, so the wind to keep us cool came from Tom's and Henry's open windows. Of course, there wasn't air-conditioning. I was sure the whole arrangement wasn't what Tom and Henry had envisioned for their road trip to Henry's old lady's place when they headed out, but I thought it served them right for trying to pick up a thirteen-year-old girl. *There's that karma again.*

Once we were all settled, Tom started off again. In about ten minutes, Henry had scooted Gerri over to his window-side knee and unwrapped his arm from around her to roll a fresh joint.

"Y'all don't mind, do ya?" It was clear he didn't care if we minded or not. Before any of us gave a solid answer, he was already puffing it to life. "Gerri, can you roll up the window for a sec?"

Tom rolled up his window, too. I had never tried it before, but I did like the smell and strained forward a little to breathe some of the smoke.

"Hey there, Tom. Pay attention to the road," said Gerri.

"Yeah, yeah. Okay," said Tom. To our surprise, he motioned to Dad in the rearview mirror, offering to pass the joint back to him. There was a pause, during which I was sure Dad would produce one of his diplomatic salesmen rejections.

So when Dad replied, "Sure, why not?" I felt my jaw practically hit the floor.

I realized he had no surprises left. He didn't think twice about whether or not smoking grass in front of his kids—or smoking grass in general—was a good thing for a father to do.

He scooted Jill over to my lap while he reached forward and pinched the shrinking joint with his forefinger and thumb. He took two experienced-looking hits before passing it back up to Henry, coughing through his thank-you.

Was there nothing too low he wouldn't do? Even in front of the twins?

"Hey, guys, hurry up with that and open the windows. We're melting back here," I said. Not to mention, the car was filling up with smoke. I didn't mind the smell, but I could tell Jill was getting a little green in the face, and the last thing I wanted was for her to barf all over me in the back.

We drove for about a half hour, listening to the three grown men acting silly and giggly.

"Hey, Henry, tell me about your old lady," I said, trying to get them to talk about something sensical. Before he could get started, we heard a familiar sound: their Pacer's engine was making some knocking and tapping noises.

I thought it was funny to hear Gerri ask Tom, "Have you put oil in the engine recently?"

Dad laughed, and Tom looked at her quizzically. "What are you, a mechanic?" he said. That got Henry going hysterical all over again.

"Well, no. But I know that sound might mean that your engine needs oil," Gerri explained. *Good one, Ger-Bear.*

"Yeah," Jill chimed in, not to be outdone. "You don't want to seize your motor or shoot a rod."

The look on Henry's face was pure comedy. He turned around, not believing his ears. "What? How do two little girls know about car engines?"

"Are you insinuating that girls can't know about cars?" I challenged.

Out of the corner of my eye, I saw Dad smirk.

Both Tom and Henry replied, "Of course not."

"Oh, that's a relief. For a minute there, I thought you might've been male chauvinist pigs."

"Actually, we're women's libbers," Henry stated. They both thought that was hilarious. He pushed his backward hat up his forehead.

"You are?" I sneered. "How so?"

"Yes. Some of our favorite people are women. For instance, Lynda Carter, otherwise known as Wonder Woman. She's a . . . wonderful woman." Tom laughed. All this was obviously a joke to them, and I realized I shouldn't take the bait. I sat back in my cramped seat, biting my tongue.

"Good one, Tom. And there's Farrah Fawcett from *Charlie's Angels*. She's a wonderful woman," Henry added. We were doing the tennis match head-turning thing, looking back and forth between them as they answered.

Dad joined in, "What about Raquel Welch? She's a wonderful woman. Va-va-va-voom, right?"

"Dad! Whose side are you on?" I asked. "What about Jane Fonda?"

"No. Not her. She's too radical," Henry said.

"Yeah, always stirrin' up trouble," Tom agreed.

"Oh, I get it. You think that appreciating sex symbols means you're a women's libber?"

"Uh . . ." was as far as Henry got. I sat back again, shaking my head. *Pathetic*.

"Men after my own heart," Dad said, and I wanted to kick his shin.

Again, it occurred to me that we could just ask Grandpa Red or Mom for some money so that we could catch a bus directly home—a safe, quick, comfortable-ish ride without Mary Jane–smoking chauvinists who thought it'd be okay to pick up a minor. The idea of secretly contacting Mom behind Dad's back via pay phone was becoming increasingly enticing.

I glared at Dad. *Men after my own heart*, he'd said. Would he have picked up a minor?

It hit home that this whole hitchhiking thing was to preserve Dad's pride. That was it. He was willing to drag us all through the mud just to save face.

At the next gas station near a little place called Hadley, Tom pulled over and told the guy, "Fill 'er up with regular, and would you check the oil?" I saw the twins had little smirks on their faces that matched mine.

While the gas station attendant went about his business, including wiping down the windshield, Tom turned around and asked Dad if he could contribute to the car-filling expenditure.

Dad reluctantly peeled out a ten-dollar bill from his wallet. That left him with twenty.

Our total had now dwindled to fifty dollars, and we were still far from home.

The attendant approached the driver's window. "The oil's pretty low, mister. I'd say you need two quarts," he revealed, and I saw a huge smile spread across Gerri's face. We attempted not to laugh.

Meanwhile, Tom looked embarrassed. He tried not to look at any of us. "Go ahead and add them. Will that be enough?"

"I think that'll do it," the attendant answered.

Tom drove fast. The predicted three-hour ride to Wichita Falls took only two and a half hours. Finally, it was over. I couldn't wait to get out of the car and unwind my limbs. As soon as Henry opened the door, Gerri bounded out as fast as a bunny chased by a fox. Jill, then I, then Dad crawled out of the back seat. Tom put the Pacer in park and walked to the back to start unloading the luggage.

"That sure was a tight squeeze," I said.

"Good luck, you guys," Henry said, slamming the hatchback and getting inside.

The Pacer sped away. They had dropped us off at the corner of 287 and Vermont Street, just past the junction with Interstate 44.

56

John Parker's Flowers

"*I'm glad Tom* and Henry picked us up, but I didn't really like sitting in the front with them," Gerri said, shaking herself like a wet dog. I bet she'd held that full-body shiver in for the whole ride. I put my arm around her, and she rested her head on my shoulder.

"Yeah, their car *stunk*," Jill said, joining us. We walked over to a little piece of lawn at the edge of Lynwood East Park, finding a shady spot under a tree.

"Let's eat lunch," I suggested.

Without a word, we all sat down in the cool grass and unrolled our lunch bags. Charlene was a star. She'd folded a paper napkin and drew a red heart and wrote our names on it with a Magic Marker. Each bag had a cheese sandwich with yellow mustard and sweet pickle slices, a little bag of potato chips, and a tart and crisp Red Delicious apple. There were even little bags with four Oreo cookies each. Boy, I *loved* Oreos. We rarely had them back home. The occasional times Mom bought them, we'd devour them as soon as the grocery bags were brought in.

"Dad, maybe we should have an avocado from Aunt Ruth as well," I suggested.

Dad seemed groggy. He took out his knife and did a very sloppy job quartering and passing out the avocado, but it tasted *deyishous* anyway. He wiped his hands and the pocketknife on the grass. I took the opportunity to apply some Campho-Phenique to my legs while I stretched them out.

"Let's find a bathroom and get back on the road again," Dad said. We used the facilities at the park and walked back to 44 and 287.

We waited and waited for a ride. Eventually, a truck driver picked us up and introduced himself as John Parker. John Parker was on his way to Birmingham, Alabama. Not really on the beeline home, but we figured that it was a good distance out of Texas and that riding in his spacious eighteen-wheeler would be an upgrade from the pot-smoking fools we'd traveled with earlier. We quickly piled into the truck, where there was a big bed in back. We three girls climbed on it, trying to keep our shoes off the bedding, and lay down. Soon, the vibrating monotony lulled me and the twins into a sound sleep.

When I woke up, I heard Dad and John Parker talking about why we were on this big around-the-country road trip without Mom. I pretended to be asleep so that they'd go on candidly. I had to admit, I was becoming quite the eavesdropper. First it was the checkbook fight, then Dad asking Grandpa Red for money, Dad and Charlotte outside the Super 8 Motel window, and now here I was listening in on Dad's explanation. Turned out I learned a heck of a lot more through eavesdropping than I ever did through asking questions, so I wasn't about to stop now.

"My wife basically kicked me out after she found out about my allegedly shady business dealings. She'd said she'd had enough of me, essentially. Couldn't put up with my job anymore. That she did all the taking care of the kids and house when I was out in the evenings—"

John Parker interrupted, "Out in the evenings doing what? Didn't you say you had four kids?"

I chuckled silently. See? It wasn't normal for dads to miss supper most nights.

"Well," Dad defended himself, "six o'clock in the evening is a good time to sell life insurance." He laughed to himself. "I'd get a free supper, maybe a cocktail, too, and make a sale. On Thursdays I have choir practice."

"Really? Didn't you like your missus's cooking or want to be with your kids?"

Dad sounded confused and stuttered, "Well, ye-yes. I like my wife's cooking. Obviously, I like being with my kids." He gestured to us in the back of the big rig's cab. "I'm traveling around the country with three of them. My son's moved out of our house already; otherwise, he'd be with us, too."

"Yeah, but that's because she kicked you out, right?"

It was hard to keep my laugh inaudible. John Parker was having none of it. They were both quiet for a minute, and I could feel the bumps on the highway passing under the eighteen wheels in irregular drumrolls.

John Parker remarked wistfully, "The main thing I miss about being married is being away from my kid. Seeing him and spending time with him every other weekend and some holidays isn't really raising a son now, is it? And that's coming from a trucker who's already away from home a lot."

"I don't suppose it is, John," Dad said. I wondered if hearing that out loud from another man would help things sink in for Dad. Here John was, talking about the reality of being divorced. None of us knew anybody who'd gotten divorced before, and it all felt so surreal, so out of reach. But now we were getting a firsthand account of it.

"A teenage boy needs a real father, not my ex-wife's new boyfriend and his prissy ways. *Harold* spends more time with my son than I do. How is that fair? And the judge will always take the mother's side. Beware, Ralph." I could sense the sadness in his forced exhalation.

I thought men just talked about football and politics and cars and inflation and the Cincinnati Reds. But after hearing them discuss real feelings and family issues, it came as no surprise to hear Dad say, "So how was your sex life?"

John Parker laughed. "Pretty nice, actually. Miss that, too."

"Well, then why did you get divorced?"

"Cuz of my job. I'm just gone too long at a stretch. She got lonely." He tilted his head, checking all the side-view mirrors. "Seems like both our wives don't like our jobs, huh?"

"Guess so," Dad said. "My wife . . . well, she doesn't have a strong sexual appetite."

There was a beat of charged silence. "Is that so?" John asked safely.

"She and I had come to an understanding," Dad said, and I cringed.

"An understanding?" I couldn't see John Parker's face, but I bet his eyebrows were up in an expression of skepticism.

"Yes, an understanding. I could seek love outside of our marriage if I was discreet."

"Were you?"

"Was I what?"

"Were you discreet?"

"Hm," Dad considered. "I guess not." They both chuckled, but maybe not because it was funny but because it was the unvarnished truth—very sad and only ironically humorous. "Yeah, well, even if I might be getting a divorce in the near future, I'd have to say that this summer has really been *ex-tra-or-din-ary*. Even if my family falls apart, they'll sure have some incredible memories from this trip."

"That's real nice," conceded John Parker.

I heard Dad give a huge sigh and then blow his nose. "Well . . . another shameful part for me about this whole situation I find myself in is that I had to grovel to my wife's hero of a father for some charity at the start of this road trip."

"Hero of a father, eh?"

"The great and mighty Mr. Ransford." Dad said the name with so much resentment. I had never heard Dad refer to Grandpa Red as Mr. Ransford before. I thought he called him Dad or Pops or Grandpa Red, like we did. The bitterness in his voice was thick enough to cut with a knife. I made sure to do a little pretend snoring.

John Parker turned his head toward the back seat to see if we were still asleep. "That sounds tough," he commented, reassured that we were. "How did that go over?"

"Well, sure enough, my perfect wife's perfect father gave me some money. Five hundred bucks. He said that it was for the girls—not for me alone, of course. To create a memorable trip for his granddaughters."

"Had your wife already told her parents about kicking you out?"

"Actually, come to think of it, she must have, because they had ice-cream sundaes and banana splits ready when we arrived."

"He sounds like a nice guy," John Parker reasoned. "Giving you the money and all." I was glad he saw him that way, too. And I was even gladder that he was willing to be straight with Dad and tell him that to his face. How could Dad resent Grandpa Red?

"I guess, if you like hoity-toity uppity folk who think they're better than you and never wanted their precious daughter to marry a scumbag like you in the first place," Dad said, and his words felt a lot like a punch to the gut. I'd never heard him talk like this. Part of me felt sorry for him. It was strange to see him feeling so vulnerable; it didn't go with the generally high opinion he held of himself. After a minute, Dad said, "Seems like a lot more folks are getting divorced nowadays, but even so, I don't know how I'd face my congregation at church if we got divorced."

"You're a pastor?" John Parker asked, startled. "I wouldn't think a pastor would be out hitchhiking with his daughters."

Dad laughed. "That came out wrong. *The* congregation, not *my* congregation. I was referring to church in general. I've tried my hand at speaking a few times—I do give sermons pretty regularly and am the lead tenor in the choir—but I'm not the pastor." He paused, bristling a bit. "I guess what my wife says about me is true: I think I'm a bigwig at church."

"I don't think you should worry about what the church folk think. You should think about what is best for the kids," John offered. "Let your wife and daughters keep the house, stay at their same schools with their routines and friends, and you go find something you can afford." What *was* best for us? I wondered.

John Parker and Dad's private conversation reminded me of my blood-sister ceremony with Meredith. They were sharing some pretty dark secrets. I felt a little guilty for listening in. If anyone had heard all the things Meredith and I had told each other, I would have been mortified. It felt wrong to continue eavesdropping on the two men now—plus, I'd heard enough, and most of it I already knew.

Wiggling around and feigning waking up with an exaggerated yawn, I said in a pretend groggy voice, "Where are we?" The twins woke up for real next to me.

When we finally made it near his destination, John Parker downshifted and air-braked to a stop near a Super 8 Motel just off I-20. *Oh no,* I thought. *Not a Super 8.* At least prostitution wasn't legal here in Alabama like it was in Nevada. But even so, this motel looked a lot like the other one, and I was getting flashbacks.

I was glad to see that it had a swimming pool, though.

Before we bid farewell to John Parker, he motioned for us to follow him around to the back of his rig, where he turned the enormous handle to open the massive doors. We were flooded with the cold, sweet scent of a million flowers. What a pleasant thing to haul across the country.

He boosted us up and said, "Go ahead. Pick yourself a bouquet." We looked at him like he was crazy. "No, really. They would never miss a couple of handfuls of flowers. Go for it. You too, Ralph. You can use the motel's ice buckets as vases."

We emerged, our hands overflowing with unique bundles of colorful and fragrant flowers.

Then he shut and locked the big back doors, walked around to the cab, checked inside to make sure we hadn't left anything, and drove off. Just like that. Standing in front of the motel, we waved to him, our flowers swishing back and forth until we couldn't see him anymore. He waved out the window and sounded his air horn in that funny shave-and-a-haircut-two-bits way.

I looked over at Dad, who was grinning from ear to ear.

57

$14.95 Plus Tax

The plump middle-aged front desk clerk looked up from her register at the Super 8 Motel and blandly announced our total. "$14.95, sir, plus tax." The four of us stood in a row, tallest to shortest, on the other side of the reception desk in the lobby, our luggage lined up with us. We'd had a little powwow in the parking lot about what to say, how to present our case.

Dad eyed her shiny Super 8 name tag and gave her a big smile. "It's pretty late, Sandra . . ."

"Sir?" Sandra's eyes narrowed.

"I'm just saying that it's so late. Doesn't look like you'll be getting any more business tonight. No one else will be checking in, and we really need a place to stay."

"We have vacancy, sir. You can stay here. No issue with that." Sandra wasn't having it.

"But we've run out of money—our car broke down in Amarillo, Texas," Dad went on, laying it on a little thicker this time. "We're far from home, and we're tired." He spread out his flower-filled hands in supplication.

"What are you asking, sir?" She looked at our pathetic appearance, mismatched hodgepodge luggage, and hands overflowing with beautiful flowers. I thought I saw her cringe.

We three girls tried to smile back at her. I imagined we looked just terrible.

"Sandra, let me be frank," Dad said. "I'm asking if you'll let us stay gratis."

She looked at him like he was crazy. "Gratis, sir?"

"You can call me Ralph."

"I thought you said Frank."

"No, it's Ralph," Dad said, "Sandra, *gratis* means—"

"I know what *gratis* means, *Ralph*." She fidgeted, clicking her ballpoint pen. I bet she was ready to get back to that crossword puzzle of hers and wasn't in the mood for our negotiations. "It's not in our Super 8 Motel policy to simply allow guests to stay without paying."

"Do you have a manager here at this late hour?" Dad looked around, surveying the reception area. "Maybe he can help us, appreciate our dire situation, and offer some Christian charity. We've heard that you Southerners have that in spades."

"Sir, I *am* the manager," Sandra huffed. "There is no one higher up than me to discuss this with."

"I see," said Dad. "Girls?"

"We're not trying to pull one over on you, Sandra. And congratulations on being the manager. It's nice for me to see a woman in charge," I offered, taking a deep breath. "But what Dad said is true. We really are down on our luck. We're just trying to get back to our mom—"

"In Ohio," Jill chimed in, taking over the story like a wrestler in a tag-team match. "We've been on a summer road trip since June, and everything was going great until our car broke down in Texas."

"And we've been hitchhiking for a couple of days now." It was Gerri's turn to jump in. At the word *hitchhiking*, Sandra raised her brows at Dad. "People have been very nice picking us up and giving us rides."

"You would have liked the Dolly Parton impersonator named Jolene who picked us up and took us in for the night," I said. "She was groovy and so kind."

Dad joined the storyline. "She even made us dinner, packed us lunches to go, and washed our clothes. Just like I said, she was oozing southern hospitality."

Sandra gave us a doubtful look. I could read her response on her face: this Super 8 wasn't her personal property to give away for free; letting us stay here wasn't the same as letting us stay with her at her home. But we desperately kept up our negotiations anyway.

"And a trucker named John Parker brought us across four states today, all the way here," I added. "You'd be the next in line of kind and giving people."

"I bet the Super 8 Motel corporation wouldn't mind and wouldn't even notice if some guests stayed overnight without paying, especially at this late hour," Dad suggested. Sandra just looked at us with wide, disbelieving eyes.

"Sir, you should be—"

"Ralph," Dad corrected her, smiling still.

"Ralph," she said, pausing to give Dad a razor-sharp critical glare. "You should be ashamed of yourself, having your children plead on your behalf like this. What do you think this is? *Paper Moon?*" She looked him over. "You're no Ryan O'Neal. What kind of example are you setting for your girls?"

"I love that movie, *Paper Moon*. That Tatum O'Neal is the cutest!" I exclaimed.

"You can't just kick us out on the street," Jill said, undeterred. "What will we do?"

"Yeah, where will we go? We had to leave our stuff in the broken-down car," Gerri said, adding a slight whine to her voice.

"We do have one small sleeping bag, a blanket, and a towel—but in a city like this, it'll be hard to find a place to camp at this late hour," Dad explained.

"Oh goodness . . ." Sandra looked at Dad. "Don't you have a credit card like everyone else in America?"

"That's a good question, but actually I don't," he confessed. "Don't like to pay interest on money I've spent before I've earned it."

Oh brother, I thought.

"You have no money at all? I find that hard to believe."

"Yep, we don't believe in credit cards," I echoed.

Jill glanced at me, startled I'd drifted from our script, and grabbed my hand. I looked back at her with an *I'm sorry* expression. Then, earnestly, she looked at Sandra and offered her the bouquet she'd selected from John Parker's truck. "How about we sell you our flowers?"

The offer was so disarmingly sweet and innocent that even Sandra's eyes melted.

Little Ger-Bear offered her bouquet, too. "They're fresh and beautiful. Here, smell them." She grasped her bunch and extended them toward the receptionist. "John Parker, the trucker, just gave them to us. He had a truckful of them and said nobody would notice. Maybe you could help us with a room for the night and nobody would notice that, either?"

"You can decorate your desk with them to look pretty for you and the other guests," Jill added, forcing a wobbly smile. "Maybe you'd end up getting twice as many guests!"

We looked at one another, suppressing hopeful smiles.

Sandra sighed. "Lord have mercy! You've won me over. It'll be our secret." She looked around, as if someone might hear her.

I could've sobbed with joy. I nearly did, in fact—I tried to exhale a sigh of relief, but it came out as more of a whimper. Jill and Gerri hugged each side of me, staying close, and Dad's hand found my shoulder, squeezing it.

"Thanks, ma'am—" Dad started, but Sandra held up her hand to him.

"I'm doing this for your children, Ralph, not for you. You should be providing them with a more upstanding role model. It doesn't look like you planned ahead for emergencies. Wait here," she said. After arranging the flowers in a couple of vases she'd procured from the back, she handed us a key to room 115. "It's the room closest to the pool." She winked at me. "Check out is at ten o'clock."

✽ ✽ ✽

To our relief and surprise, room 115 had two queen-size beds. Usually the twins slept together, but we split them up to maximize the bed space. I would sleep with Gerri, and Jill would sleep with Dad.

424

We got the twins in the tub first, and they took a rapid-fire bath with the efficiency of a pit crew, soaping up their hair and using the Super 8's brand of conditioner. I used our one single comb to get through all their tangles and, like so many times over the past weeks, gave them a couple of rows of braids each. By the time I'd finished showering, Dad had turned down the beds and was blasting the fan and the air-conditioning, making the whole experience decadent and luxurious.

"We've been going nonstop, girls," Dad said, getting into bed. We were all tucked in now, and the lights were off. "You were able to take a nap in John Parker's rig, but I'm exhausted." He yawned, then took out his dental bridge with the three yellowish molars and laid it on the nightstand along with his glasses. *Ew*.

"Let's sleep in," I suggested, snuggling into the covers. Boy, they felt wonderful. They were a million times more comfortable than dispersed camping with one single blanket and zero pillows.

"That's exactly what I was thinking." He sighed. "If the pool is open early—"

"You don't want us to get on the road early, Dad?" Gerri cut in. How come she never got in trouble for interrupting?

"What's the rush?" he said. That was surprising. "Let's make the most of this comfy situation. You can go eat breakfast in their cafeteria. We'll leave at the checkout time."

"We'll try to be quiet and keep the curtains drawn so that the sun doesn't wake you up," I added.

"If you're still asleep, we'll sneak out some toast and other things for you, Dad," Gerri told him.

"Thanks, honey." And with that, he was out like a light.

Dad was right—we'd taken a long nap, but that didn't prevent us from feeling beat anyway. The mental exhaustion of repeatedly taking leaps of faith, without any idea as to where we'd land, was wearing on me. And yet I struggled to sleep. The twins passed out as quickly as Dad. Gerri was already snoring quite peacefully alongside me. My eyes flicked to the alarm clock perched on the bedside table between the two queen-size beds, and to my surprise, it read 12:45 a.m.

My palms broke into a sweat. What were the odds? This was the exact time I'd overheard Dad and that prostitute having sex back in Wells, in the other Super 8.

But this time, things were as they should be.

I took a breath, closed my eyes, and decided to imagine flipping through My Journal of Life's many hundreds of entries and go to sleep reviewing my all-time favorites. One of the first entries to crop up was of Dad and me standing outside at dawn, my trumpet raised and ready, with the American flag about to ascend the flagpole.

58

Reverend Sally

In the end, it took us six days of hitchhiking and twenty-one rides before we finally made it home. We met some interesting people from all walks of life along the way, forever memorialized in our Slate of Dates, States, and Fates.

We still hadn't told Mom that we'd been hitchhiking all the way home from Texas. I'd had a few opportunities to call her, and I'd been more than tempted to pull the plug on the whole trip back, but I still couldn't shake the gut feeling that in some way, I'd be responsible for Mom and Dad's divorce if I did so. I know that didn't really make sense. It wasn't a sensical thing. It was a feeling—sort of like the feeling of my foot being slightly past the twins' feet into the Grand Canyon and quietly knowing in my heart that I'd gone farther.

We'd made it to this point. And if we could somehow get all the way home and have Mom be the one to make the final decision, I'd be able to live the rest of my life guilt-free. I think that for a while, even if I hadn't realized it, this had been my driving force—the one thing keeping me going.

The divorce would be bad enough; I didn't want to feel like I'd played a part in making it happen.

Our last ride brought us within two and a half hours from home. An older lady had picked us up and brought us to the Trinity United Methodist Church in Marble Cliff, Ohio. It was late at night. She'd knocked on the door of the parish house, waking the reverend. We waited a few minutes before the outside porch lights were illuminated and the door opened.

"Good evening, Reverend. I'm sorry to disturb you," the older lady said, shifting to reveal the four of us standing beside her.

"It's no trouble at all. What do we have here?"

I was confused. There was a woman in a clerical robe standing in the open door. Where was the minister?

"Reverend Sally." The lady cleared her throat and spoke quietly. "I've brought you three girls and their father. They seem to be in need of some Christian charity."

"Well, well. My goodness." Reverend Sally peered over her glasses, looking us over. We stood before her, hungry and broke, with our smattering of possessions at our feet.

"Good evening, Reverend," Dad spoke up. "As this kind lady has indicated, my girls and I are in a bit of pinch. We're at the tail end of a several-weeks-long road trip and are almost home. We're congregants of the Trinity United Methodist Church in Chesterland, near our home in Kirtland."

"I see. I'm acquainted with your minister." She smiled. "We just worked together recently at the general conference. Nice fellow. Progressive," she mused, then brought her attention back to us. "What seems to be the trouble, and furthermore, how can I be of assistance?"

Jill asked, "Are *you* the minister?"

"Indeed." Reverend Sally smiled at her gently. Jill and Gerri exchanged glances of disbelief. Since when were women allowed to be minsters of churches? I wasn't sure when, but I loved the sound of this Reverend Sally and at once warmed to the idea of staying here for the night.

"Our minister is a man," Gerri informed her.

"Yes. Most of them are." Reverend Sally chuckled mirthlessly. "Welcome to the new world."

Far-out! I thought.

Reverend Sally offered us the opportunity to spend the night in the house of God, sleeping on the pews of the church. After we scarfed down a midnight snack in her tidy kitchen, Reverend Sally gave us some woolen blankets—the kind with satin edges—and walked us to the adjacent church building. Dad reached out and held my hand, and I didn't pull away. Our footsteps, surprisingly loud on the gravelly parking lot, broke the night's silence. The church's white steeple reflected the moonlight.

As agreed, we'd sleep on the pews right in front of the altar that night. Spreading out the blanket, I reached into the pocket on the back of the pew in front of me for the familiar red hymnal, running my fingers over the worn-smooth cover, softened by the worshipping hands of hundreds of parishioners. I opened the book to the first hymn: "Oh for a Thousand Tongues to Sing." The sparse light of the moon, glinting through the stained-glass windows, provided enough light to see, but I didn't really need it. I had that hymn—plus many, many others—memorized. Just by looking at the lyrics, I could hear the organ and vocal harmonies in my head.

"I'll pray for you tonight before I go to sleep," Reverend Sally informed us as she left. "In the morning, things will look better, and we can make a plan to get you home." She walked out of the nave and through the vestibule, quietly shutting the large, ornate double doors behind her.

At this point, I was too tired to worry much about anything other than getting back home. The fear of what awaited us there stubbornly lingered and throbbed like the rash I'd gotten from the poison oak back in California, but I'd gotten better at ignoring it.

It was outside of my control. And it was inevitable.

I was ready to face whatever came next.

＊ ＊ ＊

The next morning, I woke up before everybody else, wrapped myself up like a burrito in the blanket I'd been offered, and wandered the grounds. The late-summer weather was gorgeous, and so was the exterior of the church; I'd missed its beauty last night in the dark.

"Good morning, Mary," Reverend Sally said, taking me by surprise, a big smile spreading across her face as she meandered toward me. I was delighted that she'd remembered my name. "Did you sleep well?"

"Good morning, Reverend Sally. You might be surprised, but the pew was more comfortable than you'd think. It was very peaceful in there. The others are still asleep."

"I'm not surprised you were comfortable, seeing how you slept in God's house last night. You were surrounded by the Holy Spirit. Care to take a little walk with me?"

"I'd love to," I said, following her along.

"How are you doing?" She waited for my response in that patient minister way. Should I share my troubles with her? Ministers were supposed to be like counselors, right? I decided to trust her. I really did need some help, and I'd probably never see her again.

Formulating my thoughts, I told her about my parents' fight and our ensuing trip. The good parts and the bad parts. She didn't even flinch when I told her about the prostitute and the other bad things about Dad, even though it made me cry to tell her. She nodded along, and her arm draped across my shoulder as we walked in the little woods behind the church. It felt so good to talk to someone. I told her how scared I was about what would happen if my parents got divorced.

"Would you believe that we've been hitchhiking from Texas to here for almost a week and that our mom doesn't even know about it? Dad's been afraid to talk to her," I confessed, everything spilling out of me like pus from a wound. It was painful—but the relief overshadowed the pain. Reverend Sally smiled at me in a completely nonjudgmental way. "I guess I've been afraid to call Mom, too. I feel kind of guilty, like I should have protected the twins better."

We sat down on a fallen log, and she took my hands into hers. "I'm guessing that you did your best. You sound conscientious and caring."

"I haven't done my best." I started to cry. She pulled me in and embraced me, then prayed for me. The tears came gushing.

After we finished praying, she said, "Everything will be okay, Mary," and for some reason, I felt as though I could fully believe her. Trust her. An upsurge of relief spurred me to take a deep breath, and somehow, it felt like the first breath of a new life, like I'd been reborn and forgiven just by telling her the truth.

She pushed the hair that had fallen in my face behind my ear, just like Mom did. "You will help your little sisters manage the transitions God has in store for you. If your family changes and your dad does move out, you might take on more responsibilities to help your mother, but I have no doubt that a strong girl like you can do it. Mary, God never gives you more than you can handle. Did you know that?"

I nodded silently. Dad had told me that a number of times, but only now was I really getting it.

"Think of all you've done on your road trip and in your life in preparation for that." She squeezed my hands reassuringly. "Keep your faith in God, whose will be done. He has a plan for you." I tried to smile at her encouraging words. "Remember, he works in mysterious ways, and Jesus is always there to listen to you."

I nodded, and she gazed at me with a tender, perhaps pitying, look, as though seeing something in me for the first time.

"It sounds like maybe," she went on, "you've been working on forgiving your father."

I answered with a whimper. "I have. I really have. I really, really have. He makes me so mad." I couldn't suppress another sob from escaping my throat. "And sad. How can you hate and love someone at the same time? It's true that he's so much fun, but he's so bad. He thinks he can sin left and right and then just say sorry. Like that fixes things."

She hugged me again, and I released a torrent of grief onto her shoulders. How nice it was to lay my burden down. When my crying stopped, I noticed the peaceful sound of a little brook babbling at the base of the hill.

"Everything will be okay. Forgiving him will set you free. He's one of God's children, too, with regular human problems.

You'll see," she reassured me. "No matter what happens, there will be a silver lining. You just can't see it yet."

After another embrace, I took a couple of very deep, shuddering breaths. We stood up, dusted off our derrières, and walked back to the church, hand in hand. The twins and Dad were sitting on the front steps, their blankets stacked neatly next to them.

"Good morning, Stromp family," the reverend said in greeting. Her eyes were so bright, they could've lit up a cave. "What do you say we get you home?"

The twins hopped up and down. Holding hands, they jumped off the steps and danced in circles.

Reverend Sally turned her attention to Dad. "Ralph, would you like to use the parish's phone to call your wife?"

Dad looked at me, maybe noticing my tear-lacquered face, and sheepishly accepted her offer. I thought it was great that Reverend Sally had suggested Dad call Mom. I'd expected her to arrange for a ride to get us the rest of the way home and leave it at that—but this was, in a way, the *right* way.

Dad needed to come clean. And this was the place to do it.

We three girls sat on the steps while Dad and Reverend Sally walked back to the parish. When they returned, I could tell that his phone conversation had not gone well. He looked chastised, his face sad and tired. The reverend rested her hand on his slumped shoulders as she spoke softly to him. But wouldn't you know, in a New York minute, typical Dad shook off Mom's scolding, along with his forlorn hangdog expression, and he clapped his hands, putting on a happy face for us all.

"All right. Here we go," he said, coming back to himself. "Next stop: home!"

We all cheered. I couldn't help but ask him, "What happened? What did Mom say?"

"Well . . ." He laughed. "She was none too pleased to hear about our last week. She said that we should have called her or Grandpa Red to get fare for a bus ride." *Just like I'd thought.* "But then we wouldn't have had the *ex-tra-or-din-ary* experience we've just enjoyed."

"Now what do we do?" Gerri asked.

Reverend Sally said, "How about we have a proper break-fast, and then I'll take you to the bus depot and buy you some tickets home?"

59

"Leave the Driving to Us"

We'd never been on a Greyhound bus before. It was noisy, crowded, and a little smelly—kind of like a mix of Fritos and sweaty socks—but it wasn't any worse than some of the other rides we'd had to endure recently. I waved out the window at Reverend Sally, a part of me wishing that the bus had an ooga horn. I rested my head on the cool glass of the window and flipped the business card she'd given me round and round with my nail-bitten fingers.

"Don't lose that," Dad instructed. "You might want to send a thank-you card to that address. She's an excellent minister, for a woman. Don't you think?"

"Dad! That is so chauvinist of you!" I turned to him, regretting that I had agreed to be his seat partner and let the twins sit together in front of us. "What does her being a woman have to do with anything? Jeez! I think it's high time that women can be whatever men can be."

"I'm just saying—"

I cut him off with a stop-sign hand. But I did agree with part of what he'd said. "You're right, though, about her being an excellent minister. She really helped me, and by the looks of it, she helped you, too." I paused for a second, the groan of the bus filling the silence. "I think being a minister would be a good occupation."

"I've always thought so, too. The counseling-people-in-trouble part seems okay." He frowned a little. "But the public speaking every Sunday, giving the sermon sounds grand . . . Plus, imagine all that singing as part of your job!"

I furrowed my brow at his self-centeredness. Of course, he wouldn't gravitate to the charity of the position but instead to the attention of it.

We traveled along in silence for a while, and then I broached the uncomfortable subject in a whisper. "Dad? What's going to happen when we get home?"

"What do you mean?" He could be so opaque sometimes.

"Come on. You know," I told him. "The divorce."

"Oh, that. Well . . ." He was stalling. "I've been trying to get my head around it."

"And have you come up with anything?"

"What do *you* think about it?" He turned to me and looked like he would really appreciate my opinion. Who was the kid and who was the parent here? Then I remembered what Reverend Sally had said about him being just a grown-up child of God.

"Even though it affects me and the twins—and even Skippy, to a certain degree—it shouldn't be a decision that I make."

"I'm not asking you to make a decision, Mary," he clarified softly. "I just wanted to know what you thought about it. I respect your opinion."

"Here's what I think about it." I took a calming breath, trying to put together my thoughts so that they sounded true but also spared his feelings. He was my father, after all. And even after everything was said and done, I still loved him, faults and sins be damned. "Well, I think that if it happens, somehow or other, we'd all be okay. You probably don't know this, but I heard you and that trucker, the guy with the flowers?"

"John Parker?"

"Yeah, him. Well, I pretended to be asleep when you two were talking about divorce, and I liked his suggestion. He said something about you moving out and letting me and the twins and Mom have the house. Do you remember?"

Dad sighed. "Oh yes, something like that. Seems a bit unfair, don't you think?"

"Whose fault is it that this is happening?" I asked quietly but firmly, and Dad sort of snickered at the brutal reality check. "None of this would be happening if it weren't for you, Dad. We didn't ask for any of this."

"That's true," he conceded. "Life would be very, very different. I'd sure miss you girls."

I let him put his arm around me, and he choked up a little. There's just about nothing more pitiful than seeing your dad cry.

"This has been a wonderful trip we've shared this summer—one I'll remember till my dying day. Seems like we've grown closer, and I know you all a little bit better, what with us all being together twenty-four hours a day. I'm very proud of each of you." He wiped a tear with the back of his hand, jostling his glasses askew, and chuckled again.

We sat in silence for a bit. I gazed out the window and saw that we were ten miles from Cleveland. Kirtland was only another half hour beyond that. *Holy cow! We're almost home!* After nearly two months of travel—covering around six thousand miles, twenty-one states, and two countries—we were finally, *finally* almost home.

"What do you think? Could you manage without us?" I asked. I thought that I was done with crying after my talk with Reverend Sally, but a sob swelled up in my throat.

"I just can't picture it. Know what I mean?" Dad looked at me, sadness clouding his eyes.

I nodded back; it was hard to imagine. "Mom's picking us up at the bus depot, right?" I asked, figuring we both needed a change of subject.

"Yep. In ten minutes. That's the plan."

"Good luck, Dad," I said, trying not to cry, but a little tear rolled down my cheek. "Can we stop talking about this so that I don't look like a crybaby mess when I see Mom for the first time in two months?"

We both laughed, and he reached his hand out and brushed away my tears. "Sure, sweetheart. I love you, Mare."

I choked out an "I love you, too."

"Thanks for helping make this an *ex-tra-or-din-ary* trip."

60

Home

Ten minutes later, the bus pulled up to our stop, its brakes hissing as we shrieked to a halt. All of a sudden, it was as though I couldn't move.

This was it. This was our last stop.

We were almost *home*. And somewhere, just out of sight, was Mom.

The twins didn't share my hesitation. They ran as fast as ever, darting between other passengers like a Charles Dickens child, escaping the throng of people clogging the platform. Dad and I stood, making our way toward the exit, and I happened to glance through the window to my left.

My eyes immediately found Mom in the crowd. "Wow," I said out loud, taken aback by how much she'd changed. It was as though she was standing taller—she seemed thinner, happier, and healthier than I'd seen her in years. "Look at Mom!"

Dad followed my gaze to where Mom stood outside, clasping her purse. She wore a gorgeous silk blouse and a stylish skirt. Her hair was shiny and perfectly curled. She looked a million times better than Charlotte ever could. I reluctantly peeled my gaze off her to gauge Dad's reaction. His expression was a mix of shock and hesitation, as if his brain had momentarily short-circuited. The twins got to Mom first, naturally. She enveloped them in her arms, rocking them back and forth. Dad and I drifted off the bus, weaving through the crowd. The knot of strangers loosened, and I was able to embrace Mom next.

She disentangled herself from the twins and grabbed me with both hands around my face.

"Let me have a look at you." She shook her head slowly and must have noticed the weariness I'd come to wear like a second skin. "You look so grown up, Mary." Then she gazed at my legs. "And your rash seems almost healed."

I hugged her and hugged her and hugged her. "Mom!" The word came out as a moan.

"Oh Mary. My sweet girl. You're okay. You're okay." She brushed away my hot tears with her thumb. I was a mess. "We're all going to be okay. You'll see."

The twins wrapped themselves into our hug again. I squeezed my eyes tightly shut and tried to savor every last sensation. I needed this Journal of Life entry to be vivid enough to last forever.

Dad brought up the rear, carrying what was left of our possessions. "Ginny."

"Ralph." She looked him in the eyes as she said it.

"You look really good." He smiled sheepishly at her.

"Thank you. I've been living a healthy lifestyle this summer." She gave him a once-over. "Truth be told, you look a little worse for wear." That made him laugh and nod in agreement.

As we walked to the parking lot to her station wagon, she told us that Skippy and Stacey would be coming over for supper later to hear about our adventures. The twins gripped her hands tightly, talking and laughing over each other. I don't know how she managed to process what they were saying when they spoke like that. They couldn't stop talking. I would wait my turn and have a private heart-to-heart with her once things settled down.

I decided to walk with Dad, knowing that what awaited him at home would be difficult.

"How are you doing, Dad?" I looked up at him, and what I felt was sadness and pity—not anger anymore. Just sadness . . . for all of us.

"Not bad, not bad." I think he was attempting to be reassuring.

Mom had Dad drive, and as we left the city, rolled through the suburbs, and eventually reached the countryside, the familiar sights of our hometown brought me a renewed sense of comfort. The softball fields. Gildersleeve Elementary School. The Dairy Queen on the corner of 6 and 306.

As we drove past Crary Lane, I was stunned to hear Dad remark, "I wonder how Winnie Gravvers is doing."

What? That was a first! I shook off my astonishment that he didn't call her the sexiest girl on Crary Lane and replied that I couldn't wait to call her tomorrow. Maybe I'd ride my bike to her house, and we could play in her pool.

"How's Namo, Mom?" Jill asked.

"She's had a bit of a flea problem this summer, but I gave her a bath yesterday, so she should be feeling better. I bet she'll be so happy to see you all."

"Happy as a dog with two tails, right?" Gerri asked. "Like Grandpa Red likes to say."

We all laughed.

Gosh, I wished we could be like this forever—talking and joking in such a carefree manner. Not thinking about what we had to face.

When we got home, after we'd rolled up the steep drive-way and parked the car under the poplar by the garage, Namo came running from behind the vegetable garden and knocked me over, jumping up in a frenzied greeting. She ran dizzying circles around us, a blur of tan and brown and black fur. She toppled down both twins, too. Only Dad and Mom remained standing, despite our beloved mutt's onslaught of affection. We sat on the cool grass until that crazed dog finally settled down, flopping onto her back, her tongue lolling, offering us the opportunity to pet her belly.

"Namo doesn't know whether to shit or go blind," Mom stated.

"Mom!" I scolded, but I was laughing. The twins looked on with equally shocked expressions.

Dad thought that was *hilarious*, and he laughed so hard that he kind of sounded like TeenTeen by the end with all his wheezing. "You sound like your hillbilly mother, Ginny."

"I know! I guess the apple doesn't fall far from the tree." Now it was her turn to laugh. She looked so beautiful in her new stylish outfit and hairdo.

We got up, and I noticed that the flagpole did not have the flag raised. The ballcock was crooked and looked dingy, and some of that silver paint had splintered off. It wasn't like I'd expected her to carry out the daily flag raising and lowering without us, but for some reason, I'd thought Old Glory would at least be waving for our welcome home.

As we approached the front porch, I saw that there were a couple of cardboard boxes stacked, taped closed, and labeled on the side in thick Magic Marker in Mom's neat printing: "Ralph's Pants" sat right beside "Ralph's Socks and Unmentionables."

We three girls got quiet, not sure of what to say or think. Right when I'd started to believe we'd face this reality at another time and be spared it today, it sprang out of nowhere like an ambush and forced itself to be seen. Better to get it over with, I supposed.

"I'm guessing I'm moving out, huh, Gin?" Dad sounded resigned to the inevitable.

"I think it would be best," she said in a soft and sad voice.

"How about tomorrow? I'm pretty beat." That was an understatement.

"That would be okay, Ralph." Then she directed her attention to us three. "Girls, have a seat."

We all plopped down onto the cool concrete steps. I took a deep breath, acknowledging this very moment as the real final leg of our journey. *One final push,* I told myself. *We're almost there.*

"Your father and I spoke on the phone yesterday, and I hope I'm not speaking out of turn . . ." She looked at Dad, who tried to give her a reassuring smile. I imagined this was breaking his heart. Even though he was a cheater and a liar—and one who preferred to gloss over troubles—I bet the thought of not living here with Mom and us was gut-wrenching for him.

In that moment, I couldn't help but feel a deep compassion for Mom as well. Forced into this decision by Dad's poor choices, she had put on a brave face, and although she seemed healthier these days, I knew that behind her smile must lie a heart quietly breaking, too.

"We want you all to know how proud we are of you and how much we love you."

The twins interrupted in unison, "We know that." They sounded equally irritated and cross.

Mom released her held breath. This was probably harder for her than she was letting on, and my empathy shifted off Dad and onto her again. After all, she'd loved Dad, and he'd forced her into this decision with his poor business practices, extramarital affairs, and neglect.

"Well, that's good to hear." She looked at Dad. "Like I said, we love you and are proud of all of you, and we know that you're very strong and can roll with the punches." She took a big breath and let the next words rush out in a torrent. "But your father and I think it might be best if we took a break from each other—"

"A break from each other?" Jill interrupted. "What the hell does that mean? You've had almost two months of a break from each other."

We all looked at her, aghast. Even she seemed startled by what she'd said. She had never cussed like that in front of Mom and Dad before, and she'd certainly never cussed *at* them. How bad was her punishment going to be? Soap in her mouth? A spanking? Write an apology?

Shockingly, our parents just looked at each other, snapped closed their open mouths, and didn't say a thing about it.

Eventually, Mom rallied, and I could tell she was about to give us the brutal truth of what was going to happen, only for Dad to interrupt and say, "Girls, we're considering divorce. It's the responsible, adult thing to think about—but we're not certain about anything just yet. We're going to take some additional time apart to decide."

Mom looked at Dad like she was peering back at a stranger, a wave of obvious relief crashing over her shoulders. She gave him a reassuring nod, and I could tell she was grateful that he hadn't made her be the sole bearer of the bad news. He was taking responsibility for this—as he should.

"I know this isn't ideal," he acknowledged when the twins began to tear up, "but we're going to do what we do best and roll with the punches, like Mom said. No matter what happens, we'll be all right, and we'll always love each other. Isn't that right, Gin?"

"Of course," Mom said, eyes shining. "Of course, Ralph."

"I don't want you to get a divorce," Jill said.

"Me neither," Gerri concurred, scooting over to sit closer to her twin. I was so happy they had each other. How hard would this be if either of them was alone? It was unimaginable.

"Me either," said Dad, looking over to Mom with an unrealistically hopeful smile.

"Oh. Stop this. All of you," Mom said, laughing, giving her little red curls a jiggle. Why couldn't Dad have been satisfied with just her? He'd ruined everything. If he'd been a better husband, we wouldn't all be in this situation together.

"Quit ganging up on me." She wagged her finger and gave the mom's eye to each of us in turn. "Divorce will be hard. But we are strong." The twins nodded at her words. Dad did, too.

"Our family has gone through lots of changes," Mom went on. "This is just the next transition. We'll be able to navigate this new way of being." Her pep talk was gaining traction. For some reason, she paused and asked, "Mary, how do you feel about this?"

Was she really offering me the opportunity to speak freely and openly? Or were those just words? All of them turned to me expectantly.

I looked at Dad. Then the twins. Man, we'd been through a lot of profound things this summer. Hundreds of hours of close confinement can do that to people. Those long, boring lectures. Dad's shameless flirting. Being such a cheapskate. The disregard for his safety, like with the buffalo and the trail to the ocean in Big Sur. My rash. All the dispersed camping. His general Mr. Magoo-ness. Our near deaths at Salt River. The hitchhiking.

If there was a chart of plusses and minuses about our summer, there would undeniably be a lot of things listed in the minuses column. But truthfully, there were a lot of plusses, too.

Spending time with TeenTeen and Grandpa Red. Meeting and becoming friends with Meredith and her family. The incredible places we saw: Devils Tower, the Pacific Ocean, the Grand Canyon. Mexico. Aunt Ruth and Uncle Hartery and Randy. The times we magically made meals out of nothing. The awesome people like Charlene, John Parker, and the lady at that last Super 8 who let us stay for the cost of a couple of handfuls of flowers.

"You know, Mom. You're right—we're strong." I glanced at the twins who, in that moment, didn't look very strong. In fact, they looked gaunt and exhausted. "We know how to get through bad situations and keep going."

I stood up. The twins came and stood with me at the base of the stairway, leaving Mom and Dad on the porch steps, with those two packed boxes behind them. "In a perfect world, this wouldn't be happening. But this is no perfect world, is it? What is happening is you're probably getting a divorce. Which means we're probably getting a divorce, too."

"Mary's right," Gerri said. "When parents get divorced, the kids have to get divorced, too."

"It's not really fair, is it?" Jill said.

"Not a bit," I answered. I put my arms around the girls' shoulders. "But life—"

"—is not fair!" the twins finished.

We gave one another a look of shared understanding that left Mom and Dad out. Well, good on us. If the next stage in our family's development was beginning to evolve, we three girls would have to stick together.

"The truth is we only have right now. This is the only thing that's real." I clapped my hands. "So get a divorce. We girls can deal with it. Right, girls?"

"Right," they said.

"Don't fight too much about the details. Try to be nice. It's going to be sad sometimes. And let's stop hiding our sadness and anger. No more going-to-your-rooms-until-you-come-out-with-a-smiling-face anymore."

"Yes, no more of that!" Jill shouted.

"Yes, no more of that!" Gerri echoed. "I hate that."

Wow, could our family actually turn a page and make a change?

That handed-down, from both sides of the family, no less, inherited legacy of ours might be hard to let go of, but it was worth a try, and the girls still had some childhood left. Perhaps they could be spared the lifelong ramifications of always putting on a happy face.

I wasn't exactly sure of what was going to happen with our family, but I knew that we'd be able to handle anything. We'd endured the Great Salt Lake. We'd been lashed by poison oak. We'd walked to Mexico. We'd jumped off cliffs. We'd pushed our car across a desert, for pity's sake, and we'd hitchhiked for days. We could do anything.

If there was one thing I'd learned from our Great American Road Trip, it was to expect the unexpected. To not turn on one another. To see the shades of gray in the black and white, and, most of all, to stay rooted in the present moment.

I didn't need to know what would happen next. I'd learned not to care. I'd just let the story write itself in My Journal of Life, page by unfolding page.

Epilogue

A Couple of Months Later

Dad showed up in the middle of my volleyball match against Chardon High. Crouching down, ready for the serve, I saw him walk in and find a space on our home team's bleachers. I was the starting setter on the freshman team, and Winnie Gravvers was in the back row as our defensive specialist. We were both so proud to make the high school team.

"Go, Mary!" he yelled, cupping his hands around his mouth. I pretended to be embarrassed, but in truth, I loved that he was there watching me play. He hadn't done that very often before. A couple of weeks before that, he'd attended one of our football games and cheered on the marching band during halftime. Playing my trumpet extra forte, I'd hoped he could hear me.

It'd been a few months since we'd returned from the Great American Road Trip and a month since Mom and Dad had officially decided to get a divorce. Surprisingly, it seemed to be suiting both of them just fine. Not only was Dad showing up for our sporting events, but he had found a small apartment in Euclid—near Skippy and Stacey. It was only about a half hour from our house. Skippy told me that Dad had come over for supper a few times and that they were getting along better.

Mom, of course, was thriving. She was excelling at work and felt so full of life. I realized that the *understanding* Dad suggested he'd had with her was one-sided and unwanted—without all that in her life, she was practically floating. She continued with what she called her healthy lifestyle. If I wasn't at a late-evening event at school, I'd go for a walk around the block with her after supper. We got a lot closer during those walks. I think that being married to Dad had been a depressing thing for her. She seemed freer, funnier, happier, and overall lighter on her own.

Was this the silver lining Reverend Sally predicted? It sure seemed like it.

We didn't spend *every* weekend at Dad's small apartment, but many of them we did—and we could count on him to be fun and adventurous, as usual. He took us bowling and to the Cleveland Zoo. We helped him in the kitchen since he still wasn't a very good cook. Mastering spaghetti and meat sauce was a source of pride for him.

I thought it was kind of odd that he had asked Mom to help him set up his new place, but she eagerly agreed, and with her guidance, his little apartment was really quite cozy and cute, with curtains and everything. She had stocked it with lots of stuff from our house, so for me and the girls, there was plenty of familiarity. It felt oddly like home, even though it wasn't, and a part of me loved that throughout everything, Mom and Dad were still civil and kinder to each other than they used to be.

The twins started middle school and were adjusting well. Mom had asked the counselors to allow them to be in the same homeroom and to have the same schedule so that they could support each other during our family's upheaval. They both chose the first semester of home ec and the second of shop. I looked forward to helping them with their projects and homework if they needed it.

The girls and I carried on with our helpful housekeeping, and our little home stayed tidy.

The pressure and, I hated to say it, the fear of being punished for not doing things Dad's way was lifted. Mom was a much gentler parent.

Everything felt calmer. Everything felt *better*.

Life was too busy to do the flag raising and lowering every day during the school year, but on the weekends, when we weren't at Dad's, I'd rouse the twins, and they'd rather reluctantly get out of bed and do the flag part while I played "Reveille" and "Assembly." I'd squeezed my eyes tight on the high notes and captured the moments in a new chapter of My Journal of Life.

SLATE OF...

DATES	STATES	FATES
6/21/76	Kirtland, Ohio	Bye to Mom and Namo
6/21/76	Indiana, Indianapolis	Hot and Sunny
6/21/76	Michigan	Swam in Lake Michigan
6/22/76 - 6/25/76	Clarendon Hills, Illinois	TT & GPR - Banana Splits, Big Red Bike Ride, Show, Phoebe's Ham ▓▓▓ Salad
		I dropped the Bologna on the floor, Two Packs of Dentyne!!
6/25/76 - 6/30/76	La Crosse, Wisconsin,	Bluebird Campground with the Gardeners Fun Camping Stuff
6/30/76	Minnesota	Drive to Sioux Falls - Mary drove!
6/30/76	Sioux City, Iowa	Foot Down near ▓ Sioux Falls
6/30/76	Sioux Falls, South Dakota	▓Sincére Statue of David
7/1/76	Wall, South Dakota	Wall Drug with the Gardeners! - Buffalo - Car Problems: Broken Trailer Axle and Overheated Blue Pierre - Campground in Rapid City - Dad Lost Us
7/2/76 - 7/4/76	Mount Rushmore, South Dakota	Camping with the Gardeners - Mount Rushmore Area: Crazy Horse, Caves, Fourth of July Fireworks
7/5/76	Deadwood, South Dakota	Deadwood
7/6/76	Devil's Tower, Wyoming	Devil's Tower
7/7/76	Yellowstone, Wyoming	Yellowstone - Old Faithful Geyser - Said Good-Bye to Mallory and Meredith and Mr. and Mrs. G.
7/8/76	Salt Lake City, Utah	The Great Salt Lake - Salty, Floaty, White Sand / Salt Lake City Temple and Tabernacle (Couldn't Go In!)
7/8/76	Wells, Nevada	Wells, Nevada - Stayed at Super 8 Motel Swimming Pool, Laundry and Grocery Shopping
7/10/76	Truckee and Kings Beach, California	Truckee - Five and Dime / Kings Beach - Ticklebelly, Lake Tahoe Hot Sand, Cold and Clean and Fresh Water Ice Cream at ▓▓▓ CharPit
7/10/76	Sand ▓▓▓ Harbor, Nevada	Sand Harbor - Steak Dinner and Camping Under the Stars
7/10/76	Truckee and Auburn, California	Truckee - Donner Lake Dad Dropped Glasses / Auburn - Concrete Gold Miner Statue / San Francisco - Bay Bridge on Blue Pierre Roof Human JukeBox Cable Car Crookedest Street Shrimp Cocktails and Sea Lions Dr. Jekyll and Mr. Hyde, Chinatown, Edsel Ford Fong

DATES	STATES	FATES
7/13/76	San Francisco and Santa Cruz, California	San Francisco - Officer O'Neill and Tai Chi / Breakfast Burritos / Santa Cruz - Beach Boardwalk Ferris Wheel, Giant Dipper - Tricked Ger-Bear, Corndogs and Body Surfing / Surfers / FreeCamping
7/14/76	Pfeiffer Beach, California	Big Sur - Bixby Bridge / Tried to Get To Tide Pools at Pfeiffer Beach Nearly Fell Off Cliff
7/15/76	Los Angeles, California	Los Angeles - Topanga Beach Tide Pools, Hollywood Walk of Fame, San Elijo State Beach
7/16/76	Calexico / Mexicali	Calexico / Mexicali - Walke to Mexico Hospital - Medicine for Poison Ivy, Bought Animalito Bobble Heads and Mexican Blanket
7/16/76 - 7/20/76	Phoenix, Arizona	Phoenix / Aunt Ruth, Uncle Richard, and Randy Swimming Pool, Trampoline Park, McDonald's
7/20/76	Grand Canyon, Arizona	Grand Canyon / Kaibab Trail, Ooh Aah Point
7/21/76	Salt River, Arizona	Salt River Tubing and Mud Cliff Jumping
7/23/76	Flagstaff, Arizona	Cathedral Rock, Chapel of the Holy Cross, Bell Rock, Ice Cream in Flagstaff, Painted Desert, Meteor Crater, Petroglyph National Monument
7/24/76	Bushland, Texas	Bushland / Blue Pierre Broke Down, Earl at Falcon's Stop, Started Hitchhiking / Spent the Night in Goodnight, Texas at Charlene's (Jolene/Dolly Parton) House, Sheila, Shayla, and Sheena
7/25/76	Goodnight, Texas	Goodnight, TX to Wichita Falls, TX with Tom and Henry, who were Smoking Joints
7/26/76	Wichita Falls, Texas	From Wichita Falls to Birmingham, Alabama (LONG—all day Drive) With John Parker in his Semi-Truck. He gave us Bouquets of Flowers
7/27/76	Birmingham, Alabama	Birmingham / Super 8 - Traded Flowers for Lodging Swimming Pool - Stole Some Breakfast
7/28/76	Birmingham, Alabama	Birmingham / Paul's Pied Piper Plumbing, Tour of Churches / Vulcan Statue - Climbed up 160 Steps to the Viewing Area Over the City
7/29/76	Nashville, Tennessee	Edith, Ethel, and Junior on Their Way to the Children's Hospital in Nashville to get Junior's Hemangioma Removed. Slept under a Bridge like Trolls
8/1/76	Marble Cliff, Ohio	Slept at Reverend Sally's Church (a Lady Minister!) In the Church on Pews in Front of the Altar
8/2/76	Kirtland, Ohio	Home at Last! Namo Went Crazy! Mom Told us that She and Dad are Getting a Divorce. Dad's Stuff was Already Packed When We Got Home.

Use this QR code to link to book club
discussion questions on the author's website.

SCAN ME

Author's Note

Although Bicentennial Summer was born from a real-life road trip and the unforgettable summer of 1976, it is very much a work of fiction. I've bent timelines, reshuffled events, and embroidered memories to create a story that flows — even if the facts occasionally had to hitchhike to catch up.

Some scenes are imagined, others are stitched together from scraps of truth and feeling. And some things, like the Ponderosa (or whatever the grocery store in Truckee was eventually called), simply didn't exist back then. But fiction has a funny way of borrowing from the future when the story needs a Coke and a setting.

To Ralph, Ginny, Grandpa Red, TeenTeen, Skippy, Gerri, and Jill—the real ones: I couldn't bring myself to rename you. Anything else would have felt dishonest or lesser. Jill, who is no longer with us, remains forever young and loved in these pages. And to my childhood friend Ginny—renamed Winnie in this telling—thank you for being part of the foundation I still walk on today.

Writing this book let me revisit old joys, old questions, and old wounds with fresh eyes. It's my hope that somewhere in these pages, you'll find a spark of your own growing-up summer—messy, magical, and full of unexpected turns.

—Mary Berelson

Acknowledgments

I extend my deepest gratitude to Kathy Meis, founder of Bublish, for her kindness and encouragement. When I first called with questions about publishing, it was the middle of the winter holidays and her staff was away—yet Kathy answered the phone herself. Her warm, reassuring voice gave me the confidence to take the plunge into publishing.

A heartfelt thank-you to my project manager, Shilah LaCoe, and to the gifted developmental and copy editors at Bublish for your expert guidance and insightful feedback. To the entire Bublish team: thank you for helping me bring this book to life with such care and professionalism.

To my early readers—Scott Berelson, Joanna McMullen, Gerri Conlon, Rebecca Hiremath, Hannah Red Hill, Ashton Leigh, Paige Derdowski, Marilyn Crang, Sheri McDaniel, Sonya Koster, Marjie Prisco, Heidi Reynaud, and Marina Phillips—I'm deeply grateful for your fresh eyes, thoughtful comments, and steady encouragement. Your support helped me keep going when the road felt long.

Ginny Travers, my childhood bestie—thank you for all the adventures we shared growing up. You are the heart and inspiration behind the character of Winnie Gravvers.

Reebha Hiremath, thank you for encouraging me to create an audiobook version of this story!

To Ellen Walters, my first editor—thank you for your upbeat spirit and early read-throughs. Your enthusiasm gave me early momentum and belief in the story.

A special thank-you to Kat Terrey of Tangled Roots Writing in Truckee, California, for your invaluable mentorship. Kat guided me as I transformed this book from a loose memoir into a fully formed novel. Her manuscript review and ongoing encouragement were instrumental. She also opened doors for me to speak publicly about the book, inviting me to substitute for her at Truckee's Business Network International meetings—where I found support from a broader community.

To Andy Dashe, my new eagle-eyed friend from Tennessee—thank you for jumping in after the first developmental edit to tackle a five-hundred-plus-page draft. Your sharp editorial instincts and fearless revisions helped me embrace the mantra: cut, cut, cut.

A huge shout-out to Michael Arington, who patiently guided me through countless technical hurdles—from the early stages in Scrivener to tricky behind-the-scenes setups, syncing tools, stubborn glitches, and eventually, business email and social media integration. Time after time, he showed up with calm, clarity, and expertise. I could not have navigated the tech side of this journey without him.

I hope you enjoyed *Bicentennial Summer*, and that it resonates with you.

Interview with Mary Berelson

1. *What inspired you to write* Bicentennial Summer? The novel was inspired by a real-life road trip I took with my father and siblings in 1976. It was a formative experience, full of adventure and discovery, but also a time when I started to see my father as a flawed person rather than as just a larger-than-life figure. Initially, I set out to write a memoir, but I realized that fiction gave me more freedom to explore the deeper emotional truths of that journey.

2. *How much of the story is based on real events?* The road trip itself was real, as were many of the locations we visited, but the events in *Bicentennial Summer* are fictionalized. Mary's father in the book is more reckless than my real father, and some scenes—like the motel incident in Wells, Nevada—are entirely made up. That said, the emotional core of the story, especially Mary's evolving understanding of her father, is very personal.

3. *Why did you choose to set the story in 1976?* The bicentennial was a unique moment in American history. The whole country was caught up in a mix of patriotism, celebration, and change. I wanted to capture that feeling of transition—not just nationally but also personally for Mary. It was the perfect backdrop for a coming-of-age story, especially one about family and shifting perceptions.

4. *Why did you use the real names of your family members in a fictional story?* When I first started writing, the book was meant to be a memoir, so using real names felt natural. Even after shifting to fiction, I kept them because those names held so much meaning for me. They anchored me to the emotional truth of the story, even when events were dramatized or invented. It felt like a way to honor the people who shaped my life while still allowing the book to take on a life of its own. Plus, Ger-Bear and Jilly-Bean and Jillerri just cannot be replaced with other names!

5. *What do you hope readers take away from Mary's journey?* I hope readers reflect on the complexity of family relationships—especially how we see our parents as we grow up. We start out believing they're heroes, then realize they're just people with their own flaws and struggles. I also want readers to feel a sense of nostalgia, whether it's for their own childhood road trips or for a time when cross-country travel felt like a real adventure.

6. *Music plays an important role in the book. Is that something drawn from your own life?* Yes! I've always loved music, and like Mary, I was very involved in school bands. Playing music was a way for me to express myself, and I wanted to bring that into the story. It also serves as a contrast between Mary and her father—she finds order and expression in music, whereas he tends to thrive in chaos.

7. *What was the most challenging part of writing this book?* Letting go of the idea that it had to be a perfect reflection of real life. I struggled with whether to stick to the exact details of my childhood or to allow the story to grow into its own thing. Once I embraced fiction, it became much easier to write.

8. *How did your background as a teacher influence your writing?* Spending thirty years teaching gave me a deep understanding of how young people think, grow, and process emotions. That helped me shape Mary's perspective in an

authentic way. Teaching also made me appreciate storytelling—whether through literature, music, or even the way we share personal experiences.

9. *What are you working on next?* I have an idea in the works for another novel based on a journal my sister Gerri kept while we traveled from Ohio to San Francisco. Unlike *Bicentennial Summer*, which follows a westward road trip, this journey took us east first—exploring the East Coast, then making an unexpected jaunt to Jamaica before finally heading to California. It was another adventure-filled trip, full of twists, challenges, and discoveries, and I think it has the makings of a great story. I'm still in the early stages, but I'm excited about bringing that journey to life.

10. *If you could give young Mary one piece of advice, what would it be?* Trust yourself. You don't need to have everything figured out right away, and it's okay to question things—even the people you love. Growth comes from learning to see the world in all its complexity.

About the Author

Mary Berelson is a storyteller, adventurer, and educator with a rich thirty-year teaching career. She dedicated twenty-five years to teaching kindergarten and first grade before transitioning to middle school technology for the final chapter of her career. Mary spent most of her adulthood in Truckee, California, where she and her husband raised their two daughters. Now retired in Tennessee, she draws inspiration from a life shaped by a childhood in Ohio, formative adult years in California, and her recent experiences as a Tennessean.

Mary enjoys exploring the outdoors, embarking on road trips in her and Scott's beloved VW bus, and creating stories that resonate deeply with readers. She continues to add entries to her Journal of Life. When not writing, Mary can be found tending her garden, spending precious moments with her new granddaughter, crafting in her fancy-pants crafting room, or mountain biking with her husband and dog.

This story is inspired by a road trip she took with her younger twin sisters and their father during the summer of 1976.